My Young Alcides

A Faded Photograph

by

Charlotte M. Yonge

Double9 BOOKS

My Young Alcides
A Faded Photograph
by Charlotte M. Yonge

ISBN: 978-93-68096-19-1

Published by

DOUBLE 9 BOOKS
2/13-B, Ansari Road
Daryaganj, New Delhi – 110002
info@double9books.com
www.double9books.com
Tel. 011-40042856

ABOUT THE AUTHOR

Charlotte M. Yonge was an English novelist and historian, born on August 11, 1823, in Otterbourne, Hampshire, England. She is best known for her prolific writing career, which spanned over 60 years and produced more than 160 works, including novels, children's books, and historical studies. Yonge's writing was strongly influenced by her deep religious beliefs and her interest in history and education. Many of her novels, such as "The Heir of Redclyffe" and "Heartsease," explore moral and religious themes and are known for their wholesome and uplifting tone. She also wrote numerous works for children, including the popular "Book of Golden Deeds," which features stories of heroism and selflessness. In addition to her writing, Yonge was a prominent figure in the Church of England and was involved in various philanthropic and educational endeavors. She founded a school for girls in her hometown and was a supporter of the National Society for Promoting Religious Education. Yonge died on May 24, 1901, in Otterbourne, Hampshire, England. Her legacy as a writer and educator continues to be celebrated, and her works remain popular with readers today.

CONTENTS

PREFACE

Ideas have a tyrannous power of insisting on being worked out, even when one fears they may be leading in a track already worthily preoccupied.

But the Hercules myth did not seem to me to be like one of the fairy tales that we have seen so gracefully and quaintly modernised; and at the risk of seeming to travestie the Farnese statue in a shooting-coat and wide-awake, I could not help going on, as the notion grew deeper and more engrossing.

For, whether the origin of the myth be, or be not, founded on solar phenomena, the yearning Greek mind formed on it an unconscious allegory of the course of the Victor, of whom the Sun, rejoicing as a giant to run his course, is another type, like Samson of old, since the facts of nature and of history are Divine parables.

And as each one's conquest is, in the track of his Leader, the only true Conqueror, so Hercules, in spite of all the grotesque adjuncts that the lower inventions of the heathen hung round him, is a far closer likeness of manhood—as, indeed, the proverbial use of some of his tasks testifies—and of repentant man conquering himself. The great crime, after which his life was a bondage of expiation; the choice between Virtue and Vice; the slain passion; the hundred-headed sin for ever cropping up again; the winning of the sacred emblem of purity;—then the subduing of greed; the cleansing of long-neglected uncleanness; the silencing of foul tongues; the remarkable contest with the creature which had become a foe, because, after being devoted for sacrifice, it was spared; the obtaining the girdle of strength; the recovery of the spoil from the three-fold enemy; the gaining of the fruit of life; immediately followed by the victory over the hell-hound of death; and lastly, the attainment of immortality—all seem no fortuitous imagination, but one of those when "thoughts beyond their thoughts to those old bards were given."

I have not followed all these meanings, for this is not an allegory, but a mere distant following rather of the spirit than the letter of the old Greek tale of the Twelve Tasks. Neither have I adhered to every incident of Hercules' life; and the most touching and beautiful of all—the rescue of Alcestis, would hardly bear to come in merely as an episode, in this weak and presumptuous endeavour to show that the half-divine, patient conqueror is not merely a classic invention, but that he and his labours belong in some form or other to all times and all surroundings.

C. M. YONGE.
Nov. 8, 1875.

CHAPTER I
THE ARGHOUSE INHERITANCE

One of the children brought me a photograph album, long ago finished and closed, and showed me a faded and blurred figure over which there had been a little dispute. Was it Hercules with club and lion-skin, or was it a gentleman I had known?

Ah me! how soon a man's place knoweth him no more! What fresh recollections that majestic form awoke in me—the massive features, with the steadfast eye, and low, square brow, curled over with short rings of hair; the mouth, that, through the thick, short beard, still invited trust and reliance, even while there was a look of fire and determination that inspired dread.

The thing seemed to us hideous and absurd when it was taken by Miss Horsman. I hated it, and hid it away as a caricature. But now those pale, vanishing tints bring the very presence before me; and before the remembrance can become equally obscure in my own mind, let me record for others the years that I spent with my young Alcides as he now stands before me in memory.

Our family history is a strange one. I, Lucy Alison, never even saw my twin brothers—nor, indeed, knew of their existence—during my childhood. I had one brother a year younger than myself, and as long as he lived he was treated as the eldest son, and neither he nor I ever dreamed that my father had had a first wife and two sons. He was a feeble, broken man, who seemed to my young fancy so old that in after times it was always a shock to me to read on his tablet, "Percy Alison, aged fifty-seven;" and I was but seven years old when he died under the final blow of the loss of my little brother Percy from measles.

The dear old place—house with five gables on the garden front, black timbered, and with white plaster between, and oh! such flowers in the garden—was left to my mother for her life; and she was a great deal younger than my father, so we went on living there, and it was only when I was almost a woman that I came to the knowledge that the property would never be mine, but would go in the male line to the son of one of my disinherited convict brothers.

The story, as my mother knew it, was this: Their names were Ambrose and Eustace: there was very little interval between their births, and there had been some confusion between them during the first few hours of their lives, so that the question of seniority was never entirely clear, though Ambrose was so completely the leader and master that he was always looked upon as the elder.

In their early youth they were led away by a man of Polish extraction, though a British subject, one Count Prometesky, who had thrown himself into every revolutionary movement on the Continent, had fought under Kosciusko in Poland, joined the Carbonari in Italy, and at last escaped, with health damaged by a wound, to teach languages and military drawing in England, and, unhappily, to spread his principles among his pupils, during the excitement connected with the Reform Bill. Under his teaching my poor brothers became such democrats that they actually married the two daughters of a man from Cumberland named Lewthwayte, whom Lord Erymanth had turned out of one of his farms for his insolence and radicalism; and not long after they were engaged in the agricultural riots, drilling the peasants, making inflammatory speeches, and doing all they could to bring on a revolution. Dreadful harm was done on the Erymanth estate, and the farm from which Lewthwayte had been expelled suffered especially, the whole of the ricks and buildings being burnt down, though the family of the occupant was saved, partly by Prometesky's exertions.

When the troops came, both he and my brothers were taken with arms in their hands; they were tried by the special commission and sentenced to death. Lewthwayte and his son were actually hung; but there was great interest made for Ambrose and Eustace, and in consideration of their early youth (they were not twenty-two) their sentence was commuted to transportation for life, and so was Prometesky's, because he was half a foreigner, and because he was proved to have saved life.

My father would not see them again, but he offered their wives a passage out to join them, and wanted to have had their two babies left with him, but the two young women refused to part with them; and it was after that that he married again, meaning to cast them off for ever, though, as long as their time of servitude lasted, he sent the wives an allowance, and as soon as his sons could hold property, he gave them a handsome sum with which to set themselves up in a large farm in the Bush.

And when little Percy died, he wanted again to have his eldest grandson sent home to him, and was very much wounded by the refusal which came only just before his death. His will had left the estate to the grandson, as the right heir. Everyone looked on it as a bad prospect, but no one thought of the "convict boy" as in the immediate future, as my mother was still quite a young woman.

But when I was just three-and-twenty, an attack of diphtheria broke out; my mother and I both caught it; and, alas! I alone recovered. The illness was very long with me, partly from my desolateness and grief, for, tender as my kind old servants were, and good as were my friends and neighbours, they could only make me feel what they were *not*.

Our old lawyer, Mr. Prosser, had written to my nephew, for we knew that both the poor brothers were dead; but he assured me that I might safely stay on at the old place, for it would be eight months before his letter could be answered, and the heir could not come for a long time after.

I was very glad to linger on, for I clung to the home, and looked at every bush and flower, blossoming for the last time, almost as if I were dying, and leaving them to a sort of fiend. My mother's old friends, Lady Diana Tracy and Lord Erymanth, her brother, used to bemoan with me the coming of this lad, born of a plebeian mother, bred up in a penal colony, and, no doubt, uneducated except in its coarsest vices. Lord Erymanth told at endless length all the advice he had given my father in vain, and bewailed the sense of justice that had bequeathed the property to such a male heir as could not fail to be a scourge to the country. Everyone had some story to tell of Ambrose's fiery speeches and insubordinate actions, viewing Eustace as not so bad because his mere satellite—and what must not their sons be?

The only person who had any feeling of pity or affection for them was old Miss Woolmer. She was the daughter of a former clergyman of Mycening, the little town which is almost at our park-gates. She was always confined to the house by rheumatic-gout. She had grown up with my brothers. I sometimes wondered if she had not had a little tenderness for one of them, but I believe it was almost elder-sisterly. She told me much in their excuse. My father had never been the fond, indulgent father to them that I remembered him, but a strict, stern authority when he was at home, and when he was absent leaving them far too much to their own devices; while Prometesky was a very attractive person, brilliant, accomplished, full of fire and of faith in his theories of universal benevolence and emancipation.

She thought, if the times had not been such as to bring them into action, Ambrose would have outgrown and modified all that was dangerous in his theories, and that they would have remained mere talk, the ebullition of his form of knight-errantry; for it was generous indignation and ardour that chiefly led him astray, and Eustace was always his double: but there were some incidents at the time which roused him to fury. Lewthwayte was a Cumberland man, who had inherited the stock and the last years of a lease of a farm on Lord Erymanth's property; he had done a good deal for it, and expended money on the understanding that he should have the lease renewed, but he was a man of bold, independent northern tongue, and gave great offence to his lordship, who was used to be listened to with a sort of feudal deference. He was of the fierce old Norse blood, and his daughters were tall, fair, magnificent young women, not at all uneducated nor vulgar, and it was the finding that my brothers were becoming intimate at his farm that made Lord Erymanth refuse to renew the lease and turn the family out so harshly, and with as little notice as possible.

The cruelty, as they thought it, was, Miss Woolmer said, most ill-judged, and precipitated the very thing that was dreaded. The youths rushed into the marriage with the daughters, and cast in their lot with all that could overturn the existing order of things, but Miss Woolmer did not believe they had had anything to do with the rick-burning or machine-breaking. All that was taken out of their hands by more brutal, ignorant demagogues. They were mere visionaries and enthusiasts according to her, and she said the two wives were very noble-looking, high-spirited young women. She had gone to see them several times when their husbands were in prison, and had been much struck with Alice, Ambrose's wife, who held up most bravely; though Dorothy, poor thing, was prostrated, and indeed her child was born in the height of the distress, when his father had just been tried for his life, and sentenced to death.

It was their birth and education that caused them to be treated so severely; besides, there was no doubt of their having harangued the people, and stirred them up, and they were seen, as well as Prometesky, at the fire at what had been Lewthwayte's farm; at least, so it was declared by men who turned King's evidence, and the proof to the contrary broke down, because it depended on the wives, whose evidence was not admissible; indeed that—as the law then stood—was not the question. Those who had raised the storm were responsible for all that was done in it, and it was very barely that their lives were spared.

That was the comfort Miss Woolmer gave. No one else could see any at all, except a few old women in the parish, who spoke tenderly of poor Mr. Ambrose and Mr. Eustace; but then they had sons or brothers who had been out with the rioters, and after these twenty-six years no one remembered the outrages and terrors of the time with anything but horror; and the coming of the wild lad from the Bush was looked on as the end of all comfort.

I meant, as soon as I heard he was on the way, to leave Arghouse, make visits among friends, and decide on my future home, for, alas! there was no one who wanted me. I was quite alone in the world; my mother's cousins were not near, and I hardly knew them; and my only relations were the bushrangers, as Lady Diana Tracy called them.

She was sister to Lord Erymanth, and widow to an Irish gentleman, and had settled in the next parish to us, with her children, on the death of her husband.

Her little daughter, Viola, had been spending the day with me, and it was a lovely spring evening, when we sat on the lawn, wondering whether I should ever care for anything so much as for those long shadows from the fir woods upon the sloping field, with the long grass rippling in the wind, and the border of primroses round the edge of the wood.

We heard wheels and thought it was the carriage come for Viola, much too soon, when out ran one of the maids, crying, "Oh! Miss Alison, he is come. There's ever so many of them!"

I believe we caught hold of one another in our fright, and were almost surprised when, outstripping lame old Richardson, as he announced "Mr. Alison!" there came only three persons. They were the two tallest men I had ever seen, and a little girl of eight years old. I found my hand in a very large one, and with the words "Are you my aunt Lucy?" I was, as it were, gathered up and kissed. The voice, somehow, carried a comfortable feeling in the kindness of its power and depth; and though it was a mouth bristly with yellow bristles, such as had never touched me before, the honest friendly eyes gave me an indescribable feeling of belonging to somebody, and of having ceased to be alone in the world.

"Here is Eustace," he said, "and little Dora," putting the child forward as she backed against him, most unwilling to let me kiss her. "And, I did not know I had another aunt."

"No," I said, starting between, for what would Lady Diana's feelings have been if Viola had carried home an Australian kiss? "This is Miss Tracy."

Viola's carriage was now actually coming, and as I went into the house with her, she held me, whispering to me to come home at once with her, but I told her I could not leave them in that way, and they were really my nephews.

"You are not afraid?" she said.

"What do you think he could do to me?" I asked, laughing.

"He is so big," said Viola. "I never saw any one so big, but I think he is like Coeur de Lion. Ah!" We both shrieked, for a most uncanny monster was rearing up in front of us, hopping about the hall, as far as was allowed by the chain that fastened it to the leg of a table.

"Mr. Alison brought it, ma'am," said Richardson, in a tone of disgust and horror. "Will you have the carriage out, Miss Alison, and go down to the Wyvern? Shuh! you brute! He shan't hurt you, my dear ladies. I'll stand between."

We had recovered our senses, however, enough to see that it was only a harmless kangaroo; and Dora came running out, followed by Harold, caressing the beast, calling it poor Nanny, and asking where he should shut it up for the night.

I suggested an outhouse, and we conducted the creature thither in procession, hearing by the way that the kangaroo's mother had been shot, and that the animal itself, then very young, and no bigger than a cat, had taken Harold's open shirt front for her pouch and leaped into his bosom, and that it had been brought up to its present stature tame at Boola Boola. Viola went with us, fed the kangaroo, and was so much interested and delighted, that she could hardly go away, Eustace making her a most elaborate and rather absurd bow, being evidently much impressed by the carriage and liveried servants who were waiting for her.

"Like the Governor's lady!" he said. "And I know, for I've been to a ball at Government House."

He plainly cared much more for appearances than did Harold. He was not so tall, much slighter, with darker hair, rather too shiny, and a neatly turned up moustache, a gorgeous tie and watch chain, a brilliant breast pin, a more brilliant ring, and a general air that made me conclude that he regarded himself as a Sydney beau. But Harold, in his loose, rough grey suit, was very different. His height was extraordinary, his breadth of chest and shoulder equally gigantic, though well proportioned, and with a look of easy strength, and, as Viola had said, his head was very much what one knows as the Lion Heart's, not Marochetti's trim carpet knight, but Vertue's rugged portrait from the monument at Fontevrand. There was the same massive breadth of feature, large yet not heavy, being relieved by the exceeding keenness and quickness of the light but very blue eyes, which seemed to see everywhere round in a moment, as men do in wild countries. The short thick yellow curly beard and moustache veiled the lower part of the face; but the general expression, when still, was decidedly a sad one, though a word or a trick of Dora's would call up a smile all over the browned cheeks and bright eyes. His form and colouring must have come from the Cumberland statesman, but people said his voice and expression had much of his father in them; and no one could think him ungentlemanly, though he was not like any English gentleman. He wore no gaieties like Eustace, the handkerchief loosely knotted round his neck sailor fashion was plain black, and he had a gold ring on his little finger.

Dora had the same yellow curly hair, in tight, frizzly rings all over her head, like a boy's, a light complexion, and blue eyes, in a round, pug-nosed face; and she hung so entirely on Harold that I never doubted that she was his sister till, as we were sitting down to eat, I said, "Can't you come a little way from your brother?"

Eustace gave his odd little giggle, and said, "There, Dora!"

"I'm not his sister—I'm his wife!"

"There!" and Eustace giggled again and ordered her away; but I saw Harold's brow knit with pain, and as she began to reiterate her assertion and resist Eustace, he gently sat her down on the chair near at hand, and silently made her understand that she was to stay there; but Eustace rather teasingly said:

"Aunt Lucy will teach you manners, Dora. She is my sister, and we have brought her home to send her to school."

"I won't go to school," said Dora; "Harold would not."

"You won't get away like him," returned Eustace, in the same tone.

"Yes, I shall. I'll lick all the girls," she returned, clenching a pair of red mottled fists that looked very capable.

"For shame, Dora!" said the low voice.

"Harold did," said she, looking up at me triumphantly; "he beat all the boys, and had to come back again to Boola Boola."

I longed to understand more, but I was ashamed to betray my ignorance of my near relations, for I did not even know whether their mothers were alive; but I saw that if I only listened, Eustace would soon tell everything. He had a runaway chin, and his mouth had a look at times that made me doubt whether there were not some slight want in his intellect, or at least weakness of character. However, I was relieved from the fear of the vice with which the neighbourhood had threatened us, for neither of them would touch wine or beer, but begged for tea, and drank oceans of it.

We had not long finished, when Richardson brought me a note from Lady Diana Tracy, saying she had sent the carriage for me that I might at once take refuge from this unforeseen invasion.

I felt it out of all possibility that I should thus run away, and yet I knew I owed an apology for Harold's finding me and the old servants in possession, so I began to say that my old friend had sent the carriage for me.—I had been taken by surprise, their journey (one of the first across the Isthmus) had been so much quicker than I had expected, or I should have left the house free for them.

"Why?" asked Harold. And when I answered that the place was his and I had no business there, he did not seem to see it. "It is your home," he said; "you have always lived here."

I began explaining that this was no reason at all; but he would not hear of my going away, and declared that it was I who belonged to the place, so that I confessed that I should be very thankful to stay a little while.

"Not only a little while," he said; "it is your home as much as ever, and the best thing in the world for us."

"Yes, yes," responded Eustace; "we kept on wondering what Aunt Lucy would be like, and never thought she could be such a nice *young* lady."

"Not realising that your aunt is younger than yourselves," I said.

"No," said Eustace, "the old folk never would talk of home—my father did not like it, you see—and Aunt Alice had moved off to New Zealand, so that we could not go and talk about it to her. Mr. Smith has got a school in Auckland, you know."

I did not know, but I found that a year or two after the death of my brother Ambrose, his widow had become the second wife of the master of a boarding-school at Sydney, and that it was there that Harold, at ten years old, had fought all the boys, including the step-children, and had been so audacious and uncontrollable, that she had been forced to return him to his uncle and aunt in the "Bush." Eustace had been with the Smiths at Sydney until her move to Auckland, he had even been presented, and had been to a ball at Government House, and thus was viewed as the polished member of the family, though, if he had come as master, I should never have been drawn, as I was by Harold's free, kindly simplicity, into writing my thanks to Lady Diana, and saying that I could not leave my nephews so abruptly, especially as they had brought a little sister.

It was gratifying to see that Harold was uneasy till the note was sent off and the carriage dismissed. "You are not going?" he said, as persuasively as if he were speaking to Dora, and I strove to make a wise and prudent answer, about remaining for the next few days, and settling the rest when he had made his plans.

Then I proposed to take Dora up to bed, but though manifestly very weary, the child refused, and when her brother tried to order her, she ran between Harold's knees, and there tossed her head and glared at me. He lifted her on his lap, and she drew his arm round her in defence. Eustace said he spoilt her, but he still held her, and, as she dropped asleep against his breast, Eustace related, almost in a tone of complaint, that she had cared for no one else ever since the time she had been lost in the Bush, and Harold had found her, after three days, in the last stage of exhaustion, since which time she had had neither eyes, ears, nor allegiance for any other creature, but that she must be taught something, and made into a lady.

Harold gazed down on her with his strange, soft, melancholy smile, somehow seeming to vex Eustace, who accused him of not caring how rough and uncultivated she was, nor himself either.

"We leave the polish to you," said Harold.

"Why, yes," said Eustace, simpering, "my uncle Smith gave me the first advantages in Sydney, and everyone knew my father was 'a gentleman.'"

Harold bit the hair that hung over his lip, and I guessed, what I afterwards found to be the truth, that his stepfather was no small trial to him; being, in fact, an unprosperous tutor and hanger-on on some nobleman's family, finally sent out by his patrons in despair, to keep school in Sydney.

Poor Ambrose had died of lock-jaw from a cut from an axe very soon after his emancipation, just as his energy was getting the farm into order, and making things look well with the family, and, after a year or two, Alice, deceived by the man's air and manners, and hoping to secure education for her son, had married, and the effect had been that, while Harold was provoked into fierce insubordination, Eustace became imbued with a tuft-hunting spirit, a great contrast to what might have been expected from his antecedents.

I cannot tell whether I found this out the first evening, or only gradually discovered it, with much besides. I only remember that when at last Harold carried Dora upstairs fast asleep, and my maid Colman and I had undressed her and put her into a little bed in a room opening out of mine, I went to rest, feeling rejoiced that the suspense was over and I knew the worst. I felt rather as if I had a magnificent wild beast in the house; and yet there was a wonderful attraction, partly from the drawing of kindred blood, and partly from the strength and sweetness of Harold's own face, and, aunt-like, I could not help feeling proud, of having such a grand creature belonging to me, though there might be a little dread of what he would do next.

In the morning all seemed like a dream, for Dora had vanished, leaving no trace but her black bag; but while I was dressing a tremendous cackling among my bantams caused me to look out, when I beheld them scurrying right and left at sight of the kangaroo leaping after the three strangers, and my cat on the top of the garden wall on tiptoe, with arched back, bristling tail, and glassy eyes, viewing the beast as the vengeful apotheosis of all the rats and mice she had slaughtered in her time.

From the stairs I heard Dora scouting her brother's orders to tidy herself for breakfast, adding that Harry never did, to which he merely replied, "I shall now. Come."

There was a sound of hoisting, that gave me warning rather fortunately, for he came striding upstairs with that great well-grown girl of eight perched on his shoulder as if she had been a baby, and would have run me down if I had not avoided into the nook on the landing.

All that day and the next those three were out; I never saw them but at meals, when they came in full of eager questions and comments on their discoveries in farming and other matters. These were the early bright days of spring, and they were out till after dark, only returning to eat and go to bed. I found the fascination of Harold's presence was on all the servants and dependents, except perhaps our bailiff Bullock, who disliked him from the first. All the others declared that they had no doubt about staying on, now that they saw what the young squire really was. It made a great impression on them that, when in some farmyard arrangements there was a moment's danger of a faggot pile falling, he put his shoulder against it and propped the whole weight without effort. His manhood, strength, and knowledge of work delighted them, and they declared already that he would be a good friend to the poor.

I confess that here lay what alarmed me. He was always given to few words, but I could see that he was shocked at the contrast between our poor and the Australian settlers, where food and space were plenty and the wages high. I was somewhat hurt at his way of viewing what had always seemed to me perfection, at least all that could be reasonably expected for the poor—our pet school, our old women, our civil dependents in tidy cottages, our picturesque lodges; and I did not half like his trenchant questions, which seemed to imply censure on all that I had hitherto thought unquestionable, and perhaps I told him somewhat impatiently that, when he had been a little longer here, he would understand our ways and fall naturally into them.

"That's just what I don't want," he said.

"Not want?" I exclaimed.

"Yes; I want to see clearly before I get used to things."

And as, perhaps, I seemed to wonder at this way of beginning, he opened a little, and said, "It is my father. He told me that if ever I came here I was to mind and do his work."

"What kind of work?" I asked, anxiously.

"Doing what he meant to have done," returned Harold, "for the poor. He said I should find out about it."

"You must have been too young to understand much of what he meant then," I said. "Did he not regret anything?"

"Yes, he said he had begun at the wrong end, when they were not ripe for it, and that the failure had ruined him for trying again."

"Then he did see things differently at last?" I said, hoping to find that the sentiments I had always heard condemned had not been perpetuated.

"Oh yes!" cried Eustace. "They were just brutes, you know, that nobody could do any good to, and were only bent on destroying, and had no gratitude nor sense; and that was the ruin of him and of my father too."

"They were ignorant, and easily maddened," said Harold, gravely. "He did not know how little they could be controlled. I must find out the true state of things. Prometesky said I must read it up."

"Prometesky!" I cried in despair. "Oh, Harold, you have not been influenced by that old firebrand?"

"He taught me almost all I know," was the answer, still much to my dismay; but I showed Harold to the library, and directed him to some old books of my father's, which I fancied might enlighten him on the subjects on which he needed information, though I feared they might be rather out of date; and whenever he was not out of doors, he was reading them, sometimes running his fingers through his yellow hair, or pulling his beard, and growling to himself when he was puzzled or met with what he did not like. Eustace's favourite study, meanwhile, was "Burke's Peerage," and his questions nearly drove me wild by their absurdity; and Dora rolled on the floor with my Spitz dog, for she loathed the doll I gave her, and made me more afraid of her than of either of the others.

Harold was all might and gentleness; Eustace viewed me as a glass of fashion and directory of English life and manners; but I saw they both looked to me not only to make their home, but to tame their little wild cat of a child; and that was enough to make her hate and distrust me. Moreover, she had a gleam of jealousy not far from fierce in her wild blue eyes if she saw Harold turn affectionately to me, and she always protested sullenly against the "next week," when I was to begin her education.

She could only read words of four letters, and could not, or would not, work a stitch. Harold had done all her mending. On the second day I passed by the open door of his room, and saw him at work on a great rectangular rent in her frock. I could not help stopping to suggest that Colman or I might save him that trouble, whereupon Dora slammed the door in my face.

Harold opened it again at once, saying, "You ought to beg Aunt Lucy's pardon;" and when no apology could be extracted from her, and with thanks he handed over the little dress to me, she gave a shriek of anger (she hardly ever shed tears) and snatched it from me again.

"Well, well," said Harold, patting her curly head; "I'll finish this time, but not again, Dora. Next time, Aunt Lucy will be so good as to see to it. After old Betty's eyes grew bad we had to do our own needling."

I confess it was a wonderful performance—quite as neat as Colman could have made it; and I suspect that Harold did not refrain from producing needle and thread from his fat miscellaneous pocket-book, and repairing her many disasters before they reached the domestic eye; for there was a chronic feud between Dora and Colman, and the attempts of the latter to make the child more like a young lady were passionately repelled, though she would better endure those of a rough little under-housemaid, whose civilisation was, I suppose, not quite so far removed from her own.

On Sunday, she and Harold disappeared as soon as breakfast was over, and only Eustace remained, spruce beyond all imagination, and giving himself childlike credit for not being with them; but when at church I can't say much for his behaviour. He stared unblushingly, whispered remarks and inquiries, could not find the places in his book, and appeared incapable of kneeling. Our little church at Arghouse was then a chapelry, with merely Sunday morning service by a curate from Mycening, and the congregation a village one, to the disgust of Eustace, who had expected to review his neighbours, and thought his get-up thrown away.

"No one at all to see," he observed with discontent over our luncheon, Harold and Dora having returned from roaming over Kalydon Moor.

"I go to afternoon service at Mycening, Harold," I said. "Will not you come with me?"

"There will be somebody there?" asked Eustace; to which I replied in the affirmative, but with some protest against his view of the object, and inviting the others again, but Dora defiantly answered that Harold was going to swing her on the ash tree.

"You ought to appear at church, Harry," said Eustace. "It is expected of an English squire. You see everybody, and everybody sees you."

"Well, then, go," said Harold.

"And won't you?" I entreated.

"I've promised to swing Dora," he answered, strolling out of the room, much to my concern; and though Eustace did accompany me, it was so evidently for the sake of staring that there was little comfort in that; and it was only by very severe looks that I could keep him from asking everyone's name. I hoped to make every one understand that he was not the squire, but no one came across us as we went out of church, and I had to reply to his torrent of inquiries all the way home.

It was a wet evening, and we all stayed in the house. Harold brought in one of his political economy studies from the library, and I tried to wile Dora to look at the pictures in a curious big old Dutch Scripture history, the Sunday delight of our youth.

Eustace came too, as if he wanted the amusement and yet was ashamed to take it, when he exclaimed, "I say, Harry; isn't this the book father used to tell us about—that they used to look over?"

Harold came, and stood towering above us with his hands in his pockets; but when we came to the Temptation of Eve, Dora broke out into an exclamation that excited my curiosity too much not to be pursued, though it was hardly edifying.

"Was that such a snake as Harold killed?"

"I have killed a good many snakes," he answered.

"Yes, but I meant the ones you killed when you were a little tiny boy."

"I don't remember," he said, as if to stop the subject, hating, as he always did, to talk about himself.

"No, I know you don't," said Dora; "but it is quite true, isn't it, Eustace?"

"Hardly true that Harold ever was a little tiny boy," I could not help saying.

"No, he never was *little*," said Eustace. "But it is quite true about the snakes. I seem to remember it now, and I've often heard my mother and my Aunt Alice tell of it. It was at the first place where we were in New South Wales. I came running out screaming, I believe—I was old enough to know the danger—and when they went in there was Harry sitting on the floor, holding a snake tight by the neck and enjoying its contortions like a new toy."

"Of course," said Harold, "if it were poisonous, which I doubt, the danger would have been when I let go. My mother quietly bade me hold him tight, which I suppose I had just sense enough to do, and in another moment she had snatched up the bill-hook they had been cutting wood with, and had his head off. She had the pluck."

I could but gasp with horror, and ask how old he was. About two! That was clear to their minds from the place where it happened which Harold could not recollect, though Eustace could.

"But, Harold, you surely are the eldest," I said.

"Oh no; I am six months the eldest," said Eustace, proud of his advantage.

We were to hear more of that by-and-by.

Monday afternoon brought Mr. Prosser, who was closeted with Harold, while Eustace and I devoted our faculties to pacifying Dora under her exclusion, and preventing her from climbing up to the window-sill to gaze into the library from without. She scorned submission to either of us, so Eustace kept guard by lying on the grass below, and I coaxed her by gathering primroses, sowing seeds, and using all inducements I could think of, but my resources were nearly exhausted when Harold's head appeared at the window, and he called, "Eustace! Lucy! here!"

We came at once, Dora before us.

"Come in," said Harold, admitting us at the glass door. "It is all a mistake. I am not the man. It is Eustace. Eu, I wish you joy, old chap—"

Mr. Prosser was at the table with a great will lying spread out on it. "I am afraid Mr. Alison is right, Miss Alison," he said. "The property is bequeathed to the eldest of the late Mr. Alison's grandsons born here, not specifying by which father. If I had copied the terms of the will I might have prevented disappointment, but I had no conception of what he tells me."

"But Ambrose was Harold's father," I exclaimed in bewilderment, "and he was the eldest."

"The seniority was not considered as certain," said Mr. Prosser, "and therefore the late Mr. Alison left the property to the eldest child born at home. 'Let us at least have an English-born heir,' I remember he said to me."

"And that is just what I am not," said Harold.

"I cannot understand! I have heard Miss Woolmer talk of poor Ambrose's beautiful child, several months older than Eustace's, and his name was Harold."

"Yes," said Harold, "but that one died on the voyage out, an hour or two before I was born. He was Harold Stanislas. I have no second name."

"And I always was the eldest," reiterated Eustace, hardly yet understanding what it involved.

All the needful documents had been preserved and brought home. There was the extract from the captain's log recording the burial at sea of

Harold Stanislas Alison, aged fifteen months, and the certificate of baptism by a colonial clergyman of Harold, son of Ambrose and Alice Alison, while Eustace was entered in the Northchester register, having been born in lodgings, as Mr. Prosser well recollected, while his poor young father lay under sentence of death.

It burst on him at last. "Do you mean that I have got it, and not you?"

"That's about it," said Harold. "Never mind, Eu, it will all come to the same thing in the end."

"You have none of it!"

"Not an acre. It all goes together; but don't look at me in that way. There's Boola Boola, you know."

"You're not going back there to leave me?" exclaimed Eustace, with a real sound of dismay, laying hold of his arm.

"Not just yet, at any rate," said Harold.

"No, no; nor at all," reiterated Eustace, and then, satisfied by the absence of contradiction, which did, in fact, mean a good deal from the silent Harold, he began to discover his own accession of dignity. "Then it all belongs to me. I am master. I am squire—Eustace Alison, Esquire, of Arghouse. How well it sounds. Doesn't it, Harry, doesn't it, Lucy? Uncle Smith always said I was the one cut out for high life. Besides, I've been presented, and have been to a ball at Government House."

I saw that Mr. Prosser was a little overcome with amusement, and I wanted to make my retreat and carry off Dora, but she had perched on her favourite post—Harold's knee—and I was also needed to witness Eustace's signatures, as well as on some matters connected with my own property. So I stayed, and saw that he did indeed seem lost without his cousin's help. Neither knew anything about business of this kind, but Harold readily understood what made Eustace so confused, that he was quite helpless without Harold's explanations, and rather rough directions what he was to do. How like themselves their writing was! Eustace's neat and clerkly, but weak and illegible; and Harold's as distinct, and almost as large, as a schoolboy's copy, but with square-turned joints and strength of limb unlike any boy's writing.

The dressing-bell broke up the council, and Harold snatched up his hat to rush out and stretch his legs, but I could not help detaining him to say:

"Oh, Harry, I am so sorry!"

"Why?" he said.

"What does it leave you, Harry?"

"Half the capital stock farm, twelve thousand sheep, and a tidy sum in the Sydney bank," said Harold readily.

"Then I am afraid we shall lose you."

"That depends. I shall set Eustace in the way of doing what our fathers meant; and there's Prometesky—I shall not go till I have done his business."

I hardly knew what this meant, and could not keep Harold, whose long legs were eager for a rush in the fresh air; and the next person I met was Eustace.

"Aunt Lucy," he said, "that old fellow says you are going away. You can't be?"

I answered, truly enough, that I had not thought what to do, and he persisted that I had promised to stay.

"But that was with Harry," I said.

"I don't see why you should not stay as much with me," he said. "I'm your nephew all the same, and Dora is your niece; and she must be made a proper sister for me, who have been, &c."

I don't know that this form of invitation was exactly the thing that would have kept me; but I had a general feeling that to leave these young men and my old home would be utter banishment, that there was nothing I so cared for as seeing how they got on, and that it was worth anything to me to be wanted anywhere and by anyone; so I gave Eustace to understand that I meant to stay. I rather wished Harold to have pressed me; but I believe the dear good fellow honestly thought everyone must prefer Eustace to himself; and it was good to see the pat he gave his cousin's shoulder when that young gentleman, nothing loath, exultingly settled down in the master's place.

Before long I found out what Harold meant about Prometesky's business; for we had scarcely begun dinner before he began to consult Mr. Prosser about the ways and means of obtaining a pardon for Prometesky. This considerably startled Mr. Prosser. Some cabinets, he said, were very lenient to past political offences, but Prometesky seemed to him to have exceeded all bounds of mercy.

"You never knew the true facts, then?" said Harold.

"I know the facts that satisfied the jury."

"You never saw my father's statement?"

No, Mr. Prosser had been elsewhere, and had not been employed in my brother's trial; he had only inherited the connection with our family affairs when the matter had passed into comparative oblivion.

My brothers had never ceased to affirm that he had only started for the farm that had been Lewthwayte's on hearing that an attack was to be made on it, in hopes of preventing it, and that the witness, borne against him on the trial by a fellow who had turned king's evidence, had been false; but they had been unheeded, or rather Prometesky was regarded as the most truly mischievous of all, as perhaps he really had been, since he had certainly drawn them into the affair, and his life had barely been saved in consideration of his having rescued a child from the fire at great personal peril.

Ambrose had written again and again about him to my father, but as soon as the name occurred the letter had been torn up. On their liberation from actual servitude they had sent up their statement to the Government of New South Wales; but in the meantime Prometesky had fared much worse than they had. They had been placed in hands where their education, superiority, and good conduct had gained them trust and respect, and they had quickly obtained a remission of the severer part of their sentence and become their own masters; indeed, if Ambrose had lived, he would soon have risen to eminence in the colony. But Prometesky had fallen to the lot of a harsh, rude master, who hated him as a foreigner, and treated him in a manner that roused the proud spirit of the noble. The master had sworn that the convict had threatened his life, and years of working in chains on the roads had been the consequence.

It was no time for entertaining a petition on his account, and before the expiration of this additional sentence Ambrose was dead.

By that time Eustace, now a rich and prosperous man, would gladly have taken his old tutor to his home, but Prometesky was still too proud, and all that he would do was to build a little hut under a rock on the Boola Boola grounds, where he lived upon the proceeds of such joiner's and watchmaker's work as was needed by the settlers on a large area, when things were much rougher than even when my nephews came home. No one cared for education enough to make his gifts available in that direction, except as concerned Harold, who had, in fact, learnt of him almost all he knew in an irregular, voluntary sort of fashion, and who loved him heartily.

His health was failing now, and to bring him home was one of Harold's prime objects, since London advice might yet restore him. Harold had made one attempt in his cause at Sydney, sending in a copy of his father's dying statement, also signed by his uncle; but though he was told that it had been received, he had no encouragement to hope it would be forwarded, and had been told that to apply direct to the Secretary of State, backed by persons from our own neighbourhood, would be the best chance, and on this he consulted Mr. Prosser, but without meeting much sympathy. Mr. Prosser said many people's minds had changed with regard to English or Irish demagogues, and that the Alison Brothers themselves might very probably have been pardoned, but everyone was tired of Poles, and popular tradition viewed Prometesky as the ogre of the past. Mr. Prosser did not seem as if he would even very willingly assist in the drawing up in due form a petition in the Pole's favour, and declared that without some influential person to introduce it, it would be perfectly useless.

Eustace turned round with, "There, you see, Harold, nothing can be done."

"I do not see that," said Harold, in his quiet way.

"You do not mean to do anything?"

"Yes, I do."

"But what—what? What can you do?"

"I do not yet know."

"You see it is of no use. We shall only get into a scrape with all the gentlemen of the county."

"Never mind now, Eustace," said Harold, briefly. But I knew the expression of his face by this time quite well enough to be certain that nothing would make him abandon the cause of his father's old friend; and that his silence was full of the strongest determination. I think it fascinated me, and though in my cooler senses I reverted to my old notion of Prometesky as a dangerous firebrand, I could not help feeling for and with the youth whose soul was set on delivering his friend from exile.

My turn came the next morning, before Mr. Prosser went away. He had much to say against my making Arghouse my home, telling me that I had a full independence and could live where I pleased; but that I knew already, and had decided on the amount I ought to pay towards the housekeeping.

Then he wanted me to understand how the young men were looked upon, and the dread all the neighbourhood had of them. I said I had shared this dread, but on better acquaintance I found it quite undeserved, and this being the case it was incumbent on their only relation to stand by them, and not shun them as if they had brought the leprosy.

This he allowed, calling it a generous feeling, if they were worthy of it. But what greatly amazed me was his rejoicing that Eustace had proved to be the heir, since nothing was known against him, and when the other young man was gone there was hope that any little distrusts might be allayed, and that he might ultimately take his place in the county.

The other young man! Why should there be any distrust of Harold? I grew hot and indignant, and insisted on knowing what was meant; but Mr. Prosser declared that he knew nothing, only there were vague reports which made him rejoice that Mr. Harold Alison was not called to be the manager of the property, and would make him question whether a young lady would find it expedient to be long an inmate of the same house.

What reports could he mean? No—I could get no more out of him; he was too cautious to commit himself, and seemed to be satisfied by observing that if I changed my mind, I could at any time leave my nephews.

"Her nephews," I heard him mutter to himself; "yes, her nephews. No one has any right to object, and she can but judge for herself—there's no harm done."

I shall always believe, however, that he set on my friends to remonstrate, for letters began coming in, in all the senses of the imperative mood, commanding and entreating me to leave Arghouse. There was one such as only Lord Erymanth could write. He was an old man, and never could make short work of anything. They say that his chief political value was to be set on when anyone was wanted to speak against time. I know he was very dreadful at all the platforms in the county; but he was very good and conscientious, and everyone looked up to him as a sort of father of the country.

But oh! that letter! Such a battery of heavy arguments against my unprecedented step in taking up my residence with these unfortunate young men, who, though they had not themselves openly transgressed the law of the land, yet were the offspring of unhallowed unions with the children of a felon. I cannot go through it all, but it hinted that besides their origin, there was some terrible stain on Harold, and that society could not admit them; so that if I persisted in casting in my lot with them, I should share the ban. Indeed, he would have thought my own good sense and love of decorum would have taught me that the abode of two such youths would be no fit place for the daughter of such respected parents, and there was a good deal more that I could not understand about interceding with his sister, and her overlooking my offence in consideration of my inexperience and impulsiveness.

On my first impulse I wrote to thank my old friend, but to say I could see no harm in an aunt's being with her nephews, and that I was sure he had only to know them to lay aside all doubts of their being thorough gentlemen and associates for anybody. My little niece required my care, and I should stay and give it to her till some other arrangement was made. If Lady Diana were displeased with me, I was very sorry, but I could see no reason for it.

When I looked over the old Earl's letter, before closing mine, some expressions wound out of the mist that made me uncomfortable, especially when I recollected that though it was a week since their arrival, no one had attempted to call but Mr. Crosse, the vicar of Mycening, a very "good man in the pulpit," as the servants said, and active in the parish, but underbred and no companion.

Our neighbourhood was what is called very clannish. There were two families, the Horsmans and the Stympsons, who seemed to make up all the society. The sons either had the good livings, or had retired from their professions into cottages round and about, and the first question after any party was, how many of each. The outsiders, not decidedly of inferior rank, were almost driven into making a little clique—if so it might be called—of their own, and hanging together the more closely. Lord Erymanth of course predominated; but he was a widower of many years' standing, and his heir lived in a distant county. His sister, Lady Diana, had been married to an Irish Mr. Tracy, who had been murdered after a few years by his tenants, upon which she had come with her three children to live at Arked House. I never could guess how she came to marry an Irish landlord, and I always thought she must have exasperated his people. She was viewed as the perfection of a Lady Bountiful and pattern of excellence; but, I confess, that I always thought of her when I heard of the devout and honourable women who were stirred up against St. Paul. She was a person who was admired more than she was liked, and who was greatly praised and honoured, but somehow did not proportionably endear herself on closer acquaintance, doing a great deal of good, but all to large masses rather than individuals. However, all the neighbourhood had a pride in her, and it was a distinction to be considered a fit companion for Diana and Viola Tracy. I never cared for Di, who was her mother over again, and used to set us to rights with all her might; but she had married early, a very rich man—and Viola and I had always been exceedingly fond of one another, so that I could not bear to be cut off from her, however I might be disposed to defy her mother.

The upshot of my perplexities was that I set off to Mycening to lay them before Miss Woolmer, another of the few belonging to neither clan, to know what all this meant, as well as to be interested in my nephews.

Mycening is one of the prettiest country towns I know, at least it was twenty years ago. There is a very wide street, unpaved, but with a broad smooth gravelled way, slightly sloping down towards the little clean stone-edged gutters that border the carriage road along the centre, which is planted on each side with limes cut into arches. The houses are of all sorts, some old timbered gable-ended ones with projecting upper stories, like our own, others of the handsome old Queen Anne type with big sash windows, and others quite modern. Some have their gardens in front, some stand flush with the road, and the better sort are mixed with the shops and cottages.

Miss Woolmer lived in a tiny low one, close to the road, where, from her upstairs floor, she saw all that came and went, and, intellectual woman as she certainly was, she thoroughly enjoyed watching her neighbours, as by judiciously-arranged looking-glasses, she could do all up and down the street. I believe she had been a pretty woman, though on a small scale, and now she had bright eyes, and a very sweet bright look, though in complexion she had faded into the worn pallor that belongs to permanent ill health. She dressed nicely, and if she had been well, might, at her age, scarcely above forty, have been as much a young lady as Philippa Horsman; but I fancy the great crush of her life had taken away her girlhood and left her no spring of constitution to resist illness, so that she had sunk into a regular crippled invalid before I could remember, though her mind was full of activity.

"You are come to tell me about them, my dear," was her greeting. "I've seen them. No, I don't mean that they have been to see me. You'll bring them some day, won't you? I'm sure Ambrose's boy would come to see a sick woman. I watched one of them yesterday pick up old Molly's oranges for her in the street, when her basket got upset by a cart, and he then paid her for them, and gave them among the children round. It did my heart good, I'd not seen such a sight since the boys were sent away."

"Harold would do anything kind," I said, "or to see an old friend of his father. The worst of it is that there seem to be so few who wish to see him, or can even forgive me for staying with him."

I showed her Lord Erymanth's letter, and told her of the others, asking her what it meant. "Oh, as to Lady Diana," she said, "there is no doubt about that. She was greatly offended at your having sent away her carriage and not having taken her advice, and she goes about saying she is disappointed in you."

For my mother's sake, and my little Viola, and Auld Lang Syne besides, I was much hurt, and defended myself in a tone of pique which made Miss Woolmer smile and say she was far from blaming me, but that she thought I ought to count the cost of my remaining at Arghouse. And then she told me that the whole county was up in arms against the new comers, not only from old association of their name with revolutionary notions, but because the old Miss Stympsons, of Lake Side, who had connections in New South Wales, had set it abroad that the poor boys were ruffians, companions of the double-dyed villain Prometesky, and that Harold in especial was a marked man, who had caused the death of his own wife in a frenzy of intoxication.

At this I fairly laughed. Harold, at his age, who never touched liquor, and had lived a sort of hermit life in the Bush, to be saddled with a wife only to have destroyed her! The story contradicted itself by its own absurdity; and those two Miss Stympsons were well-known scandal-mongers. Miss Woolmer never believed a story of theirs without sifting, but she had been in a manner commissioned to let me know that society was determined not to accept Eustace and Harold Allson, and was irate at my doing so. Mothers declared that they should be very sorry to give poor Lucy Alison up, but that they could not have their children brought into contact with young men little better than convicts, and whom they would, besides, call my cousins, instead of my nephews. "I began to suspect it," I said, "when nobody left cards but Mr. Lawless and Peter Parsons."

"And that is the society they are to be left to?"

"But I shall not leave them," I cried. "Why should I, to please Miss Stympson and Lord Erymanth? I shall stand by my own brothers' sons against all the world."

"And if they be worthy, Lucy, your doing so is the best chance of their weathering the storm. See! is not that one of them? The grand-looking giant one, who moves like a king of men. He is Ambrose's son, is he not? What a pity he is not the squire!"

Harold was, in effect, issuing from the toy-shop, carrying an immense kite on his arm, like a shield, while Dora frisked round in admiration, and a train of humbler admirers flocked in the rear.

I hurried down into the street to tell Harold of my old friend's wish to see them, and he followed me at once, with that manner which was not courtesy, because, without being polished, it was so much more. Dora was much displeased, being ardent on the kite's tail, and followed with sullen looks, while Harold had to stoop low to get into the room, and brushed the low ceiling with his curly hair as he stood upright, Miss Woolmer gazing up to the very top of him. I think she was rather disappointed that he had not taken more after his father; and she told him that he was like his uncle Lewthwayte, looking keenly to see whether he shrunk from the comparison to a man who had died a felon's death; but he merely answered, "So I have been told."

Then she asked for his mother, and he briefly replied that she was well and in New Zealand. There was an attempt at noticing Dora, to which she responded like the wild opossum that she was, and her fidgeting carried the day. Harold only made answer to one or two more observations, and then could not but take leave, promising on the entreaty of the old lady, to come and see her again. I outstayed them, being curious to hear her opinion.

"A superb being," she said, with a long breath; "there's the easy strength of a Greek demi-god in every tread."

"He seems to me more like Thor in Nifelheim," I said, "being, no doubt, half a Viking to begin with."

"They are all the same, as people tell us now," she said, smiling. "Any way, he looks as if he was a waif from the heroic age. But, my dear, did not I hear him call you Lucy?"

"They generally do."

"I would not let them. Cling to your auntship; it explains your being with them. A grand creature! I feel like the people who had had a visit from the gods of old."

"And you understand how impossible it would be to run away," I said.

She smiled, but added, "Lucy, my dear, that looked very like a wedding-ring!"

I could not think it possible. Why, he was scarcely five-and-twenty! And yet the suggestion haunted me, whenever my eyes fell on his countenance in repose, and noted the habitual sadness of expression which certainly did not match with the fine open face that seemed fitted to express the joy of strength. It came on me too when, at the lodge, a child who had been left alone too long and had fallen into an unmitigated agony of screaming, Harry had actually, instead of fleeing from the sound, gone in, taken the screamer in his arms, and so hushed and pacified it, that on the mother's return she found it at perfect rest.

"One would think the gentleman was a father himself, ma'am," she had said to me; and thereupon Harold had coloured, and turned hastily aside, so that the woman fancied she had offended him and apologised, so that he had been forced to look back again and say, "Never mind," and "No harm done," with a half laugh, which, as it now struck me, had a ring of pain in it, and was not merely the laugh of a shy young man under an impossible imputation. True, I knew he was not a religious man, but to believe actual ill of him seemed to me impossible.

He had set himself to survey the Arghouse estate, so as to see how those dying wishes of his father could best be carried out, and he was making himself thoroughly acquainted with every man, woman, child, and building, to the intense jealousy of Bullock, who had been agent all through my mother's time, and had it all his own way. He could not think why "Mr. Harold" should be always hovering about the farms and cottages, sometimes using his own ready colonial hand to repair deficiencies, and sometimes his purse, and making the people take fancies into their heads that were never there before, and which would make Mr. Alison lose hundreds a year if they were attended to. And as Mr. Alison always did attend to his cousin, and gave orders accordingly, the much-aggrieved Bullock had no choice but in delaying their execution and demonstrating their impracticability, whereas, of course, Harold did not believe in impossibilities.

It was quite true, as he had once said, that though he could not bring about improvements as readily as if he had been landlord, yet he could get at the people much better, and learn their own point of view of what was good for them. They were beginning to idolise him; for, indeed, there was a fascination about him which no one could resist. I sometimes wondered what it was, considering that he was so slow of speech, and had so little sunshine of mirth about him.

I never did enforce my title of Aunt, in spite of Miss Woolmer's advice. It sounded too ridiculous, and would have hindered the sisterly feeling that held us together.

Eustace was restless and vexed at not being called upon, and anxious to show himself on any occasion, and I was almost equally anxious to keep him back, out of reach of mortification. Both he and Harold went to London on business, leaving Dora with me. The charge was less severe than I expected. My first attempts at teaching her had been frustrated by her scorn of me, and by Harold's baffling indulgence; but one day, when they had been visiting one of the farms, the children had been made to exhibit their acquirements, which were quite sufficient to manifest Dora's ignorance. Eustace had long declared that if she would not learn of me she must either have a governess or go to school, and I knew she was fit for neither. Harold, I believe, now enforced the threat, and when he went away, left her a black silk necktie to be hemmed for him, and a toy book with flaming illustrations, with an assurance that on her reading it to him on his return, depended his giving her a toy steam-engine.

Dora knew that Harold kept his word, even with her. I think she had a great mind to get no one's assistance but the kitchenmaid's, but this friendship was abruptly terminated by Dora's arraying the kangaroo in Sarah's best bonnet and cloak, and launching it upon a stolen interview between her and her sweetheart. The screams brought all the house together, and, as the hero was an undesirable party who had been forbidden the house, Sarah viewed it as treachery on Miss Dora's part, and sulked enough to alienate her.

Dora could make out more to herself in a book than she could read aloud, and one day I saw her spelling over the table of degrees of marriage in a great folio Prayer-Book, which she had taken down in quest of pictures.

Some time later in the day, she said, "Lucy, are you Harry's father's sister?" and when I said yes, she added, with a look of discovery, "A man cannot marry his father's sister."

It was no time to protest against the marriage of first cousins. I was glad enough that from that time the strange child laid aside her jealousy of me; and that thenceforth her resistance was simply the repugnance of a wild creature to be taught and tamed. Ultimately she let me into the recesses of that passionate heart, and, as I think, loved me better than anybody else, except Harold; but even so, at an infinite distance from that which seemed the chief part of her whole being.

CHAPTER II
THE LION OF NEME HEATH

The work was done. The sixteen pages of large-type story book were stumbled through; and there was a triumphant exhibition when the cousins came home—Eustace delighted; Harold, half-stifled by London, insisting on walking home from the station to stretch his legs, and going all the way round over Kalydon Moor for a whiff of air!

If we had not had a few moors and heaths where he could breathe, I don't know whether he could have stayed in England; and as for London, the din, the dinginess, the squalor of houses and people, sat like a weight on his heart.

"They told me a great deal had been done for England. It is just nothing," he said, and hardly anything else that whole evening; while Eustace, accoutred point-device by a London tailor, poured forth volumes of what he had seen and done. Mr. Prosser made up a dinner party for them, and had taken them to an evening party or two—at least, Eustace; for after the first Harold had declined, and had spent his time in wandering about London by gas-light, and standing on the bridges, or trying how far it was on each side to green fields, and how much misery lay between.

Eustace had evidently been made much of, and had enjoyed himself greatly. It grieved me that his first entrance into society should be under no better auspices than those of the family solicitor; but he did not yet perceive this, and was much elated. "I flatter myself it was rather a success," was the phrase he had brought home, apropos to everything he had worn or done, from his tie to his shoe-buckles. He told me the price of everything, all the discussions with his tradesmen, and all the gazes fixed on him, with such simplicity that I could not help caring, and there sat Harold in his corner, apparently asleep, but his eye now and then showing that he was thinking deeply.

"Lucy," he said, as we bade one another good-night, "is nothing being done?"

"About what?" I asked.

"For all that wretchedness."

"Oh yes, there are all sorts of attempts," and I told him of model cottages, ragged schools, and the like, and promised to find him the accounts; but he gave one of his low growls, as if this were but a mockery of the direful need.

He had got his statement of Prometesky's case properly drawn up, and had sent up a copy, but in vain; and had again been told that some influential person must push it to give it any chance. Mr. Prosser's acquaintance lay in no such line; or, at least, were most unlikely to promote the pardon of an old incendiary.

"What will you do?" I asked. "Must you give it up?"

"Never! I will make a way at last."

Meantime, he was necessary to Eustace in accomplishing all the details of taking possession. Horses were wanted by both, used to riding as they had always been, and there was an old-fashioned fair on Neme Heath, just beyond Mycening, rather famous for its good show of horses, where there was a chance of finding even so rare an article as a hunter up to Harold's weight, also a pony for Dora.

An excellent show of wild beasts was also there. Harold had been on the heath when it was being arranged in the earliest morning hours, and had fraternised with the keepers, and came home loquacious far more than usual on the wonders he had seen. I remember that, instead of being disappointed in the size of the lions and tigers, he dwelt with special admiration on their supple and terrible strength of spine and paw.

He wanted to take Dora at once to the menagerie, but I represented the inexpedience of their taking her about with them to the horse-fair afterwards, and made Eustace perceive that it would not do for Miss Alison; and as Harold backed my authority, she did not look like thunder for more than ten minutes when she found we were to drive to Neme Heath, and that she was to go home with me after seeing the animals. Eustace was uncertain about his dignity, and hesitated about not caring and not intending, and not liking me to go alone, but made up his mind that since he had to be at the fair, he would drive us.

So we had out the barouche, and Eustace held the reins with infinite elation, while Harold endured the interior to reconcile Dora to it, and was as much diverted as she was at the humours of the scene, exclaiming at every stall of gilt gingerbread, every see-saw, and merry-go-round, that lined the suburbs of Mycening, and I strongly suspect meditating a private expedition to partake of their delights. Harold was thoroughly the great child nature meant him for, while poor Eustace sat aloft enfolded in his dignity, not daring to look right or left, or utter a word of surprise, lest he should compromise himself in the eyes of the coachman by his side.

The fair was upon the heath, out to which the new part of the town was stretching itself, and long streets of white booths extended themselves in their regular order. We drove on noiselessly over the much-trodden turf, until we were checked by the backward rush of a frightened crowd, and breathless voices called out to Eustace, "Stop, sir; turn, for Heaven's sake. The lion! He's loose!"

Turning was impossible, for the crowd was rushing back on us, blocking us up; and Eustace dropped the reins, turning round with a cry of "Harry! Harry! I see him. Take us away!"

Harold sprang on the back seat as the coachman jumped down to run to the horses' heads. He saw over the people's heads, and after that glance made one bound out of the carriage. I saw then what I shall never forget, across the wide open space round which the principal shows were arranged, and which was now entirely bare of people. On the other side, between the shafts of a waggon, too low for him to creep under, lay the great yellow lion, waving the tufted end of his tail as a cat does, when otherwise still, showing the glassy glare of his eyes now and then, growling with a horrible display of fangs, and holding between those huge paws a senseless boy as a sort of hostage. From all the lanes between the booths the people were looking in terror, ready for a rush on the beast's least movement, shrieking calls to someone to save the boy, fetch a gun, bring the keeper, &c.

That moment, with the great thick carriage-rug on his arm, Harold darted forward, knocking down a gun which some foolish person had brought from a shooting-gallery, and shouting, "Don't! It will only make him kill the boy!" he gathered himself up for a rush; while I believe we all called to him to stop: I am sure of Eustace's "Harry! don't! What shall I do?"

Before the words were spoken, Harold had darted to the side of the terrible creature, and, with a bound, vaulted across its neck as it lay, dealing it a tremendous blow over the nose with that sledge-hammer fist, and throwing the rug over its head. Horrible roaring growls, like snarling thunder, were heard for a second or two, and one man dashed out of the frightened throng, rifle in hand, just in time to receive the child, whom Harold flung to him, snatched from the lion's grasp; and again we saw a wrestling, struggling, heaving mass, Harry still uppermost, pinning the beast down with his weight and the mighty strength against which it struggled furiously. Having got free of the boy, his one ally was again aiming his rifle at the lion's ear, when two keepers, with nets and an iron bar, came on the scene, one shouting not to shoot, and the other holding up the bar and using some word of command, at which the lion cowered and crouched. The people broke into a loud cheer after their breathless silence, and it roused the already half-subdued lion. There was another fierce and desperate struggle, lasting only a moment, and ended by the report of the rifle.

In fact, the whole passed almost like a flash of lightning from the moment of our first halt, till the crowd closed in, so that I could only see one bare yellow head, towering above the hats, and finally cleaving a way towards us, closely followed by Dermot Tracy, carrying the rifle and almost beside himself with enthusiasm and excitement. "Lucy—is it you? What, he is your cousin? I never saw anything like it! He mastered it alone, quite alone!"

And then we heard Harry bidding those around not touch him, and Dora screamed with dismay, and I saw he had wrapped both hands in his handkerchief. To my frightened question, whether he was hurt, he answered, "Only my hands, but I fancy the brute has done for some of my fingers. If those fellows could but have held their tongues!"

He climbed into the carriage to rid himself of the crowd, who were offering all sorts of aid, commiseration, and advice, and Dermot begged to come too, "in case he should be faint," which made Harry smile, though he was in much pain, frowning and biting his lip while the coachman took the reins, and turned us round amid the deafening cheers of the people, for Eustace was quite unnerved, and Dora broke into sobs as she saw the blood soaking through the handkerchiefs—all that we could contribute. He called her a little goose, and said it was nothing; but the great drops stood on his brow, he panted and moved restlessly, as if sitting still were unbearable, and he could hardly help stamping out the bottom of the carriage. He shouted to Eustace to let him walk, but Dermot showed him how he would thus have the crowd about him in a moment. It was the last struggle that had done the mischief, when the lion, startled by the shout of the crowd, had turned on him again, and there had been a most narrow escape of a dying bite, such as would probably have crushed his hand itself beyond all remedy; and, as it was, one could not but fear he was dreadfully hurt, when the pain came in accesses of violence several times in the short distance to Dr. Kingston's door.

No, Dr. Kingston was not at home; nor would be in for some time; but while we were thinking what to do, a young man came hastily up, saying "I am Dr. Kingston's partner; can I do anything?"

Harold sprang out on this, forbidding Eustace to follow him, but permitting Dermot; and Mrs. Kingston, an old acquaintance of mine, came and invited us all to her drawing-room, lamenting greatly her husband's absence, and hoping that Mr. Yolland, his new partner, would be able to supply his place. The young man had very high testimonials and an excellent education. She was evidently exercised between her own distrust of the assistant and fear of disparaging him. Seeing how much shaken we were, she sent for wine, and I was surprised to see Eustace take some almost furtively, but his little sister, though still sobbing, glared out from behind the knuckles she was rubbing into her eyes, and exclaimed, "Eustace, I shall tell Harry."

"Hold your tongue," said Eustace, petulantly; "Harry has nothing to do with it."

Mrs. Kingston looked amazed. I set to work to talk them both down, and must have given a very wild, nervous account of the disaster. At last Dermot opened the door for Harry, who came in, looking very pale, with one hand entirely covered and in a sling, the other bound up all but the thumb and forefinger. To our anxious inquiries, he replied that the pain was much better now, and he should soon be all right; and then, on being further pressed, admitted that the little finger had been so much crushed that it had been taken off from the first joint, the other three fingers had been broken and were in splints, and the right hand was only torn and scratched. Mrs. Kingston exclaimed at this that Mr. Yolland should have waited for the doctor to venture on such an operation, but both Dermot and Harold assured her that he could not have waited, and also that it could not have been more skilfully done, both of which assurances she must have heard with doubts as to the competence of the judges, and she much regretted that she could not promise a visit from her doctor that evening, as he was likely to be detained all night.

Dermot came downstairs with us, and we found Mr. Yolland waiting at the door to extract a final promise that Harold would go to bed at once on coming home. It seemed that he had laughed at the recommendation, so that the young surgeon felt bound to enforce it before all of us, adding that it was a kind of hurt that no one could safely neglect. There was something in his frank, brusque manner that pleased Harold, and he promised with half a smile, thanking the doctor hastily as he did so, while Dermot Tracy whispered to me, "Good luck getting him; twice as ready as the old one;" and then vehemently shaking all our hands, to make up for Harold's not being fit to touch, he promised to come and see him on the morrow. The moment we were all in the carriage—Eustace still too much shaken to drive home—his first question was, who *that* was?

"Mr. Tracy," I answered; and Eustace added, "I thought you called him Dermont?"

"Dermot—Dermot Tracy. I have known him all our lives."

"I saw he was a gentleman by his boots," quoth Eustace with deliberation, holding out his own foot as a standard. "I saw they were London made."

"How fortunate that you had not on your Sydney ones," I could not help saying in mischief.

"I took care of that," was the complacent answer. "I told Richardson to take them all away."

I don't think Harold saw the fun. They had neither of them any humour; even Harold was much too simple and serious.

Eustace next treated us to a piece of his well-conned manual, and demonstrated that Dermot St. Glear Tracy, Esquire, of Killy Marey, County Cavan, Ireland, was grandson to an English peer, great grandson to an Irish peer, and nephew to the existing Edward St. Glear, 6th Earl of Erymanth. "And a very fashionable young man," he went on, "distinguished in the sporting world."

"An excellent good fellow, with plenty of pluck," said Harold warmly. "Is he not brother to the pretty little girl who was with you when we came?"

I answered as briefly as I could; I did not want to talk of the Tracys. My heart was very sore about them, and I was almost relieved when Dora broke in with a grave accusing tone: "Harry, Eustace drank a glass of wine, and I said I would tell you!"

"Eustace has no reason to prevent him," was Harold's quiet answer.

"And, really, I think, in my position, it is ridiculous, you see," Eustace began stammering, but was wearily cut short by Harold with, "As you please."

Eustace could never be silent long, and broke forth again: "Harold, your ring."

By way of answer Harold, with his available thumb and finger, showed the ring for a moment from his waistcoat pocket. Instantly Dora sprang at it, snatched it from his finger before he was aware, and with all her might flung it into the river, for we were crossing the bridge.

There was strength in that thumb and finger to give her a sharp fierce shake, and the low voice that said "Dora" was like the lion's growl.

"It's Meg's ring, and I hate her!" she cried.

"For shame, Dorothy."

The child burst into a flood of tears and sobbed piteously, but it was some minutes before he would relent and look towards her. Eustace scolded her for making such a noise, and vexing Harold when he was hurt, but that only made her cry the more. I told her to say she was sorry, and perhaps Harold would forgive her; but she shook her head violently at this.

Harold relented, unable to bear the sight of distress. "Don't tease her," he said, shortly, to us both. "Hush, Dora; there's an end of it."

This seemed to be an amnesty, for she leant against his knee again.

"Dora, how could you?" I said, when we were out of the carriage, and the two young men had gone upstairs together.

"It was Meg's ring, and I hate her," answered Dora, with the fierce wild gleam in her eyes.

"You should not hate anyone," was, of course, my answer.

"But she's dead!" said Dora, triumphantly as a little tigress.

"So much the worse it is to hate her. Who was she?"

"His wife," said Dora.

I durst not ask the child any more questions.

"Eustace, who is Meg?"

I could not but ask that question as we sat tete-a-tete after dinner, Dora having gone to carry Harold some fruit, and being sure to stay with him as long as he permitted.

Eustace looked round with a startled, cautious eye, as if afraid of being overheard, and said, as Dora had done, "His wife."

"Not alive?"

"Oh, no—thank goodness."

"At his age!"

"He was but twenty when he married her. A bad business! I knew it could not be otherwise. She was a storekeeper's daughter."

Then I learnt, in Eustace's incoherent style, the sad story I understood better afterwards.

This miserable marriage had been the outcome of the desolate state of the family after the loss of all the higher spirits of the elder generation. For the first few years after my brothers had won their liberation, and could hold property, they had been very happy, and the foundations of their prosperity at Boola Boola had been laid. Had Ambrose lived he would, no doubt, have become a leading man in the colony, where he had heartily embraced his lot and shaped his career.

Poor Eustace was, however, meant by nature for a quiet, refined English gentleman, living in his affections. He would never have transgressed ordinary bounds save for his brother's overmastering influence. He drooped from the time of Ambrose's untimely death, suffered much from the loss of several children, and gradually became a prey to heart complaint. But his wife was full of sense and energy, and Ambrose's plans were efficiently carried on, so that all went well till Alice's marriage; and, a year or two later on, Dorothy's death, in giving birth to her little girl, no woman was left at the farm but a rough though kind-hearted old convict, who did her best for the motherless child.

Harold, then sixteen, and master of his father's half of the property, was already its chief manager. He was, of course, utterly unrestrained, doing all kinds of daring and desperate things in the exuberance of his growing strength, and, though kind to his feeble uncle, under no authority, and a thorough young barbarian of the woods; the foremost of all the young men in every kind of exploit, as marksman, rider, hunter, and what-not, and wanting also to be foremost in the good graces of Meg Cree, the handsome daughter of the keeper of the wayside store on the road to Sydney, where young stock-farmers were wont to meet, with the price of their wool fresh in their hands. It was the rendezvous for all that was collectively done in the district; and many were the orgies and revelries in which Harold had shared when a mere boy in all but strength and stature, and ungovernable in proportion to the growing forces within him.

Of course she accepted him, with his grand physical advantages and his good property. There was rivalry enough to excite him, her beauty was sufficient to fire his boyish fancy; and opposition only maddened his headstrong will. A loud, boisterous, self-willed boy, with already strength, courage, and power beyond those of most grown men; his inclination light and unformed, as the attachments of his age usually are, was so backed that he succeeded where failure would have been a blessing.

My poor brother Eustace! what must not Harold's marriage have been to him! Into the common home, hitherto peaceful if mournful, was brought this coarse, violent, uneducated woman, jealous of him and his family, unmeasured in rudeness, contemning all the refinements to which he clung, and which even then were second nature to the youths, boasting over him for being a convict, whereas her father was a free settler, and furious at any act of kindness or respect to him from her husband.

She must have had a sort of animal jealousy, for the birth of her first child rendered her so savagely intolerant of poor Dora's fondness for Harold, that the offer of a clergyman's wife to take charge of the little girl was thankfully accepted by her father, though it separated him from his darling by more than fifty miles.

The woman's plan seemed to be to persecute the two Eustaces out of her house, since she could not persuade Harold that it was not as much theirs as his own. They clung on, as weak men do, for want of energy to make a change, and Eustace said his father would never complain; but Harold never guessed how much she made him suffer. Home had become a wretched place to all, and Harold was more alienated from it, making long expeditions, staying out as long and as late as he could whenever business or pleasure called him away, and becoming, alas, more headlong and reckless in the pursuit of amusement. There were fierce hot words when he came home, and though a tender respect for his uncle was the one thing in which he never failed, the whole grand creature was being wrecked and ruined by the wild courses to which home misery was driving him.

After about three years of this kind of life, Meg, much against his will, went to her father's station for the birth of her second child; lingered in the congenial atmosphere there far longer than was necessary after her recovery, and roused Harold's jealousy to a violent pitch by her demeanour towards a fellow of her own rank, whom she probably would have married but for Harold's unfortunate advantages, and whom she now most perilously preferred.

The jollification after the poor child's long-deferred christening ended in furious language on both sides, Meg insisting that she would not go home while "the old man" remained at Boola Boola, Harold swearing that she should come at once, and finally forcing her into his buggy, silencing by sheer terror her parents' endeavours to keep them at least till morning, rather than drive in his half-intoxicated condition across the uncleared country in the moonlight.

In the early morning Harold stood at their door dazed and bleeding, with his eldest child crushed and moaning in his arms. Almost without a word he gave it to the grandmother, and then guided the men at hand, striding on silently before them, to the precipitous bank of a deep gulley some twelve miles off. In the bottom lay the carriage broken to pieces, and beside it, where Harold had dragged them out, Meg and her baby both quite dead—where he had driven headlong down in the darkness.

The sun was burning hot when they brought her back in the cart, Harold walking behind with the little one in his arms, and when he had laid it down at home, the elder one waited till he took it. It was a fine boy of two years old, the thing he loved best in the world; but with a broken spine there was no hope for it, and for a whole day and night he held it, pacing the room, and calling it, speaking to and noticing no one else, and touching no food, only slaking his thirst with the liquor that stood at hand, until the poor little thing died in convulsions.

Unhappily, he had scarcely laid it down beside its mother and brother, when he saw his rival in the outer room of the store, and with one deadly imprecation, and a face which Eustace could not think of without horror, challenged him to fight, and in a second or two had struck him down, with a fractured skull. But the deed was done in undoubted brain fever. That was quite established, and for ten days after he was desperately ill and in the wildest delirium, probably from some injury to the head in the fall, aggravated by all that followed.

Neiher magistrate nor doctor was called in, but Prometesky came to their help, and when he grew calmer, brought him home, where his strength rallied, but his mind was for some time astray. For weeks he alternated between moods of speechless apathy and hours of frenzy, which, from his great strength, must have been fatal to someone if he had not always known his gentle, feeble old uncle, and obeyed his entreaties, even when Prometesky lost power with him.

In this remote part of the country no one interfered; the Crees, whose presence maddened him, were afraid to approach, and only Prometesky sustained the hopes of the two Eustaces by his conviction that this was not permanent insanity, but a passing effect of the injury; and they weathered that dreadful time till the frantic fits ceased, and there was only the dull, silent, stoniness of look and manner, lasting on after his health had entirely returned, and he had begun mechanically to attend to the farm and stock, and give orders to the men.

The final cure was the message that Dora was lost in the Bush. Harold had the keen sagacity of a black fellow, and he followed up the track with his unwearied strength until, on the third day, he found her, revived her with the food he had brought with him, and carried her home. There was only just nourishment enough to support her, and he took none himself, so that when he laid her down beside her father, he was so spent that, after a mouthful or two, he slept for twenty hours without moving, as he had never rested since the accident; and when he woke, and Dora ran up and stroked his face, it was the first time he had been seen to smile. Ever since he had been himself again, though changed from the boy of exuberant spirits, and the youth of ungovernable inclinations, into a grave, silent man, happier apparently in Dora's vehement affection than in anything else, and, at any rate, solaced, and soothed by the child's fondness and dependence upon him. This was two years ago, and no token of mental malady had since shown itself.

My poor brother Eustace! My heart yearned to have been able to comfort him. His tender nature had been all along the victim of others, and he was entirely shattered by these last miseries; an old man when little more than forty, and with heart disease so much accelerated by distress and agitation, that he did not live a month after Dora's adventure; but at least he had the comfort of seeing Harold's restoration, and being able to commit the other two to his charge, being no doubt aware that his son was at the best a poor weak being, and that Harold's nature would rise under responsibility which would call out its generosity.

Harold had never touched liquor since the day of his child's death, nor spoken of it; but when his dying uncle begged him to watch over his young cousins, he took up the Bible that lay on the bed, and, unsolicited, took a solemn oath to taste nothing of the kind for the rest of his life.

Afterwards the three had lived on together at Boola Boola. Then had come the tidings of the inheritance supposed to be Harold's, and with the relief of one glad to make a new beginning, to have a work to do, and leave old things behind, he had taken both the others with him.

So it was true! My noble-looking Harold had those dark lines in his spectrum. Wild ungovernable strength had whirled him in mere boyhood at the beck of his passions, and when most men are entering freshly upon life, he was already saddened and sobered by sin and suffering. The stories whispered of him were more than true. I remember I cried over them as I sat alone that evening. Eustace had not told all with the extenuations that I discovered gradually, some even then by cross-questioning, and much by the tuition of that sisterly affection that had gone out from me to Harold, and fastened on him as the one who, to me, represented family ties.

I never thought of breaking with him. No, if I had been told he might be insane that very night, it would have bound me to him the more. And when I went to bid him "Good-night" and take away Dora, and saw the massive features in their stillness light up into a good-natured smile of thanks at my inquiries, I could believe it all the less. He was lying cornerwise across the bed, with a stool beyond for his feet to rest on, and laughed a little as he said he always had to contrive thus, he never found a bed long enough; and our merriment over this seemed to render what Eustace had told me even more incongruous in one so scrupulously gentle.

That gentleness was perhaps reactionary in one who had had such lessons in keeping back his strength. He had evidently come forth a changed man. But that vow of his—was it the binding of a worse lion than that he had fought with to-day? Yet could such things be done in the might of a merely human will? And what token was there of the higher aid being invoked? My poor Harold! I could only pray for him! Alas! did he pray for himself?

I was waked in early morning by Dora's vociferous despair at the disappearance of her big patient, and then Eustace's peremptory fretful tone was heard silencing her by explaining that Harold's hurts had become so painful that he had walked off to Mycening to have the bandages loosened.

Indeed, when we met at breakfast, Eustace seemed to think himself injured by the interruption of his slumbers by Harold's coming to him for assistance in putting on his clothes, and stared at my dismay at his having permitted such an exertion. Before long, however, we saw an unmistakable doctor's gig approaching, and from it emerged Harold and Mr. Yolland. I saw now that he was a sturdy, hard-working-looking young man of seven or eight and twenty, with sandy hair, and an honest, open, weather-beaten face. He had a rather abrupt manner, but much more gentleman-like than that of the usual style of young Union doctors, who are divided between fine words and affectation and Sawbones roughness.

He said he had come in to enforce on us what he could not get his patient to believe—that it was madness to take such liberties with himself, while such serious wounds were so fresh; and certainly Harold did not seem to suppose a two mile walk more of an exertion than a turn on the terrace; indeed, but for Mr. Yolland, he would have set off again after breakfast for the interrupted quest of horses at the fair. This, however, was forbidden, with a hint about even the strongest constitution not being able to defy tetanus. This made us all look grave, and submission being promised, the young doctor took his leave, saying he would come in the evening and dress the hands again for the night.

"Why *did* you go to that fellow?" asked Eustace. "It is the old doctor who attends *gentlemen*; he is only the partner."

"He is good enough for me," said Harold. "I was right glad to meet him."

Then it appeared that as Harold was striding into town, half distracted with the pain of his hands, in the sunrise of that April morning, he had had the good fortune to meet Mr. Yolland just coming from the cottage where the poor little boy lay who had been injured by the lion. The fright and shock had nearly killed the mother, and the young doctor had been up all night, trying to save her, while on the floor, in a drunken sleep, lay the father, a navvy, who had expended the money lavished on the child by the spectators of the accident, in a revel at the public house. If any were left, it was all in the brute's pocket, and the only hope of peace was when he should have drunk it up.

Eustace went off to the fair to look at horses, Harold impressing on him to do nothing final in haste; and I could see that, while proud of doing anything on his own account, he was almost afraid of the venture alone. Tired by his sleepless night and morning walk, Harold, when we went into the hall for Dora's lessons, lay down on the white bear-skin, let us build a pile of cushions for his head, and thanked us with "That's nice." I suppose he had never been waited on before, he smiled with such a grateful look, almost of surprise.

Have I not said that ours was a black oak-panelled hall, with a wide fireplace, a gallery and oriel window, matted, and so fitted up as to be a pleasant resort for summer days. Our lessons took place there, because I had found that my old schoolroom, out of sight and sound of everything, was such an intolerable prison to my little wild Bush girl, that she really could not learn there, since her very limited attention could only be secured, under the certainty that Harold did not leave the house without her.

He bade her let him hear how well she could read, but he was very soon fast asleep, and I was persuading her that the multiplication table could not disturb his slumbers, when, at the sound of horses' feet, she darted from my side, like an arrow from a bow, to the open front door, and there waved her hand in command, calling to the rider in a hushed voice, "He is asleep."

I followed, expecting to see Eustace; but the rider was instead Dermot Tracy, who in unfeigned alarm asked if he were seriously ill; and when I laughed and explained, he gave his horse, to the groom, and came quietly enough, to satisfy Dora, into the hall with us.

There he stood transfixed, gazing at the great sleeping figure with a passion of enthusiasm in his dark-grey eyes. "Glorious!" he said. "Splendid fellow! Worthy of the deed, Lucy! It was the most plucky thing I ever saw!"

"You distinguished yourself too," I said.

"I? Why, I had a rifle. I galloped down to Grice's for mine at the first, when I saw the menagerie people were cowed. What's that to going at him alone, and mastering him too, as he had done before those idiots thought proper to yell?"

Being talked about, of course, awoke Harold; his eyes opened, and he answered for himself, greeting Dermot heartily. Only then did we understand the full history of what had happened. The lion-tamer, whose part it was to exhibit the liberty he could take with the animals, was ill, and his assistant, after much bravado as to his equal power, had felt his courage quail, and tried to renew it with drink. Thus he was in no state to perceive that he had only shot-to the bolt of the door of the cage; and his behaviour had so irritated the beast that, after so dealing with him that he lay in a most dangerous state, he had dashed out at the door in rage and terror, and, after seizing the hindmost of the flying crowd, had lain down between the shafts of the waggon, as we had seen him.

The keepers had lost their heads in the panic, and no one durst go near him. The lion-tamer had to be called from his bed, in lodgings in the town, and only came on the scene just as Dermot's rifle had finished the struggle. The master had quite seen the necessity, but was in great despair at the loss of so valuable an animal.

"I'll share in making it good to him," said Harold.

"You? You are the last to do so. If you had only been let alone, the beast would have been captured unhurt. No, no! I settled all that, as it was I who meddled in the matter when, I believe, you could have settled him yourself."

"I don't know that," said Harold. "I was glad enough to see your rifle at his ear. But I should like to have his skin, if they would sell it."

Dermot explained that he had been bargaining for the skin, and hoped Mr. Alison would accept it from him, but here Harold's resolution won the day, much as Dermot evidently longed to lay the trophy at his feet. Poor Dermot, I could see hero-worship growing in his eyes, as they talked about horses, endlessly as men can and do talk of them, and diligent inquiries elicited from Harold what things he had done with the unbroken animal in Australia.

I went off the scene at once, but when I returned to luncheon they were at it still. And Eustace's return with two steeds for Harold's judgment renewed the subject with double vigour. Dermot gave his counsel, and did not leave Arghouse without reiterating an invitation to the cousins to come to-morrow to his cottage at Biston, to be introduced to his stables, let doctors say what they might, and Eustace was in raptures at the distinguished acquaintance he fancied he had made for himself. He had learnt something of Mr. Tracy's sporting renown, and saw himself introduced to all the hunting world of the county, not to say of England.

It gave me a great deal to consider, knowing, as I did full well, that poor Dermot's acquaintance was not likely to bring him into favour with society, even if it were not dangerous in itself. And my poor mother would not have been delighted at my day, a thing I had totally forgotten in the pleasantness of having someone to talk to; for it was six weeks since I had spoken to anyone beyond the family, except Miss Woolmer. Besides, it was Dermot! And that was enough to move me in itself.

I think I have said that his father was an Irish landlord, who was shot at his own hall-door in his children's infancy. Lady Diana brought them back to her old neighbourhood, and there reigned over one of her brother's villages, with the greatest respect and admiration from all, and viewed as a pattern matron, widow, and parent. My mother was, I fancy, a little bit afraid of her, and never entirely at ease with her. I know I was not, but she was so "particular" about her children, that it was a great distinction to be allowed to be intimate with them, and my mother was proud of my being their licensed playfellow, when Horsmans and Stympsons were held aloof. But even in those days, when I heard the little Tracys spoken of as pattern children, I used to have an odd feeling of what it was to be behind the scenes, and know how much of their fame rested on Di. I gloried in the knowledge how much more charming the other two were than anyone guessed, who thought them models of propriety.

In truth, Dermot did not keep that reputation much longer than his petticoats. Ere long he was a pickle of the first order, equalling the sublime naughtiness of Holiday House, and was continually being sent home by private tutors, who could not manage him. All the time I had a secret conviction that, if he had been my own mother's son, she could have managed him, and he would never have even wished to do what she disapproved; but Lady Diana had no sympathy or warmth in her, and while she loved her children she fretted them, and never thawed nor unbent; and when she called in her brother's support, Dermot's nerves were driven frantic by the long harangues, and his relief was in antics which of course redoubled his offence. After he had put crackers into his uncle's boots, peppered the coachman's wig, inserted a live toad in the centre of a fortification of clear jelly at a great luncheon, and had one Christmas painted the two stone wild boars that guard the iron gates of Erymanth Castle into startling resemblance of the porkers as displayed in butchers' shops, with a little tin pail at the snout of each, labelling each sevenpence-ha'penny per pound, his uncle had little more hope of him.

Dreading his father's fate for him, Lady Diana put him into the Guards, to prevent him from living in Ireland, and there he fell into all the usual temptations of his kind, so that everybody came to look on him as a black sheep, and all the time I knew that, if any one had taken him in the right way, he might have been kept out of it. Why there was one talk that he and I had at a picnic on Kalydon Moor, which showed me how hopeless he was of ever really pleasing or satisfying his mother without being, what he could never be, like his uncle in his youth, and how knowing that I cared really might make a difference to him. But mamma and Lady Diana were both very much vexed about that talk; mamma was angry with me; and when Dermot, in a poetical game a little after, sent me some verses—well, with a little more blarney and tenderness than the case required—there was a real uproar about them. Di showed them to her mother, who apologised in her lofty way for my having been insulted. Oh! how angry it did make me; and mamma absolutely cried about it. It seems foolish to say so, but if they would have let us alone I could have done something towards inducing him to keep straight, whereas the way he was treated by his mother and Di only made him worse. Poor mamma! I don't wonder at her, when even his own mother and uncle would not stand up for him; but I knew, whenever we met afterwards at ball or party, that it was pain and grief to her for me to speak a word to him, and that she thought me wrong to exchange anything beyond bare civility. He was vexed, too, and did not try; and we heard worse and worse of him, especially when he went over to his place in Ireland.

Then came the Crimean war, and all the chances of showing what I knew he really was; but at the Alma he was wounded, not very dangerously, but just touching his lungs, and after a long illness in London, the doctors said he must not go back to Sebastopol, for to serve in the trenches would be certain death to him. He wanted to go back all the same, and had an instinct that it would be better for him, but his mother and uncle prevented him and made him sell out, and after that, when he had nothing to do—oh! there's no need to think of it.

In the course of this last year he had taken the shooting of Kalydon Moor, and a house with it, with immense stables, which one of the Horsmans had made for his hunters, and had ruined himself and died. He had not quarrelled with his mother—indeed nobody could quarrel with Dermot—and he used to go over to see her, but he would not live at home, and since he had been at Biston I had never once met him till I saw him run up to attack the lion, the only man in all the fair except Harold who had courage to do so! I could not help my heart bounding at the thought, and afterwards enjoying the talk with him that I could not help. But then it made me feel undutiful to my dear mother, and then there was the further difficulty to be faced. It would have been all very well to live with my nephews if we had been in a desert island, but I could not expect them not to make friends of their own; and if mine chose to drop me, how would it be for me, at my age, all alone in the house?

Harold was forced to confess that he had done too much that first day. His hand was inflamed, and pain and weariness forbade all thought of spending a long day from home; and, besides, there arrived letters by the morning's post which left grave lines on his brow.

So Eustace drove off alone, a good deal elated at such an expedition, and I took Harold to my own little sitting-room, so despised by Dora, for the convenience of bathing the flesh wounds on the right hand, which, though really the least injured, was a much greater torment than the broken fingers, and had allowed him very little sleep.

It was the first time he had been in the room, and on the chimney-piece stood open a miniature-case containing a portrait, by Thorburn, of my little brother Percy, in loose brown holland. Harold started as he came in, and exclaimed, "Where did that come from?" I told him, and he exclaimed, "Shut it up, please," and sat down with his back to it, resigning his hand to me, and thanking me warmly when the fomentation brought some relief, and when I asked if I could do any more for him he seemed undecided, extracted some letters from his pocket with his two-fifths of a hand, and sent Dora to his room for his writing-case. I offered to write anything for him, but he said, "Let me try," and then endeavoured; but he found that not only did the effort hurt him unbearably, but that he could not guide the pen for more than a word or two; so he consented to make use of me, saying, however, "Dora, it is no use your staying in; you had better go out."

Dora, of course, wanted to stay; but I devised that she should go, under the escort of one of the maids, to carry some broth to the wounded boy, an expedition which would last her some time, and which Harold enforced with all his might as a personal favour, till she complied.

"Thank you," said Harold; "you see this must be done at once, or we shall have them coming over here."

He gave me the sheet he had begun with "Dear Mother," and went on dictating. It was not at all after Julius Caesar's fashion of dictating. He sat with his eyes on his own letter, and uttered one brief but ponderous sentence after another, each complete in all its parts, and quite unhesitating, though slowly uttered. I gathered it up, wrote it down, said "Well," and waited for more in silence, till, after I had looked at him once or twice to see whether he were asleep or in a reverie, another such sentence followed, and I began to know him very much better.

After saying "My hands have been lamed for a few days, and my aunt is so good as to write for me," he went on to say, in forcible and not very affectionate terms, that "Smith must not think of coming home; Eustace could do nothing for him there, but as long as the family remained at Nelson their allowance should be increased by one hundred pounds a year." I filled up an order, which he signed on a Sydney bank for the first quarter. "It must not be more," he said, as he told me the sum, "or they will be taking their passage with it."

"No more?" I asked, when he prepared to conclude this short letter.

"No. Smith reads all her letters."

"That is very hard on you."

"She meant to do well for me, but it was a great mistake. If Smith comes home to prey upon Eustace, it will be a bad business."

"But he has no claim on Eustace, whatever he may think he has on you."

"He is more likely to come now. He knows he can get nothing out of me—" Then, as I looked at the order, he added, "Beyond my mother's rights. Poor mother!"

I found that the schoolmaster had been induced to marry Alice Alison in the expectation that her share in the proceeds of Boola Boola would be much larger than it proved to be. He had fawned on the two Eustaces, and obtained all he could from the elder, but, going too far at last, had been detected by the Sydney bank in what amounted to an embezzlement. Prosecution was waived, and he was assisted to leave Australia and make a fresh start in New Zealand, whence he had never ceased to endeavour to gain whatever he could from Boola Boola. He could twist Eustace round his finger, and Harold, though loathing and despising him, would do anything for his mother, but was resolved, for Eustace's sake, to keep them at a distance, as could only be done by never allowing them a sufficient sum at once to obtain a passage home, and he knew the habits of Smith and his sons too well to expect them to save it. In fact, the letter before him, which he ended by giving me to read, had been written by the poor woman at her husband's dictation, in the belief that Harold was the heir, to demand their passage-money from him, and that there was a sad little postscript put in afterwards, unknown to her tyrant. "My boy, don't do it. It will be much better for you not;" and, brave woman as she was, she added no entreaty that his refusal might be softened. I asked if she had had any more children. "No, happily," was Harold's answer. "If I might only wring that fellow's neck, I could take care of her." In fact, I should think, when he wanted to come within Harold's grasp, he hardly knew what he asked.

This finished, it appeared that Harold wanted to have a letter finished to Prometesky which he had begun some days before. This astonished me more, both by the questions Prometesky had been asking, and the answers Harold was returning, as to the state of the country and the condition of the people. They did much to relieve my mind of the fears I had sometimes entertained of Harold's being a ferocious demagogue incited thereto by his friend.

Who would have thought there was so much depth in his brain? He ended by saying, "Eustace takes kindly to his new position, and is gone today to see Mr. Tracy, nephew to Lord Erymanth, but who does not appear disposed to carry on the same hostility to us."

I exclaimed at his having said nothing of the lion either to his mother or his friend, and asked leave to add it, which he did not refuse, though saying there was no use in it, and that he wanted me to do one thing more for him—namely, to write to his agent in Sydney an order which he signed for the transmission of some money to England. He had learnt from Mr. Yolland that morning that the "Dragon's Head" and some adjoining houses at Mycening were for sale, and that the purchaser could have immediate possession.

"What are you going to do with it?"

"Shut it up."

"You can't do much good by shutting up one public-house."

"Eustace will do the same with those on his property."

"I am very much afraid your crusade will not succeed, unless you can put something better into people's minds."

"I shall see about that," he answered, thinking, I believe, that I was going to suggest religion, from all mention of which he shrank, as if it touched a wound. "Smith talked of religion," he once said, with a shudder. Besides, he was a creature in the superabundance of all human faculties to whom their exercise seemed for a time all-sufficient, and the dark shade of horror and remorse in the depths of his heart made him unwilling to look back or think. At any rate, he silenced me on that head; but, thinking, perhaps, that he had been unkindly blunt, he resumed, "There is no risk for Eustace in this acquaintance?"

In spite of the pang that smote me, I felt that this was the only time I might have for that word of warning which seemed incumbent on me. "I do not think there is danger in his going to-day, but it does seem right to tell you that poor Dermot Tracy is said to be very extravagant, and to lead a wild life. And Harold, though I have known him all my life, I have been thinking that it will not do for me to be here, if this should become a resort of the set of people he has made friends of."

Harold answered in his steady, grave way, "I see. But, Lucy, I suppose none of them have been so bad as I have been?"—rather as if he were wondering over the matter.

"But you belong to me," I answered, and I saw a look of real pleasure meet my smile.

"I wish I knew what was best for Eustace," he said, after a few more moments' thought. "Is it doing him harm for me to be here? I could go back to New South Wales at once, only in some ways I don't think the old fellow could get on without me, till he is more used to it all, and in safe hands."

I had no hesitation in answering that Eustace would be much worse off without his cousin, and that the treatment we were receiving was chiefly on account of the fathers of both, not personal to Harold.

"Then you think it would not help him for me to leave him?"

"I think he is far more likely to live it down with you to help him."

"But, Lucy, are you being given up by all your friends for our sakes? We did not know it meant that when we asked you to stay with us!"

"No more did I. But don't be uneasy about that, Harold dear. Don't you think one's own flesh and blood is more than all such friends?"

"I should not have thought two fellows like us could have been worth much to you," said Harold, gravely pondering. "That pretty little thing who was with you the night we came; she has never been here again. Don't you miss her?"

"It is not her fault," I said. "Besides, nothing is like the tie of blood."

I shall never forget the look that was in Harold's eyes. I was standing over him, putting some fresh warm water on his hand. He put back his head and looked up earnestly in my face, as if to see whether I meant it, then said, "We are very thankful to you for thinking so."

I could not help bending and touching his forehead with my lips. His eyes glistened and twinkled, but he said nothing for a little space, and then it was, "If any one like you had been out there—"

I don't think I ever had a compliment that gave me more pleasure, for there was somehow an infinite sense of meaning in whatever Harold said, however short it might be, as if his words had as much force in them as his muscles.

After a good deal more of silent sponging and some knitting of his brows, either from thought or from pain, he said, "Then, as I understand, you cast in your lot with us, and give us the blessing of your presence and care of poor little Dora, to help to set Eustace in his proper place in society. I see then that it is your due that we should bring no one here of whom you do not fully approve."

"It is not only a matter of approval," I explained. "There are many with whom I could freely associate in general society, or if I had any lady with me, whom I ought not to have constantly here with only you two."

"England is different from the Bush," he answered, and meditated for ten minutes more, for no doubt it was the Australian practice to offer free quarters to all comers without Mrs. Grundy, who had hardly yet had her free passage. My heart smote me lest I were acting unkindly for her sake, but then surely I was saving my allegiance to my dead mother, and while I was still thinking it over, Harold said:

"You are more to us than any one could be; Eustace shall see the thing rightly, and while you are good enough to make this our home, I promise you that no one shall be invited here but as you like."

It was a bold promise, especially as it turned out that Eustace had been making large invitations to the Arghouse fishing to Dermot Tracy and some officer friends whom he had found at Biston, and who seemed to have made themselves very pleasant. I bade Harold never mind about that sort of invitation, as it need not affect Dora or me, since we could keep out of the way of it, being unconcerned with gentlemen's parties. Miss Woolmer said I had done right, and gave us a general invitation to spend the evening with her if Eustace wished to entertain his friends, though she hinted, "Don't be too ready to leave the coast clear. Remember that you are a wholesome check."

CHAPTER III
THE "DRAGON'S HEAD"

Harold's right hand healed quickly, and was free in a few days, but the left had to be kept for some time in a sling, and be daily attended to, though he heeded it but little, walking miles to look at horses and to try them, for he could manage them perfectly with one hand, and in this way he saw a good deal of Dermot Tracy, who exerted himself to find a horse to carry the mighty frame.

The catastrophe at the fair had gained him two friends, entirely unlike one another—Dermot, who thenceforward viewed him with unvarying hero-worship, and accepted Eustace as his appendage; and George Yolland, the very reverse of all Dermot's high-bred form of Irishism, and careless, easy self-indulgence.

A rough-hewn, rugged young man, intensely in earnest, and therefore neither popular nor successful was that young partner of Dr. Kingston. Had Harold been squire, the resignation of the patient into his hands would have been less facile; but as a mere Australian visitor, he was no prize, and might follow his own taste if he preferred the practitioner to whom club, cottage, and union patients were abandoned.

By him Harold was let into those secrets of the lower stratum of society he had longed to understand. Attention to the poor boy who had been torn by the lion brought him into the great village of workmen's huts, that had risen up round the Hydriot clay works on the Lerne.

These had been set up by a company about eighteen years before, much against all our wills. With Lord Erymanth at our head, we had opposed with all our might the breaking up of the beautiful moorland that ran right down into Mycening, and the defilement of our pure and rapid Lerne; but modern progress had been too strong for us. Huge brick inclosures with unpleasant smoky chimneys had arisen, and around them a whole colony of bare, ugly little houses, filled with squalid women and children, little the better for the men's wages when they were high, and now that the Company was in a languishing state, miserable beyond description. We county people had simply viewed ourselves as the injured parties by this importation, bemoaned the ugliness of the erections, were furious at the interruptions to our country walks, prophesied the total collapse of the Company, and never suspected that we had any duties towards the potters. The works were lingering on, only just not perishing; the wages that the men did get, such as they were, went in drink; the town in that quarter was really unsafe in the evening; and the most ardent hope of all the neighbourhood was, that the total ruin constantly expected would lead to the migration of all the wretched population.

Mr. Yolland, who attended most of their sicknesses, used to tell fearful things of the misery, vice, and hardness, and did acts of almost heroic kindness among them, which did not seem consistent with what, to my grief and dismay, was reported of this chosen companion of Harold—that physical science had conducted him into materialism. The chief comfort I had was that Miss Woolmer liked him and opened her house to him. She was one of the large-hearted women who can see the good through the evil, and was interested by contact with all phases of thought; and, moreover, the lad should not be lost for want of the entree to something like a home, because the upper crust of Mycening considered him as "only Dr. Kingston's partner," and the Kingstons themselves had the sort of sense that he was too much for them which makes a spider dislike to have a bluebottle in his web.

She was interested, too, rather sadly in the crusade without the cross that the two young men were trying to undertake against the wretchedness of those potters.

It was much in their favour that the landlord, who was also the owner of the "Dragon's Head," was invited to join a brother in America without loss of time, and was ready to sell and give immediate possession; so that Harry actually owned it in a fortnight from first hearing of the offer, having, of course, given a heavy price for it.

The evening it came into his possession he went down, and, standing at the door, tried to explain why he had closed it, and why he could not bear to see its frequenters spending their wages on degrading themselves and making their homes miserable. In no mood for a temperance harangue, the men drowned, or would have drowned aught but his short incisive sentences, in clamours for their beer, and one big bully pushed forward to attack him. His left hand was still in the sling, but with the other he caught hold of the fellow by the collar, and swung him over the side of the stone steps as helpless as a puppy dog, shaking him till his teeth chattered ere setting him on his feet. "If you wish for any more," he said, "we'll have it out as soon as this hand is well."

That made them cheer him, and the fellow slunk away; while Harold, having gained a hearing, told them that he meant to make the former "Dragon's Head" a place where they might smoke, read the papers, play games, and have any refreshment such as coffee, tea, or ginger-beer, at which they hissed, and only one or two observed, "I am sure you wishes us well, sir."

It was a good-sized house, and he meant to put in a steady couple to keep it, giving up two upper rooms to make a laboratory for Mr. Yolland, whose soul was much set on experiments for which his lodgings gave him no space; but the very day when Harold opened his coffee-rooms, as he went down the street, an "Original Dragon's Head" and a "Genuine Dragon's Head" grinned defiance at him, in the full glory of teeth, fiery breath, and gilded scales, on the other side of the way. I believe they had been beershops before; but, be that as it may, they devoured quite as many as their predecessor, and though newspapers and draught-boards lay all about the place, they attracted only two clients!

And the intended closing of all the beer-houses on the Arghouse property, except the time-honoured "Blue Boar" on the village green, seemed likely to have the same effect; for the notices to their holders, grimly resisted by Bullock, seemed only to cause dozens of householders to represent the absolute need of such houses whenever they did not belong to us.

"To destroy one is to produce two," sighed Harold.

"There's nothing to be done but to strike at the root," I said.

"What's that?" said Harold.

"Man's evil propensities," I said.

"Humph," said Harold. "If I could manage the works now! They say the shares are to be had for an old song."

"Oh, Harry, don't have anything to do with them," I entreated. "They have ruined every creature who has meddled with them, and done unmitigated mischief."

Harold made no answer, but the next day he was greatly stimulated by a letter from Prometesky, part of which he read to me, in its perfect English, yet foreign idiom.

"I long to hear of the field of combat we had to quit, because one party was too stolid, the other too ardent. I see it all before me with the two new champions freshly girded for the strife, but a peaceful strife, my friend. Let our experience be at least profitable to you, and let it be a peaceful contention of emulation such as is alone suited to that insular nation which finds its strongest stimulus in domestic comfort and wealth. Apropos, has some one pursued a small discovery of mine, that, had I not been a stranger of a proscribed nation, and had not your English earl and the esquires been hostile to all save the hereditary plough, might have found employment for thousands and prevented the history of your fathers and of myself? That bed of argillaceous deposit around the course of your Lerne, which I found to be of the same quality as the porcelain clay of Meissen, does it still merely bear a few scanty blades of corn, or is its value appreciated, and is it occupying hundreds of those who starved and were discontented, to the great surprise of their respectable landlords? I wonder whether a few little figures that I modelled in the clay for specimens, and baked in my hostess's oven, are still in existence. The forms of clay were there. Alas! I asked in vain of your English magnates for the fire from heaven to animate the earth, or rather I would have brought it, and I suffered."

It was amusing to see how much delighted honest Harold was with this letter, and how much honoured he seemed by his dear old Prometesky having spent so much time and thought upon writing to him. It fired him with doubled ardour to investigate the Hydriot Company, and he could hardly wait till a reasonable hour the next day. Then he took Eustace down with him and returned quite talkative (for him) with the discoveries he had made, from one of the oldest workmen who had become disabled from the damp of working in the clay.

The Company had been set up by a clever speculating young attorney, but the old man remembered that "that there foreign gentleman, the same as was sent to foreign parts with the poor young squires," was "always a-puddling about in it; and they did say as how he tried to get my lord, and Squire Horsman, and Squire Stympson to see to setting up summut there; but they wasn't never for 'speriments, and there was no more talk of it not till that there young Crabbe got hold, they say, of some little images as he had made, and never rested till he had got up the Company, and begun the works, having drawn in by his enthusiasm half the tradesmen and a few of the gentlemen of the place."

Three years of success; then came a bad manager; young Crabbe struggled in vain to set things right, broke down, and died of the struggle; and ever since the unhappy affair had lingered on, starving its workmen, and just keeping alive by making common garden pots and pans and drain-tiles. Most people who could had sold out of it, thanking the Limited Liabilities for its doing them no further harm; and the small remnant only hung on because no one could be found to give them even the absurdly small amount that was still said to be the value of their shares.

That they would find now Harold had fallen in with young Yolland, who had been singing the old song, first of Prometesky, then of Crabbe, and had made him listen to it. Five pounds would now buy a share that used to be worth a hundred, and that with thanks from the seller that he got anything from what had long ceased to pay the ghost of a dividend. And loose cash was not scarce with Harold; he was able to buy up an amount which perfectly terrified me, and made me augur that the Hydriot would swallow all Boola Boola, and more too; and as to Mr. Yolland's promises of improvements, no one, after past experience, could believe in them.

"Now, Harold, you know nothing of all this intricate business; and as to these chemical agencies, I am sure you know nothing about them."

"I shall learn."

"You will only be taken in," I went on in my character as good aunt, "and utterly ruined."

"No matter if I am."

"Only please, at least, don't drag in Eustace and Arghouse."

"Eustace will only have five shares standing in his name to enable him to be chairman."

"Five too many! Harold! I cannot see why you involve yourself in all this. You are well off! You don't care for these foolish hopes of gain."

"I can't see things go so stupidly to wrack."

The truth was that he saw in it a continuation of Prometesky's work and his father's, so expostulations were vain. He had been thoroughly bitten, and was the more excited at finding that Dermot and Viola Tracy were both shareholders. Their father had been a believer in Crabbe, and had taken a good many shares, and these had been divided between them at his death. They could not be sold till they were of age, and by the time Dermot was twenty-one, no one would buy them; and now, when they were recalled to his mind, he would gladly have made Harold a present of them, but Harold would not even buy them; he declared that he wanted Dermot's vote, as a shareholder, to help in the majority; and, in fact, the effective male shareholders on the spot were only just sufficient to furnish directors. Mr. Yolland bought two shares that he might have a voice; Eustace was voted into the chair, and the minority was left to consist of the greatly-soured representative of the original Crabbe, and one other tradesman, who held on for the sake, as it seemed, of maintaining adherence to the red pots and pans, as, at any rate, risking nothing.

Of course I hated and dreaded it all, and it was only by that power which made it so hard to say nay to Harold, that he got me down to look at the very lair of the Hydriot Company. It was a melancholy place; the buildings were so much larger, and the apparatus so much more elaborate than there was any use for; and there were so few workmen, and those so unhealthy and sinister-looking.

I remember the great red central chimney with underground furnaces all round, which opened like the fiery graves where Dante placed the bad Popes; and how dreadfully afraid I was that Dora would tumble into one of them, so that I was glad to see her held fast by the fascination of the never-superseded potter and his wheel fashioning the clay, while Mr. Yolland discoursed and Harold muttered assents to some wonderful scheme that was to economise fuel—the rock on which this furnace had split.

It has been explained to me over and over again, and I never did more than understand it for one moment, and if I did recollect all about it, like a scientific dialogue, nobody would thank me for putting it in here, so it will be enough to say that it sounded to me very bewildering and horribly dangerous, not so much to the body as to the pocket, and I thought the Hydriot bade fair to devour Boola Boola and Harold, if not Arghouse and Eustace into the bargain.

They meant to have a Staffordshire man down to act as foreman and put things on a better footing.

"I'll write to my brother to send one," said Mr. Yolland. "He's a curate in the potteries; has a wonderful turn for this sort of thing."

"Have you a brother a clergyman?" I said, rather surprised, and to fill up Harold's silence.

"Yes, my brother Ben. It's his first curacy, and his two years are all but up. I don't know if he will stay on. He's a right down jolly good fellow is Ben, and I wish he would come down here."

Neither of us echoed the wish. Harold had no turn for clergymen after the specimen of Mr. Smith; and Mr. Yolland, though I could specify nothing against him but that he was rough and easy, had offended me by joining us, when I wanted Harold all to myself. Besides, was he not deluding my nephews into this horrid Hydriot Company, of which they would be the certain victims?

The Staffordshire man came, and the former workmen looked very bitter on him. After a meeting, in which the minority made many vehement objections, Eustace addressed the workmen in the yards—that is to say, he thought he did; but Harold and Mr. Yolland made his meaning more apparent. A venture in finer workmanship, imitating Etruscan ware, was to be made, and, if successful, would much increase trade and profits, and a rise in wages was offered to such as could undertake the workmanship. Moreover, it was held out to them that they might become the purchasers of shares or half shares at the market price, and thus have an interest in the concern, whereat they sneered as at some new dodge of the Company for taking them in. It did not seem to me that much was done, save making Harry pore over books and accounts, and run his hands through his hair, till his thick curls stood up in all directions.

And Miss Woolmer herself was sorry. She remembered the old story—nay, she had one of Prometesky's own figures modelled in terra cotta, defective, of course, as a work of art, but with that fire that genius can breathe into the imperfect. She believed it had been meant for the Hope of Poland. Alas! the very name reminded one of the old word for despair, "Wanhope." But Harold admired it greatly, and both he and George Yolland seemed to find inspiration in it.

But one summer evening, when the young men were walking up and down the garden, smoking, we heard something that caused us to look round for a thunder-cloud, though none could be seen in the clear sky, and some quarter of an hour after, Richardson hurried out to us with the tidings, "I beg your pardon, sir, but there is a person come up to say there has been an explosion at the Hydriot works."

"Impossible!" said Harold. "There's nothing to explode!"

"I beg your pardon, sir, but it is Mr. Yolland they say has blowed himself up with his experiments, and all the old 'Dragon's Head' in Lerne Street, and he is buried under the ruins. It is all one mass of ruin, sir, and he under it."

Harold rushed off, without further word or query, and Eustace after him, and I had almost to fight to hold back Dora, and should hardly have succeeded if the two had not disappeared so swiftly that she could not hope to come up with them.

I let her put on her things and come down with me to the lodge-gate to watch. I was afraid to go any farther, and there we waited, without even the relief of a report, till we had heard the great clock strike quarter after quarter, and were expecting it to strike eleven, when steps came near at last, and Eustace opened the gate. We threw ourselves upon him, and he cried out with surprise, then said, "He is alive!"

"Who! Harold?"

"Harold! Nonsense. What should be the matter with Harold? But he is going to stay with him—Yolland I mean—for the night! It was all his confounded experiments. It was very well that I went down—nothing was being done without a head to direct, but they always know what to be at when *I* come among them."

No one there knew the cause of the accident, except that it had taken place in Mr. Yolland's laboratory, where he had been trying experiments. The house itself had been violently shattered, and those nearest had suffered considerably. Happily, it stood in a yard of its own, so that none adjoined it, and though the fronts of the two opposite "Dragon's Heads" had broken windows and torn doors, no person within them had been more than stunned and bruised. But the former "Dragon's Head" itself had become a mere pile of stones, bricks, and timbers. The old couple in charge had happily been out, and stood in dismay over the heap, which Harold and a few of the men were trying to remove, in the dismal search for Mr. Yolland and the boy he employed to assist him. The boy was found first, fearfully burnt about the face and hands, but protected from being crushed by the boards which had fallen slantwise over him. And under another beam, which guarded his head, but rested on his leg, lay young Yolland.

Harold's strength had raised the beam, and he was drawn out. He revived as the night air blew on his face, looked up as Harold lifted him, said, "I have it," and fainted the next moment. They had taken him to his lodgings, where Dr. Kingston had set the broken leg and bound the damaged rib, but could not yet pronounce on the other injuries, and Harold had taken on himself the watch for the night.

The explanation that we all held by was, that the damage was caused by an officious act of the assistant, who, perceiving that it was growing dark, fired a match, and began to light the gas at the critical moment of the experiment, by which the means of obtaining the utmost heat at the smallest expense of fuel was to be attained. It was one of those senseless acts that no one would have thought of forbidding; and though the boy, on recovering his senses, owned that the last thing he remembered was getting the matches and Mr. Yolland shouting to stop him, there were many who never would believe anything but that it was blundering of his, and that he was a dangerous and mischievous person to have in the town.

Harold came home for a little while just as we were having breakfast, to bring a report that his patient had had a much quieter night than he expected, and to say that he had telegraphed for the brother and wanted Eustace to meet him at the station. The landlady was sitting with the patient now, and Harold had come home for ice, strawberries, and, above all, to ask for help in nursing, for the landlady could not, and would not, do much. I mentioned a motherly woman as, perhaps, likely to be useful, but Harold said, "I could do best with Dora."

He had so far learnt that it was not the Bush as not to expect me to offer, and was quite unprepared for the fire that Eustace and I opened on him as to the impossibility of his request. "Miss Alison, *my* sister," as Eustace said, "going down to a little, common, general practitioner to wait on him;" while I confined myself to "It won't do at all, Harold," and promised to hunt up the woman and to send her to his aid. But when I had seen her, arranged my housekeeping affairs, and called Dora to lessons, she was nowhere to be found.

"Then she has gone after Harold!" indignantly exclaimed Eustace. "It is too bad! I declare I will put a stop to it! To have *my* sister demeaning herself to put herself in such a situation for a little Union doctor!"

I laughed, and observed that no great harm was done with so small a person, only I could not think what use Harold could make of her; at which Eustace was no less surprised, for a girl of eight or nine was of no small value in the Bush, and he said Dora had been most helpful in the care of her father. But his dignity was so much outraged that he talked big of going to bring her home—only he did not go. I was a little wounded at Harold having taken her in the face of my opposition, but I found that that had not been the case, for Eustace had walked to the lodge with him, and she had rushed after and joined him after he was in the town. And at luncheon Eustace fell on me with entreaties that I would come with him and help him meet "this parson," whom he seemed to dread unreasonably, as, in fact, he always did shrink from doing anything alone when he could get a helper. I thought this would be, at least, as queer as Dora's nursing of the other brother; but it seemed so hard for the poor man, coming down in his anxiety, to be met by Eustace either in his vague or his supercilious mood, that I consented at last, so that he might have someone of common sense, and walked down with him.

We could not doubt which was the right passenger, when a young clergyman, almost as rough-looking as his brother, and as much bearded, but black where he was yellow, sprang out of a second-class with anxious looks. It was I who said at one breath, "There he is! Speak to him, Eustace! Mr. Yolland—he is better—he will do well—"

"Thank—thank you—" And the hat was pushed back, with a long breath; then, as he only had a little black bag to look after, we all walked together to the lodgings, while the poor man looked bewildered and unrealising under Eustace's incoherent history of the accident—a far more conjectural and confused story than it became afterwards.

I waited till Harold came down with Dora; and to my "How could you?" and Eustace's more severe and angry blame, she replied, "He wanted me; so of course I went."

Harold said not a word in defence of her or of himself; but when I asked whether she had been of any use, he said, smiling affectionately at her, "Wasn't she?"

Then we went and looked at the shattered houses, and Harold showed us where he had drawn out his poor friend, answering the aggrieved owners opposite that there would be an inquiry, and means would be found for compensation.

And when I said, "It is a bad beginning for the Hydriot plans!" he answered, "I don't know that," and stood looking at the ruins of his "Dragon's Head" in a sort of brown study, till we grew impatient, and dragged him home.

CHAPTER IV
THE WRATH OF DIANA

Harold did not like clergymen. "Smith was a clergyman," he said, with an expressive look; and while George Yolland had his brother and the nurse I had sent, he merely made daily inquiries, and sometimes sat an hour with his friend.

Mr. Crosse's curate had kindred in Staffordshire, and offered to exchange a couple of Sundays with Mr. Benjamin Yolland, and this resulted in the visitor being discovered to have a fine voice and a great power of preaching, and as he was just leaving his present parish, this ended in Mr. Crosse begging him to remain permanently, not much to Harold's gratification; but the two brothers were all left of their family, and, different as their opinions were, they were all in all to each other.

The agreement with Mr. Crosse would hardly have been made, had the brothers known all that was coming. George Yolland was in a strange stupefied state for the first day or two, owing, it was thought, to the effects of the gas; but he revived into the irritable state of crankiness which could not submit in prudent patience to Dr. Kingston's dicta, but argued, and insisted on his own treatment of himself, and his own theory of the accident, till he as good as told the doctor that he was an old woman. Whether it were in consequence or not, I don't know, but as soon as Dr. Kingston could persuade himself that a shock would do no harm, he wrote a polite letter explaining that the unfortunate occurrence from which Mr. Yolland was suffering had so destroyed the confidence of his patients, that he felt it due to them to take steps to dissolve the partnership.

Perhaps it was no wonder. Such things were told and believed, that those who had never yet been attended by George Yolland believed him a wild and destructive theorist. Miss Avice Stympson asked Miss Woolmer how she could sleep in her bed when she knew he was in the town, and the most astonishing stories of his practice were current, of which I think the mildest was, that he had pulled out all a poor girl's teeth for the sake of selling them to a London dentist, and that, when in a state of intoxication, he had cut off a man's hand, because he had a splinter in his finger.

However, the effect was, that Harold summoned a special meeting of the shareholders, the same being nearly identical with the Directors of the Hydriot Company, and these contrived to get George Yolland, Esquire, appointed chemist and manager of the works, with a salary of 70 pounds per annum, to be increased by a percentage on the sales! Crabbe objected vehemently, but was in the minority. The greater number were thoroughly believers in the discovery made on that unlucky night, or else were led away by that force of Harold's, which was almost as irresistible by mind as by matter. But the tidings were received with horror by the town. Three nervous old ladies who lived near the Lerne gave notice to quit, and many declared that it was an indictable offence.

Small as the salary was, it was more than young Yolland was clearing by his connection with Dr. Kingston; and as he would have to spare himself during the next few months, and could not without danger undertake the exertions of a wide field of Union practice, the offer was quite worth his acceptance. Moreover, he had the enthusiasm of a practical chemist, and would willingly have starved to see his invention carried out, so he received the appointment with the gruff gratitude that best suited Harold; and he and his brother were to have rooms in the late "Dragon's Head," so soon as it should have been rebuilt on improved principles, with a workman's hall below, and a great court for the children to play in by day and the lads in the evening.

Of the clerical Yolland we saw and heard very little. Harold was much relieved to find that even before his brother could move beyond the sofa he was always out all day, for though he had never spoken a word that sounded official, Harold had an irrational antipathy to his black attire. Nor did I hear him preach, except by accident, for Arghouse chapelry was in the beat of the other curate, and in the afternoon, when I went to Mycening old church, he had persuaded Mr. Crosse to let him begin what was then a great innovation—a children's service, with open doors, in the National School-room. Miss Woolmer advised me to try the effect of this upon Dora, whose Sundays were a constant perplexity and reproach to me, since she always ran away into the plantations or went with Harold to see the horses, and if we did succeed in dragging her to church, there behaved in the most unedifying manner.

"I don't like the principle of cutting religion down for children," said my old friend. "They ought to be taught to think it a favour to be admitted to grown-up people's services, and learn to follow them, instead of having everything made to please them. It is the sugar-plum system, and so I told Mr. Ben, but he says you must catch wild heathens with sugar; and as I am afraid your poor child is not much better, you had better try the experiment."

I did try it, and the metrical litany and the hymns happily took Dora's fancy, so that she submitted to accompany me whenever Harold was to sit with George Yolland, and would not take her.

One afternoon, when I was not well, I was going to send her with Colman, and Harold coming in upon her tempest of resistance, and trying to hush it, she declared that she would only go if he did, and to my amazement he yielded and she led him off in her chains.

He made no comment, but on the next Sunday I found him pocketing an immense parcel of sweets. He walked into the town with us, and when I expected him to turn off to his friend's lodging, he said, "Lucy, if you prefer the old church, I'll take Dora to the school. I like the little monkeys."

He went, and he went again and again, towering among the pigmies in the great room, kneeling when they knelt, adding his deep bass to the curate's in their songs, responding with them, picking up the sleepy and fretful to sit on his knee during the little discourse and the catechising; and then, outside the door, solacing himself and them with a grand distribution of ginger-bread and all other dainty cakes, especially presenting solid plum buns, and even mutton pies, where there were pinched looks and pale faces.

It was delightful, I have been told, to see him sitting on the low wall with as many children as possible scrambling over him, or sometimes standing up, holding a prize above his head, to be scrambled for by the lesser urchins. It had the effect of rendering this a highly popular service, and the curate was wise enough not to interfere with this anomalous conclusion to the service, but to perceive that it might both bless him that gave and those that took.

In the early part of the autumn, one of the little members of the congregation died, and was buried just after the school service. Harold did not know of it, or I do not think he would have been present, for he shrank from whatever renewed the terrible agony of that dark time in Australia.

But the devotions in the school were full of the thought, the metrical litany was one specially adapted to the occasion, so was the brief address, which dwelt vividly, in what some might have called too realising a strain, upon the glories and the joys of innocents in Paradise. And, above all, the hymns had been chosen with special purpose, to tell of those who—

> For ever and for ever
> Are clad in robes of white.

I knew nothing of all this, but when I came home from my own church, and went to my own sitting-room, I was startled to find Harold there, leaning over the table, with that miniature of little Percy, which, two months before, he had bidden me shut up, open before him, and the tears streaming down his face.

In great confusion he muttered, "I beg your pardon," and fled away, dashing his handkerchief over his face. I asked Dora about it, but she would tell nothing; I believe she was half ashamed, half jealous, but it came round through Miss Woolmer, how throughout the address Harold had sat with his eyes fixed on the preacher, and one tear after another gathering in his eyes. And when the concluding hymn was sung—one specially on the joys of Paradise—he leant his forehead against the wall, and could hardly suppress his sobs. When all was over, he handed his bag of sweets to one of the Sunday-school teachers, muttering "Give them," and strode home.

From that time I believe there never was a day that he did not come to my sitting-room to gaze at little Percy. He chose the time when I was least likely to be there, and I knew it well enough to take care that the coast should be left clear for him. I do believe that, ill-taught and unheeding as the poor dear fellow had been, that service was the first thing that had borne in upon him any sense that his children were actually existing, and in joy and bliss; and that when he had once thus hearkened to the idea, that load of anguish, which made him wince at the least recollection of them, was taken off. It was not his nature to speak in the freshness of emotion, and, after a time, there was a seal upon his feelings; but there was an intermediate period when he sometimes came for sympathy, but that was so new a thing to him that he did not quite know how to seek it.

It was the next Sunday evening that I came into my room at a time I did not expect him to be there, just as it was getting dark, that he seemed to feel some explanation due. "This picture," he said, "it is so like my poor little chap."

Then he asked me how old Percy had been when it was taken; and then I found myself listening, as he leant against the mantelpiece, to a minute description of poor little Ambrose, all the words he could say, his baby plays, and his ways of welcoming and clinging to his father, even to the very last, when he moaned if anyone tried to take him out of Harold's arms. It seemed as though the dark shadow and the keen sting had somehow been taken away by the assurance that the child might be thought of full of enjoyment; and certainly, from that time, the peculiar sadness of Harold's countenance diminished. It was always grave, but the air of oppression went away.

I said something about meeting the child again, to which Harold replied, "You will, may be."

"And you, Harold." And as he shook his head, and said something about good people, I added, "It would break my heart to think you would not."

That made him half smile in his strange, sad way, and say, "Thank you, Lucy;" then add, "But it's no use thinking about it; I'm not that sort."

"But you are, but you are, Harold!" I remember crying out with tears. "God has made you to be nobler, and greater, and better than any of us, if you only would—"

"Too late," he said. "After all I have been, and all I have done—"

"Too late! Harry—with a whole lifetime before you to do God real, strong service in?"

"It won't ever cancel that—"

I tried to tell him what had cancelled all; but perhaps I did not do it well enough, for he did not seem to enter into it. It was a terrible disadvantage in all this that I had been so lightly taught. I had been a fairly good girl, I believe, and my dear mother had her sweet, quiet, devotional habits; but religion had always sat, as it were, outside my daily life. I should have talked of "performing my religious duties" as if they were a sort of toll or custom to be paid to God, not as if one's whole life ought to be one religious duty. That sudden loss, which left me alone in the world, made me, as it were, realise who and what my Heavenly Father was to me; and I had in my loneliness thought more of these things, and was learning more every day as I taught Dora; but it was dreadfully shallow, untried knowledge, and, unfortunately, I was the only person to whom Harold would talk. Mr. Smith's having been a clergyman had given him a distaste and mistrust of all clergy; nor do I think he was quite kindly treated by those around us, for they held aloof, and treated him as a formidable stranger with an unknown ill repute, whose very efforts in the cause of good were untrustworthy.

I thought of that mighty man of Israel whom God had endowed with strength to save His people, and how all was made of little avail because his heart was not whole with God, and his doings were self-pleasing and fitful. Oh! that it might not be thus with my Harold? Might not that little child, who had for a moment opened the gates to him, yet draw him upwards where naught else would have availed?

As to talking to me, he did it very seldom, but he had a fashion of lingering to hear me teach Dora, and I found that, if he were absent, he always made her tell him what she had learnt; nor did he shun the meeting me over Percy's picture in my sitting-room in the twilight Sunday hour. Now and then he asked me to find him some passage in the Bible which had struck him in the brief instruction to the children at the service, but what was going on in his mind was entirely out of my reach or scope; but that great strength and alertness, and keen, vivid interest in the world around, still made the present everything to him. I think his powerfulness, and habit of doing impossible things, made the thought of prayer and dependence—nay, even of redemption—more alien to him, as if weakness were involved in it; and though to a certain extent he had, with Prometesky beside him, made his choice between virtue and vice beside his uncle's death-bed; yet it was as yet but the Stoic virtue of the old Polish patriot that he had embraced.

And yet he was not the Stoic. He had far more of the little child, the Christian model in his simplicity, his truth, his tender heart, and that grand modesty of character which, though natural, is the step to Christian humility. How one longed for the voice to say to him, "The Lord is with thee, thou mighty man of valour."

And so time went on, and we were still in solitude. People came and went, had their season in London and returned, but it made no difference to us. Dermot Tracy shot grouse, came home and shot partridges, and Eustace and Harold shared their sport with him, though Harold found it dull cramped work, and thought English gentlemen in sad lack of amusement to call that sport. Lady Diana and Viola went to the seaside, and came back, and what would have been so much to me once was nothing now. Pheasant shooting had begun and I had much ado to prevent Dora from joining the shooting parties, not only when her brother and cousin were alone, but when they were going to meet Mr. Tracy and some of the officers to whom he had introduced them.

On one of these October days, when I was trying to satisfy my discontented Dora by a game at ball upon the steps, to my extreme astonishment I beheld a white pony, led by Harold, and seated on the same pony, no other than my dear little friend, unseen for four months, Viola Tracy!

I rushed, thinking some accident had happened, but Harold called out in a tone of exultation, "Here she is! Now you are to keep her an hour," and she held out her arms with "Lucy, Lucy, dear old Lucy!" and jumped down into mine.

"But Viola, your mother—"

"I could not help it," she said with a laughing light in her eyes. "No, indeed, I could not. I was riding along the lane by Lade Wood, on my white palfrey, when in the great dark glade there stood one, two, three great men with guns, and when one took hold of the damsel's bridle and told her to come with him, what could she do?"

I think I said something feeble about "Harold, how could you?" but he first shook his head, and led off the pony to the stable, observing, "I'll come for you in an hour," and Dora rushing after him.

And when I would have declared that it was very wrong, and that Lady Diana would be very angry, the child stopped my mouth with, "Never mind, I've got my darling Lucy for an hour, and I can't have it spoilt."

Have I never described my Viola? She was not tall, but she had a way of looking so, and she was not pretty, yet she always looked prettier than the prettiest person I ever saw. It was partly the way in which she held her head and long neck, just like a deer, especially when she was surprised, and looked out of those great dark eyes, whose colour was like that of the lakes of which each drop is clear and limpid, and yet, when you look down into the water, it is of a wonderful clear deep grey.

Those eyes were her most remarkable feature; her hair was light, her face went off suddenly into rather too short a chin, her cheeks wanted fulness, and were generally rather pale. So people said, but plump cheeks would have spoilt my Viola's air, of a wild, half-tamed fawn, and lessened the wonderful play of her lips, which used often to express far more than ever came out of them in words. Lady Diana had done her utmost to suppress demonstrativeness, but unless she could have made those eyes less transparent, the corners of that mouth less flexible, and hindered the colour from mantling in those cheeks, she could not have kept Viola's feelings from being patent to all who knew her.

And now the child was really lovely, with the sweet carnation in her cheeks, and eyes dancing with the fear and pretence at alarm, and the delight of a stolen interview with me.

"Forth stepped the giant! Fee! fo! fum!" said she; "took me by the bridle, and said, 'Why haven't you been to see my Aunt Lucy?'"

"I must not," she said.

"And I say you must," he answered. "Do you know she is wearying to see you?"

Then I fancy how Viola's tears would swim in her eyes as she said, "It's not me; it's mamma."

And he answered, "Now, it is not you, but I, that is taking you to see her."

"Should auld acquaintance be forgot!" was whistled out of the wood; and the whistle Viola knew quite well enough to disarm me when I came to the argument what was to become of her if she let such things be done with her; and she had quite enough of Dermot's composition in her to delight in a "little bit of naughtiness that wasn't too bad," and when once she had resigned herself into the hands of her captor she enjoyed it, and twittered like a little bird; and I believe Harold really did it, just as he would have caught a rare bird or wild fawn, to please me.

"Then you were not frightened?" I said.

"Frightened? No. It was such fun! Besides, we heard how he mastered the lion to save that poor little boy, and how he has looked after him ever since, and is going to bind him apprentice. Oh, mind you show me his skin—the lion's, I mean. Don't be tiresome, Lucy. And how he goes on after the children's service with the dear little things. I should think him the last person to be afraid of."

"I wish your mother saw it so."

Viola put on a comically wise look, and shook her head, as she said, "You didn't go the right way to work. If you had come back in the carriage, and consulted her, and said it was a mission—yes, a mission—for you to stand, with a lily in your hand, and reform your two bush-ranger nephews, and that you wanted her consent and advice, then she would have let you go back and be good aunt, and what-not. Oh, I wish you had, Lucy! That was the way Dermot managed about getting the lodge at Biston. He says he could consult her into going out hunting."

"For shame, Viola! O fie! O Vi!" said I, according to an old formula of reproof.

"Really, I wanted to tell you. It might not be too late if you took to consulting her now; and I can't bear being shut up from you. Everything is grown so stupid. When one goes to a garden-party there are nothing but Horsmans and Stympsons, and they all get into sets of themselves and each other, and now and then coalesce, especially the Stympsons, to pity poor Miss Alison, wonder at her not taking mamma's advice, and say how horrid it is of her to live with her cousins. I've corrected that so often that I take about with me the word 'nephews' written in large text, to confute them, and I've actually taught Cocky to say, 'Nephews aren't Cousins.' Dermot is the only rational person in the neighbourhood. I'm always trying to get him to tell me about you, but he says he can't come up here much without giving a handle to the harpies."

I had scarcely said how good it was in Dermot, when he sauntered in. "There you are, Vi; I'm come to your rescue, you know," he said, in his lazy way, and disposed himself on the bear-skin as we sat on the sofa. I tried again to utter a protest. "Oh Dermot, it was all your doing."

"That's rather too bad. As if I could control your domestic lion-tamer."

"You abetted him. You could have prevented him."

"Such being your wish."

"I am thinking of your mother."

"Eh, Viola, is the meeting worth the reckoning?"

"You should not teach her your own bad ways," said I, resisting her embrace.

"Come, we had better be off, Dermot," she said, pouting; "we did not come here to be scolded."

"I thought you did not come of your own free will at all," I said, and then I found I had hurt her, and I had to explain that it was the disobedience that troubled me; whereupon they both argued seriously that people were not bound to submit to a cruel and unreasonable prejudice, which had set the country in arms against us. "Monstrous," Dermot said, "that two fellows should suffer for their fathers' sins, and such fellows, and you too for not being unnatural to your own flesh and blood."

"But that does not make it right for Viola to disobey her mother."

"And how is it to be, Lucy?" asked Viola. "Are we always to go on in this dreadful way?"

By this time Eustace could no longer be withheld from paying his respects to the lady guest, and Harold and Dora came with him, bringing the kangaroo, for which Viola had entreated; and she also made him fetch the lion-skin, which had been dressed and lined and made into a beautiful carriage-rug; and to Dora she owed the exhibition of the great scar across Harold's left palm, which, though now no inconvenience, he would carry through life. It was but for a moment, for as soon as he perceived that Dora meant anything more than her usual play with his fingers, he coloured and thrust his hand into his pocket.

We all walked through the grounds with Viola, and when we parted she hung about my neck and assured me that now she had seen me she should not grieve half so much, and, let mamma say what she would, she could not be sorry; and I had no time to fight over the battle of the sorrow being for wrongdoing, not for reproof, for the pony would bear no more last words.

Eustace had behaved all along with much politeness; in fact, he was always seen to most advantage with strangers, for his manners had some training, and a little constraint was good for him by repressing some of his sayings. His first remark, when the brother and sister were out of hearing, was, "A very sweet, lively young lady. I never saw her surpassed in Sydney!"

"I should think not," said Harold.

"Well, you know I have been presented and have been to a ball at Government House. There's an air, a tournure about her, such as uncle Smith says belongs to the real aristocracy; and you saw she was quite at her ease with me. We understand each other in the higher orders. Don't be afraid, Lucy, we shall yet bring back your friend to you."

"I'm glad she is gone," said Dora, true to her jealousy. "I like Dermot; he's got some sense in him, but she's not half so nice and pretty as Lucy."

At which we all laughed, for I had never had any attempt at beauty, except, I believe, good hair and teeth, and a habit of looking good-humoured.

"She's a tip-topper," pronounced Eustace, "and no wonder, considering who she is. Has she been presented, Lucy?"

Though she had not yet had that inestimable advantage, Eustace showed himself so much struck with her that, when next Harold found himself alone with me, he built a very remarkable castle in the air—namely, a wedding between Eustace and Viola Tracy. "If I saw him with such happiness as that," said Harold, "it would be all right. I should have no fears at all for him. Don't you think it might be, Lucy?"

"I don't think you took the way to recommend the family to Lady Diana," I said, laughing.

"I had not thought of it then," said Harold; "I'm always doing something wrong. I wonder if I had better go back and keep out of his way?"

He guessed what I should answer, I believe, for I was sure that Eustace would fail without Harold, and I told him that his cousin must not be left to himself till he had a good wife. To which Harold replied, "Are all English ladies like that?"

He had an odd sort of answer the next day, when we were all riding together, and met another riding party—namely, the head of the Horsman family and his two sisters, who had been on the Continent when my nephews arrived. Mamma did not like them, and we had never been great friends; but they hailed me quite demonstratively with their eager, ringing voices: "Lucy! Lucy Alison! So glad to see you! Here we are again. Introduce us, pray."

So I did. Mr. Horsman, Miss Hippolyta, and Miss Philippa Horsman—Baby Jack, Hippo, and Pippa, as they were commonly termed—and we all rode together as long as we were on the Roman road, while they conveyed, rather loudly, information about the Dolomites.

They were five or six years older than I, and the recollection of childish tyranny and compulsion still made me a little afraid of them. They excelled in all kinds of sports in which we younger ones had not had nearly so much practice, and did not much concern themselves whether the sport were masculine or feminine, to the distress of the quiet elder half-sister, who stayed at home, like a hen with ducklings to manage.

They spoke of calling, and while I could not help being grateful, I knew how fallen my poor mother would think me to welcome the notice of Pippa and Hippo.

Most enthusiastic was the latter as she rode behind with me, looking at the proportions of Harry and his horse, some little way on before, with Dora on one side, and Pippa rattling on the other.

"Splendid! Splendiferous! More than I was prepared for, though I heard all about the lion—and that he has been a regular stunner in Australia—eh, Lucy, just like a hero of Whyte-Melville's, eh?"

"I don't think so."

"And, to complete it all, what has he been doing to little Viola Tracy? Oh, what fun! Carrying her off bodily to see you, wasn't it? Lady Diana is in such a rage as never was—says Dermot is never to be trusted with his sister again, and won't let her go beyond the garden without her. Oh, the fun of it! I would have gone anywhere to see old Lady Di's face!"

CHAPTER V
THE CAPTURE IN THE SNOW

I do not recollect anything happening for a good while. Our chief event was the perfect success of Mr. Yolland's concentrated fuel, which did not blow up anything or anybody, and the production of some lovely Etruscan vases and tiles, for which I copied the designs out of a book I happily discovered in the library. They were sent up to the porcelain shops in London, and orders began to come in, to the great exultation of Harold and Co., an exultation which I could not help partaking, even while it seemed to me to be plunging him deeper and deeper in the dangerous speculation.

We put the vases into a shop in the town and wondered they did not sell; but happily people at a distance were kinder, and native genius was discovered in a youth, who soon made beautiful designs. But I do not think the revived activity of the unpopular pottery did us at that time any good with our neighbours.

Harold and Eustace sent in their subscriptions to the hunt and were not refused, but there were rumours that some of the Stympsons had threatened to withdraw.

I had half a mind to ride with them to the meet, but I could not tell who would cut me, and I knew the mortification would be so keen to them that I could not tell how they would behave, and I was afraid Eustace's pride in his scarlet coat might be as manifest to others as to us, and make me blush for him. So I kept Dora and myself at home.

I found that by the management of Dermot Tracy and his friends, the slight had been less apparent than had been intended, when all the other gentlemen had been asked in to Mr. Stympson's to breakfast, and they had been left out with the farmers; Dermot had so resented this that he had declined going into the house, and ridden to the village inn with them.

To my surprise, Eustace chose to go on hunting, because it asserted his rights and showed he did not care; and, besides, the hard riding was almost a necessity to both the young men, and the Foling hounds, beyond Biston, were less exclusive, and they were welcomed there. I believe their horsemanship extorted admiration from the whole field, and that they were gathering acquaintance, though not among those who were most desirable. The hunting that was esteemed hard exercise here was nothing to them. They felt cramped and confined even when they had had the longest runs, and disdained the inclosures they were forced to respect. I really don't know what Harold would have done but for Kalydon Moor, where he had a range without inclosures of some twelve miles. I think he rushed up there almost every day, and thus kept himself in health, and able to endure the confinement of our civilised life.

A very hard winter set in unusually early, and with a great deal of snow in December. It was a great novelty to our Australians, and was not much relished by Eustace, who did not enjoy the snow-balling and snow fortification in which Harold and Dora revelled in front of the house all the forenoon. After luncheon, when the snowstorm had come on too thickly for Dora to go out again, Harold insisted on going to see how the world looked from the moor. I entreated him not to go far, telling him how easy it was to lose the way when all outlines were changed in a way that would baffle even a black fellow; but he listened with a smile, took a plaid and a cap and sallied forth. I played at shuttle-cock for a good while with Dora, and then at billiards with Eustace; and when evening had closed darkly in, and the whole outside world was blotted out with the flakes and their mist, I began to grow a little anxious.

The hall was draughty, but there was a huge wood fire in it, and it seemed the best place to watch in, so there we sat together, and Eustace abused the climate and I told stories—dismal ones, I fear—about sheep and shepherds, dogs and snowdrifts, to the tune of that peculiar howl that the wind always makes when the blast is snow-laden; and dinner time came, and I could not make up my mind to go and dress so as to be out of reach of—I don't know what I expected to happen. Certainly what did happen was far from anything I had pictured to myself.

Battling with the elements and plunging in the snow, and seeing, whenever it slackened, so strange and new a world, was a sort of sport to Harold, and he strode on, making his goal the highest point of the moor, whence, if it cleared a little, he would be able to see to a vast distance. He was curious, too, to look down into the railway cutting. This was a sort of twig from a branch of the main line, chiefly due to Lord Erymanth, who, after fighting off the railway from all points adjacent to his estate, had found it so inconvenient to be without a station within reasonable distance, that a single line had at last been made from Mycening for the benefit of the places in this direction, but not many trains ran on it, for it was not much frequented.

Harold came to the brow of the cutting, and there beheld the funnel of a locomotive engine, locomotive no more, but firmly embedded in the snowdrift into which it had run, with a poor little train of three or four carriages behind it, already half buried. Not a person was to be seen, as Harold scrambled and slid down the descent and lighted on the top of one of the carriages; for, as it proved, the engineer, stoker, and two or three passengers had left the train an hour before, and were struggling along the line to the nearest station. Harold got down on the farther side, which was free of snow, and looked into all the carriages. No one was there, till, in a first-class one, he beheld an old gentleman, well wrapped up indeed, but numb, stiff, and dazed with the sleep out of which he was roused.

"Tickets, eh?" he said, and he dreamily held one out to Harold and tried to get up, but he stumbled, and hardly seemed to understand when Harold told him it was not the station, but that they had run into the snowdrift; he only muttered something about being met, staggered forward, and fell into Harold's arms. There was a carriage-bag on the seat, but Harold looked in vain there for a flask. The poor old man was hardly sensible. Ours was the nearest house, and Harold saw that the only chance for the poor old gentleman's life was to carry him home at once. Even for him it was no small effort, for his burthen was a sturdy man with the solidity of years, and nearly helpless, save that the warmth of Harold's body did give him just life and instinct to hold on, and let himself be bound to him with the long plaid so as least to impede his movements; but only one possessed of Harold's almost giant strength could have thus clambered the cutting at the nearest point to Arghouse and plodded through the snow. The only wonder is that they were not both lost. Their track was marked as long as that snow lasted by mighty holes.

It was at about a quarter-past seven that all the dogs barked, a fumbling was heard at the door, and a muffled voice, "Let me in."

Then in stumbled a heap of snow, panting, and amid Spitz's frantic barks, we saw it was Harold, bent nearly double by the figure tied to him. He sank on his knee, so as to place his burthen on the great couch, gasping, "Untie me," and as I undid the knot, he rose to his feet, panting heavily, and, in spite of the cold, bathed in perspiration.

"Get something hot for him directly," he said, falling back into an arm-chair, while we broke out in exclamations. "Who—where did you find him? Some poor old beggar. Not too near the fire—call Richardson—hot brandy-and-water—bed. He's some poor old beggar," and such outcries for a moment or two, till Harold, recovering himself in a second, explained, "Snowed up in the train. Here, Lucy, Eustace, rub his hands. Dora, ask

Richardson for something hot. Are you better now, sir?" beginning to pull off the boots that he might rub his feet; but this measure roused the traveller, who resisted, crying out, "Don't, don't, my good man, I'll reward you handsomely. I'm a justice of the peace."

Thick and stifled as it was, the voice was familiar. I looked again, and screamed out, "Lord Erymanth, is it you?"

That roused him, and as I took hold of both hands and bent over him, he looked up, dazzled and muttering, "Lucy, Lucy Alison! Arghouse! How came I here?" and then as the hot cordial came at last, in the hand of Richardson, who had once been in his service, he swallowed it, and then leant back and gazed at me as I went on rubbing his hands. "Thank you, my dear. Is it you? I thought I was snowed up, and I have never signed that codicil about little Viola, or I could die easily. It is not such a severe mode, after all."

"But you're not dying, you're only dreaming. You are at Arghouse. Harold here found you and brought you to us."

And then we agreed that he had better be put to bed at once in Eustace's room, as there was already a fire there, and any other would take long in being warmed.

Harold and Eustace got him upstairs between them, and Richardson followed, while I looked out with dismay at the drifting snow, and wondered how to send either for a doctor or for Lady Diana in case of need. He had been a childless widower for many years, and had no one nearer belonging to him. Dora expressed her amazement that I did not go to help, but I knew this would have shocked him dreadfully, and I only sent Colman to see whether she could be of any use.

Harold came out first, and on his way to get rid of his snow-soaked garments, paused to tell me that the old gentleman had pretty well come round, and was being fed with hot soup and wine, while he seemed half asleep. "He is not frost-bitten," added Harold; "but if he is likely to want the doctor, I'd better go on to Mycening at once, before I change my things."

But I knew Lord Erymanth to be a hale, strong man of his years, little given to doctors, and as I heard he had said "No, no," when Eustace proposed to send for one, I was glad to negative the proposal from a man already wet through and tired—"well, just a little."

Our patient dropped asleep almost as soon as he had had his meal, in the very middle of a ceremonious speech of thanks, which sent Eustace down to dinner more than ever sure that there was nothing like the aristocracy, who all understood one another; and we left Richardson to watch over him, and sleep in the dressing-room in case of such a catastrophe as a rheumatic waking in the night.

We were standing about the fire in the hall, our usual morning waiting-place before breakfast, and had just received Richardson's report that his lordship had had a good night, seemed none the worse, and would presently appear, but that he desired we would not wait breakfast, when there was a hasty ring at the door, and no sooner was it opened than Dermot Tracy, battered and worn, in a sou'-wester sprinkled with snow and with boots up to his thighs, burst into the hall.

"Alison, you there? All right, I want you," shaking hands in an agitated way all round, and speaking very fast with much emotion. "I want you to come and search for my poor uncle. He was certainly in the train from Mycening that ran into a drift. Men went to get help; couldn't get back for three hours. He wasn't there—never arrived at home. My mother is in a dreadful state. Hogg is setting all the men to dig at the Erymanth end. I've got a lot to begin in the Kalydon cutting; but you'll come, Alison, you'll be worth a dozen of them. He might be alive still, you see."

"Thank you, Dermot, I am happy to say that such is the case," said a voice from the oak staircase, and down it was slowly proceeding Lord Erymanth, as trim, and portly, and well brushed-up as if he had arrived behind his two long-tailed bays.

Dermot, with his eyes full of tears, which he was squeezing and winking away, and his rapid, broken voice, had seen and heard nothing in our faces or exclamations to prepare him. He started violently and sprang forward, meeting Lord Erymanth at the foot of the stairs, and wringing both his hands—nay, I almost thought he would have kissed him, as he broke out into some incoherent cry of scarcely-believing joy, which perhaps surprised and touched the old man. "There, there, Dermot, my boy, your solicitude is—is honourable to you; but restrain—restrain it, my dear boy—we are not alone." And he advanced, a little rheumatically, to us, holding out his hand with morning greetings.

"I must send to my mother. Joe is here with the sleigh," said Dermot. "Uncle, how did you come here?" he added, as reflection only made his amazement profounder.

"It is true, as you said just now, that Mr. Harold Alison is equal to a dozen men. I owe my preservation, under Providence, to him," said Lord Erymanth, who, though not a small man, had to look far up as Harold stood towering above us all. "My most earnest acknowledgments are due to him," he added, solemnly holding out his hand.

"I might have expected that!" ejaculated Dermot, while Harold took the offered hand with a smile, and a mutter in his beard of "I am very glad."

"I'll just send a line to satisfy my mother," said Dermot, taking a pen from the inkstand on the hall-table. "Joe's here with the sleigh, and we must telegraph to George St. Glear."

Lord Erymanth repeated the name in some amazement, for he was not particularly fond of his heir.

"Hogg telegraphed to him this morning," and as the uncle observed, "Somewhat premature," he went on: "Poor Hogg was beside himself; he came to Arked at ten o'clock last night to look for you, and, luckily, I was there, so we've been hallooing half the night along the line, and then getting men together in readiness for the search as soon as it was light. I must be off to stop them at once. I came in to get the Alisons' help—never dreamt of such a thing as finding you here. And, after all, I don't understand—how did you come?"

"I cannot give you a detailed account," said his lordship. "Mr. Harold Alison roused me from a drowsiness which might soon, very probably, have been fatal, and brought me here. I have no very distinct recollection of the mode, and I fear I must have been a somewhat helpless and encumbering burthen."

Dora put in her oar. "Harry can carry anything," she said; "he brought you in so nicely on his back—just as I used to ride."

"On his back!"

"Yes," said Dora, who was fond of Mr. Tracy, and glad to impart her information, "on his back, with his boots sticking out on each side, so funnily!"

Lord Erymanth endeavoured to swallow the information suavely by the help of a classical precedent, and said, with a gracious smile, "Then I perceive we must have played the part of AEneas and Anchises—" But before he had got so far, the idea had been quite too much for Dermot, who cried out, "Pick-a-back! With his boots sticking out on both sides! Thank you, Dora. Oh! my uncle, pick-a-back!" and went off in an increasing, uncontrollable roar of laughter, while Harold, with a great tug to his moustache, observed apologetically to Lord Erymanth, "It was the only way I could do it," which speech had the effect of so prolonging poor Dermot's mirth, that all the good effect of the feeling he had previously displayed for his uncle was lost, and Lord Erymanth observed, in his most dry and solemn manner, "There are some people who can see nothing but food for senseless ridicule in the dangers of their friends."

"My dear Lord Erymanth," I said, almost wild, "do just consider Dermot has been up all night, and has had nothing to eat, and is immensely relieved to find you all safe. He can't be expected to quite know what he is about when he is so shaken. Come to breakfast, and we shall all be better."

"That might be a very sufficient excuse for you or for Viola, my dear Lucy," returned Lord Erymanth, taking, however, the arm I offered. "Young *ladies* may be very amiably hysterical, but a young man, in my day, who had not trifled away his manliness, would be ashamed of such an excuse."

There was a certain truth in what he said. Dermot was not then so strong, nor had he the self-command he would have had, if his life had been more regular; but he must always have had a much more sensitive and emotional nature than his uncle could ever understand. The reproach, however, sobered him in a moment, and he followed us gravely into the dining-room, without uttering a word for the next quarter of an hour; neither did Harold, who was genuinely vexed at having made the old man feel himself ridiculous, and was sorry for the displeasure with his friend. Nobody did say much except Eustace, who was delighted at having to play host to such distinguished guests, and Lord Erymanth himself, who was so gracious and sententious as quite to restore Dermot's usual self by the time breakfast was over, and he saw his servant bringing back his sleigh, in which he offered to convey his uncle either home or to Arked. But it was still fitfully snowing, and Lord Erymanth was evidently not without touches of rheumatism, which made him lend a willing ear to our entreaties to him not to expose himself. Harold then undertook to go in search of his portmanteau either to the scene of the catastrophe or the Hall.

"My dear sir, I could not think of exposing you to a repetition of such inclement weather as you have already encountered. I am well supplied here, my young friend—I think I may use the term, considering that two generations ago, at least, a mutual friendship existed between the houses, which, however obscured for a time—hum—hum—hum—may be said still to exist towards my dear friend's very amiable young daughter; and although I may have regretted as hasty and premature a decision that, as her oldest and most experienced—I may say paternal—friend, I ventured to question—you will excuse my plain speaking; I am always accustomed to utter my sentiments freely—yet on better acquaintance—brought about as it was in a manner which, however peculiar, and, I may say, unpleasant—cannot do otherwise than command my perpetual gratitude—I am induced to revoke a verdict, uttered, perhaps, rather with a view to the antecedents than to the individuals, and to express a hope that the ancient family ties may again assert themselves, and that I may again address as such Mr. Alison of Arghouse."

That speech absolutely cleared the field of Harold and Dermot both. One strode, the other backed, to the door, Dermot hastily said, "Good-bye then, uncle, I shall look you up to-morrow, but I must go and stop George St. Glear," and Harold made no further ceremony, but departed under his cover.

Probably, Richardson had spoken a word or two in our favour to his former master, for, when Lord Erymanth was relieved from his nephew's trying presence, he was most gracious, and his harangues, much as they had once fretted me, had now a familiar sound, as proving that we were no longer "at the back of the north wind," while Eustace listened with rapt attention, both to the long words and to anything coming from one whose name was enrolled in his favourite volume; who likewise discovered in him likenesses to generations past of Alisons, and seemed ready to admit him to all the privileges for which he had been six months pining.

At the first opportunity, Lord Erymanth began to me, "My dear Lucy, it is a confession that to some natures may seem humiliating, but I have so sedulously cultivated candour for my whole term of existence, that I hope I may flatter myself that I am not a novice in the great art of retracting a conclusion arrived at under premises which, though probable, have proved to be illusory. I therefore freely confess that I have allowed probability to weigh too much with me in my estimation of these young men." I almost jumped for joy as I cried out that I knew he would think so when he came to know them.

"Yes, I am grateful to the accident that has given me the opportunity of judging for myself," quoth Lord Erymanth, and with a magnanimity which I was then too inexperienced to perceive, he added, "I can better estimate the motives which made you decide on fixing your residence with your nephews, and I have no reluctance in declaring them natural and praiseworthy." I showed my satisfaction in my old friend's forgiveness, but he still went on: "Still, my dear, you must allow me to represent that your residence here, though it is self-innocent, exposes you to unpleasant complications. I cannot think it well that a young lady of your age should live entirely with two youths without female society, and be constantly associating with such friends as they may collect round them."

I remember now how the unshed tears burnt in my eyes as I said the female society had left me to myself, and begged to know with whom I had associated. In return I heard something that filled me with indignation about his nephew, Dermot Tracy, not being exactly the companion for an unchaperoned young lady, far less his sporting friends, or that young man who had been Dr. Kingston's partner. He was very sorry for me, as he saw my cheeks flaming, but he felt it right that I should be aware. I told him how I had guarded myself—never once come across the sportsmen, and only seen Mr. Yolland professionally when he showed me how to dress Harold's hand, besides the time when he went over the pottery with us. Nay, Dermot himself had only twice come into my company—once about his sister, and once to inquire after Harold after the adventure with the lion.

There I found I had alluded to what made Lord Erymanth doubly convinced that I must be blinded; my sight must be amiably obscured, as to the unfitness—he might say, the impropriety of such companions for me. He regretted all the more where his nephew was concerned, but it was due to me to warn, to admonish, me of the true facts of the case.

I did not see how I could want any admonition of the true facts I had seen with my own eyes.

He was intensely astonished, and did not know how to believe that I had actually seen the lion overpowered; whereupon I begged to know what he had heard. He was very unwilling to tell me, but it came out at last that Dermot and Harold—being, he feared, in an improperly excited condition—had insisted on going to the den with the keeper, and had irritated the animal by wanton mischief, and he was convinced that this could not have taken place in my presence.

I was indignant beyond measure. Had not Dermot told him the true story? He shook his head, and was much concerned at having to say so, but he had so entirely ceased to put any confidence in Dermot's statements that he preferred not listening to them. And I knew it was vain to try to show him the difference between deliberate falsehood, which was abhorrent to Dermot, and the exaggerations and mystifications to which his uncle's solemnity always prompted him. I appealed to the county paper; but he had been abroad at the time, and had, moreover, been told that the facts had been hushed up.

Happily, he had some trust in my veracity, and let me prove my perfect alibi for Harold as well as for Dermot. When I represented how those two were the only men among some hundreds who had shown either courage or coolness, he granted it with the words, "True, true. Of course, of course. That's the way good blood shows itself. Hereditary qualities are sure to manifest themselves."

Then he let me exonerate Harold from the charge of intemperance, pointing out that not even after the injury and operation, nor after yesterday's cold and fatigue, had he touched any liquor; but I don't think the notion of teetotalism was gratifying, even when I called it a private, individual vow. Nor could I make out whether his Australian life was known, and I was afraid to speak of it, lest I should be betraying what need never be mentioned. Of Viola's adventure, to my surprise, her uncle did not make much, but he had heard of that from the fountain-head, unpolluted by Stympson gossip; and, moreover, Lady Diana had been so disproportionately angry as to produce a reaction in him. Viola was his darling, and he had taken her part when he had found that she knew her brother was at hand. He allowed, too, that she might fairly be inspired with confidence by the voice and countenance of her captor, whom he seemed to view as a good-natured giant. But even this was an advance on "the prize-fighter," as Lady Diana and the Stympsons called him.

It was an amusing thing to hear the old earl moralising on the fortunate conjunction of circumstances, which had brought the property, contrary to all expectation, to the most suitable individual. Much did I long for Harold to return and show what he was, but only his lordship's servant, letters, and portmanteau came on an improvised sleigh. He had an immense political, county, and benevolent correspondence, and was busied with it all the rest of the day. Eustace hovered about reverentially and obligingly, and secured the good opinion which had been already partly gained by the statement of the police at the Quarter Sessions, whence Lord Erymanth had been returning, that they never had had so few cases from the Hydriot potteries as during this last quarter. Who could be complimented upon this happy state of things save the chairman? And who could appropriate the compliment more readily or with greater delight? Even I felt that it would be cruel high treason to demonstrate which was the mere chess king.

Poor Eustace! Harold had infected me enough with care for him to like to see him in such glory, though somewhat restless as to the appearances of this first state dinner of ours, and at Harold's absence; but, happily, the well-known step was in the hall before our guest came downstairs, and Eustace dashed out to superintend the toilette that was to be as worthy of meeting with an earl as nature and garments would permit. "Fit to be seen?" I heard Harold growl. "Of course I do when I dine with Lucy, and this is only an old man."

Eustace and Richardson had disinterred and brushed up Harold's only black suit (ordered as mourning for his wife, and never worn but at his uncle's funeral); but three years' expansion of chest and shoulder had made it pinion him so as to lessen the air of perfect ease which, without being what is called grace, was goodly to look upon. Eustace's studs were in his shirt, and the unnatural shine on his tawny hair too plainly revealed the perfumeries that crowded the young squire's dressing-table. With the purest intentions of kindness Eustace had done his best to disguise a demigod as a lout.

We had a diner a la Russe, to satisfy Eustace's aspirations as to the suitable. I had been seeking resources for it all the afternoon and building up erections with Richardson and Colman; and when poor Harold, who had been out in the snow with nothing to eat since breakfast, beheld it, he exclaimed, "Lucy, why did you not tell me? I could have gone over to Mycening and brought you home a leg of mutton."

"Don't expose what a cub you are!" muttered the despairing Eustace. "It is a deena a la Roos."

"I thought the Russians ate blubber," observed Harold, somewhat unfeelingly, though I don't think he saw the joke; but I managed to reassure him, sotto voce, as to there being something solid in the background. He was really ravenous, and it was a little comedy to see the despairing contempt with which he regarded the dainty little mouthfuls that the cook viewed with triumph, and Eustace in equal misery at his savage appetite; while Lord Erymanth, far too real a gentleman to be shocked at a man's eating when he was hungry, was quite insensible of the by-play until Harold, reduced to extremity at sight of one delicate shaving of turkey's breast, burst out, "I say, Richardson, I must have some food. Cut me its leg, please, at once!"

"Harry," faintly groaned Eustace, while Lord Erymanth observed, "Ah! there is no such receipt for an appetite as shooting in the snow. I remember when a turkey's leg would have been nothing to me, after being out duck-shooting in Kalydon Bog. Have you been there to-day? There would be good sport."

"No," said Harold, contented at last with the great leg, which seemed in the same proportion to him as a chicken's to other men. "I have been getting sheep out of the snow."

I elicited from him that he had, in making his way to Erymanth, heard the barking of a dog, and found that a shepherd and his flock had taken refuge in a hollow of the moor, which had partly protected them from the snow, but whence they could not escape. The shepherd, a drover who did not know the locality, had tried with morning light to find his way to help, but, spent and exhausted, would soon have perished, had not Harold been attracted by the dog. After dragging him to the nearest farm, Harold left the man to be restored by food and fire, while performing his own commission at the castle, and then returned to spend the remainder of the daylight hours in helping to extricate the sheep, and convey them to the farmyard, so that only five had been lost.

"An excellent, not to say a noble, manner of spending a winter's day," quoth the earl.

"I am a sheep farmer myself," was the reply.

Lord Erymanth really wanted to draw him out, and began to ask about Australian stock-farming, but Harold's slowness of speech left Eustace to reply to everything, and when once the rage of hunger was appeased, the harangues in a warm room after twenty miles' walk in the snow, and the carrying some hundreds of sheep one by one in his arms, produced certain nods and snores which were no favourable contrast with Eustace's rapt attention.

For, honestly, Eustace thought these speeches the finest things he had ever heard, and though he seldom presumed to understand them, he listened earnestly, and even imitated them in a sort of disjointed way. Now Lord Erymanth, if one could manage to follow him, was always coherent. His sentences would parse, and went on uniform principles—namely, the repeating every phrase in finer words, with all possible qualifications; whereas Eustace never accomplished more than catching up some sonorous period; but as his manners were at their best when he was overawed, and nine months in England had so far improved his taste that he did not once refer to his presentation at Government House, he made such an excellent impression that Lord Erymanth announced that he was going to give a ball to introduce his niece, Miss Tracy, on her seventeenth birthday, in January, and invited us all thereto.

Eustace's ecstacy was unbounded. He tried to wake Harold to share it, but only produced some murmurs about half-inch bullets: only when the "Good-night" came did Harold rouse up, and then, of course, he was wide awake; and while Eustace was escorting the distinguished guest to his apartment, we stood over the hall fire, enjoying his delight, and the prospect of his being righted with the county.

"And you will have your friends again, Lucy," added Harold.

"Yes, I don't suppose Lady Diana will hold out against him. He will prepare the way."

"And," said Eustace, coming downstairs, "it is absolutely necessary that you go and be measured for a dress suit, Harry."

"I will certainly never get into this again," he said, with a thwarted sigh; "it's all I can do to help splitting it down the back. You must get it off as you got it on."

"Not here!" entreated Eustace, alarmed at his gesture. "Remember the servant. Oh Harold, if you could but be more the gentleman! Why cannot you take example by me, instead of overthrowing all the advantageous impressions that such—such a service has created? I really think there's nothing he would not do for me. Don't you think so, Lucy?"

"Could he do anything for Prometesky?" asked Harold.

"He could, more than anyone," I said; "but I don't know if he would."

"I'll see about that."

"Now, Harold," cried Eustace in dismay, "don't spoil everything by offending him. Just suppose he should not send us the invitation!"

"No great harm done."

Eustace was incoherent in his wrath and horror, and Harold, too much used to his childish selfishness to feel the annoyance, answered, "I am not you."

"But if you offend him?"

"Never fear, Eu, I'll take care you don't fare the worse."

And as he lighted his candle he added to poor Eustace's discomfiture by the shocking utterance under his beard:

"You are welcome to him for me, if you can stand such an old bore."

CHAPTER VI
OGDEN'S BUILDINGS

When I came downstairs the next morning, I found Lord Erymanth at the hall window, watching the advance of a great waggon of coal which had stuck fast in the snow half way up the hill on which the house stood. Harold, a much more comfortable figure in his natural costume than he had been when made up by Eustace, was truly putting his shoulder to the wheel, with a great lever, so that every effort aided the struggling horses, and brought the whole nearer to its destination.

"A grand exhibition of strength," said his lordship, as the waggon was at last over its difficulties, and Harold disappeared with it into the back-yard; "a magnificent physical development. I never before saw extraordinary height with proportionate size and strength."

I asked if he had ever seen anyone as tall.

"I have seen one or two men who looked equally tall, but they stooped and were not well-proportioned, whereas your nephew has a wonderfully fine natural carriage. What is his measure?" he added, turning to Eustace.

"Well, really, my lord, I cannot tell; mine is six feet two and five-sixteenths, and I much prefer it to anything so out of the way as his, poor fellow."

The danger that he would go on to repeat his tailor's verdict "that it was distinguished without being excessive," was averted by Harold's entrance, and Dora interrupted the greetings by the query to her cousin, how high he really stood; but he could not tell, and when she unfraternally pressed to know whether it was not nice to be so much taller than Eustace, he replied, "Not on board ship," and then he gave the intelligence that it seemed about to thaw.

Lord Erymanth said that if so, he should try to make his way to Mycening, and he then paid his renewed compliments on the freedom of the calendar at the Quarter Sessions from the usual proportion of evils at Mycening. He understood that Mr. Alison was making most praiseworthy efforts to impede the fatal habits of intoxication that were only too prevalent.

"I shall close five beer-houses at Christmas," said Eustace. "I look on it as my duty, as landlord and man of property."

"Quite right. I am glad you see the matter in its right light. Beer-shops were a well-meaning experiment started some twenty years ago. I well remember the debate, &c."

Harold tried with all his might to listen, though I saw his chest heave with many a suppressed yawn, and his hand under his beard, tweaking it hard; but substance could be sifted out of what Lord Erymanth said, for he had real experience, and his own parish was in admirable order.

Where there was no power of expulsion, as he said, there would always be some degraded beings whose sole amusement was intoxication; but good dwelling-houses capable of being made cheerful, gardens, innocent recreations, and instruction had, he could testify from experience, no small effect in preventing such habits from being formed in the younger population, backed, as he was sure (good old man) that he need not tell his young friends, by an active and efficient clergyman, who would place the motives for good conduct on the truest and highest footing, without which all reformation would only be surface work. I was glad Harold should hear this from the lips of a layman, but I am afraid he shirked it as a bit of prosing, and went back to the cottages.

"They are in a shameful state," he said.

"They are to be improved," exclaimed Eustace, eagerly. "As I told Bullock, I am quite determined that mine shall be a model parish. I am ready to make any sacrifices to do my duty as a landlord, though Bullock says that no outlay on cottages ever pays, and that the test of their being habitable is their being let, and that the people are so ungrateful that they do not deserve to have anything done for them."

"You are not led away by such selfish arguments?" said Lord Erymanth.

"No, assuredly not," said Eustace, decidedly; "though I do wish Harold would not disagree so much with Bullock. He is a very civil man, and much in earnest in promoting my interests."

"That's not all," put in Harold.

"And I can't bear Bullock," I said. "'Our interest' has been always his cry, whenever the least thing has been proposed for the cottage people; and I know how much worse he let things get than we ever supposed."

On which Lord Erymanth spoke out his distinct advice to get rid of Bullock, telling us how he had been a servant's orphan whom my father had intended to apprentice, but, being placed with our old bailiff for a time, had made himself necessary, and ingratiated himself with my father so as to succeed to the situation; and it had been the universal belief, ever since my mother's widowhood, that he had taken advantage of her seclusion and want of knowledge of business to deal harshly by the tenants, especially the poor, and to feather his own nest.

It was only what Harold had already found out for himself, but it disposed of his scruples about old adherents, and it was well for Eustace to hear it from such oracular lips as might neutralise the effect of Bullock's flattery, for it had become quite plain to my opened eyes that he was trying to gain the squire's ear, and was very jealous of Harold.

I knew, too, that to listen to his advice was the way to Lord Erymanth's heart, and rejoiced to hear Harold begging for the names of recent books on drainage, and consulting our friend upon the means of dealing with a certain small farm in a tiny inclosed valley, on an outlying part of the property, where the yard and outhouses were in a permanent state of horrors; but interference was alike resented by Bullock and the farmer, though the wife and family were piteous spectacles of ague and rheumatism, and low fever smouldered every autumn in the hamlet.

Very sound advice was given and accepted with pertinent questions, such as I thought must convince anyone of Harold's superiority, when he must needs produce a long blue envelope, and beg Lord Erymanth to look at it and tell him how to get it presented to the Secretary of State.

It was graciously received, but no sooner did the name of Stanislas Prometesky strike the earl's eyes than he exclaimed, "That rascally old demagogue! The author of all the mischief. It was the greatest error and weakness not to have had him executed."

"You have not seen my father's statement?"

"Statement, sir! I read statements till I was sick of them, absolutely disgusted with their reiteration, and what could they say but that he was a Pole? A Pole!" (the word uttered with infinite loathing). "As if the very name were not a sufficient conviction of whatever is seditious and treasonable, only that people are sentimental about it, forsooth!"

Certainly it was droll to suspect sentiment in the great broad giant, who indignantly made reply, "The Poles have been infamously treated."

"No more than they deserved," said Lord Erymanth, startled for once into brevity. "A nation who could never govern themselves decently, and since they have been broken up, as they richly deserved, though I do not justify the manner—ever since, I say, have been acting the incendiary in every country where they have set foot. I would as soon hear of an infernal machine in the country as a Pole!"

"Poles deserve justice as well as other men," said Harold, perhaps the more doggedly because Eustace laid a restraining hand on his arm.

"Do you mean to tell me, sir, that every man has not received justice at the tribunal of this country?" exclaimed Lord Erymanth.

Perhaps he recollected that he was speaking to the son of a convict, for there was a moment's pause, into which I launched myself. "Dear Lord Erymanth," I said, "we all know that my poor brothers did offend against the laws and were sentenced according to them. They said so themselves, and that they were mistaken, did they not, Harold?"

Harold bent his head.

"And owing to whom?" demanded Lord Elymanth. "I never thought of blaming those two poor lads as I did that fellow who led them astray. I did all I could to save their lives; if they were alive this moment I would wish nothing better than to bring them home, but as to asking me to forward a petition in favour of the hoary old rebel that perverted them, I should think it a crime."

"But," I said, "if you would only read this, you would see that what they wanted to explain was that the man who turned king's evidence did not show how Count Prometesky tried to withhold them."

"Count, indeed! Just like all women. All those Poles are Counts! All Thaddeuses of Warsaw!"

"That's hard," I said. "I only called him Count because it would have shocked you if I had given him no prefix. Will you not see what poor Ambrose wanted to say for him?"

"Ah!" said Lord Erymanth, after a pause, in which he had really glanced over the paper. "Poor boys! It goes to my heart to think what fine fellows were lost there, but compassion for them cannot soften me towards the man who practised on their generous, unsuspecting youth. I am quite aware that Prometesky saved life at the fire, and his punishment was commuted on that account, contrary to my judgment, for it is a well-known axiom, that the author of a riot is responsible for all the outrages committed in it, and it is undeniable that the whole insurrection was his work. I am quite aware that the man had amiable, even fascinating qualities, and great enthusiasm, but here lay the great danger and seduction to young minds, and though I can perfectly understand the warm sympathy and generous sentiment that actuates my young friends, and though I much regret the being obliged to deny the first request of one to whom, I may say, I owe my life, I must distinctly refuse to take any part in relieving Count Stanislas Prometesky from the penalty he has incurred."

Harold's countenance had become very gloomy during this peroration. He made no attempt at reply, but gathered up his papers, and, gnawing his fringe of moustache, walked out of the room, while Eustace provoked me by volunteering explanations that Prometesky was no friend of his, only of Harold's. His lordship declared himself satisfied, provided no dangerous opinions had been imbibed, and truly Eustace might honestly acquit himself of having any opinions at all.

That afternoon he drove Lord Erymanth to Mycening, whence the railway was now open. Harold could nowhere be found, and kind messages were left for him, for which he was scarcely grateful when he came in late in the evening, calling Lord Erymanth intolerably vindictive, to bear malice for five-and-twenty years.

I could not get him to see that it was entirely judicial indignation, and desire for the good of the country, not in the least personal feeling; but Harold had not yet the perception of the legislative sentiment that actuates men of station in England. His strong inclination was not to go near the old man or his house again, but this was no small distress to Eustace, who, in spite of all his vaunting, dreaded new scenes without a protector, and I set myself to persuade him that it was due to his cousin not to hide himself, and avoid society so as to give a colour to evil report.

"It might be best to separate myself from him altogether and go back." On this, Eustace cried out with horror and dismay, and Harold answered, "Never fear, old chap; I'm not going yet. Not till I have seen you in good hands."

"And you'll accept the invitation," said Eustace, taking up one of the coroneted notes that invited us each for two nights to the castle.

"Very well."

"And you'll come up to town, and have a proper suit."

"As you please."

Eustace went off to the library to find some crested paper and envelopes worthy to bear the acceptance, and Harold stood musing. "A good agent and a good wife would set him on his feet to go alone," he said.

"Meantime he cannot do without you."

"Not in some ways."

"And even this acquaintance is your achievement, not his."

"Such as it is."

I pointed out that though Lord Erymanth refused to assist Prometesky, his introduction might lead to those who might do so, while isolation was a sort of helplessness. To this he agreed, saying, "I must free him before I go back."

"And do you really want to go back?" said I, fearing he was growing restless.

His face worked, and he said, "When I feel like a stone round Eustace's neck."

"Why should you feel so? You are a lever to lift him."

"Am I? The longer I live with you, the more true it seems to me that I had no business to come into a world with such people in it as you and Miss Tracy."

Eustace came back, fidgeting to get a pen mended, an operation beyond him, but patiently performed by the stronger fingers. We said no more, but I had had a glimpse which made me hope that the pilgrim was beginning to feel the burthen on his back.

Not that he had much time for thought. He was out all day, looking after the potteries, where orders were coming in fast, and workmen increasing, and likewise toiling in the fields at Ogden's farm, making measurements and experiments on the substrata and the waterfall, on which to base his plans for drainage according to the books Lord Erymanth had lent him.

After the second day he came home half-laughing. Farmer Ogden had warned him off and refused to listen to any explanation, though he must have known whom he was expelling—yes, like a very village Hampden, he had thrust the unwelcome surveyor out at his gate with such a trembling, testy, rheumatic arm, that Harold had felt obliged to obey it.

Eustace, angered at the treatment of his cousin, volunteered to come and "tell the ass, Ogden, to mind what he was about," and Harold added, "If you would come, Lucy, you might help to make his wife understand."

I came, as I was desired, where I had never been before, for we had always rested in the belief that the Alfy Valley was a nasty, damp, unhealthy place, with "something always about," and had contented ourselves with sending broth to the cottages whenever we heard of any unusual amount of disease. If we had ever been there!

We rode the two miles, as I do not think Dora and I would ever have floundered through the mud and torrents that ran down the lanes. It was just as if the farm had been built in the lower circle, and the cottages in Malebolge itself, where the poor little Alfy, so pure when it started from Kalydon Moor, brought down to them all the leakage of that farmyard. Oh! that yard, I never beheld, imagined, or made my way through the like, though there was a little causeway near the boundary wall, where it was possible to creep along on the stones, rousing up a sleeping pig or a dreamy donkey here and there, and barked at in volleys by dogs stationed on all the higher islets in the unsavoury lake. If Dora had not been a colonial child, and if I could have feared for myself with Harold by my side, I don't think we should ever have arrived, but Farmer Ogden and his son came out, and a man and boy or two; and when Eustace was recognised, they made what way they could for us, and we were landed at last in a scrupulously clean kitchen with peat fire and a limeash floor, where, alas! we were not suffered to remain, but were taken into a horrid little parlour, with a newly-lighted, smoking fire, a big Bible, and a ploughing-cup. Mrs. Ogden was a dissenter, so we had really no acquaintance, and, poor thing, had long been unable to go anywhere. She was a pale trembling creature, most neat and clean, but with the dreadful sallow complexion given by perpetual ague. She was very civil, and gave us cake and wine, to the former of which Dora did ample justice, but oh! the impracticability of those people!

The men had it all out of doors, but when I tried my eloquence on Mrs. Ogden I found her firmly persuaded not only that her own ill health and the sickness in the hamlet were "the will of the Lord," but in her religious fatalism, that it was absolutely profane to think that cleansing and drainage would amend them; and she adduced texts which poor uninstructed I was unable to answer, even while I knew they were a perversion; and, provoked as I was, I felt that her meek patience and resignation might be higher virtues than any to which I had yet attained.

Her husband, who, I should explain, was but one remove above a smock-frock farmer, took a different line. He had unsavoury proverbs in which he put deep faith. "Muck was the mother of money," and also "Muck was the farmer's nosegay." He viewed it as an absolute effeminacy to object to its odorous savours; and as to the poor people, "they were an ungrateful lot, and had a great deal too much done for them," the small farmer's usual creed. Mr. Alison could do as he liked, of course, but his lease had five years yet to run, and he would not consent to pay no more rent, not for what he didn't ask for, nor didn't want, and Mr. Bullock didn't approve of—that he would not, not if Mr. Alison took the law of him.

His landlord do it at his own expense? That made him look knowing. He was evidently certain that it was a trick for raising the rent at the end of the lease, if not before, upon him, whose fathers had been tenants of Alfy Vale even before the Alisons came to Arghouse; and, with the rude obstinacy of his race, he was as uncivil to Harold as he durst in Eustace's presence. "He had no mind to have his fields cut up just to sell the young gentleman's drain-pipes, as wouldn't go off at them potteries."

"Well, but all this stuff would be doing much more good upon your fields than here," Eustace said. "I—I really must insist on this farmyard being cleansed."

"You'll not find that in the covenant, sir," said the farmer with a grin.

"But, father," began the son, a more intelligent-looking man, though with the prevailing sickly tint.

"Hold your tongue, Phil," said Ogden. "It's easy to talk of cleaning out the yard; I'd like to see the gentleman set about it, or you either, for that matter."

"Would you?" said Harold. "Then you shall."

Farmer Ogden gaped. "I won't have no strange labourers about the place."

"No more you shall," said Harold. "If your son and I clean out this place with our own hands in the course of a couple of days, putting the manure in any field you may appoint, will you let the drainage plans be carried out without opposition?"

"It ain't a bet?" said the farmer; "for my missus's conscience is against bets."

"No, certainly not."

"Nor a trick?" he said, looking from one to another.

"No. It is to be honest work. I am a farmer, and know what work is, and have done it too."

Farmer Ogden, to a certain extent, gave in, and we departed. His son held the gate open for us, with a keen look at Harold, full of wonder and inquiry.

"You'll stand by me?" said Harold, lingering with him.

"Yes, sir," said Phil Ogden; "but I doubt if we can do it. Father says it is a week's work for five men, if you could get them to do it."

"Never fear," said Harold. "We'll save your mother's life yet against her will, and make you all as healthy as if you'd been born in New South Wales."

This was Friday, and Phil had an engagement on the Monday, so that Tuesday was fixed, much to Eustace's displeasure, for he did not like Harold's condescending to work which labourers would hardly undertake; and besides, he would make his hands, if not himself, absolutely unfit for the entertainment on Thursday. On which Harold asked if there were no such thing as water. Eustace implored him to give it up and send half-a-dozen unemployed men, but to this he answered, "I should be ashamed."

And when we went home he rode on into Mycening, to see about his equipment, he said, setting Eustace despairing, lest he, after all, meant to avoid the London tailor, and to patronise Mycening; but the equipment turned out to be a great smock-frock. And something very different came home with him—namely, a little dainty flower-pot and pan, with an Etruscan pattern, the very best things that had been turned out of the pottery, adorned with a design in black and white, representing a charming little Greek nymph watering her flowers.

"Don't you think, Lucy, Miss Tracy being a shareholder, and it being her birthday, the chairman might present this?" he inquired.

I agreed heartily, but Eustace, with a twist of his cat's-whisker moustache, opined that they were scarcely elegant enough for Miss Tracy; and on the Monday, when he did drag Harold up to the tailor's, he brought down a fragile little bouquet of porcelain violets, very Parisian, and in the latest fashion, which he flattered himself was the newest thing extant, and a much more appropriate offering. The violets could be made by a pinch below to squirt out perfume!

"Never mind, Harold," I said, "you can give your flower-pot all the same."

"You may," said Harold.

"Why should not you?"

He shook his head. "I've no business," he said; "Eustace is chairman."

I said no more, and I hardly saw Harold the two following days, for he was gone in the twilight of the January morning and worked as long as light would allow, and fortunately the moon was in a favourable quarter; and Phil, to whom the lighter part of the task was allotted, confided to his companion that he had been wishing to get father to see things in this light for a long time, but he was that slow to move; and since Harold had been looking about, Mr. Bullock had advised him not to give in, for it would be sure to end in the raising of his rent, and young gentlemen had new-fangled notions that only led to expense and nonsense, and it was safest in the long run to trust to the agent.

However, the sight of genuine, unflinching toil, with nothing of the amateur about it, had an eloquence of its own. Farmer Ogden looked on grimly and ironically for the first two hours, having only been surprised into consent in the belief that any man, let alone a gentleman, must find out the impracticability of the undertaking, and be absolutely sickened. Then he brought out some bread and cheese and cider, and was inclined to be huffy when Harold declined the latter, and looked satirical when he repaired to wash his hands at the pump before touching the former. When he saw two more hours go by in work of which he could judge, his furrowed old brow grew less puckered, and he came out again to request Mr. Harold to partake of the mid-day meal. I fancy Harold's going up to Phil's room, to make himself respectable for Mrs. Ogden's society, was as strange to the farmer as were to the Australian the good wife's excuses for making him sit down with the family in the kitchen; but I believe that during the meal he showed himself practical farmer enough to win their respect; and when he worked harder than ever all the afternoon, even till the last moment it was possible to see, and came back with the light the next morning, he had won his cause; above all, when the hunt swept by without disturbing the labour.

The farmer not only turned in his scanty supply of men to help to finish off the labour, and seconded contrivances which the day before he would have scouted, but he gave his own bowed back to the work. A pavement of the court which had not seen the day for forty years was brought to light; and by a series of drain tiles, for which a messenger was dispatched to the pottery, streams were conducted from the river to wash these up; and at last, when Harold appeared, after Eustace had insisted on waiting no longer for dinner, he replied to our eager questions, "Yes, it is done."

"And Ogden?"

"He thanked me, shook hands with me, and said I was a man."

Which we knew meant infinitely more than a gentleman.

Harold wanted to spend Thursday in banking up the pond in the centre of the yard, but the idea seemed to drive Eustace to distraction. Such work before going to that sublime region at Erymanth! He laid hold of Harold's hands—shapely hands, and with that look of latent strength one sees in some animals, but scarred with many a seam, and horny within the fingers—and compared them with those he had nursed into dainty delicacy of whiteness, till Harold could not help saying, "I wouldn't have a lady's fingers."

"I would not have a clown's," said Eustace.

"Keep your gloves on, Harold, and do not make them any worse. If you go out to that place to-day, they won't even be as presentable as they are."

"I shall wash them."

"Wash! As if oceans of Eau-de-Cologne would make them fit for society!" said Eustace, with infinite disgust, only equalled by the "Faugh!" with which Harold heard of the perfume. In fact, Eustace was dreadfully afraid the other hunters had seen and recognised those shoulders, even under the smock-frock, as plainly as he did, and he had been wretched about it ever since.

"You talk of not wanting to do me harm," he said, "and then you go and grub in such work as any decent labourer would despise."

So miserable was he, that Harold, who never saw the foolery in Eustace that he would have derided in others, yielded to him so far as only to give directions to Bullock for sending down the materials wanted for the pond, and likewise for mending the roof of a cottage where a rheumatic old woman was habitually obliged to sleep under a crazy umbrella.

CHAPTER VII
THE BIRDS OF ILL OMEN

Nothing stands out to me more distinctly, with its pleasures and pains, than the visit to Erymanth Castle—from our arrival in the dark—the lighted hall—the servants meeting us—the Australians' bewilderment at being ushered up to our rooms without a greeting from the host—my lingering to give a last injunction in Eustace's ear, "Now, Eustace, *I won't* have Harold's hair greased; and put as little stuff as you can persuade yourself to do on your pocket-handkerchief"—orders I had kept to the last to make them more emphatic; then dashing after the housekeeper, leaving them to work—my great room, where it was a perfect journey from the fire to the toilet-table—my black lace dress, and the silver ornaments those dear nephews had brought me from London—and in the midst of my hair-doing dear little Viola's running in to me in one of her ecstacies, hugging me, to the detriment of Colman's fabric and her own, and then dancing round and round me in her pretty white cloudy tulle, looped up with snowdrops. The one thing that had been wanting to her was that her dear, darling, delightful Lucy should be at her own ball—her birthday ball; and just as she had despaired, it had all come right, owing to that glorious old giant of ours; and she went off into a series of rapturous little laughs over Dermot's account of her uncle's arrival pick-a-back. It was of no use to look cautious, and sign at Colman; Viola had no notion of restraint; and I was thankful when my dress was complete, and we were left alone, so that I could listen without compunction to the story of Lord Erymanth's arrival at Arked House, and solemn assurance that he had been most hospitably received, and that his own observation and inquiry had convinced him that Mr. Alison was a highly estimable young man, in spite of all disadvantages, unassuming, well-mannered, and grateful for good advice. Dermot had shown his discernment in making him his friend, and Lucy had, in truth, acted with much courage, as well as good judgment, in remaining with him; "and that so horrified mamma," said Viola, "that she turned me out of the room, so I don't know how they fought it out; but mamma must have given in at last, though she has never said one word to me about it, not even that you were all to be here. What a good thing it is to have a brother! I should never have known but for Dermot. And, do you know, he says that my uncle's pet is the cousin, after all—the deferential fool of a cousin, he says."

"Hush, hush, Viola!"

"I didn't say so—it was Dermot!" said the naughty child, with a little arch pout; "he says it is just like my uncle to be taken with a little worship from—well, he is your nephew, Lucy, so I will be politer than Dermot, who does rage because he says Mr. Alison has not even sense to see that he is dressed in his cousin's plumes."

"He is very fond of Harold, Viola, and they both of them do it in simplicity; Harold does the things for Eustace, and never even sees that the credit is taken from him. It is what he does it for."

"Then he is a regular stupid old jolly giant," said Viola. "Oh, Lucy, what delicious thing *is* this?"

It was the little flower-pot, in which I had planted a spray of lemon-scented verbena, which Viola had long coveted. I explained how Harold had presided over it as an offering from the Hydriot Company to its youngest shareholder, and her delight was extreme. She said she would keep it for ever in her own room; it was just what she wanted, the prettiest thing she had had—so kind of him; but those great, grand giants never thought anything too little for them. And then she went into one of her despairs. She had prepared a number of Christmas presents for the people about the castle to whom she had always been like the child of the house, and her maid had forgotten to bring the box she had packed, nor was there any means of getting them, unless she could persuade her brother to send early the next morning.

"Is Dermot staying here?"

"Oh yes—all night; and nobody else, except ourselves and Piggy. Poor Piggy, he moves about in more awful awe of my uncle than ever—and so stiff! I am always expecting to see him bristle!"

There came a message that my lady was ready, and was asking for Miss Tracy to go down with her. Viola fluttered away, and I waited till they should have had time to descend before making my own appearance, finding all the rooms in the cleared state incidental to ball preparations—all the chairs and tables shrunk up to the walls; and even the drawing-room, where the chaperons were to sit, looking some degrees more desolate than the drawing-room of a ladyless house generally does look.

Full in the midst of an immense blue damask sofa sat Lady Diana, in grey brocade. She was rather a small woman in reality, but dignity made a great deal more of her. Eustace, with a splendid red camellia in his coat, was standing by her, blushing, and she was graciously permitting the presentation of the squirting violet. "Since it was a birthday, and it was a kind attention," &c., but I could see that she did not much like it; and Viola, sitting on the end of the sofa with her eyes downcast, was very evidently much less delighted than encumbered with the fragile china thing.

Lord Erymanth met me, and led me up to his sister, who gave me a cold kiss, and we had a little commonplace talk, during which I could see Viola spring up to Harold, who was standing beside her brother, and the colour rising in his bronzed face at her eager acknowledgments of the flower-pot; after which she applied herself to begging her brother to let his horse and groom go over early the next morning for the Christmas gifts she had left behind, but Dermot did not seem propitious, not liking to trust the man he had with him with the precious Jack o'Lantern over hills slippery with frost; and Viola, as one properly instructed in the precariousness of equine knees, subsided disappointed; while I had leisure to look up at the two gentlemen standing there, and I must say that Harold looked one of Nature's nobles even beside Dermot, and Dermot a fine, manly fellow even beside Harold, though only reaching to his shoulder.

I was the greatest stranger, and went in to the dining-room with his lordship, which spared me the sight of Eustace's supreme satisfaction in presenting his arm to Lady Diana, after she had carefully paired off Viola with her cousin Piggy—i.e., Pigou St. Glear, the eldest son of the heir-presumptive, a stiff, shy youth in the Erymanth atmosphere, whatever he might be out of it, and not at all happy with Viola, who was wont to tease and laugh at him.

It was a save-trouble dinner, as informal as the St. Glear nature and servants permitted. Lord Erymanth carved, and took care that Harold should not starve, and he was evidently trying to turn the talk into such a direction as to show his sister what his guests were; but Eustace's tongue was, of course, the ready one, and answered glibly about closed beershops, projected cottages, and the complete drainage of the Alfy—nay, that as to Bullock and Ogden hearing reason, he had only to go over in person and the thing was done; the farmyard was actually set to rights, and no difficulty at all was made as to the further improvements now that the landlord had once shown himself concerned. That was all that was wanting. And the funny part of it was that he actually believed it.

Dermot could not help saying to Harold, "Didn't I see you applying a few practical arguments?"

Harold made a sign with his head, with a deprecatory twinkle in his eye, recollecting how infra dig Eustace thought his exploit. The party was too small for more than one conversation, so that when the earl began to relate his experiences of the difficulties of dealing with farmers and cottagers, all had to listen in silence, and I saw the misery of restless sleepiness produced by the continuous sound of his voice setting in upon Harold, and under it I had to leave him, on my departure with Lady Diana and her daughter, quaking in my satin shoes at the splendid graciousness I saw in preparation for me; but I was kept all the time on the outer surface; Lady Diana did not choose to be intimate enough even to give good advice, so that I was very glad when the carriages were heard and the gentlemen joined us, Harold hastily handing to Viola the squirting violets which she had left behind her on the dining-table, and which he had carefully concealed from Eustace, but, alas! only to have them forgotten again, or, maybe, with a little malice, deposited in the keeping of the brazen satyr on the ante-room chimney-piece.

Dermot had already claimed my first dance, causing a strange thrill of pain, as I missed the glance which always used to regret without forbidding my becoming his partner. Viola was asked in due form by Eustace, and accepted him with alacrity, which he did not know to be due to her desire to escape from Piggy. Most solicitously did our good old host present Eustace to every one, and it was curious to watch the demeanour of the different classes—the Horsmans mostly cordial, Hippa and Pippa demonstratively so; but the Stympsons held aloof with the stiffest of bows, not one of them but good-natured Captain George Stympson would shake hands even with me, and Miss Avice Stympson, of Lake House, made as if Harold were an object invisible to the naked eye, while the kind old earl was doing his best that he should not feel neglected. Eustace had learnt dancing for that noted ball at Government House, but Harold had disavowed the possibility. He had only danced once in his life, he said, when Dermot pressed him, "and that counted for nothing." To me the pain on the bent brow made it plain that it had been at the poor fellow's wedding.

However, he stood watching, and when at the end of our quadrille Dermot said, "Here lies the hulk of the Great Harry," there was an amused air about him, and at the further question, "Come, Alison, what do you think of our big corroborees?" he deliberately replied, "I never saw such a pretty sight!" And on some leading exclamation from one of us, "It beats the cockatoos on a cornfield; besides, one has got to kill them!"

"Mr. Alison looks at our little diversion in the benevolent spirit of the giant whose daughter brought home ploughman, oxen, and all in her apron for playthings," said Viola, who with Eustace had found her way to us, but we were all divided again, Viola being carried off by some grandee, Eustace having to search for some noble damsel to whom he had been introduced, and I falling to the lot of young Mr. Horsman, a nice person in himself, but unable to surmount the overcrowing of the elder sisters, who called him Baby Jack, and publicly ordered him about. Even at the end of our dance, at the sound of Hippa's authoritative summons, he dropped me suddenly, and I found myself gravitating towards Harold like a sort of chaperon. I was amazed by his observing, "I think I could do it now. Would you try me, Lucy?"

After all, he was but five-and-twenty, and could hardly look on anything requiring agility or dexterity without attempting it, so I consented, with a renewal of the sensations I remembered when, as a child, I had danced with grown-up men, only with alarm at the responsibility of what Dermot called "the steerage of the Great Harry," since collision with such momentum as ours might soon be would be serious; but I soon found my anxiety groundless; he was too well made and elastic to be clumsy, and had perfect power over his own weight and strength, so that he could dance as lightly and safely as Dermot with his Irish litheness.

"Do you think I might ask Miss Tracy?" he said, in return for my compliments.

"Of course; why not?"

When he did ask, her reply was, "Oh, will you indeed? Thank you." Which naivete actually raised her mother's colour with annoyance. But if she had a rod laid up, Viola did not feel it then; she looked radiant, and though I don't believe three words passed between the partners, that waltz was the glory of the evening to her.

She must have made him take her to the tea-room for some ice, and there it was that, while I was standing with my partner a little way off, we heard Miss Avice Stympson's peculiarly penetrating attempt at a whisper, observing, "Yes, it is melancholy! I thought we were safe here, or I never should have brought my dear little Birdie.... What, don't you know? There's no doubt of it—the glaze on the pottery is dead men's bones. They have an arrangement with the hospitals in London, you understand. I can't think how Lord Erymanth can be so deceived. But you see the trick was a perfect success. Yes, the blocking up the railway. A mercy no lives were lost; but that would have been nothing to him after the way he has gone on in Australia.—Oh, Lord Erymanth, I did not know you were there."

"And as I could not avoid overhearing you," said that old gentleman, "let me remind you that I regard courtesy to the guest as due respect to the host, and that I have good reason to expect that my visitors should have some confidence in my discrimination of the persons I invite them to meet."

Therewith both he and Miss Stympson had become aware of the head that was above them all, and the crimson that dyed the cheeks and brow; while Viola, trembling with passion, and both hands clasped over Harold's arm, exclaimed, in a panting whisper, "Tell them it is a wicked falsehood—tell them it is no such thing!"

"I will speak to your uncle to-morrow. I am obliged to him."

Everybody heard that, and all who had either feeling or manners knew that no more ought to be said. Only Lord Erymanth made his way to Harold to say, "I am very sorry this has happened."

Harold bent his head with a murmur of thanks, and was moving out of the supper-room, when Dermot hastily laid a hand on him with, "Keep the field, Harry; don't go."

"I'm not going."

"That's right. Face it out before the hags. Whom shall I introduce you—There's Birdie Stympson—come."

"No, no; I don't mean to dance again."

"Why not? Beard the harpies like a man. Dancing would refute them all."

"Would it?" gravely said Harold.

Nor could he be persuaded, save once at his host's bidding, but showed no signs of being abashed or distressed, and most of the male Stympsons came and spoke to him. The whole broke up at three, and we repaired to our rooms, conscious that family prayers would take place as the clock struck nine as punctually as if nothing had happened, and that our characters depended on our punctuality. Viola was in time, and so was Eustace; I sneaked in late and ashamed; and the moment the servants had filed out Viola sprang to Eustace with vehement acknowledgments; and it appeared that just before she came down her missing box of gifts had been brought to her room, and she was told that Mr. Alison had sent for them. Eustace smirked, and Lady Diana apologised for her little daughter's giddy, exaggerated expressions, by which she had given far more trouble than she ever intended.

"No trouble," said Eustace. "Harold always wants to work off his steam."

"What, it was he?" said Viola.

"Yes, of course; he always does those things," said Eustace, speaking with a tone of proprietorship, as if Harold had been a splendid self-acting steam-engine. "I am very glad to have gratified you, Miss Tracy—"

"Only he did, and not you," said Viola, boldly, luckily without being heard by her mother, while Eustace murmured out, rather bewildered, "It is all the same."

Viola evidently did not think so when Harold came in with beads of wet fringing his whiskers, though he had divested himself of the chief evidences of the rivers of muddy lane through which he had walked to Arked House, full four miles off.

Viola's profuse thanks were crossed by Lady Diana's curt apologies; and as poor Piggy, who had genuinely overslept himself, entered with his apologies—poor fellow—in a voice very much as if he was trying to say "Grumph, grumph," while he could only say "Wee, wee," they were received solemnly by his uncle with, "The antipodes are a rebuke to you, Pigou. I am afraid the young men of this hemisphere have no disposition to emulate either such chivalrous attentions or exertions as have been Mr. Harold Alison's excuse."

When so much was said about it, Harold probably wished he had let the whole matter alone, and was thankful to be allowed to sit down in peace to his well-earned breakfast, which was finished before Dermot lounged in—not waited for by his uncle, who offered an exhibition of his model-farm-buildings, machines, cattle, &c. Fain would Viola and I have gone in the train of the gentlemen, but the weather, though not bad enough to daunt a tolerably hardy man, was too damp for me, and we had to sit down to our work in the drawing-room, while Piggy, always happier without his great-uncle, meandered about until Lady Diana ordered off Viola to play at billiards with him, but kept me, for, as I perceived, the awful moment was come, and the only consolation was that it might be an opportunity of pleading Harold's cause.

With great censure of the Stympsons' ill-breeding and discourtesy to her brother (which seemed to affect her far more than the direct injury to Harold), and strong disclaimers of belief in them, still my mother's old friend must inquire into the character of these young men and my position with regard to them. If she had been tender instead of inquisitorial, I should have answered far more freely, and most likely the air of defiance and defence into which she nettled me had a partisan look; but it was impossible not to remember that Miss Woolmer had always said that, however she might censure the scandal of the Stympsons, they only required to dish it up with sauce piquant to make her enjoy it heartily.

And really and truly it did seem as if there was nothing in the whole lives of those poor youths on which those women had not contrived to cast some horrid stain; working backwards from the dead men's bones in the pottery (Dermot had told her they used nothing but live men's bones), through imputations on Mr. George Yolland's character, and the cause of the catastrophe at the "Dragon's Head;" stories of my associating with all the low, undesirable friends they picked up at Mycening, or in the hunting-field; and as to the Australian part of the history, she would hardly mention to me all she had heard, even to have it confuted.

I was not sure how far she did believe my assurances, or thought me deceived, when I strenuously denied all evil intent from Harold towards his poor wife, and explained that he had merely driven over a precipice in the dark, and had a brain fever afterwards; all I could see was that, though not perfectly satisfied or convinced, she found that her brother would not allow the separation to be kept up, and therefore she resumed her favourite office of adviser. She examined me on the religious habits of my nephews and niece, impressing on me that it was for the sake of the latter that my presence at Arghouse was excusable; but insisting that it was incumbent on me to provide her with an elderly governess, both for her sake and my own. I was much afraid of having the governess at once thrust upon me; but, luckily, she did not happen to have one of a chaperon kind of age on her list, so she contented herself with much advice on what I was teaching Dora, so that perhaps I grew restive and was disposed to think it no concern of hers, nor did I tell her that much of the direction of Dora's lessons was with a view to Harold; but she could not have been wholly displeased, since she ended by telling me that mine was a vast opportunity, and that the propriety of my residence at Arghouse entirely depended on the influence I exerted, since any acquiescence in lax and irreligious habits would render my stay hurtful to all parties. She worried me into an inclination to drop all my poor little endeavours, since certainly to have tried to follow out all the details of her counsel would have alienated all three at once.

Never was I more glad than when the luncheon-bell put a stop to the conversation, and the sun struggling out dispensed me from further endurance, and set me free to go with Viola to bestow her gifts, disposing on the way of the overflow of talk that had been pent up for months past. In the twilight, near the lodge of a favourite old nurse of Dermot's, we encountered all the younger gentlemen, and not only did Viola drag her brother in but Harold also, to show to whom was owing the arrival of her wonderful tea-pot cozy.

The good woman was just going to make her tea. Viola insisted on showing the use of her cozy, and making everybody stay to nurse's impromptu kettledrum, and herself put in the pinches of tea. Dermot chaffed all and sundry; Viola bustled about; Harold sat on the dresser, with his blue eyes gleaming in the firelight with silent amusement and perfect satisfaction, the cat sitting on his shoulder; and nurse, who was firmly persuaded that he had rescued her dear Master Dermot from the fangs of the lion, was delighted to do her best for his entertainment. Viola insisted on displaying all the curiosities—the puzzle-cup that could not be used, the horrid frog that sprang to your lips in the tankard, the rolling-pin covered with sentimental poetry, and her extraordinary French pictures on the walls. Dermot kept us full of merriment, and we laughed on till the sound of the dressing-bell sent us racing up to the castle in joyous guilt. That kettledrum at the lodge is one of the brightest spots in my memory.

We were very merry all the evening in a suppressed way over the piano, Viola, Dermot, and I singing, Harold looking on, and Eustace being left a willing victim to the good counsel lavished by my lord and my lady, who advised him nearly out of his senses and into their own best graces.

But we had not yet done with the amenities of the Stympsons. The morning's post brought letters to Lady Diana and Lord Erymanth, which were swallowed by the lady with only a flush on her brow, but which provoked from the gentleman a sharp interjection.

"Scandalous, libellous hags!"

"The rara Avis?" inquired Dermot.

And in spite of Lady Diana's warning, "Not now," Lord Erymanth declared, "Avice, yes! A bird whose quills are quills of iron dipped in venom, and her beak a brazen one, distilling gall on all around. I shall inform her that she has made herself liable to an action for libel. A very fit lesson to her."

"What steps shall I take, my lord?" said Eustace, with much importance. "I shall be most happy to be guided by you."

"It is not you," said Lord Erymanth.

"Oh! if it is only *he*, it does not signify so much."

"Certainly not," observed Dermot. "What sinks some floats others."

Lady Diana here succeeded in hushing up the subject, Harold having said nothing all the time; but, after we broke up from breakfast, I had a private view of Lady Diana's letter, which was spiteful beyond description as far as we were concerned; making all manner of accusations on the authority of the Australian relations; the old stories exaggerated into horrible blackness, besides others for which I could by no means account. Gambling among the gold-diggers, horrid frays in Victoria, and even cattle-stealing, were so impossible in a man who had always been a rich sheep farmer, that I laughed; yet they were told by the cousins with strange circumstantiality. Then came later tales—about our ways at Arghouse—all as a warning against permitting any intercourse of the sweet child's, which might be abused. Lady Diana was angered and vexed, but she was not a woman who rose above the opinion of the world. Her daughter, Di Enderby, was a friend of Birdie Stympson, and would be shocked; and she actually told me that I must perceive that, while such things were said, it was not possible—for her own Viola's sake—to keep up the intimacy she would have wished.

For my part it seemed to me that, in Lady Diana's position, unjust accusations against a poor young girl were the very reason for befriending her openly; but her ladyship spoke in a grand, authoritative, regretful way, and habitual submission prevented me from making any protest beyond saying coldly, "I am very sorry, but I cannot give up my nephews."

Viola was not present. It was supposed to be so shocking that she could know nothing about it, but she flew into my room and raged like a little fury at the cruel wickedness of the Stympsons in trying to turn everyone's friends against them, and trumping up stories, and mamma giving up as if she believed them. She wished she was Dermot—she wished she was uncle Erymanth—she wished she was anybody, to stand up and do battle with those horrid women!—anybody but a poor little girl, who must obey orders and be separated from her friends. And she cried, and made such violent assurances that I had to soothe and silence her, and remind her of her first duty, &c.

Lord Erymanth was a nobler being than his sister, and had reached up to clap Harold on the shoulder, while declaring that these assertions made no difference to him, and that he did not care the value of a straw for what Avice Stympson might say, though Harold had no defence but his own denial of half the stories, and was forced to own that there was truth in some of the others. He was deeply wounded. "Why cannot the women let us keep our friends?" he said, as I found him in the great hall.

"It is very hard," I said, with grief and anger.

"Very hard on the innocent," he answered.

Then I saw he was preparing to set off to walk home, twelve miles, and remonstrated, since Lake Valley would probably be flooded.

"I must," he said; "I must work it out with myself, whether I do Eustace most harm or good by staying here."

And off he went, with the long swift stride that was his way of walking off vexation. I did not see him again till I was going up to dress, when I found him just inside the front door, struggling to get off his boots, which were perfectly sodden; while his whole dress, nay, even his hair and beard, was soaked and drenched, so that I taxed him with having been in the water.

"Yes, I went in after a dog," he said, and as he gave a shiver, and had just pulled off his second boot, I asked no more questions, but hunted him upstairs to put on dry clothes without loss of time; and when we met at dinner, Eustace was so full of our doings at the castle, and Dora of hers with Miss Woolmer, that his bath was entirely driven out of my head.

But the next day, as I was preparing for my afternoon's walk, the unwonted sound of our door-bell was heard. "Is our introduction working already?" thought I, little expecting the announcement—"The Misses Stympson."

However, there were Stympsons and Stympsons, so that even this did not prepare me for being rushed at by all three from Lake House—two aunts and one niece—Avice, Henny, and Birdie, with "How is he?" "Where is he? He would not take anything. I hope he went to bed and had something hot." "Is he in the house? No cold, I hope. We have brought the poor dear fellow for him to see. He seems in pain to-day; we thought he would see him."

At last I got in a question edgeways as to the antecedents, as the trio kept on answering one another in chorus, "Poor dear Nep—your cousin—nephew, I mean—the bravest—"

Then it flashed on me. "Do you mean that it was for your dog that Harold went into the water yesterday!"

"Oh, the bravest, most generous, the most forgiving. So tender-handed! It must be all a calumny. I wish we had never believed it. He could never lift a hand against anyone. We will contradict all rumours. Report is so scandalous. Is he within?"

Harold had been at the Hydriot works ever since breakfast, but on my first question the chorus struck up again, and I might well quail at the story. "Lake Mill; you know the place, Miss Alison?"

Indeed I did. The lake, otherwise quiet to sluggishness, here was fed by the rapid little stream, and at the junction was a great mill, into which the water was guided by a sharp descent, which made it sweep down with tremendous force, and, as I had seen from the train, the river was swelled by the thaw and spread far beyond its banks. "The mill-race!" I cried in horror.

"Just observe. Dear Nep has such a passion for the water, and Birdie thoughtlessly threw a stick some way above the weir. I never shall forget what I felt when I saw him carried along. He struggled with his white paws, and moaned to us, but we could do nothing, and we thought to have seen him dashed to pieces before our eyes, when, somehow, his own struggles I fancy—he is so sagacious—brought him up in a lot of weeds and stuff against the post of the flood-gates, and that checked him. But we saw it could not last, and his strength was exhausted. Poor Birdie rushed down to beg them to stop the mill, but that could never have been done in time, and the dear dog was on the point of being sucked in by the ruthless stream, moaning and looking appealingly to us for help, when, behold! that superb figure, like some divinity descending, was with us, and with one brief inquiry he was in the water. We called out to him that the current was frightfully strong—we knew a man's life ought not to be perilled; but he just smiled, took up the great pole that lay near, and waded in. I cannot describe the horror of seeing him breasting that stream, expecting, as we did, to see him borne down by it into the wheel. The miller shouted to him that it was madness, but he kept his footing like a rock. He reached the place where the poor dog was, and the fury of the stream was a little broken by the post, took up poor Nep and put him over his shoulder. Nep was so good—lay like a lamb—while Mr. Alison fought his way back, and it was harder still, being upwards. The miller and his men came out and cheered, thinking at least he would come out spent and want help; but no, he came out only panting a little, put down the dog, and when it moaned and seemed hurt he felt it all over so tenderly, found its leg was broken, took it into the miller's kitchen, and set it like any surgeon. He would take nothing but a cup of tea, whatever they said, and would not change his clothes—indeed, the miller is a small man, so I don't see how he could—but I hope he took no harm. He walked away before we could thank him. But, oh dear! what a wicked thing scandal is! I will never believe anything report says again."

To the end of their days the Misses Stympson believed that it was the convenient impersonal rumour which had maligned Harold—not themselves.

I was just parting with them when Harold appeared, and they surrounded him, with an inextricable confusion of thanks—hopes that he had not caught cold, and entreaties that he would look at his patient, whom they had brought on the back seat of the barouche to have his leg examined. Harold said that his was self-taught surgery, but was assured that the dog would bear it better from him than any one, and could not but consent.

I noticed, however, that when he had to touch the great black Newfoundland dog, a strong shudder ran through his whole frame, and he had to put a strong force on himself, though he spoke to it kindly, and it wagged its tail, and showed all the grateful, wistful affection of its kind, as he attended to it with a tender skill in which his former distaste was lost; and the party drove away entreating him to come and renew the treatment on the Monday, and asking us all to luncheon, but not receiving a distinct answer in Eustace's absence, for he was very tenacious of his rights as master of the house.

I was quite touched with the dog's parting caress to his preserver. "So you have conquered the birds with iron quills!" I cried, triumphantly.

"Who were they?" asked Harold, astonished.

"Surely you know them? I never thought of introducing you."

"You don't mean that they were those women?"

"Of course they were. I thought you knew you were performing an act of heroic forgiveness."

Harold's unfailing politeness towards me hindered him from saying "heroic fiddlesticks," but he could not suppress a "Faugh!" which meant as much, and that mortified me considerably.

"Come now, Harry," I said, "you don't mean that you would not have done it if you had known?"

"I should not have let the poor beast drown because his mistresses were spiteful hags." And there was a look on his face that made me cry out in pain, "Don't, Harry!"

"Don't what?"

"Don't be unforgiving. Say you forgive them."

"I can't. I could as soon pardon Smith."

"But you ought to pardon both. It would be generous. It would be Christian."

I was sorry I had said that, for he looked contemptuously and said, "So they teach you. I call it weakness."

"Oh, Harry! dear Harry, no! The highest strength!"

"I don't understand that kind of talk," he said. "You don't know what that Smith is to my poor mother!"

"We won't talk of him; but, indeed, the Misses Stympson are grateful to you, and are sorry. Won't you go to them on Monday?"

"No! I don't like scandal-mongers."

"But you have quite conquered them."

"What do you mean? If we are the brutes they tell those who would have been our friends, we are not less so because I pulled a dog out of the river."

The hard look was on his face, and to my faint plea, "The poor dog!"

"The dog will do very well." He went decisively out of the way of further persuasions, and when a formal note of invitation arrived, he said Eustace and I might go, but he should not. He had something to do at the potteries; and as to the dog, the less it was meddled with the better.

"I know you hate black dogs," said Eustace; "I only wonder you ever touched it."

Harold's brow lowered at this, and afterwards I asked Eustace to account for the strange dislike. He told me that the dogs at the store had run yelping after the buggy on that fatal drive, and this and the melancholy howl of the dingoes had always been supposed to be the cause of the special form of delirious fancy that had haunted Harold during the illness following—that he was pursued and dragged down by a pack of black hounds, and that the idea had so far followed him that he still had a sort of alienation from dogs, though he subdued it with a high hand.

He would still not go with us to Lake House, for go we did. An invitation was stimulating to Eustace, and though I much disliked the women, I knew we could not afford to reject an advance if we were not to continue out of humanity's reach.

So I went, and we were made much of in spite of the disappointment.

Had not Mr. Harold Alison been so kind as to come over both Sunday and Monday morning and see to poor Nep in his kennel before they were down? Oh, yes, they had heard of it from the stable-boy, and had charged him to take care the gentleman came in to breakfast, but he could not persuade him. Such a pity he was too busy to come to-day!

Eustace gave learned and elaborate opinions on Nep, and gained the hearts of the ladies, who thenceforth proclaimed that Mr. Alison was a wonderfully finished gentleman, considering his opportunities; but Mr. Harold was at the best a rough diamond, so that once more his conquest had been for Eustace rather than for himself. They showed me, in self-justification, letters from their relations in Melbourne, speaking of the notorious Harry Alison as a huge bearded ruffian, and telling horrid stories of his excesses in no measured terms. Of course we denied them, and represented that some other man must have borne the same name, and gratitude made them agree;

but the imputation lay there, ready to revive at any time. And there had been something in the whole affair that had not a happy effect on Harold. He was more blunt, more gruff, less tolerant or ready to be pleased; Eustace's folly was no longer incapable of provoking him; and even his gentleness towards Dora and me was with a greater effort, and he was plainly in an irritable state of suppressed suffering of mind or temper, which only the strong force he put upon himself kept in check. My poor Harold, would he see that there were moral achievements higher than his physical ones, and would he learn that even his strength was not equal to them, unaided?

CHAPTER VIII
BULLOCK'S CHASTISEMENT

The next frosty day Dora and I set forth for a visit to the double cottage, where, on one side, dwelt a family with a newly-arrived baby; on the other was Dame Jennings', with the dilapidated roof and chimney. I was glad to see Dora so happily and eagerly interested over the baby as to be more girl-like than I had yet seen her, though, comparing her to what she had been on her arrival, she was certainly a good deal softened and tamed. "Domesticated" would really not have been so inappropriate a word in her case as it is in advertisements of companions.

We had come to the door, only divided from Mrs. Jennings's by a low fence and a few bushes, when voices struck on our ears, and we saw Bullock's big, sturdy, John Bull form planted in a defiant attitude in the garden-path before the door, where the old woman stood courtesying, and mingling entreating protestations against an additional sixpence a week on her rent with petitions that at least the chimney might be made sound and the roof water-tight.

There is no denying that I did stand within the doorway to listen, for not only did I not wish to encounter Bullock, but it seemed quite justifiable to ascertain whether the current whispers of his dealings with the poor were true; indeed, there was no time to move before he replied with a volley of such abuse, as I never heard before or since, at her impudence in making such a demand.

I was so much shocked that I stood transfixed, forgetting even to draw Dora away from the sound, while the old woman pleaded that "Mr. Herod" had made the promise, and said nothing of increasing her rent. Probably Bullock had been irritated by the works set on foot at Ogden's farm, for he brought out another torrent of horrid imprecations upon "the meddling convict fellow," the least intolerable of the names he used, and of her for currying favour, threatening her with instant expulsion if she uttered a word of complaint, or mentioned the increase of her rent, and on her hesitation actually lifting his large heavy stick.

We both cried out and sprang forward, though I scarcely suppose that he would have actually struck her. But much more efficient help was at hand. Bullock's broad back was to the gate, and he little knew that at the moment he raised his stick Harold, attracted by his loud railing voice, leaped over the gate, and with one bound was upon the fellow, wresting the stick from his hand and laying it about his shoulders with furious energy. We all screamed out. Dora, it was suspected, bade him go on and give it to him well, and perhaps my wrath with the man made me simply shriek; but the sense of our presence did (whatever we wished) check Harold's violence so far that he ceased his blows, throwing the man from him with such force that he fell prone into the poor dame's gooseberry-bush, and had to pick himself up through numerous scratches, just as we had hurried round through the garden.

He had regained his feet, and was slinking up to the gate as we met him, and passionately exclaimed: "Miss Alison, you have seen this; I shall call on you as my witness."

Dora called out something so vituperative that my energies went in silencing her, nor do I think I answered Bullock, though at least it was a relief to see that, having a great sou'-wester over all his other clothes, the force of the blows had been so broken that he could not have any really serious injury to complain of. It was not unfortunate, however, that he was so shaken and battered that he went first to exhibit himself to Dr. Kingston's new partner, and obtain a formidable scientific account of his sprains and bruises; so that Eustace had heard an account of the affray in the first place, and Dora, with a child's innate satisfaction in repeating personalities, had not spared the epithets with which Bullock had mentioned the "fool of a squire." The said squire, touched to the quick, went out invulnerable to his interview, declaring that the agent had been rightly served, only wishing he had had more, and indignantly refusing Bullock's offer to abstain from prosecuting Mr. Harold Alison on receiving a handsome compensation, and a promise never to be interfered with again. Eustace replied—too much, I fear, in his own coin—with orders to send in his accounts immediately and to consider himself dismissed from his agency from that hour; and then came back to us like a conquering hero, exulting in his own magnanimous firmness, which "had shown he was not to be trifled with."

But he did not like it at all when Richardson came in trying to look quite impassive, and said to Harold, "Some one wants to speak to you sir."

Harold went, and returned without a word, except, "You are wanted too, Lucy," and I was not equally silent when I found it was to serve on me an order to appear as witness before the magistrates the next day, as to the assault upon Bullock.

Eustace was very much annoyed, and said it was disgraceful, and that Harold was always getting into scrapes, and would ruin him with all the county people, just as he was beginning to make way with them—a petulant kind of ingratitude which we had all learnt to tolerate as "old Eu's way," and Dora announced that if he was put in prison, she should go too.

It was only a Petty Sessions case, heard in the justice-room at Mycening, and on the way the prisoner was chiefly occupied in assuring the witness that there was nothing to be nervous about; and the squire, that it would hurt nobody but himself; and, for his part, fine him as they would, he would willingly pay twenty times as much to rid the place of Bullock.

The bench—who sat at the upper end of a table—were three or four Horsmans and Stympsons, with Lord Erymanth in the chair par excellence, for they all sat on chairs, and they gave the like to Eustace and me while we waited, poor Harold having put himself, in the custody of a policeman, behind the rail which served as bar.

When our turn came, Harold pleaded "Guilty" at once, not only for truth's sake, but as meaning to spare me the interrogation; and Crabbe, who was there on Bullock's behalf, looked greatly baffled and disappointed; but the magistrates did not let it rest there, since the amount of the fine of course would depend on the degree of violence, &c., so both Mrs. Jennings and I, and the doctor, were examined as witnesses.

I came first; and at first I did not find the inquiries half so alarming as I expected, since my neighbours spoke to me quite in a natural way, and it was soon clear that my account of the matter was the best possible defence of Harold in their eyes. The unpleasant part was when Crabbe not only insisted on my declaring on oath that I did not think Bullock meant to strike the old woman, but on my actually repeating the very words he had said, which he probably thought I should flinch from doing; but he thereby made it the worse for himself. No doubt he and Crabbe had reckoned on our general unpopularity, and had not judged it so as to discover the reaction that had set in. An endeavour to show that we were acting as spies on the trustworthy old servant, in order to undermine him with his master, totally failed, and, at last, the heavy fine of one shilling was imposed upon Harold—as near an equivalent as possible to dismissing the case altogether. Lord Erymanth himself observed to Eustace, "that he felt, if he might say so, to a certain degree implicated, since he had advised the dismissal of Bullock, but scarcely after this fashion." However, he said he hoped to have Eustace among them soon in another capacity, and this elevated him immensely.

The case had taken wind among the workmen at the potteries; and as we came out at their dinner-hour, there was a great assemblage, loudly cheering, "Alison, the poor man's friend!"

Eustace stood smiling and fingering his hat, till Captain Stympson, who came out with us, hinted, as he stood between the two young men, that it had better be stopped as soon as possible. "One may soon have too much of such things," and then Eustace turned round on Harold, and declared it was "just his way to bring all the Mycening mob after them." Whereat Harold, without further answer, observed, "You'll see Lucy home then," and plunged down among the men, who, as if nothing had been wanting to give them a fellow-feeling for him but his having been up before the magistrates, stretched out hands to shake; and as he marched down between a lane of them, turned and followed the lofty standard of his head towards their precincts.

Bullock, in great wrath and indignation, sent in his accounts that night with a heavy balance due to him from Eustace, which Harold saw strong cause to dispute. But that battle, in which, of course, Crabbe was Bullock's adviser, and did all he could to annoy us, was a matter of many months, and did not affect our life very closely. Harold was in effect Eustace's agent, and being a very good accountant, as well as having the confidence of the tenants, all was put in good train in that quarter, and Mr. Alison was in the way to be respected as an excellent landlord and improver. People were calling on us, and we were evidently being taken into our proper place. Lady Diana no longer withheld her countenance, and though she only called on me in state she allowed Viola to write plenty of notes to me.

But I must go on to that day when Harold and Eustace were to have a hunting day with the Foling hounds, and dine afterwards with some of the members of the hunt at the Fox Hotel at Foling, a favourite meet. They were to sleep at Biston, and I saw nothing of them the next day till Eustace came home alone, only just in time for a late dinner, and growled out rather crossly that Harold had chosen to walk home, and not to be waited for. Eustace himself was out of sorts and tired, eating little and hardly vouchsafing a word, except to grumble at us and the food, and though we heard Harold come in about nine o'clock, he did not come in, but went up to his room.

Eustace was himself again the next morning, but Harold was gone out. However, as, since he had been agent, he had often been out and busy long before breakfast, this would not have been remarkable, but that Eustace was ill at ease, and at last said, "The fact is, Lucy, he has been 'screwed' again, and has not got over it."

I was so innocent that only Dora's passion with her brother revealed to me his meaning, and then I was inexpressibly horrified and angry, for I did not think Harold could have broken his own word or the faith on which I had taken up my abode with them, and the disappointment in him, embittered, I fear, by the sense of personal injury, was almost unbearable.

Eustace muttered something in excuse which I could not understand, and I thought was only laxity on his part. I told him that, if such things were to happen, his house was no home for me. And he began, "Come now, Lucy, I say, that's hard, when 'twas Harold, and not me, and all those fellows—"

"What fellows?"

"Oh, Malvoisin and Nessy Horsman, you know."

I knew they were the evil geniuses of Dermot's life. Lord Malvoisin had been his first tempter as boys at their tutor's, and again in the Guards; and Ernest, or Nessy, Horsman was the mauvais sujet of the family, who never was heard of without some disgraceful story. And Dermot had led my boys among these. All that had brightened life so much to me had suddenly vanished.

It was Ash Wednesday, and I am afraid I went through my Lenten services in the spirit of the elder son, nursing my virtuous indignation, and dwelling chiefly on what would become of me if Arghouse were to be made uninhabitable, as I foresaw.

I was ashamed to consult Miss Woolmer, and spent the afternoon in restless attempts to settle to something, but feeling as if nothing were worth while, not even attending to Dora, since my faith in Harold had given way, and he had broken his word and returned to his vice.

Should I go to church again, and spare myself the meeting him at dinner? I was just considering, when Mr. George Yolland came limping up the drive, and the sight was the first shock to the selfish side of my grief. "Is anything the matter?" I asked, trying to speak sternly, but my heart thumping terribly.

"No—yes—not exactly," he said hastily; "but can you come, Miss Alison? I believe you are the only person who can be of use."

"Then is he ill?" I asked, still coldly, not being quite sure whether I ought to forgive.

"Not bodily, but his despair over what has taken place is beyond us all. He sits silent over the accounts in his room at the office; will talk to none of us. Mr. Alison has tried—I have—Ben and all of us. He never looks up but to call for soda-water. If he yields again, it will soon be acute dipsomania, and then—" he shrugged his shoulders.

"But what do you mean? What can I do?" said I, walking on by his side all the time.

"Take him home. Give him hope and motive. Get him away, at any rate, before those fellows come. Mr. Tracy was over at Mycening this morning, and said they talked of coming to sleep at the 'Boar,' for the meet to-morrow, and looking him up."

"Lord Malvoisin?" I asked.

And as I walked on, Mr. Yolland told me what I had not understood from Eustace, that there had been an outcry among the more reckless of the Foling Hunt that so good a fellow should be a teetotaller. Dermot Tracy had been defied into betting upon the resolute abstinence of his hero—nay, perhaps the truth was that these men had felt that their victim was being attracted from their grasp, and a Satanic instinct made them strive to degrade his idol in his eyes.

So advantage was taken of the Australian's ignorance of the names of liqueurs. Perhaps the wine in the soup had already caused some excitement in the head—unaccustomed to any stimulant ever since the accident and illness which had rendered it inflammable to a degree no one suspected. When once the first glass was swallowed, the dreadful work was easy, resolution and judgment were obscured, and the old habits and cravings of the days when poor Harold had been a hard drinker had been revived in full force. Uproarious mirth and wild feats of strength seemed to have been the consequence, ending by provoking the interference of the police, who had locked up till the morning such of the party as could not escape. Happily, the stupefied stage had so far set in that Harold had made it no worse by offering resistance, and Dermot had managed to get the matter hushed up by the authorities at Foling. This was what he had come to say, but Harold had been very brief and harsh with him; though he was thoroughly angered and disgusted at the conduct of his friends, and repeated, hotly, that he had been treated with treachery such as he could never forgive.

So we came to the former "Dragon's Head," where Harold had fitted up a sort of office for himself. Mr. Yolland bade me go up alone, and persuade him to come home with me. I was in the greater fright, because of the selfishness which had mingled with the morning's indignation, but I had just presence of mind enough for an inarticulate prayer through the throbbings of my heart ere knocking, and at once entering the room where, under a jet of gas, Harold sat at a desk, loaded with papers and ledgers, on which he had laid down his head. I went up to him, and laid my hand as near his brow as his position would let me. Oh, how it burnt!

He looked up with a face half haggard, half sullen with misery, and hoarsely said, "Lucy, how came you here?"

"I came in to get you to walk home with me."

"I'll get a fly for you."

(This would be going to the "Boar," the very place to meet these men.)

"Oh no! please don't. I should like the walk with you."

"I can't go home yet. I have something to do. I must make up these books."

"But why? There can't be any haste."

"Yes. I shall put them into Yolland's hands and go by the next mail."

"Harold! You promised to stay till Eustace was in good hands."

He laughed harshly. "You have learnt what my promise is worth!"

"Oh Harold! don't. You were cheated and betrayed. They took a wicked advantage of you."

"I knew what I was about," he said, with the same grim laugh at my folly. "What is a man worth who has lost his self-command?"

"He may regain it," I gasped out, for his look and manner frightened me dreadfully.

He made an inarticulate sound of scorn, but, seeing perhaps the distress in my face, he added more gently, "No, Lucy, this is really best; I am not fit to be with you. I have broken my word of honour, and lost all that these months had gained. I should only drag Eustace down if I stayed."

"Why? Oh, why? It was through their deceit. Oh, Harry! there is not such harm done that you cannot retrieve."

"No," he said, emphatically. "Understand what you are asking. My safeguard of an unbroken word is gone! The longing for that stuff—accursed though I know it—is awakened. Nothing but shame at giving way before these poor fellows that I have preached temperance to withholds me at this very moment."

"But it does withhold you! Oh, Harold! You know you can be strong. You know God gives strength, if you would only try."

"I know you say so."

"Because I know it. Oh, Harold! try my way. Do ask God to give you what you want to stand up against this."

"If I did, it would not undo the past."

"Something else can do that."

He did not answer, but reached his hat, saying something again about time, and the fly. I must make another effort. "Oh, Harold! give up this! Do not be so cruel to Dora and to me. Have you made us love you better than anybody, only to go away from us in this dreadful way, knowing it is to give yourself up to destruction? Do you want to break our hearts?"

"Me!" he said, in a dreamy way. "You don't really care for me?"

"I? Oh, Harry, when you have grown to be my brother, when you are all that I have in this world to lean on and help me, will you take yourself away?"

"It might be better for you," he said.

"But it *will* not," I said; "you will stay and go on, and God will make your strength perfect to conquer this dreadful thing too."

"You shall try it then," he said, and he began to sweep those accounts into a drawer as if he had done with them for the night, and as he brought his head within my reach, I could not but kiss his forehead as I said, "Thank you, my Harry."

He screwed his lips together, with a strange half-smile very near tears, emptied the rest of a bottle of soda-water into a tumbler, gulped it down, opened the door, turned down the gas, and came down with me. Mr. Yolland was watching, I well knew, but he discreetly kept out of sight, and we came out into a very cold raw street, with the stars twinkling overhead, smiling at us with joy I thought, and the bells were ringing for evening service.

But our dangers were not over. We had just emerged into the main street when a dog-cart came dashing up, the two cigars in it looming red. It was pulled up. Harold's outline could be recognised in any light, but I was entirely hidden in his great shadow, and a voice called out:

"Halloo, Alison, how do? A chop and claret at the 'Boar'—eh? Come along."

"Thank you," said Harold, "but I am walking home with Miss Alison—"

The two gentlemen bowed, and I bowed, and oh! how I gripped Harold's arm as I heard the reply; not openly derisive to a lady, but with a sneer in the voice, "Oh! ah! yes! But you'll come when you've seen her home. We'll send on the dog-cart for you."

"No, thank you," said Harold. His voice sounded firm, but I felt the thrill all through the arm I clung to. "Good night."

He attempted no excuse, but strode on—I had to run to keep up with him—and they drove on by our side, and Nessy Horsman said, "A prior engagement, eh? And Miss Alison will not release you? Ladies' claims are sacred, we all know."

What possessed me I don't know, nor how I did it, but it was in the dark and I was wrought up, and I answered, "And yours can scarcely be so! So we will go on, Harold."

"A fair hit, Nessy," and there was a laugh and flourish of the whip. I was trembling, and a dark cloud had drifted up with a bitter blast, and the first hailstones were falling. The door of the church was opened for a moment, showing bright light from within; the bells had ceased.

"My dear Lucy," said Harold, "you had better go in here for shelter."

"Not if you leave me! You must come with me," I said, still dreading that he would leave me in church, send a fly, and fall a victim at the "Boar;" and, indeed, I was shaking so, that he would not withdraw his arm, and said, soothingly, "I'm coming."

Oh! that blessed hailstorm that drove us in! I drew Harold into a seat by the door, keeping between him and that, that he might not escape. But I need not have feared.

Ben Yolland's voice was just beginning the Confession. It had so rarely been heard by Harold that repetition had not blunted his ears to the sound, and presently I heard a short, low, sobbing gasp, and looked round. Harold was on his knees, his hands over his face, and his breath coming short and thick as those old words spoke out that very dumb inarticulate shame, grief, and agony, that had been swelling and bursting in his heart without utterance or form—"We have erred and strayed—there is no health in us—"

We were far behind everyone else—almost in the dark. I don't think anyone knew we were there, and Harold did not stand up throughout the whole service, but kept his hands locked over his brow, and knelt on. Perhaps he heard little more, from the ringing of those words in his ears, for he moved no more, nor looked up, through prayers or psalms, or anything else, until the brief ceremony was entirely over, and I touched him; and then he looked up, and his eyes were swimming and streaming with tears.

We came to the door as if he was in a dream, and there a bitterly cold blast met us, though the rain had ceased. I was not clad for a night walk. Harold again proposed fetching a carriage from the "Boar," but I cried out against that—"I would much, much rather walk with him. It was fine now."

So we went the length of the street, and just then down came the blast on us; oh! such a hurricane, bringing another hailstorm on its wings, and sweeping along, so that I could hardly have stood but for Harold's arm; and after a minute or two of labouring on, he lifted me up in his arms, and bore me along as if I had been a baby. Oh! I remember nothing so comfortable as that sensation after the breathless encounter with the storm. It always comes back to me when I hear the words, "A man shall be as a hiding-place from the tempest, a covert from the wind."

He did not set me down till we were at the front door. We were both wet through, cold, and spent, and it was past nine, so long as it had taken him to labour on in the tempest. Eustace came out grumbling in his petulant way at our absence from dinner. I don't think either of us could bear it just then: Harold went up to his room without a word; I stayed to tell that he had seen me home from church, and say a little about the fearful weather, and then ran up myself, to give orders, as Mr. Yolland had advised me, that some strong hot coffee should be taken at once to Harold's room.

I thought it would be besetting him to go and see after him myself, but I let Dora knock at his door, and heard he had gone to bed. To me it was a long night of tossing and half-sleep, hearing the wild stormy wind, and dreaming of strange things, praying all the time that the noble soul might be won for God at last, and almost feeling, like the Icelander during the conversion of his country, the struggle between the dark spirits and the white.

I had caught a heavy cold, and should have stayed in bed had I not been far too anxious; and I am glad I did not, for I had not been many minutes in my sitting-room before there was a knock at the door, and Harold came in, and what he said was, "Lucy, how does one pray?"

Poor boys! Their mothers, in the revulsion from all that had seemed like a system of bondage, had held lightly by their faith, and in the cares and troubles of their life had heeded little of their children's devotions, so that the practical heathenism of their home at Boola Boola had been unrelieved save by Eustace the elder, when his piety was reckoned as part of his weak, gentlemanly refinement. The dull hopeless wretchedness was no longer in Harold's face, but there was a wistful, gentle weariness, and yet rest in it, which was very touching, as he came to me with his strange sad question, "How does one pray?"

I don't know exactly how I answered it. I hardly could speak for crying, as I told him the very same things one tells the little children, and tried to find him some book to help; but my books no more suited him than my clothes would have done, till he said, "I want what they said in church yesterday."

And as we knelt together, and I said it, the 51st Psalm came to my mind, and I went through it, oh! how differently from when I had said it the day before. "Ah!" he said at the end, "thank you."

And then he stood and looked at the picture which was as his child's to him, turned and said, "Well for him that he is out of all this!"

Presently, when I had marked a Prayer Book for him, he said, "And may I ask that the—the craving I told you of may not come on so intolerably?"

"'Ask, and it shall be given,'" I said. "It may not go at once, dear Harold. Temptation does come, but only to be conquered; and you will conquer now."

We went down to breakfast, where Eustace appeared in full hunting trim, but Harold in the rough coat and long gaiters that meant farming work; and to Eustace's invitations to the run, he replied by saying he heard that Phil Ogden had been to ask him about some difficulty in the trenching work, and he was going to see to it. So he spent the daylight hours in one of those digging and toiling tasks of his "that three day-labourers could not end." I saw him coming home at six o'clock, clay up to the eyes, and having achieved wholesome hunger and wholesome sleepiness.

Eustace had come in cross. He had been chaffed about Harold's shirking, and being a dutiful nephew, and he did not like it at all. He thought Harold ought to have come out for his sake, and to show they did not care. "I do care," said Harold. And when Eustace, with his usual taste, mentioned that they had laughed at the poor fellow led meekly home by his aunt, Harold laid a kind hand on mine, which spoke more than words. I had reason to think that his struggle lasted some time longer, and that the enemy he had reawakened was slow of being laid to rest, so that he was for weeks undergoing the dire conflict; but he gave as little sign as possible, and he certainly conquered.

And from that time there certainly was a change. He was not a man without God any longer. He had learnt that he could not keep himself straight, and had enough of the childlike nature to believe there was One who could. I don't mean that he came at once to be all I could have wished or figured to myself as a religious man. He went to church on Sunday morning now, chiefly, I do believe, for love of the Confession, which was the one voice for his needs; and partly, too, because I had pressed for that outward token, thinking that it would lead him on to more; but it generally seemed more weariness than profit, and he never could sit still five minutes without falling asleep, so that he missed even those sermons of Mr. Ben Yolland's that I thought must do him good.

I tried once, when, feeling how small my powers were beside his, to get him to talk to this same Mr. Yolland, whose work among the pottery people he tried to second, but he recoiled with a tone half scorn, half reserve, which showed that he would bear no pressure in that direction. Only he came to my sitting-room every morning, as if kneeling with me a few moments, and reading a few short verses, were to be his safeguard for the day, and sometimes he would ask me a question. Much did I long for counsel in dealing with him, but I durst seek none, except once, when something Mr. Ben Yolland said about his having expressed strong affection for me, made me say, "If only I were fitter to deal with him," the answer was, "Go on as you are doing; that is better for him as yet than anything else."

CHAPTER IX
THE CHAMPION'S BELT

After all, the fates sent us a chaperon. A letter came addressed to my mother, and proved to be from the clergyman of a village in the remotest corner of Devonshire, where a cousin of my father had once been vicar. His widow, the daughter of his predecessor, had lived on there, but, owing to the misdoings of her son and the failure of a bank, she was in much distress. All intercourse with the family had dropped since my father's death, but the present vicar, casting about for means of helping her, had elicited that the Arghouse family were the only relations she knew of, and had written to ask assistance for her.

"I will go and see about her," said Harold. So he shouldered his bag, walked into Mycening, and started in the tender, the only place where he could endure railway travelling. Four days later came this note:

> "Thursday.
>
> "My Dear Lucy,—Send the carriage to meet Mrs. Alison at 4.40 on Saturday. Your affectionate
>
> "H. A."

I handed the note to Eustace in amazement, but I perceived that he, like his cousin, thought it quite simple that the home of the head of the family should be a refuge for all its waifs and strays, and as I was one myself, I felt rebuked.

I went to Mycening in the carriage, and beheld Harold emerge from a first-class, extracting therefrom one basket after another, two bird-cages, a bundle, an umbrella, a parcel, a cloak, and, finally, a little panting apple-cheeked old lady. "Here's Lucy! that's right." And as both his hands were full, he honoured me with a hasty kiss on the forehead. "She'll take care of you, while I get the rest of it."

"But, oh!—my dear man—my pussy—and—and your wadded cloak—and, oh—my sable muff—your poor papa's present, I would not lose it for a thousand pounds!"

I found the muff, which could not easily be overlooked, for it was as big as a portmanteau, and stuffed full of sundries. "Oh dear yes, my dear, thank you, so it is; but the cat—my poor pussy. No, my dear, that's the bantams—very choice. My poor little Henry had them given to him when he was six years old—the old ones I mean—and I've never parted with them. 'Take them all,' he said—so good; but, oh dear. Tit! Tit! Tittie! He was playing with her just now. Has anyone seen a tabby cat? Bless me, there it goes! So dreadful! It takes one's breath away, and all my things. Oh! where is he?"

"All right," said Harold. "There are your boxes, and here's your cat," showing a striped head under his coat. "Now say what you want to-night, and I'll send for the rest."

She looked wildly about, uttering an incoherent inventory, which Harold cut short by handing over articles to the porter according to his own judgment, and sweeping her into the carriage, returning as I was picking up the odds and ends that had been shed on the way. "You have had a considerable charge," said I, between amusement and dismay.

"Poor old thing, comfort her! She never saw a train before, and is regularly overset."

He put me into the carriage, emptied his pockets of the cat and other trifles, and vanished in the twilight, the old lady gaspingly calling after him, and I soothing her by explaining that he always liked walking home to stretch his legs, while she hoped I was sure, and that it was not want of room. Truly a man of his size could not well have been squeezed in with her paraphernalia, but I did my best to console the old lady for the absence of her protector, and I began at last to learn, as best I could from her bewildered and entangled speech, how he had arrived, taken the whole management of her affairs, and insisted on carrying her off; but her gratitude was strangely confused with her new railway experiences and her anxieties about her parcels. I felt as if I had drifted a little bit farther from old times, when we held our heads rather fastidiously high above "odd people."

But old Mrs. Samuel Alison *was* a lady, as even Lady Diana allowed; but of a kind nearly extinct. She had only visited London and Bath once, on her wedding tour, in the days of stage-coaches; there was provincialism in her speech, and the little she had ever been taught she had forgotten, and she was the most puzzle-headed woman I ever encountered. I do not think she ever realised that it was at Harold's own expense that her rent and other little accounts had been paid up, nor that Eustace was maintaining her. She thought herself only on a long visit, and trusted the assurances that Harold was settling everything for ever. The L30 income which remained to her out of one of L200 served for her pocket-money, and all else was provided for her, without her precisely understanding how; nor did she seem equal to the complications of her new home. She knew our history in a certain sort of way, but she spoke of one of us to the other as "your brother," or "your sister," and the late Mr. Sam always figured as "your poor papa." We tried at first to correct her, but never got her farther than "your poor uncle," and at last we all acquiesced except Eustace, who tried explanations with greater perseverance than effect. Her excuse always was that Harold was so exactly like her poor dear little Henry, except for his beard, that she could almost think she was speaking to him! She was somewhat deaf, and did not like to avow it, which accounted for some of her blunders. One thing she could never understand, namely, why Harold and Eustace had never met her "poor little Henry" in Australia, which she always seemed to think about as big as the Isle of Wight. He had been last heard of at Melbourne; and we might tell her a hundred times that she might as well wonder we had not met a man at Edinburgh; she always recurred to "I do so wish you had seen my poor dear little Henry!" till Harold arrived at a promise to seek out the said Henry, who, by all appearances, was an unmitigated scamp, whenever he should return to Australia.

On the whole, her presence was very good for us, if only by infusing the element of age. She liked to potter about in the morning, attending to her birds and bantams, and talking to the gardening men, weeding women, and all the people in the adjacent hamlet; and, afterwards, the fireside, with her knitting and a newspaper, sufficed her. Not the daily papers—they were far too much for her; but the weekly paper from her own town, which lasted her till a new one came, as she spelled it through, and communicated the facts and facetiae as she thought them suited to our capacity. She was a better walker than I, and would seldom come out in the carriage, for she always caught cold when she did so. A long nap after dinner ended in her resuming her knitting quite contentedly in silence. She wanted no more, though she was pleased if any one said a few kindly words to her. Nothing could be more inoffensive, and she gave us a centre and something needing consideration. I feared Dora might be saucy to her, but perhaps motherliness was what the wild child needed, for she drew towards her, and was softened, and even submitted to learn to knit, for the sake of the mighty labour of making a pair of socks for Harold.

The respectability her presence gave in our pew, and by our hearth, was a great comfort to our friends of all degrees. She was a very pretty old lady, with dark eyes, cheeks still rosy, lovely loose waves of short snowy curls, and a neat, active little figure, which looked well in the good black silks in which I contrived to invest her.

Good old woman, she thought us all shockingly full of worldliness, little guessing how much gaiety was due to her meek presence among us. We even gave dinner-parties in state, and what Richardson and I underwent from Eustace in preparation, no tongue can tell, nor Eustace's complacence in handing down Lady Diana!

The embargo on intercourse with Arked House was over before Viola was taken to London to be introduced. Eustace wanted much to follow them, be at the levee, and spend the season in town. Had he not been presented at Government House, and was it not due to the Queen? Dora more practically offered to follow the example of the Siberian exile, and lay a petition for Prometesky's release at her Majesty's feet, but Harold uttered his ponderous "No" alike to both, proving, in his capacity as agent, that Eustace had nothing like the amount this year which could enable him to spend two or three months even as a single man in London society. The requisite amount, which he had ascertained, was startling, even had Eustace been likely to be frugal; nor could this year's income justify it, in spite of Boola Boola. The expense of coming into the estate, together with all the repairs and improvements, had been such that the Australian property had been needed to supplement the new. Eustace was very angry and disappointed, and grumbled vehemently. It was all Harry's fault for making him spend hundreds on his own maggots, that nobody wanted and nobody cared about, and would be the ruin of him. Poor Bullock would have raised the sum fast enough, and thought nothing of it.

Harry never said how much of his own funds from Boola Boola had supplemented Eustace's outlay; he did not even say how much better it was to be a good landlord than a man about town; all he did was to growl forth to his spoilt child, "There'll be more forthcoming next year."

Eustace protested that he did not believe it, and Harold replied, "No legacy duty—no stock to purchase—Hydriots' dividend—"

It did not check the murmur, and Eustace sulked all the rest of the day; indeed, this has always seemed to me to have been the first little rift in his adherence to his cousin, but at that time his dependence was so absolute, and his power of separate action so small, that he submitted to the decree even while he grumbled; and when he found that Lord Erymanth viewed it as very undesirable for a young man to come up to London without either home or business, or political views, took to himself great credit for the wise decision.

Indeed, Lord Erymanth did invite us all for a fortnight to his great old mansion in Piccadilly to see the Exhibition, and, as he solemnly told me, "to observe enough of our institutions as may prepare my young friends for future life." Even Dora was asked, by special entreaty from Viola, who undertook to look after her—rather too boldly, considering that Di—i.e. Mrs. Enderby—was mistress of Viola's movements, and did not leave her much time to waste upon us.

In fact, Mrs. Enderby, though perfectly civil, was evidently hostile to us, and tried to keep her sister out of our way as much as she could, thickening engagements upon her, at which Viola made all the comical murmurs her Irish blood could prompt, but of course in vain. Eustace's great ambition was to follow her to her parties, and Lady Diana favoured him when she could; but Harold would have nothing to do with such penances. He never missed a chance of seeing Viola come down attired for them, but, as he once said, "that was enough for him." He did not want to see her handed about and grimaced at by a lot of fine gentlemen who did not seem to think anything worth the trouble; and as to the crowd and the stifling, they made him feel ready to strike out and knock everyone down.

So much Eustace and I elicited in short sentences one day, when we were rather foolishly urging on him to let himself be taken with us to an evening party. No, he went his own way and took Dora with him, and I was quite sure that they were safe together, and that after his year's experience he was to be trusted to know where it was fitting to take her. They saw a good deal that was more entertaining than we could venture on; and, moreover, Harold improved his mind considerably in the matters of pottery, porcelain, and model lodging-houses.

Dermot was in London too, not staying with uncle or sister, for both of whom he was much too erratic, though he generally presented himself at such times as were fittest for ascertaining our movements for the day, when it generally ended in his attaching himself to some of us, for Harold seemed to have passed an act of oblivion on the doings of that last unhappy meeting, and allowed himself to be taken once or twice with Eustace into Dermot's own world; but not only was he on his guard there, but he could not be roused to interest even where horseflesh was concerned. Some one said he was too great a barbarian, and so he was. His sports and revelries had been on a wilder, ruder, more violent scale, such as made these seem tame. He did not understand mere trifling for amusement's sake, still less how money could be thrown away for it and for fashion, when it was so cruelly wanted by real needs; and even Dermot was made uncomfortable by his thorough earnestness. "It won't do in 'the village' in the nineteenth century," said he to me. "It is like—who was that old fellow it was said of—a lion stalking about in a sheepfold."

"Sheep!" said I, indignantly. "I am afraid some are wolves in sheep's clothing."

Dermot shrugged his shoulders and said, "How is one to help oneself if one has been born some two thousand years too late, or not in the new half-baked hemisphere where demigods still walk the earth in their simplicity?"

"I want you not to spoil the demigod when he has walked in among you."

"I envy him too much to do that," said Dermot with a sigh.

"I believe you, Dermot, but don't take him among those who want to do so."

"That's your faith in your demigod," said Dermot, not able to resist a little teasing; but seeing I was really pained, he added: "No, Lucy, I'll never take him again to meet Malvoisin and Nessy Horsman. In the first place, I don't know how he might treat them; and in the next, I would die sooner than give them another chance, even if he would. I thought the men would have been struck with him as I was; but no, it is not in them to be struck with anyone. All they think of is how to make him like themselves."

"Comus' crew!" said I. "Oh! Dermot, how can you see it and be one of them?"

"I'm not happy enough to be an outer barbarian," he said, and went his way.

There was a loan exhibition of curious old objects in plate and jewellery, to which Lady Diana took me, and where, among other things, we found a long belt crusted thickly with scales of gold, and with a sort of medal at the clasp.

"Just look here, mamma," said Viola; "I do believe this is the archery prize."

And sure enough on the ticket was, "Belt, supposed to be of Peruvian workmanship. Taken in the Spanish Armada, 1588. Champion belt at the Northchester Archery Club. Lent by Miss Hippolyta Horsman."

Lady Diana came to look with some interest. She had never had an opportunity of examining it closely before, and she now said, "I am much inclined to believe that this is the belt that used to be an heirloom in the Jerfield family, and which ought to be in yours, Lucy."

My father's first wife had been the last of the Jerfields, and I asked eager questions. Lady Diana believed that "those unhappy young men" had made away with all their mother's jewels, but she could tell no more, as our catastrophe had taken place while she was living at Killy Marey. Her brother, she said, could tell us more; and so he did, enough to set Eustace on fire.

Yes, the belt had been well known. It was not taken in the Armada, but in a galleon of the Peruvian plunder by an old Jerfield, who had been one of the race of Westward Ho! heroes. The Jerfields had not been prosperous, and curious family jewels had been nearly all the portion of the lady who had married my father. The sons had claimed them, and they were divided between them, and given to the two wives; and in the time of distress, when far too proud to accept aid from the father, as well as rather pleased at mortifying him by disposing of his family treasures, Alice and Dorothy Alison had gradually sold them off. And, once in the hands of local jewellers, it was easy for the belt to pass into becoming the prize held by the winner in the Archery Club every year. Lord Erymanth would go with Eustace the next morning to identify it; but what would be the use of that? Eustace at first fancied he could claim it, but soon he saw that his proposal was viewed as so foolish that he devoured it, and talked of giving an equivalent; but, as Lord Erymanth observed, it would be very difficult to arrange this with an article of family and antiquarian value, in the hands of an archery club—an impersonal body.

"The thing would be to win it," said Viola. "Could not some of us?"

"Well done, little Miss Tell," returned Dermot. "Hippo has won that same belt these four years, to my certain knowledge, except once, when Laurie Stympson scored two more."

"I'll practise every day; won't you, Lucy? And then, between us, there will be two chances."

"I am sure I am very much nattered by Miss Tracy's kindness," put in Eustace; "but is the match solely between ladies?"

No, for the last two years, after a match between ladies and between gentlemen, there had a final one taken place between the two winners, male and female, in which Hippo had hitherto always carried off the glory and the belt. So Eustace intimated his full intention of trying for himself, endeavouring to be very polite to Viola and me, but implying that he thought himself a far surer card, boasting of his feats as a marksman in the Bush, until Dora broke in, "Why, Eustace, that was Harry; wasn't it, Harry?"

"Comme a l'ordinaire," muttered Dermot. Eustace made a little stammering about the thing being so near that no one could tell, and Dora referred again to Harold, who put her down with a muttered "Never mind" under his beard.

What was to be done with it if it were won? "Get a fac-simile made, and an appropriate inscription," recommended Lord Erymanth. "Probably they would take that willingly."

"But what would you do with it?" asked Harold. "You can't wear it."

"I tell you it is an heirloom," quoth Eustace. "Have you no feeling for an heirloom? I am sure it was your mother who sold it away from me."

The sight of the belt, with Lord Erymanth's lecture on it, inflamed Eustace's ardour all the more, and we made extensive purchases of bows and arrows; that is to say, Eustace and I did, for Lady Diana would not permit Viola to join in the contest. She did not like the archery set, disapproved of public matches for young ladies, and did not choose her daughter to come forward in the cause. I did not fancy the matches either, and was certain that my mere home pastime had no chance with Hippo and Pippa, who had studied archery scientifically for years, and aimed at being the best lady shots in England; but Eustace would never have forgiven me if I had not done my best. So we subscribed to the Archery Club as soon as we went home; and Eustace would have had me practise with him morning, noon, and night, till I rebelled, and declared that if he knocked me up my prowess would be in vain, and that I neither could nor would shoot more than an hour and a half a day.

His ardour, however, soon turned into vituperations of the stupid sport. How could mortal man endure it? If it had been pistol or rifle-shooting now, it would have been tolerable, and he should have been sure to excel; but a great long, senseless, useless thing like an arrow was only fit for women or black fellows; the string hurt one's fingers too—always slipping off the tabs.

"No wonder, as you hold it," said Harold, who had just turned aside to watch on his way down to the potteries, and came in time to see an arrow fly into the bank a yard from the target. "Don't you see how Lucy takes it?"

I had already tried to show him, but he had pronounced mine to be the ladies' way, and preferred to act by the light of nature. Harry looked, asked a question or two, took the bow in his own hands, and with "This way, Eustace; don't you see?" had an arrow in the outer white.

"Yes," said Eustace, "of course, stupid thing, anybody can do it without any trouble."

"It is pretty work," said Harry, taking up the third arrow, and sending it into the inner white.

"Much too easy for men," was Eustace's opinion, and he continued to despise it until, being capable of perseverance of a certain kind, and being tutored by Harold, he began to succeed in occasionally piercing the target, upon which his mind changed, and he was continually singing the praises of archery in the tone (whispered Viola) of the sparrow who killed Cock Robin with his bow and arrow!

We used to practise for an hour every afternoon, and the fascination of the sport gained upon Harold so much that he sent for a bow and arrows, and shot with us whenever he was not too busy, as, between the agency and the potteries, he often was. He did not join the club, nor come to the weekly meetings at Northchester with Eustace and me, until, after having seen a little of the shooting there, I privately hinted to him that there was not the smallest chance of the champion belt changing hands unless he took up the family cause. Whereupon, rather than that Eustace should be disappointed, he did ask to be admitted, and came once with us to the meeting, when, to tell the truth, he did not shoot as well as usual, for—as afterwards appeared—in riding into Northchester he had stopped to help to lift up a great tree that was insecure on its timber waggon, and even his hands shook a little from the exertion. Besides, Eustace had discovered that Harold's new bow shot better than his, and had insisted on changing, and Harold had not so proved the powers of Eustace's as to cure it of its inferiority.

Eustace really came to shooting so tolerably as to make him look on the sport with complacency, and like the people he met there. All this hardly seems worth telling, but events we little thought of sprang from those archery practices. For the present we found them a great means of getting acquainted with the neighbours. I bowed now to many more people than ever I had done before, and we had come into great favour since the Hydriots had astonished the county by announcing a dividend. It was only three per cent., but that was an immense advance upon nothing, and the promise of the future was great; the shares had gone up nearly to their original value in the most sanguine days; and the workmen—between prosperity, good management, the lecture-room at the "Dragon's Head," and the work among them done by the clerical, as well as the secular, Yolland—were, not models by any means, but far from the disorderly set they had been. They did take some pride in decent houses and well-dressed children, and Harold's plans for the improvement of their condition were accepted as they never would have been from one whose kindly sympathy and strength of will did not take them, as it were, captive. "Among those workmen you feel that he is a born king of men," said Ben Yolland.

And as Bullock had been bailiff as well as agent, Harry had all the home-farming matters on his hands, and attended to them like any farmer, so that it was no wonder that he gave little time to the meetings for archery practice, which involved the five miles expedition, and even to our own domestic practice, answering carelessly, when Eustace scolded him about letting a chance go by, and his heedlessness of the honour of the family, "Oh, I take a shot or two every morning as I go out, to keep my hand in."

"You'll get your arrows spoilt in the dew," said Eustace.

"They don't go into the dew," said Harold. And as he was always out with the lark, even Dora seldom saw this practice; but there were always new holes very near the centre of the target, which Eustace said proved how true was his own aim.

Harvest came, and in the middle of it the great archery match of the year, which was held in the beautiful grounds of Mr. Vernon, the member for Northchester, a little way from the town.

"I suppose Harry may as well go," said Eustace; "but he has not practised at all, so it will be of little avail. Now if I had not grazed my hand, I should have scored quite as much as Miss Horsman last week. It all lies in caring about it."

And severe was his lecture to Harold against foolishly walking in and making his hand unsteady. Yet, after all, when the carriage came to the door, Harold was not to be found, though his bow and arrows were laid ready with ours to be taken. He endured no other apparatus. The inside of his fingers was like leather, and he declared that tabs and guard only hampered him. Lady Diana had yielded to her daughter's entreaties, and brought her to see the contest, though only as a spectator. As I stood shy and far from sanguine among the lady archers, I felt out of my natural place, and glad she was under her mother's wing, she looked so fair and innocent in her delicate blue and white, and was free for such sweet ardour in our cause, all the prettier and more arch because its demonstrations were kept down with the strong hand of her mother.

Hippolyta and Philippa Horsman were in tightly-made short-skirted dresses, pork-pie hats, and strong boots, all black picked out with scarlet, like Hippo's own complexion. She was tall, with a good active figure, and handsome, but she had reached the age when the colouring loses its pure incarnadine and becomes hard and fixed, and she had a certain likeness to all those creatures whose names are compounded of tiger. But she was a good-natured being, and of late I had begun to understand better her aspirations towards doing and becoming something more than the mere domestic furniture kind of young lady.

Her aberrations against good taste and reticence were, I began to understand, misdirected outbreaks of the desire to be up and doing. Even now, as we ladies drew for our turn, she was saying, half sadly, "I'm tired of it all. What good comes of getting this belt over and over again? If it were rifle or pistol shooting it might be of use, but one could hardly organise a regiment of volunteers with the long bows when the invasion comes off."

Wit about the Amazonian regiment with the long bow was current all the time we ladies were shooting, and Eustace was worrying me to such a degree, that nervousness made me perform ten degrees worse than usual, but that mattered little, for Hippolyta, with another of her cui bono sighs, carried off the Roman mosaic that was the ladies' prize, telling Pippa that it should be hers when the belt was won.

"Don't be too sure."

"Bosh! There's no one here who can handle a bow but Charlie Stympson. One Alison is a spoon, and the other is a giant made to be conquered. When he shot before, his arrows went right over the grounds, and stuck into a jackdaw's nest on the church tower! I can't think why he came."

"To make a feather in your cap."

"What a substantial one!"

There I escaped to a seat by Lady Diana, where Viola could expend her enthusiasm in clutches and squeezes of my hand. Eustace was by this time wrought up to such a state that he hardly knew what he was doing, and his first arrow wavered and went feebly aside. Two or three more shot, and then the tall figure came to the front; one moment, and the cry was "Gold," while Viola's clap of the hands brought on her a frown from her mother, who thought demonstrativeness improper. She had to content herself with pinching my fingers every time one of those shafts went home to the heart of the target, and Harold stood, only too facile princeps, while Eustace sauntered up to us with the old story about the sun or the damp, I forget which, only it was something that had spoilt his archery.

Hippolyta was undaunted. The small target and longer range had thrown out many a competitor before now, and her not very low-pitched tone was heard observing that no dumb giant should beat her at her own tools.

Whatever had been her weariness of her successes before, it was gone now, and she shot splendidly. Never had such shooting been known in the annals of the club, and scarcely a word passed as the two went pacing between the two little targets, Harold with his calm, easy movement, business-like but without effort, and Hippolyta with excitement beginning to tell on her. Each time she passed us we saw her step more impetuous, the glow on her cheeks deeper, and at last that her eyes were full of tears; and after that, one arrow went into the outer white, and the last even into the green; while Harry's final shot was into that one great confluent hole that the centre of the target had become.

"Heard ye the arrow hurtle through the sky?
Heard ye the dragon monster's deathful cry?"

whispered Viola. "Mamma won't let me cheer, and I must have it out somehow."

And as I sprang up and hurried to Harold, she came with me, taking care to cast no look behind, for fear of detaining glances; and she put out both hands to shake his, as he stood with the smile lighting up his face as he saw the pleasure he had given; though Eustace never came forward, unable to rejoice where he had been so palpably and publicly excelled.

Hippolyta behaved well. She came up holding out her hand, and saying, "Well, Mr. Alison, if one is to fall, it is a pleasure to have so mighty a victor. But why did you never let me see before what a Palnatoke (if I must not say Tell) I had to deal with?"

"I had no time for the practices," said Harold, puzzled as to who Palnatoke was.

"Worse and worse! You don't mean that you shoot like this without practice?"

"Lucy taught me a little."

"Well, if heaven-born archers come down on one, there's nothing for it but submitting. Robin Hood must prevail," said Hippolyta, as the belt was handed over to Harold, with a sigh that made him say in excuse, "I would not have done it, but that Eustace wanted to have it in his hands, for family reasons."

"Then let him look to it; I mean to get it again next year. And, I say, Mr. Alison, I have a right to some compensation. All you archers are coming to lunch at Therford on Thursday, if the sun shines, to be photographed, you know. Now you must come to breakfast, and bring your lion's skin and your bow—to be done alone. It is all the consolation I ask. Make him, Lucy. Bring him."

There was no refusing; and that was the way the photograph came to be taken. We were reminded by a note after we went home, including in the invitation Eustace, who, after being a little sulky, had made up his mind that a long range was easier to shoot at than a short one, and so that he should have won the prize if he had had the chance; and the notion of being photographed was, of course, delightful to him.

"In what character shall you take me?" he asked of Miss Horsman, when we were going out on the lawn, and it dawned on him that Harry was to be a Hercules.

"Oh! as Adonis, of course," said Hippo.

"Or Eurystheus," whispered her sister.

Eustace did not understand, and looked pleased, saying something about a truly classical get up; but Harold muttered to me, "Aren't they making game of him?"

"They will take care not to vex him," I said.

But Harold could not overlook it, and took a dislike to the Horsmans on the spot, which all Hippolyta's genuine admiration of him could not overcome. She knew what the work of his eighteen months in England had been, and revered him with such enthusiasm for what she called his magnificent manhood and beneficence, as was ready on the least encouragement to have become something a good deal warmer; but whatever she did served to make her distasteful to him. First, she hastily shuffled over Eustace's portrait, because, as she allowed us to hear, "he would give her no peace till he was disposed of." And then she not only tormented her passive victim a good deal in trying to arrange him as Hercules, but she forgot the woman in the artist, and tried to make him bare his neck and shoulder in a way that made him blush while he uttered his emphatic "No, no!" and Baby Jack supported him by telling her she "would only make a prize-fighter of him." Moreover, he would have stood more at ease if the whole of Therford had not been overrun with dogs. He scorned to complain, and I knew him too well to do so for him; but it was a strain on his self-command to have them all smelling about his legs, and wanting to mumble the lion skin, especially Hippo's great bloodhound, Kirby, as big as a calf, who did once make him start by thrusting his long cold nose into his hand. Hippo laughed, but Harold could do nothing but force out a smile.

And I always saw the disgusted and bored expression most prominently in her performance, which at the best could never have given the grandeur of the pose she made him take, with the lion skin over his shoulder, and the arrows and bow in his hand. He muttered that a rifle would be more rational, and that he could hold it better, but withdrew the protest when he found that Hippo was ready to implore him to teach her to shoot with pistol, rifle—anything.

"Your brother can show you. You've only to fire at a mark," was all that could be got out of him.

Nor would he be entrapped into a beneficent talk. His great talent for silence served him well, and though I told him afterwards that he had not done Hippo justice—for she honestly wanted an opening for being useful—he was not mollified. "I don't like tongue," was all he further said of her.

But whatever Hippo was, or whatever she did, I shall always be grateful to her for that photograph.

CHAPTER X
DERMOT'S MARE

All this time Dermot Tracy had been from home. He had not come back after the season, but had been staying with friends and going to various races, in which, as usual, he had heavy stakes. He persuaded my two nephews to meet him at Doncaster, where he ran one of the horses bred on his Irish estate, and afterwards to go and make him a visit at Killy Marey, County Kildare, where he used to stay about once a year, shooting or hunting, as the season might be, and always looking after his horses and entertaining all the squires and squireens of the neighbourhood, and many of the officers from the Curragh. The benefit of those visits was very doubtful both as to morals and purses, and Lord Erymanth pointedly said he was sorry when he heard that Harold and Eustace were of the party.

I do not know whether Lady Diana viewed them as bad companions for her son, or her son as a bad companion for them; but she was very severe about it, and when I thought of the hunt dinner at Foling, my heart sank, even while I was indignant at any notion of distrusting Harold; and it did indeed seem to me that he had learnt where to look for strength and self-command, and that he had a real hatred and contempt of evil. Yet I should have been more entirely happy about him if he had not still held aloof from all those innermost ordinances, of which he somehow did not feel the need, or understand the full drift. Nor would he bow himself to give to any man the confidence or the influence over him he had given to an incapable girl like me. And if I should have feared for the best brought up, most religious of young men, in such scenes as I was told were apt to take place at Killy Marey, how could I not be anxious for my nephews? But nothing ever turns out as one expects.

I was at Arked one day, and Lady Diana was telling me of the great rambling house at Killy Marey, and how, when she arrived as a bride, none of the doors would shut except two that would not open, behind one of which lived the family ghost; how the paper hung in festoons on the walls, and the chairs were of the loveliest primrose-coloured brocade; and how the green of the meadows was so wonderful, that she was always remembering it was the Emerald Isle; but how hopeless and impossible it was to get anything properly done, and how no good could be done where the Romish priests had interfered. All the old story of course. In the midst, a telegraph paper was brought to her; she turned deadly white, and bade me open it, for she could not. I knew she thought her son had met his father's fate, and expected to astonish her with the tidings that he was coming home by the next steamer, or that he had sent some game, or the like. Alas! no; the mother's foreboding had been too near the truth. The telegram was from Eustace: "Tracy has had a bad horse accident. The doctor wishes for you."

There was nothing for it but to speed the mother and daughter on their hurried start to catch the Holyhead packet and cross that night. I went home to await in terror and trembling the despatch I might receive, and to be enlivened by Mrs. Sam Alison's cheering accounts of all the accidents she could recollect. "Horses are dangerous creatures to meddle with, and your poor papa never would let me take the reins when we kept a gig—which was when he was living, you know, my dear. 'You never can trust their heels,' he used to say; and it was only last week little Cocker was kicked off, but that was a donkey, and they were using him shamefully," &c. &c. &c. I felt as if a swarm of bees were humming in my ears, and walked about to make the suspense more tolerable, but I absolutely had no news at all till Viola's letter came. It was a long one, for she could be of no service as yet, and to write letters was at once her use and her solace.

Among the horses which Dermot's Irish agent had been buying for training purposes was a mare, own sister to Harold's hunter—a splendid creature of three years old, of wonderful beauty, power, and speed, but with the like indomitable temper. She would suffer no living thing to approach her but one little stable-boy, and her own peculiar cat, which slept on her back, and took all sorts of liberties with her. Her value would be great if she could be trained, but the training was the problem. Harold, who, partly from early familiarity, partly from the gentleness of fearless strength, had a matchless power over horses, had made acquaintance with her one evening, had been suffered in her box, had fed her, caressed her cat, and led her round the stable-yard as a first stage in the conquest of horse by man.

In the early morning, Dermot, quite as fearless, and unwilling that anyone should do or dare more than himself, had gone alone to make the same attempt, but no sooner did the mare find him beside her, than she seized him by the shoulder with her teeth, threw him down, and kicked and trampled on him. None of the grooms could succeed in rescuing him, and it was only when Eustace's cry had summoned Harold, that, grasping the mare's halter and forcing her back with his arm of iron, he made it possible for Eustace and a groom to drag out poor Dermot's senseless form, in a state that at first appeared to be death itself. For several days his condition was so extremely precarious, that Harold never once left him till his mother arrived, and even after that was his most effective nurse. He sent me a message, in Viola's letter, that he had not had a moment to write, and hoped I had not been too anxious.

After this, Viola wrote every day, and told of gradual improvement in her brother, and at last how he had been lifted to the sofa, and mamma hoped in a fortnight or three weeks he might be able to be taken home. By the next post came a note from Harold, saying he could be spared, and was coming home, and that very evening he walked into the house, and was welcomed by Dora with shrieks of ecstatic joy.

He said Dermot was better, but he looked worn, and had the indefinable expression of pain which made me sure that something had gone wrong, and presently I found out that the bite in the shoulder was a very bad business, still causing much suffering, but that the most serious matter was, that a kick in the side had renewed the damage left by the old Alma bullet, and that great care would be needed all the winter. But Harold seemed more reluctant to open his mouth than ever, and only, by most diligent pumping, did Mrs. Alison get out of him what doctors they had called in, and whether they had used all the recipes for wounds and bruises that she had entrusted to me to be sent, and which had for the most part remained in my blotting-book.

The next morning, to my grief and distress, he did not come to my room, but I found he had been up and out long before it was light, and he made his appearance at eleven o'clock, saying he had promised to go and give Lord Erymanth an account of his nephew, and wanted me to come with him "to do the talking, or he should never stand it." If I did not object to the dog-cart and Daniel O'Rourke immediately, we should be there by luncheon time. I objected to nothing that Harry drove, but all the way to Erymanth not ten words passed, and those were matters of necessity. I had come to the perception that when he did not want to speak it was better to let him take his own time.

Lord Erymanth was anxious, not only about Dermot's health, and his sister's strength and spirits, but he wanted to hear what Harold thought of the place and of the tone of the country; and, after our meal, when he grew more confidential, he elicited short plain answers full of information in short compass, and not very palatable. The estate was "not going on well." "Did Harold think well of the agent?" "He had been spoilt." "How?" "By calls for supplies." "Were the people attached to Dermot?" "To a certain degree." "Would it be safe for him to live there?" "He ought."

Lord Erymanth entirely assented to this, and we found that he had all along held that his sister had been in error for not having remained at Killy Marey, and brought up her son to his duties as a landlord, whatever the danger; though of course she, poor thing, could hardly be expected to see it in that light. He evidently viewed this absenteeism as the cause of the wreck of Dermot's youth, and those desultory habits of self-indulgence and dissipation which were overcoming that which was good and noble in him; and the good old man showed that he blamed himself for what he had conceded to his sister in the first shock of her misfortune. Harold had told him of the warm feeling shown by the tenantry when Dermot was lying in danger of his life, and their rejoicing when he turned the corner and began to recover, and he asked anxiously whether all this affection might not awaken a responsive chord, and draw him to "what was undoubtedly his proper sphere."

"It will," said Harold.

"You think so? And there is little doubt but that your cousin's influence at such a critical period may have great effect in turning the scale?"

Harold nodded.

"More especially as, from the intelligence I have received, I have little doubt that the connection will be drawn a good deal closer before long," said Lord Erymanth with a benignant smile at us both. "I suppose we must not begin to congratulate one another yet, for I may conclude that nothing had actually taken place when you came away."

"Nothing."

"When my sister became conscious of the condition of affairs and wrote to consult me, I had no hesitation in replying that, though Viola's connections might warrant greater expectations in a worldly point of view, yet I thought that there was every reason for promoting an attachment to a gentleman of family equal to her own on one side at least, and whose noble exertions during the past two years for the welfare of all concerned with him, not only obliterate all recollection of past disadvantages, but in every way promise honour and happiness to all connected with him."

I was not a little excited, but one of the worst fits of restlessness under Lord Erymanth's harangues had come upon Harold. He only sat it out by pulling so many hairs out of his beard that they made an audible frizzle in the fire when he brushed them off his knee, and stood up, saying gruffly, "You are very good; he deserves it. But I must get Lucy home in good time. May I go and speak to your coachman? Tracy gave me a message for him."

Harold was off, and Lord Erymanth observed, "A very fine young man that. It is much to be regretted that he did not employ the advantages he enjoyed at Sydney as his cousin Eustace did, and left himself so rugged and unpolished."

"You must learn to like him, dear Lord Erymanth," I said. "He is all a very dear brother could be to me."

And allegiance to him kept back every word of that infinite superiority, which was never more shown than by the opinion of Eustace, which his great unselfish devotion continued, without the least deceit, to impress on most people. Lord Erymanth rejoiced, and we agreed that it was very lucky for me that I preferred Harold, since I should have had to yield up my possession of Eustace. The old gentleman was most kind and genial, and much delighted that the old breach with the Alisons should be healed, and that his niece should make a marriage which he greatly preferred to her sister's, and together we sung the praises of our dear Viola, where we had no difference of opinion.

Harold only came back when the carriage came round, and no sooner had we driven off than I broke out—"Harry, I had no notion matters had gone so far. Fancy, Lady Diana consulting her brother! It must be very near a crisis. I can't think why you did not stay to see it."

"Because I am a fool."

The horse flew on till we were nearly out at the park-gates, and a bewildered sense of his meaning was coming before me. "You wished it," said I rather foolishly.

"I did. I do. Only I don't want to see it."

"My poor dear Harold!"

"Pshaw!"—the sound was like a wild beast's, and made the horse plunge—"I shall get over it."

Then, presently, in a more natural voice, "I must go out again in the spring. There are things to be looked to at Boola Boola for both of us. I shall only wait till Tracy is well enough to go with me."

"He! Dermot Tracy?"

"Yes. It will be the best way to break out of the old lines."

"I can fancy that. Oh, Harold! are you going to save him? That will be the most blessed work of all!" I cried, for somehow a feeling like an air of hope and joy came over me.

"I don't know about that," said he, in a smothered tone; but it was getting dark enough to loose his tongue, and when I asked, "Was it his illness that made him wish it?" he answered, "It was coming before. Lucy, those horses have done worse for him than that wound in his shoulder. They had almost eaten the very heart out of him!"

"His substance I know they have," I said; "but not his good warm heart."

"You would say so if you saw the poor wretches on his property," said Harold. "The hovels in the Alfy Valley were palaces compared with the cabins. Such misery I never saw. They say it is better since the famine. What must it have been then? And he thinking only how much his agent could squeeze from them!"

I could only say he had been bred up in neglect of them, and to think them impracticable, priest-ridden traitors and murderers. Yes, Lady Diana had said some of this to Harold already, It was true that they had shot Mr. Tracy, but Harold had learnt that after a wild, reckless, spendthrift youth, he had become a Protestant and a violent Orangeman in the hottest days of party strife, so that he had incurred a special hatred, which, as far as Harold could see, was not extended to the son, little as he did for his tenants but show them his careless, gracious countenance from time to time.

Yet peril for the sake of duty would, as all saw now, have been far better for Dermot than the alienation from all such calls in which his mother had brought him up. When her religious influence failed with him, there was no other restraint. Since he had left the army, he had been drawn, by those evil geniuses of his, deep into speculations in training horses for the turf, and his affairs had come into a frightful state of entanglement, his venture at Doncaster had been unsuccessful, and plunged him deeper into his difficulties, and then (as I came to know) Harold's absolute startled amazement how any living man could screw and starve men, women, and children for the sake of horseflesh, and his utter contempt for such diversions as he had been shown at the races, compared with the pleasure of making human beings happy and improving one's land, had opened Dermot's eyes with very few words.

The thought was not new when the danger of death made him look back on those wasted years; and resolution began with the dawning of convalescence, that if he could only free himself from his entanglements—and terrible complications they were—he would begin a new life, worthy of having been given back to him. In many a midnight watch he had spoken of these things, and Harold had soothed him by a promise to use that accountant's head of his in seeing how to free him as soon as he was well enough. Biston and the horses would be sold, and he could turn his mind to his Irish tenants, who, as he already saw, loved him far better than he deserved. He caught eagerly at the idea of going out to Australia with Harold, and it did indeed seem that my brave-hearted nephew was effecting a far greater deliverance for him than that from the teeth and hoofs of wicked Sheelah.

"But you will not stay, Harold? You will come home?" I said.

"I mean it," he answered.

"Then I don't so much mind," said I, with infinite relief; and he added, thinking that I wanted further reassurance, that he should never give up trying to get Prometesky's pardon; and that this was only a journey for supplies, and to see his old friend, and perhaps to try whether anything could be done about that other unhappy Harry. I pressed him to promise me that he would return and settle here, but though he said he would come back, to settling at home he answered, "That depends;" and though I could not see, I knew he was biting his moustache, and guessed, poor dear fellow, that it depended on how far he should be able to endure the sight of Eustace and Viola married. I saw now that I had been blind not to perceive before that his heart had been going out to Viola all this time, while he thought he was courting her for Eustace, and I also had my thoughts about Viola, which made it no very great surprise to me, when, in a few days more, intelligence came that Eustace might be expected at home, and he made his appearance in a petulant though still conceited mood, that made me suspect his wooing had not been prosperous, though I knew nothing till Harold told me that he was not out of heart, though Viola had cut him short and refused to listen to him, for her mother said she was a mere child who was taken by surprise, and that if he were patient and returned to the charge she would know her own mind better.

Harold was certainly more exhilarated than he chose to avow to himself on this discovery, and the next week came a letter from Lady Diana, and a short note from Dermot himself, both saying he had not been so well, and begging Harold to come and assist in the removal, since Dermot protested that otherwise he could not bear the journey, and his mother declared that she should be afraid to think of it for him.

Viola's hitherto constant correspondence had ceased; I drew my own auguries, but I had to keep them to myself, for Harold started off the next day in renewed spirits, and I had Eustace on my hands in a very strange state, not choosing or deigning to suppose himself rejected, and yet exceedingly, angry with all young ladies for their silliness and caprices, while he lauded Lady Diana up to the skies, and abused Dermot, who, I think, had laughed at him visibly enough to be at least suspected by himself. And, oddly enough, Dora was equally cross, and had a fit of untowardness unequalled since the combats at her first arrival, till I was almost provoked into acquiescence in Eustace's threat of sending her to school.

The journey was at last accomplished; Harold only parted with the Tracys at Arked House, after having helped to carry Dermot to the room that had been prepared for him on the ground-floor.

I rode over the next afternoon to inquire, and was delighted to meet Viola close within the gate. We sent away my horse, and she drew me into her favourite path while answering my questions that Dermot had had a good night and was getting up; I should find him in the drawing-room if I waited a little while. She could have me all to herself, for mamma was closeted with Uncle Ery, talking over things—and on some word or sound of mine betraying that I guessed what things, it broke out.

"How could you let him do it, Lucy? You, at least, must have known better."

"My dear, how could I have stopped him, with all St. George's Channel between us?"

"Well, at any rate, you might persuade them all to have a little sense, and not treat me as if I was one of the elegant females in 'Pride and Prejudice,' who only refuse for fun! Is not that enough to drive one frantic, Lucy? Can't you at least persuade the man himself?"

"Only one person can do that, Viola."

"But I can't! That's the horrid part of it. I can't get rid of it. Mamma says I am a foolish child. I could tell her of other people more foolish than I am. I can see the difference between sham and reality, if they can't."

"I don't think he means to be sham," I rambled into defence of Eustace.

"Means it! No, he hasn't the sense. I believe he really thinks it was he who saved Dermot's life as entirely as mamma does."

"No. Now do they really?"

"Of course, as they do with everything. It's always 'The page slew the boar, the peer had the gloire.'"

"It's the page's own fault," I said. "He only wants the peer to have the gloire."

"And very disagreeable and deceitful it is of him," cried Viola; "only he hasn't got a scrap of deceit in him, and that's the reason he does it so naturally. No, you may tell them that borrowed plumes won't always serve, and there are things that can't be done by deputy."

And therewith Viola, perhaps perceiving what she had betrayed, turned more crimson than ever, and hid her face against me with a sob in her breath, and then I was quite sure of what I did not dare to express, further than by saying, while I caressed her, "I believe they honestly think it is all the same."

"But it isn't," said Viola, recovering, and trying to talk and laugh off her confusion. "I don't think so, and poor Dermot did not find it so when the wrong one was left to lift him, and just ran his great stupid arm into the tenderest place in his side, and always stepped on all the boards that creak, and upset the table of physic bottles, and then said it was Harold's way of propping them up! And that's the creature they expect me to believe in!"

We turned at the moment and saw a handkerchief beckoning to us from the window; and going in, found Dermot established on a couch under it, and Harold packing him up in rugs, a sight that amazed both of us; but Dermot said, "Yes, he treats me like Miss Stympson's dog, you see. Comes over by stealth when I want him."

Dermot did look very ill and pain-worn, and his left arm lay useless across him, but there was a kind of light about his eyes that I had not seen for a long time, as he made Harold set a chair for me close to him, and he and Viola told the adventures of their journey, with mirth in their own style, and Harold stood leaning against the shutter with his look of perfect present content, as if basking in sunshine while it lasted.

When the mother and uncle came in, it was manifestly time for us to convey ourselves away. Harold had come on foot from Mycening, but I was only too glad to walk my pony along the lanes, and have his company in the gathering winter twilight.

"You have spoken to her?" he said.

"Yes. Harold, it is of no use. She will never have him."

"Her mother thinks she will."

"Her mother knows what is in Viola no more than she knows what is in that star. Has Dermot never said anything—"

"Lady Diana made everyone promise not to say a word to him."

"Oh!"

"But, Lucy, what hinders it? There's nothing else in the way, is there?"

I did not speak the word, but made a gesture of assent.

"May I know who it is," said Harold in a voice of pain. "Our poor fellow shall never hear."

"Harold," said I, "are you really so ridiculous as to think any girl could care for Eustace while you are by?"

"Don't!" cried Harold, with a sound as of far more pain than gladness.

"But why not, Harry? You asked me."

"Don't light up what I have been struggling to quench ever since I knew it."

"Why?" I went on. "You need not hold back on Eustace's account. I am quite sure nothing would make her accept him, and I am equally convinced—"

"Hush, Lucy!" he said in a scarcely audible voice. "It is profanation. Remember—"

"But all that is over," I said. "Things that happened when you were a mere boy, and knew no better, do not seem to belong to you now."

"Sometimes they do not," he said sadly; "but—"

"What is repented," I began, but he interrupted.

"The fact is not changed. It is not fit that the purest, gentlest, brightest creature made by Heaven should be named in the same day with one stained with blood—aye, and deeds I could not speak of to you."

I could not keep from crying as I said, "If I love you the more, Harry, would not she?"

"See here, Lucy," said Harry, standing still with his hand on my rein; "you don't know what you do in trying to inflame what I can hardly keep down. The sweet little thing may have a fancy for me because I'm the biggest fellow she knows, and have done a thing or two; but what I am she knows less than even you do; and would it not be a wicked shame either to gain the tender heart in ignorance, or to thrust on it the knowledge and the pain of such a past as mine?" And his groan was very heavy, so that I cried out:

"Oh, Harry! this is dreadful. Do you give up all hope and joy for ever because of what you did as an ungovernable boy left to yourself?"

We went on for some time in silence; then he said in an indescribable tone, between wonder, disgust, and pity, "And I thought I loved Meg Cree!"

"You knew no one else," I said, feeling as if, when Dora threw away that ring, the wild, passionate animal man had been exorcised; but all the answer I had was another groan, as from the burthened breast, as if he felt it almost an outrage to one whom he so reverenced to transfer to her the heart that had once beat for Meg Cree. There was no more speech for a long time, during which I feared that I had merely made him unhappy by communicating my conjecture, but just as we were reaching our own grounds he said, "You will say nothing, Lucy?"

"No, indeed."

"I thought it was all over, and for ever," he said, pausing; "it ought to have been. But the gates of a new world were opened to me when I saw her and you walking in the garden! If it had only been five or six years sooner!"

He could not say any more, for Dora, who had been watching, here burst on us with cries of welcome, and it was long before there was any renewal of the conversation, so that I could not tell whether he really persuaded himself that he had no hopes, or was waiting to see how matters should turn out.

It was never easy to detect expressions of feeling or spirits on his massive face, and he could hardly be more silent than usual; but it was noticeable that he never fell asleep after his former wont when sitting still. Indeed, he seldom was still, for he had a great deal of business both for the estate and the potteries on his hands, and stayed up late at night over them; and not only over them, for my room was next to his, and I heard the regular tramp, tramp of his feet, and the turn at the end of the room, as he walked up and down for at least an hour when the rest of the house were asleep, or the closing of the door when he returned from wandering on the moor at night. And in the early morning, long before light, he always walked or rode over to Arked House, bestowed on Dermot's hurts the cares which both had come to look on as essential, and stayed with him till the family were nearly ready to appear at their nine o'clock breakfast, not seeing Viola at all, unless any special cause led to a meeting later in the day, and then his eyes glowed, and he would do her devoted, unobserved service—no, not unobserved by her, whom it made blush and sparkle—and utter little words of thanks, not so gay as of old, but deeper, as if for a great honour and delight. And then he would bow his head, colour, and draw into the background, where, with folded arms, he could watch her.

Once, when Dora, in her old way, claimed to be his wife, Harold told her with some impatience that she was growing too old for that nonsense. The child looked at him with bent brows and questioning eyes for a moment, then turned and fled. An hour later, after a long search, I found her crouched up in the corner of the kangaroo's stall among the straw, having cried herself to sleep, with her head on the creature's soft back.

As soon as Dermot was able to bear any strain on mind or attention, he gave his keys to Harold. All his long and unhappy accumulation of bills and bonds were routed out from their receptacles at Biston, and brought over by Harold to his office, where he sorted them, and made them intelligible, before harassing his friend with the questions he alone could explain. An hour a day was then spent over them—hours that cost poor Dermot more than he was equal to; but his mind was made up, as he told me, "to face anything rather than go on in the old miserable way." It was much that he had learnt to think it miserable.

Lady Diana was not much obliged to Harold. She could not think why her patient was so often left out of spirits, and with a headache after those visits, while he was in a feverish state of anxiety about them, that made it worse to put them off than to go through with them; and then, when she had found out the cause, the family pride much disliked letting an outsider into his involvments, and she thought their solicitor would have done the thing much better.

Poor woman, it was hard that, when she thought illness was bringing her son back to her, she found his confidence absorbed by the "bush-ranger," whom she never liked nor trusted, and his reformation, if reformation it were to prove, not at all conducted on her views of visible repentance and conversion. Dermot was responsive to her awakened tenderness, but he was perversely reticent as to whether repentance or expedience prompted him. She required so much religious demonstration, that she made him shrink from manifesting his real feelings as "humbug," and Viola knew far more that his repentance was real than she did. Those proofs of true repentance—confession and restitution—I am sure he gave, and that most bravely, when, after weeks of weary and sorrowful work on Harold's part and his, the whole was sufficiently disentangled to make a lucid statement of his affairs.

He made up his mind to make an arrangement with his creditors, giving up Biston, all his horses—everything, in fact, but Killy Marey, which was entailed on his Tracy cousins. And this second year of George Yolland's management had made the shares in the Hydriot Company of so much value, that the sale of them would complete the clearance of his obligations. The full schedule of his debts, without reserve, and the estimate of his means of paying them off, was then given by Dermot to his mother, and sent to his uncle, who went over them with his solicitor.

Lady Diana writhed under the notion of selling Biston. It seemed to her to be the means of keeping her son from the place in Ireland, which she disliked more than ever, and she hoped her brother would advance enough to prevent this from being needful; but for this Lord Erymanth was far too wise. He said, as Dermot felt, that Biston had never been anything but an unjustifiable and pernicious luxury and temptation; but he did voluntarily, since it joined his property, propose to purchase it himself, and at such a sum as secured the possibility of a real payment of the debts when the other sales should have been effected.

And they were carried out. It was well for Dermot that, as a convalescent in his mother's house, he was sheltered from all counter influences, such as his easy good nature might not have withstood; and under that shelter it was his purpose to abide until the voyage which would take him out of reach for a time, and bring him home ready for his fresh start.

Of course Lady Diana hated the notion of the voyage, and though her brother advised her not to oppose it, yet to the last I think she entertained hopes that it would end in Harold's going alone.

When Harold came in and told me that Dermot Tracy's horses, English and Irish, were all sold, and named the sum that they had realised, my spirits leaped up, and I was certain, after such a voluntary sacrifice, the dear old companion of my childhood would be a joy and exultation to us all, instead of a sorrow and a grief.

CHAPTER XI
THE RED VALLEY CATTLE STEALERS

In the Easter recess our Northchester member had his house full, and among his guests was one of the most influential men of the day, who, though not a cabinet minister himself, was known to have immense influence with Government and in Parliament, from his great weight and character.

Eustace and I were invited to meet him, also Lady Diana and her daughter and son, who was called well now, though far from strong. When the gentlemen came out of the dining-room, Eustace and Dermot came up to us, the former much excited, and saying, "Lucy, you must make preparations. They are all coming to luncheon to-morrow at Arghouse."

"Ah!"

"Yes, Sir James (the great man himself), and Mr. Vernon, and the General, and all the party. I asked them all. Sir James has heard of the potteries, and of my system, and of the reformation I have effected, and there being no strikes, and no nothing deleterious—undesirable I mean—and the mechanics having an interest, he wants to see for himself—to inspect personally—that he may name it in Parliament in illustration of a scheme he is about to propose. So Mr. Vernon will bring him over to see the Hydriot works to-morrow, and I have asked them to luncheon. Only think—named in Parliament! Don't you think now it might lead to a baronetcy, Tracy?"

"Or a peerage," quoth naughty Viola, out of reach of mother or Harold. "My Lord Hardbake would be a sweet title."

"I should revive the old honours of the family," said Eustace, not catching the bit of wickedness. "Calldron of Arghouse was an old barony. Lord Calldron of Arghouse! Should you object, Miss Tracy?"

"Earthen pot or copper kettle? Which?" laughed Viola. "Ah! there's Miss Vernon going to sing. I want to hear her," and she jumped up.

"Sit down, Dermot, in my place; you are not to stand."

She threaded her way to the piano, followed by Eustace, who still viewed himself as her suitor.

"Poor little Vi!" said Dermot, who by this time was aware of the courtship, and regarded it with little favour.

"She will rub him off more easily among numbers," I said, as he settled down by me. "But is this really so, Dermot?"

"What, is she to be my Lady Calldron? I am afraid my hopes of that elevation are not high. But as to the luncheon, you will really have to slaughter your turkeys, and declare war on your surviving cocks and hens. He has been inviting right and left. And tell Harold from me that if he votes the thing a bore, and keeps out of the way for fear of having to open his mouth, he'll be doing serious damage. If respect to the future baronetcy makes him get into the background, tell him, with my compliments, the whole thing will be a muddle, and I'll never speak a good word for him again."

"Then you have been speaking good words?"

"When Sir James began to inquire about the Hydriots, Mr. Alison was called on to answer him, and you are aware that, except to certain constitutions of intellect, as my uncle would say, certain animals cannot open their mouths without proclaiming themselves. The most sensible thing he said was the invite to come and see. Really, he made such mulls with the details that even I had to set him right, and that led to Sir James talking it out with me, when I had the opportunity of mentioning that a certain person, not the smallest of mankind, had been entirely overlooked. Yes I did, Lucy. I up and told him how our friend came over as heir; and when he was done out of it, set to work as agent and manager and improver-general, without a notion of jealousy or anything but being a backbone to this cousin of his, and I could not say what besides to all that came in his way; but I flatter myself there's one man in the room who has some notion of the difference there is between the greater and the less."

"Harold would not thank you," I said.

"Not he. So much the more reason that you should take care he comes to the front."

Dermot did Eustace a little injustice in fancying he wanted to suppress Harold. He never did. He was far too well satisfied with his own great personality to think that anyone could interfere with it; and having asked everyone in the room, ladies and all, to the inspection and the luncheon, discoursed to me about it all the way home, and would almost have made me and all the servants stay up all night to prepare. Harold, who was still up when we came home, received the tidings equably, only saying he would go down to Yolland the first thing in the morning and get things made tidy. "And don't bother Lucy," he added, as we went upstairs.

Well, the supplies were contrived, and the table laid without anyone being quite distracted. From Richardson downwards, we all had learnt to take our own way, while the master talked, and Mrs. Alison was really very happy, making delicate biscuits after a receipt of her own. Things came to a point where I was sure they would finish themselves off more happily without either of us, and though one idle female more might not be desirable, I thought at least I might prevent Harold's effacement, and went down to Mycening with Eustace to receive the guests.

Sure enough, Harold was not in the entrance yard, nor the superintendent's office. Mr. Yolland was there, looking grim and bored, and on inquiry being made, said that Mr. Harold had insisted on his being on the spot, but was himself helping the men to clear the space whence it would be easiest to see the action of the machinery. I made a rush after him, and found him all over dust, dragging a huge crate into a corner, and to my entreaty he merely replied, pushing back his straw hat, "I must see to this, or we shall have everything smashed."

The carriages were coming, and I could only pick my way back by the shortest route, through stacks of drain-tiles and columns of garden-pots, to Eustace, who, becoming afraid it would seem as if he were keeping shop, was squeezing down the fingers of his left-hand glove, while impressing on Mr. Yolland and me that everyone must understand he was only there as chairman of the directors.

The people came, and were conducted round, and peeped about and made all sorts of remarks, wise and foolish. Eustace was somewhat perplexed between the needful attentions to Mrs. Vernon and to Sir James, who, being much more interested in the men than the manufacture, was examining Mr. Yolland on their welfare, spirit, content, &c.; and George Yolland might be trusted for making Mr. Harold Alison the prominent figure in his replies, till at last he could say, "But here is Mr. Harold Alison, Sir James. He can reply better than I." (Which was not strictly true, for George Yolland had by far the readiest tongue.) But he had managed to catch Harold in the great court, moving back one of his biggest barrels of heavy ingredients, with face some degrees redder and garments some degrees dustier than when I had seen him ten minutes before. It really was not on purpose, or from any wish to hide, but the place needed clearing, there was little time, and his strength could not be spared.

I am sorry to say that a chattering young lady, who stood close to Eustace, exclaimed, "Dear me, what a handsome young foreman!" making

Eustace blush to the eyes, and say, "It is my cousin—he is so very eccentric—you'll excuse him."

Sir James, meantime, had heartily shaken the hand which, though begrimed at the moment, Harold held out to him, and plunged into inquiries at once, not letting him go again; for Harold, with the intuition that nothing was idly asked, and that each observation told, answered to the point as no man could do better, or in fewer words. When the round was over, and Eustace was prepared with the carriage to drive the grandees the mile up to Arghouse, Sir James returned his thanks, but he was going to walk up with Mr. Harold Alison, who was going to show him his workmen's reading-room, cottages, &c. Eustace looked about for someone to whom to resign the reins, but in vain, and we all had to set off, my housewifely mind regretting that time and Eustace had combined to make the luncheon a hot instead of a cold one.

We found the Tracys when we arrived at home. Dermot was not equal to standing about at the pottery, but Lady Diana had promised to come and help me entertain the party, and very kindly she did so during the very trying hungry hour to which we had to submit, inasmuch as, when Sir James at last appeared, it turned out that he never ate luncheon, and was in perfect ignorance that we were waiting for him.

He offered me his arm and we went to the long-deferred luncheon. I listened to his great satisfaction with what he had seen, and the marvel he thought it; and meanwhile I looked for Harold, and saw him presently come in, in exactly that condition of dress, as he considered due to me, and with the long blue envelope I knew full well in one hand, in the other the little figure of the Hope of Poland which Miss Woolmer had given him; and oh! what a gladness there was in his eyes. He put them both down beside Sir James, and then retreated to a side table, where Dora had been set to entertain a stray school-boy or two.

I longed to hear Sir James's observations, but his provoking opposite neighbour began to talk, and I got nothing more to myself, and I had to spend the next half-hour in showing our grounds to Mrs. Vernon, who admired as if she were electioneering, and hindered me from knowing what anybody was about, till the people had had their cups of coffee and their carriages had come.

We three found ourselves in the porch together when Eustace had handed in Mrs. Vernon, and Sir James, turning for a last shake of Harold's hand, said, "I shall expect you this day week." Then, with most polite thanks to the master of the house, he was driven off, while Harold, beaming down on us, exclaimed, "It is as good as done. I am to go up and see the Secretary of State about it next week."

I had no doubt what it was, and cried out joyfully to ask how he had done it. "I told him who first discovered the capabilities of the clay, and laid the state of the case before him. He was very much touched, said it was just such a matter as needed severity at the time, but was sure to be pardoned now."

"Pardoned! What do you mean?" exclaimed Eustace. "You don't mean that you have not done with that wretched old Prometesky yet? I thought at least, when you took up Sir James all to yourself, spoiling the luncheon and keeping everyone waiting, you were doing something for the benefit of the family."

As Harold seemed dumb with amazement, I asked what he could possibly have been expected to do for the good of the family, and Eustace mumbled out something about that supposed Calldron barony, which seemed to have turned his head, and I answered sharply that Sir James had nothing at all to do with reviving peerages; besides, if this one had ever existed, it would have been Harold's. I had much better have held my tongue. Eustace never recovered that allegation. That day, too, was the very first in which it had been impossible for Harold to avoid receiving marked preference, and the jealousy hitherto averted by Eustace's incredible vanity had begun to awaken. Moreover, that there had been some marked rebuff from Viola was also plain, for, as the Arked carriage was seen coming round, and I said we must go in to the Tracys, Eustace muttered, "Nasty little stuck-up thing; catch me making up to her again!"

It was just as well that Harold did not hear, having, at sight of the carriage, gone off to fetch a favourite cup, the mending of which he had contrived for Viola at the potteries. When we came into the drawing-room, I found Lady Diana and Mrs. Alison with their heads very close together over some samples of Welsh wool, and Dermot lying on the sofa, his hands clasped behind his head, and his sister hanging over him, with her cheeks of the colour that made her beautiful.

The two elder ladies closed on Eustace directly to congratulate him on the success of his arrangements, and Dermot jumped up from the sofa, while Viola caught hold of my hand, and we all made for the window which opened on the terrace. "Tell her," said Viola to her brother, as we stood outside.

Dermot smiled, saying, "Only that Sir James thinks he has to-day seen one of the most remarkable men he ever met in his life."

"And he has promised to help him to Prometesky's pardon," I said; while Viola, instead of speaking, leaped up and kissed me for joy. "He is to go to London about it."

"Yes," Dermot said. "Sir James wants him to meet some friends, who will be glad to pick his brains about New South Wales. Hallo, Harry! I congratulate you. You've achieved greatness."

"You've achieved a better thing," said Viola, with her eyes beaming upon him.

"I hope so," he said in an under tone.

"I am so glad," with a whole heart in the four words.

"Thank you," he said. "This was all that was wanting."

The words must have come out in spite of himself, for he coloured up to the roots of his hair as they ended. And Viola not only coloured too, but the moisture sprang into her fawn-like eyes. Dermot and I looked at each other, both knowing what it meant.

That instant Lady Diana called, and Dermot, the first of all, stooped under the window to give his sister time, and in the little bustle to which he amiably submitted about wraps and a glass of wine, Lady Diana failed to look at her daughter's cheeks and eyes. Viola never even thanked Harold for the cup, which he put into her lap after she was seated beside Dermot's feet on the back seat of the carriage. She only bent her head under her broad hat, and there was a clasp of the two hands.

I turned to go up to my sitting-room. Harold came after me and shut the door.

"Lucy," he said, "may one give thanks for such things?"

The words of the 107th Psalm came to my lips: "Oh that men would therefore praise the Lord for His goodness, and declare the wonders that He doeth for the children of men."

He put his hands over his face, and said presently, in a smothered voice, "I had just begun to pray for the old man."

I could not say any more for happy tears, less for "the captive exile" than for my own Harry.

Soon he looked up again, and said with a smile, "I shan't fight against it any longer."

"I don't think it is of any use," was my answer, as if pretending to condole; and where another man would have uttered a fervent rhapsody, he exclaimed, "Lovely little darling!"

But after another interval he said, "I don't mean to speak of it till I come back." And on my question, "From London?" "No, from Boola Boola."

He had evidently debated the whole matter during his midnight tramps, and had made up his mind, as he explained, that it would be cruel to Viola to touch the chord which would disclose her feelings to herself. She was a mere child, and if her fancy were touched, as he scarcely allowed himself to believe, it was hard to lay fully before her those dark pages in his history which she must know before she could be allowed to give herself to him. Besides, her mother and uncle would, even if there were nothing else amiss, be sure to oppose a match with one who had nothing in England but his cousin's agency and a few shares in the potteries; and though Harold had plenty of wealth at Boola Boola, it was certain that he should not have a moment's audience from the elders unless he could show its amount in property in England. If things went well, he would buy a piece of Neme Heath, reclaim it, and build a house on it; or, perhaps, an estate in Ireland, near Killy Marey, where the people had gained his heart. Till, however, he could show that he had handsome means in a form tangible to Lady Diana, to express his affection would only be exposing Viola to displeasure and persecution. Moreover, he added, his character was not cleared up as much as was even possible. He had told Lord Erymanth the entire truth, and had been believed, but it was quite probable that even that truth might divide for ever between him and Viola, and those other stories of the Stympsons both cousins had, of course, flatly denied, but had never been able otherwise to confute.

I asked whether it had ever struck him that it was possible that the deeds of Henry Alison might have been charged on his head. "Yes," he said, and he thought that if he could trace this out, with Dermot as a witness, the authorities might be satisfied so far as to take him for what he was, instead of for what he had never been. But the perception of the storm of opposition which speaking at present would provoke, made me allow that he was as wise as generous in sparing Viola till his return, since I knew her too well to fear that her heart would be given away in the meantime. Still I did hint, "Might not she feel your going away without saying anything?"

"Not at all likely," said Harold. "Besides, she would probably be a happier woman if she forgot all about me."

In which, of course, there was no agreeing; but he had made up his mind, and it was plain it was the nobler part—nay, the only honest part, since it was plainly of no use to speak openly. I wondered a little that his love was so self-restrained. It was an intense glow, but not an outbreak; but I think that having gone through all the whirlwind of tempestuous passion for a mere animal like poor Meg made him the more delicately reverent and considerate for the real love of the higher nature which had now developed in him. He said himself that the allowing himself to hope, and ceasing to crush his feelings, was so great a change as to be happiness enough for him; and I guarded carefully against being forced into any promise of silence, being quite determined that, if I saw Viola unhappy, or fancying herself forgotten, I would, whether it could be called wise or foolish, give her a hint of the true state of things.

Nothing was to be said to Eustace. He would have the field to himself, and it was better that he should convince himself and Lady Diana that there was no hope for him. Harold thought he could safely be commended to George Yolland and me for his affairs and his home life; and, to our surprise, he did not seem half so reluctant to part with his cousin as we had expected. He had gone his own way a good deal more this winter and spring, as Harold seldom had time to hunt, and did not often drive out, and he had grown much more independent. His share of Boola Boola was likewise to be sold, for neither cousin felt any desire to keep up the connection with the country where they had never had a happy home; and he gave Harold full authority to transact the sale.

Perhaps we all had shared more or less in Dora's expectation that Harold would come home from London with Prometesky's pardon in his pocket; though I laughed at her, and Eustace was furious when we found she thought he was to kneel before the Queen, present his petition, and not only receive the pardon, but rise up Sir Harold Alison! It did fall flat when he came back, having had very satisfactory interviews, but only with the Secretaries of State, and having been assured that Prometesky would be certainly pardoned, but that, as a matter of form, some certificates of conduct and recommendations must be obtained from New South Wales before the pardon could be issued.

This precipitated Harold's departure. Dermot was just well enough to be likely to be the better for a voyage, and the first week in May was fixed for their setting forth. A great box appeared in my sitting-room, where Harold began to stow all manner of presents of various descriptions for friends and their children, but chiefly for the shepherds' families at Boola Boola; and in the midst, Mrs. Alison, poor thing, brought a whole box of beautifully-knitted worsted stockings, which she implored Harold to carry to her dear Henry; and he actually let her pack them up, and promised that, if he ever found Henry, they should be given. "And this little Bible," said the good old lady; "maybe he has lost his own. Tell him it is his poor papa's, and I know he will bring it back to me."

"He shall if I can make him," said Harold.

"And Harold, my dear," said Mrs. Alison, with her hand on his shoulder, as he knelt by his box, "you'll go to see your own poor mamma?"

Harold started and winced. "My mother is in New Zealand," he said.

"Yes, my dear," said the old lady triumphantly; "but that's only the other side of the way, for I looked in Lucy's map."

"And she has a husband," added Harold between his teeth, ignoring what the other side of the way might mean.

"Yes, my dear, I know he is not a nice man, but you are her only one, aren't you?"

"Yes."

"And I know what that is—not that I ever married anyone but your poor uncle, nor ever would, not if the new rector had asked me, which many expected and even paid their compliments to me on, but I always said 'No, no.' But you'll go and see her, my dear, and comfort her poor heart, which, you may depend, is longing and craving after you, my dear; and all the more if her new gentleman isn't quite as he should be."

Harold could not persuade himself to bring out any answer but "I'll see about it;" and when we were alone, he said with a sigh, "If I should be any comfort to her poor heart."

"I should think there was no doubt of that."

"I am afraid of committing murder," answered Harold, almost under his breath, over the trunk.

"Oh, Harold! Not now."

"I don't know," he said.

"You have not seen him for ten years. He may be altered as much as you."

"And for the worse. I could almost say I dare not."

"There's nothing you don't dare, God helping you," I said.

"I shall think. If it is my duty, I suppose God will help me. Hitherto, I have thought my rage against the brutes made it worse for her, and that I do best for her by keeping out of the way."

"I think they would respect you now too much to do anything very bad before you."

"She would fare the worse for it afterwards."

"I am of Mrs. Alison's opinion, that she would be willing for the sake of seeing her son, and such a son."

Harold sighed.

"But it could not have been so dreadful when Eustace lived with them, and was so fond of the man."

"He nattered Eustace to curry favour with him and his father. He has sunk much lower. Then he lived like a decent clergyman. He has thrown all that off in New Zealand, and fallen entirely under the dominion of that son. I could wish I had quite throttled that Dick when I so nearly did so at school."

"If you say such things, I shall think you ought not to trust yourself there."

"That is it—I am afraid. I have crimes enough already."

It was too great a responsibility to persuade him to put himself into temptation, even now that he knew what prayer was. I longed to have seen him come yet nearer, and taken the means of strengthening and refreshing. But he said, "I cannot; I have not time to make fit preparation." And when I pleaded that I could not bear to think of his encountering danger without fulfilling that to which the promise of Everlasting Life is attached, I struck the wrong key. What he was not ready to do for love, he would not do for fear, or hurry preparation beyond what his conscience approved, that he might have what I was representing as the passport of salvation. Whether he were right or wrong I know not even now, but it was probably through the error of the very insufficient adviser the poor fellow had chosen in me. It may seem strange, but I had never thought of his irreligion as an obstacle with Viola, for, first, I knew him to be a sincere learner, as far as he went; and next, her sister's husband had none of the goodness that Lady Diana's professions would have led one to expect in her chosen son-in-law.

We all met and parted at the railway-station, whither Viola came with her brother. Dora had been only allowed to come upon solemn promises of quietness, and at the last our attention was more taken up with her than anyone else, for she was very white, and shook from head to foot with the effort at self-restraint, not speaking a word, but clinging to Harold with a tight grip of his hand, and, when that was not attainable, of his coat. Fortunately the train was punctual, and the ordeal did not last long. Harold put in all his goods and Dermot's, and finally he lifted the poor child up in his arms, held her close, and then, as her hands locked convulsively round his neck, Eustace unclasped them, and Harold put her down on my lap as I sat down on the bench, left a kiss on my brow, wrung Eustace's hand, pressed Viola's, saying, "I'll take care of your brother," and then, with one final impulse, carried the hand to his lips and kissed it, before springing into the carriage, which was already in motion. Poor Dora was actually faint, and never having experienced the feeling before, was frightened, and gasped out, "Hasn't it killed me, Lucy?"

The laugh that was unavoidable did us all good, and I sent Eustace for some restorative from the refreshment-room. The child had to be carried to the carriage, and was thoroughly out of order for several days. Poor little girl, we neither of us knew that it was the beginning of her darker days!

Of Harold's doings in Australia I can tell less than of those at home. He kept his promise, dear fellow, and wrote regularly. But, alas! his letters are all gone, and I can only speak from memory of them, and from what Dermot told me.

Making no stay in Sydney, they pushed on to Boola Boola, avoiding a halt at Cree's Station, but making at once for Prometesky's cottage, a wonderful hermitage, as Dermot described it, almost entirely the work of the old man's ingenious hands. There he lived, like a philosopher of old, with the most sternly plain and scanty materials for comfort—a mat, a table, and a chair; but surrounded by beautiful artistic figures and intricate mathematical diagrams traced on his floor and wall, reams of essays and poems where he had tried to work out his thought; fragments of machines, the toys of his constructive brain, among which the travellers found him sitting like a masculine version of Albert Durer's Melancholia, his laughing jackass adding tones of mockery to the scene, perched on the bough, looking down, as his master below took to pieces some squatter's crazy clock.

When Harold's greeting had aroused him, Dermot said, nothing could be more touching than the meeting with Prometesky, who looked at him as a father might look at a newly-recovered son, and seemed to lose the joy of the prospect of his own freedom in the pride and exultation of his own boy, his Ambrose's son, having achieved it. The beauty of the place enchanted Dermot, and his first ride round the property made him marvel how man could find it in his heart to give up this free open life of enterprise for the tameness of an old civilised country. But Harold smiled, and said he had found better things in England.

Harold found that there were serious losses in the numbers of the sheep of the common stock, and that all the neighbouring settlers were making the like complaint. Bushranging, properly so called, had been extinguished by the goldfind in Victoria, but as my brothers had located themselves as far as possible from inhabited districts, Boola Boola was still on the extreme border of civilisation, and there was a long, wide mountain valley, called the Red Valley, beyond it, with long gulleys and ravines branching up in endless ramifications, where a gang of runaway shepherds and unsuccessful gold diggers were known to haunt, and were almost certainly the robbers. The settlers and mounted police had made some attempts at tracking them out, but had always become bewildered in the intricacies of the ravines, and the losing one's way in those eucalyptus forests was too awful a danger to be encountered.

A fresh raid had taken place the very night before Harold arrived at Boola Boola, upon a flock pasturing some way off. The shepherds were badly beaten, and then bailed up, and a couple of hundred sheep were driven off.

Now Harold had, as a lad, explored all the recesses of these ravines, and was determined to put an end to the gang; and when it became known that Harold Alison was at home, and would act as guide, a fully sufficient party of squatters, shepherds, and police rallied for the attack, and Dermot, in great delight, found himself about to see a fight in good earnest.

A very sufficient guide Harold proved himself, and they came, not to any poetical robber's cavern, but within sight of a set of shanties, looking like any ordinary station of a low character. There a sudden volley of shot from an ambush poured upon them, happily without any serious wounds, and a hand-to-hand battle began, for the robbers having thus taken the initiative, it was hardly needful to display the search warrant with which the party had come armed. And to the amazement of all, the gang was headed by a man who seemed the very counterpart of Harold, not, perhaps, quite so tall, but with much the same complexion and outline, though he was somewhat older, and had the wild, fierce, ruffianly aspect of a bushranger. This man was taking deliberate aim at the magistrate who acted as head of the party, when Harold flung down his own loaded rifle, sprang upon him, and there was the most tremendous wrestling match that Dermot said he could have imagined. Three times Harold's antagonist touched the earth, three times he sprang from it again with redoubled vigour, until, at last,

Harold clasped his arms round him, lifted him in the air, and dashed him to the ground, where he lay senseless. And then, to the general amusement, Harold seemed astonished at his state as he lay prone, observing, "I did not want to hurt him;" and presently told Dermot, "I believe he is old Mrs. Sam Alison's son."

And so it proved. He was the Henry or Harry Alison of whose deeds the Stympsons had heard. The gang was, after all, not very extensive; two had been shot in the fray, one was wounded, and one surrendered. Alison, though not dead, was perfectly helpless, and was carried down the rocky valley on an extemporary litter, Harold taking his usual share of the labour. The sheep and cattle on whom were recognised the marks of the Alisons of Boola Boola, and of sundry of their neighbours, were collected, to be driven down and reclaimed by their owners, and the victory was complete.

CHAPTER XII
THE GOLDEN FRUIT

While all this was passing on the other side the world, Eustace fulfilled his wish for a season in London, was presented by Lord Erymanth, went to a court ball, showed his horses in the Park, lived at a club, and went to Ascot and Epsom. He fulfilled Harold's boast that he might be trusted not to get into mischief, for he really had no taste for vice, and when left to himself had the suspicious dislike to spending money which is so often found where the intellect is below the average. Vanity and self-consequence were the poor fellow's leading foibles, and he did not find that they were gratified when among his equals and superiors in station. Sensible men could not make him a companion, and the more dangerous stamp of men, when they could not fleece him, turned him into ridicule, so that he came home discontented.

It was not for my sympathy or company that he came home. He should have had it, for I had grown really fond of him, and was he not a charge left me by Harold? But he did not want me more than as lady of the house when he gave a dinner-party; and after his experiences of club dinners his requirements had become so distracting as to drive our old servants away and me nearly crazy. Also he was constantly in a state of discontent with Mr. Yolland about the management of the estate, always grumbling about expenses and expecting unreasonable returns, and interfering with the improvements Harold had set in hand, till Mr. Yolland used to come and seek private interviews with me, to try to get me to instil the explanations in which he had failed. Once or twice I made peace, but things grew worse and worse. I heard nothing but petulant abuse of George Yolland on one side, and on the other I knew he would have thrown up the agency except for Harold.

When at Michaelmas Eustace informed him that the estate should no longer go on without a regular responsible agent, and that one was engaged who had been recommended by Mr. Horsman, I do not know whether he was most hurt or relieved, though I could hardly forgive the slight to his cousin, far less the reply, when I urged the impropriety. "Harold can't expect to domineer over everything. He has put me to expense enough already with his fancies."

In truth Eustace had been resorting all this time to the companionship of the Horsmans. Hunting, during the previous winter, had thrown him with them more than we knew, and when he found me far more of a champion for Harold's rights than he wished, and, I fear too, much less tolerant of his folly and petulance than when his cousin was present to make the best of them by his loyal love, he deserted home more and more for Therford Hall. Dora and I were hardly sorry, for he was very cross to her, and had almost forgotten his deference to me; but I certainly was not prepared for the announcement of his engagement to Hippolyta Horsman.

From sheepishness and want of savoir faire, he had not even properly withdrawn his suit from Viola Tracy, thus making Lady Diana and Lord Erymanth very angry, though the damsel herself was delighted. I had ventured to give one little hint of how the land lay with Harold, and she had glowed with a look of intense gladness as of being confirmed in a happy belief. I don't even now think it was wrong. It might have been imprudent, but it made that year of her life full of a calm bright hope and joy that neither she nor I can ever regret.

As far as could be guessed, Hippolyta's first and strongest attraction had been towards Harold; but when it had been met by distaste and disregard, she had turned her attention to the squire, who could be easily gained by judicious flattery. In those days, I could see no excuse for Hippolyta, and ascribed no motives to her but fortune-hunting and despair at being a spinster so long; but I have since learnt to think that she had a genuine wish to be in a position of usefulness rather than to continue her aimless life of rattle and excitement, and that she had that impulse to take care of Eustace and protect him which strong-minded women sometimes seem to feel for weak men.

The courtship was conducted at archery meetings, and afterwards at shooting parties, out of my sight and suspicion, though the whole neighbourhood was talking of it, and Miss Avice Stympson had come to Arghouse to inquire about it, and impart her great disapproval of Hippo, long before it was officially announced to me, and Eustace at the same time kindly invited Mrs. Alison and me to remain where I was till after the wedding. I understood that this had been dictated to him, and was an intimation which I scarcely needed, that Arghouse would be our home no longer.

Just as I was thinking what proposal to make to Mrs. Alison came Harold's letters about his unfortunate Australian double. His first letter to the poor old lady merely told her that he had found her son, and that he was at Sydney, laid up by a bad accident received in a fray with the police. His back was hurt, but there was no cause to fear danger. He sent his love, and Harold would write again. Viola sent me Dermot's letter with full particulars, but I kept silence through all the mother's agitations of joy and grief.

The next mail brought me full details of the skirmish, and of what Harold had learnt of Henry Alison's course. It had been a succession of falls lower and lower, as with each failure habits of drunkenness and dissipation fastened on him, and peculation and dishonesty on that congenial soil grew into ruffianism. Expelled from the gold diggings for some act too mean even for that atmosphere, he had become the leader of a gang of runaway shepherds in the recesses of the Red Valley, and spread increasing terror there until the attack on him in his stronghold, when Harold's cousinly embrace (really intended to spare his life, as well as that of the magistrate) had absolutely injured his spine, probably for life. He had with great difficulty been carried to Sydney, and there placed in the hospital instead of the jail; since, disabled as he was, no one wished to prosecute the poor wretch, and identification was always a difficulty. Harold had been taking daily care of him, and had found him in his weak and broken state ready to soften, nay, to shed tears, at the thought of his mother; evincing feelings that might be of little service if he had recovered, but if he were crippled for life might be the beginning of better things. Harold had given him the Bible, and the stockings, and had left him alone with them. The Bible was as yet left untouched, as if he were afraid of it, but he had ever since been turning over and fondling the stockings, as though all the love that the poor mother had been knitting into them for years and years, apparently in vain, were exhaling like the heat and colours stored by the sun in ages past in our coals.

Harold was wondering over the question whether a man in his state could or ought to be brought to England, or whether it could be possible to send his mother out to him, when the problem was solved by his falling in with a gentleman whose wife was a confirmed invalid, and who was ready to give almost any salary to a motherly, ladylike woman, beyond danger of marrying, who would take care of her and attend to the household. He would even endure the son, and lodge him in one of the dependencies of his house, which had large grounds looking into beautiful Sydney Bay, provided he could secure such a person.

Even an escort had been arranged, as a brother of the gentleman was in England, and about to return with his wife to Australia; so that I was at once to communicate with them, pack her up, and consign her to them. To Mrs. Alison herself Harold wrote with the offer of the situation, and a representation of her son's need and longing for her, telling her the poor fellow's affectionate messages, and promising himself to meet her at Sydney on her arrival.

He must needs await the arrival of Prometesky's pardon, in answer to the recommendations that had gone by this very mail, and which he had had no difficulty in obtaining. The squatters round Boola Boola would have done anything for the man who had delivered them from the Red Valley gang; and, besides, there was no one who had been long enough in the country to remember anything adverse to the old hermit mechanist, and most of them could hardly believe that he "had not come out at his own expense." And at Sydney, as a visitor, highly spoken of by letters from the Colonial Secretary, and in company with an English gentleman connected as was Mr. Tracy, Harold found himself in a very different sphere from that of the wild young sheep-farmer, coming down half for business, half for roistering diversion. He emulated Eustace's grandeur by appearances at Government House, and might have made friends with many of the superior families, if, after putting things in train for the sale of Boola Boola, he had not resolved on spending his waiting time on a journey to New Zealand to see his mother.

He trusted himself the more from having visited the Crees, and having found he could keep his temper when they sneered at him as a swell and a teetotaller—nay, even wounded him more deeply by the old man's rejection of his offers of assistance, as if he had wanted to buy the family off from denouncing him as having been the death of their daughter. Often Harold must have felt it well for him that Dermot Tracy knew the worst beforehand—nay, that what he learnt in New South Wales was mild compared with the Stympson version. Dermot himself wrote to his uncle the full account of what he had learnt from Cree and from Prometesky of Harold's real errors, and what Henry Alison had confessed of those attributed to him, feeling that this was the best mode of clearing the way for those hopes which Harold had not concealed from him. Dermot was thoroughly happy, enchanted with the new world, more enthusiastic about his hero than ever, and eager to see as much as possible; but they renewed their promise to be in Sydney in time to greet poor old Mrs. Alison.

Dear old body, what a state she was in, between joy and grief, love and terror, heart and brain. She never wavered in her maternal eagerness to go to "poor little Henry," but what did she not imagine as to Botany Bay? She began sewing up sovereigns in chamois-leather bags to be dispersed all over her person against the time when she should have to live among the burglars; and Dora, who was desperately offended, failed to convince her that she might as well expect robbers at home. However, the preparations were complete at last, and I took her myself to the good people who were to have the charge of her. I had no fears in sending her off, since Harold was sure to arrange for her maintenance and comfort, in case of her situation not being a success; and though I had learnt to love her, and lost in her my chaperon, I was glad to be so far unencumbered; and to be freed from the fear that Eustace and Hippolyta might do something harshly inconsiderate by her, in their selfish blindness to all save themselves.

Hippolyta's fortune was in a complicated state, which made her settlements long in being made out; and as Eustace did not wish to turn me out till the wedding, I had time to wait to ascertain what Harold would like me to do. I hoped that Dora was so inconvenient an appendage that I should be allowed to keep her, but I found that Hippolyta had designs on her—saying, truly enough, that she could neither write nor spell and knew not a word of any language. "Poor Lucy Alison, what could be expected of her!" So Dora was to go to the married cousins in London, who, by thus taking her in, would be enabled to have a superior governess for their own tribe. Poor Dora! how fiercely she showed her love for me all those weeks of reprieve, and how hard I laboured to impress upon her that her intended system of defiance to the whole Horsman family was not, by any means, such a proof of affection as either Harry or I should relish.

More letters from our travellers from New Zealand turned our attention from our own troubles. They had reached Dunedin, and there found Harold's letter, to announce his coming, waiting at the post-office. The Smith family had left the place, and Mr. Smith only came or sent from time to time when Harold's regular letters, containing remittances, were due. By inquiry, they were traced to the goldfields; and thither Harold and Dermot repaired, through curious experiences and recognitions of old army and London friends of Dermot's, now diggers or mounted police. Save for one of these gentlemen, much better educated than Harold, but now far rougher looking, they would never have found the house where "Parson Smith" (a title that most supposed to be entirely unfounded) made a greater profit by selling the necessaries of life to the diggers, than did his son by gold-digging and washing.

Poor Alice, the stately farmhouse beauty of thirty years ago, was a stooping, haggard, broken-down wreck—not a slattern, but an overworked drudge, with a face fitter for seventy than for fifty years old, and a ghastly look of long-continued sickness.

Her husband was out, and she sat, propped up in a chair behind the board that served for a counter, still attending to the shop; and thus it was that her son beheld her when he stooped under the low doorway, with the one word, "Mother."

Dermot had waited outside, but Harold called him in the next moment. "He will mind the shop, mother. I'll carry you to your bed. You are not fit to be here a moment."

And Dermot found himself selling tobacco, tin cups, and knives to very rough-looking customers, some of whom spoke in as refined a voice as he could do, and only asked what green chum the parson could have picked up instead of the sickly missus.

Alice Smith was indeed far gone in illness, the effect of exposure, drudgery, and hard usage. Perhaps her husband might have had mercy on her, but they were both cowed by the pitiless brute of a step-son, whose only view was to goad her into driving their profitable traffic to her last gasp. But there was no outbreak between them and Harold. The father's nature was to cringe and fawn, and the son estimated those thews and muscles too well to gratify his hatred by open provocation, and was only surly and dogged, keeping himself almost entirely out of the way. Alice wanted nothing but to look at her son—"her beautiful boy," "her Harry come back to her at last;" and kind and tender to her and loving, as he had never been since his baby days; but he would have moved heaven and earth to obtain comforts and attendance for her. Dermot rode a fabulous distance, and brought back a doctor for a fabulous fee, and loaded his horse with pillows and medicaments; but the doctor could only declare that she had a fatal disease of long standing and must die, though care and comfort might a little while prolong her life. It was welcome news to poor Alice, provided she might only die while her boy was still with her, shutting out all that had so long made her life one ground-down course of hopeless wretchedness.

Smith's most profitable form of employment was carrying dinners out to the men at work; and for an hour or two at noon the little store was entirely free from customers. The day after the doctor's visit, Dermot came in at this time to speak to Harold, and as soon as Alice knew of his presence (there was a mere partition of slab between her bed and the shop), she eagerly and nervously bade him stay and keep watch that no one should come near to see or hear. Then, when certain that she was alone with her son, she produced from hiding-places about her person what appeared to be three balls of worsted—her eyes gleaming, and her whole person starting at every sound. She laid her skeleton fingers over them with a start of terror, as Harold, puzzled at first, would have unwound one; but made him weigh them, parted the covering with her nail, and showed for one instant a yellow gleam. Each held a nugget of unusual size! Her urgency and her terror were excessive till they were out of sight in his pockets, though he protested that this was but to satisfy her for the moment; he could not keep them. She laid her head so close to his that she could whisper, and told him they were not meant for him. They were payment for the L200 of which her husband had defrauded the elder Eustace, and which had been a heavy weight ever since on her high-spirited pride. By one of the strange chances that often befell in the early days of the goldfields, she, going to draw water at a little stream soon after her first arrival, had seen these lying close together in the bed of the shallow rivulet—three lumps of gold formed by a freak of nature into the likeness of the golden pippins her father used to be so proud of, and the gathering of which had been the crisis of the courtship of the two handsome lads from Arghouse.

With the secretiveness that tyranny had taught her, Alice hid her treasure; and with the inborn honest pride which had, under Smith's dominion, cost her so much suffering, she swore to herself that they should go to Eustace to wipe out the fraud against his father. She had sought opportunities ever since, and believed that she should have to send for some man in authority when she was dying, and no one could gainsay her, and commit them to him, little guessing that it was in her own son's hands that she should place them.

As little did she reckon on what Harold chose to do. He said that for him to conceal them, and take them away without her husband's knowledge, would be mere robbery; but that he would show them to Smith, and sign a receipt for them, "for Eustace Alison," in payment of the sum of L200 due from James Smith to his father. Mr. Tracy and his friend, the policeman, should be witnesses, and the nuggets themselves should be placed in charge of the police, when their weight and value would be ascertained, and any overplus returned to Smith. The poor woman trembled exceedingly—Dermot heard the rustling as he stood outside; and he also heard Harold's voice soothing her, and assuring her that she should not be left to the revenge of young Dick Smith. No, she feared not that; she was past the dread of Dick for herself, but not for Harold. He laughed, and said that they durst not touch him.

For his mother's relief, and for Dermot's safety, he, however, waited to say anything till the assistance of the gentleman of the police force had been secured, so that there might be no delay to allow Dick Smith to gather his fellows for revenge or recovery of the gold.

And with these precautions all went well. Harold, in the grave, authoritative way that had grown on him, reminded Mr. Smith of a heavy debt due to his uncle; and when the wretched man began half to deny and half to entreat in the same breath, Harold said that he had received from his mother a deposit in payment thereof, and that he had prepared a receipt, which he requested Mr. Smith to see him sign in presence of the two witnesses now waiting.

Smith's resentment and disappointment at the sight of the treasure his wife had hidden from him were unspeakable. He was not an outwardly passionate man, and he was in mortal fear, not only of the giant who seemed to fill up all his little room, but also of anything that could compromise him with the police. So he suppressed his passion, aware that resistance would bring out stories that could not bear the light. Harold signed, and the golden apples were carried away to the office, where Mr. Smith was invited to come the next day and see them weighed.

That night Harold kept watch over his mother; and Dermot, who was thought to be at his friend's shanty, kept watch near the door: but Dick Smith, hating Harold's presence, had gone on an excursion lasting some days, and before his father went in quest of him in the morning, Harold had a proposal ready—namely, to continue to pay Smith what he already allowed his mother, with an addition, provided he were allowed to take her with him to Dunedin, and, if possible, home.

Smith haggled, lamented, and pretended to hesitate, but accepted the terms at last, and then showed considerable haste in setting the party off on their journey before his son should come home, fearing, perhaps, some deadly deed if Dick should discover what a prey the poor woman had concealed from him, while she was within his reach; and as the worth of the apples was estimated at about twenty pounds beyond the debt, Harold paid this to him at once, and they left him in the meek, plausible, tearful stage of intoxication, piteously taking leave of his wife as if she were the very darling of his heart, and making fine speeches about his resolution to consign her to her son for the sake of her health. So contemptible had the poor creature become, that Harold found it easier to pity than to hate him.

Besides, Harold had little thought then to spare from the eager filial and maternal affection that had been in abeyance all the years since poor Alice's unhappy marriage. For a little while the mother and son were all in all to each other. The much-enduring woman, used to neglected physical suffering, bore the journey apparently well, when watched over and guarded with a tender kindness recalling that of the husband of her youth; and Harold wrote to me from Dunedin full of hope and gladness, aware that his mother could never be well again, but trusting that we might yet give her such peace and rest as she had never yet tasted.

Again came bitter vexation in Eustace's way of receiving the intelligence. "I hope he does not mean to bring her here. It would be so extremely inconvenient—not a widow even! It would just confirm all the scandals *I* have surmounted."

"I thought she had been almost as much a mother to you as your own?"

"Oh, that was when I was at school, and they were paid for it. Besides, what a deceitful fellow Smith was, and how he defrauded me."

"And how she has restored it!"

"I hope Harold will not go and get those nuggets changed into specie. They would make splendid ornaments—so distingue with such a story attached to them."

I could only again tell myself that my first impression had been right, and that he must be underwitted to be so absolutely impervious to gratitude. How Harold must have bolstered him up to make him so tolerable as he had been.

He need not have feared. Alice's improvement was but a last flash of the expiring flame. She grew worse the very day after Harold wrote to me, and did not live three weeks after he brought her into the town, though surrounded by such cares as she had never known before. She died, they said, more from being worn out than from the disease. She had done nothing her whole lifetime but toil for others; and if unselfishness and silent slavery can be religion in a woman, poor Alice had it. But!

Harold once asked her the saddest question that perhaps a son could ask: "Mother, why did you never teach me to say my prayers?"

She stared at him with her great, sunken, uncomplaining eyes, and said, "I hadn't time;" and as he gave some involuntary groan, she said, "You see we never got religion, not Dorothy and me, while we were girls; and when our troubles came, I'm sure we'd no time for such things as that. When your father lay a-dying, he did say, 'Alice, take care the boy gets to know his God better than we have done;' but you were a great big boy by that time, and I thought I would take care you was taught by marrying a parson and a schoolmaster; but there, I ought to have remembered there was none so hard on us as the parsons!"

Nor would she see a clergyman. She had had enough of that sort, she said, with the only petulance she ever showed to Harold when he pressed it. She did not object to his reading to her some of those passages in the Bible and Prayer-Book which had become most dear to him, but she seemed rather to view it as one of the wonderful performances of her boy—a part of his having become "as good an English gentleman as ever his poor father was, and able to hold up his head with any of them." She was too ill to be argued with; she said "she trusted in God," whatever she meant by that; and so she died, holding Harold's hand as long as her fingers could clasp, and gazing at him as long as her eyes could see.

He wrote to me all out of his overflowing heart, as he could never have spoken by word of mouth, on his voyage between New Zealand and Australia; and on his arrival there, finding our letters just before the mail went out, he added the characteristic line to the one he had written to Eustace, "All right, old chap, I wish you joy;" and to me he wrote, that since I asked what he wished, he thought I had better take a house by the year in, or near, Mycening, and see how things would turn out. He hoped I should keep Dora. We need not write again, for he should leave Sydney before our letters could arrive.

I found a little house called Mount Eaton, on the Neme Heath side of Mycening, with a green field between it and the town, and the heath stretching out beyond, where Harold might rush out and shake his mane instead of feeling cribbed and confined. It wanted a great deal of painting and papering, which I set in hand at once, but of course it was a more lingering business than I expected. All the furniture and books that had belonged to my own mother had been left to me, and it had been settled by the valuation, when I knew little about it, what these were; and all that remained was to face Eustace's disgust at finding how many of "the best things" it comprised. Hippolyta showed to advantage there. I believe she was rather glad to get rid of them, and to have the opportunity of getting newer and more fashionable ones; but, at any rate, she did it with a good grace, and made me welcome not only to my own property, but to remain at Arghouse till my new abode should be habitable, which I hoped would be a day or two after the wedding.

The great grievance was, however, that I had put myself and Dora into mourning, feeling it very sad that this last of the four exiles should be the only one of whose death I even knew. Eustace thought the whole connection ought to be forgotten, and that, whatever I might choose to do, it was intolerable that his sister, the present Miss Alison of Arghouse, should put on mourning for the wife of a disgraced fellow, a runaway parson turned sharper!

I am afraid I was not as patient or tolerant as I ought to have been, and it ended in the time of reprieve being put an end to, and Dora being carried off by the Horsmans to her new schoolroom in London, her resistance, and the home-truths she told her brother, only making him the more inexorable. Poor little girl! I do not like to think of the day I put her into Hippolyta's hands.

CHAPTER XIII
THE BLOODHOUND

It was a broiling evening in early June, very beautiful, but so hot that I dreaded the fatigue and all the adjuncts of the morrow's wedding, when I was to be a bridesmaid, and should see my poor little Dora again. I was alone, for Eustace was sleeping at Therford Vicarage, but I had not time for sentiment over the old home and old gardens. I was turning out the old Indian cabinets, which were none of mine, though they had always been called so, and putting into cotton wool and paper all my treasures there, ready for transport, when a shadow fell on me from the open window. I looked up, and there stood Harold!

Oh, how unlike it was from the way in which we had met three years before as bewildered strangers! I do not think that sister could ever have met brother with more entire feeling that home, and trust, and staff, and stay were come back to her, than when I found Harold's arm round me, his head bending down to me. I was off my own mind!

When our greeting was over, Harold turned and said, "Here he is."

I saw a fine-looking old man, with a certain majesty of air that one could not define. He was pale, wrinkled, and had deep furrows of suffering on cheek and brow, but his dark eyes, under a shaggy white penthouse, were full of keen fire and even ardour. His bald forehead was very fine, and his mouth—fully visible, for he was closely shaven—had an ineffable, melancholy sweetness about it, so that the wonderful power of leading all with whom he came in contact was no longer a mystery to me; for, fierce patriot and desperate republican as he might have been, nothing could destroy the inborn noble, and instinctively I bent to him with respect as I took his hand in welcome.

After the hasty inquiries, "Where's Dora?" "Where's Eustace?" "Where's Dermot Tracy?" had been answered, and I had learnt that this last had gone on to London, where his family were, Harold hurried out to see about sending for the luggage, and Prometesky, turning to me, almost took my breath away by saying, "Madam, I revere you. You have done for the youth so dear to me what I could never have done, and have transformed him from a noble savage to that far higher being—the Christian hero."

I did not take this magnificent compliment as if I had been of the courtly continental blood of him who made it: it made me hot and sheepish, yet even now I still feel warm at the heart when I remember it; for I know he really meant it, little as I deserved it, for the truth was what I faltered out: "It was all in him."

"It was all in him. That is true; but it needed to be evoked, so as not to be any longer stifled and perverted by the vehemence of his physical nature. When he left me, after the great catastrophe which changed him from the mere exaggerated child, gratifying every passion with violence, I knew it depended on what hands he would fall into, whether the spiritual or the animal would have the mastery. Madam, it was into your hands that he fell, and I thank God for it, even more than for the deliverance that my dear pupil has gained for me."

He had tears in his eyes as he took my hand and kissed it, and very much overpowered I was. I had somewhat dreaded finding him a free-thinker, but there was something in both speeches that consoled me, and he afterwards said to me: "Madam, in our youth intellectual Catholics are apt to reject what our reason will not accept. We love not authority. In age we gain sympathy with authority, and experience has taught us that there can be a Wisdom surpassing our own. We have proved for ourselves that love cannot live without faith."

And Harold told me on the evening of their return, with much concern, that the old man had made up his mind that, so soon as his health should be sufficiently restored, he would make retreat among the monks of La Trappe experimentally, and should probably take the vows. "I don't see that his pardon has done much good," he said, and did not greatly accept my representation of the marvellous difference it must make to a Roman Catholic to be no longer isolated from the offices of religion. He had made up his mind to come into Sydney to die, but he was too poor to have lived anywhere but under the Boola Boola rock.

It was a very quietly glad evening, as we three sat round the open window, and asked and answered questions. Harold said he would come to the wedding with me the next day; he must see old Eu married; and, besides, he wanted to give up to him the three nuggets, which had been rather a serious charge. Harold, Prometesky, and Dermot had each carried one, in case of any disaster, that there might be three chances; but now they were all three laid in my lap—wonderful things, one a little larger than the others, but all curiously apple-like in form, such gifts as a bride has seldom had.

There was the account of the sale of Boola Boola to be rendered up too; and the place had risen so much in value that it had brought in far more than Harold had expected when leaving England, so that he and Eustace were much richer men than he had reckoned on being.

Mrs. Sam Alison had arrived safely, but rather surprised not to find people walking on their heads, as she had been told everything was upside down. Her son had so far recovered that he could undertake such employment in writing as it was possible to procure. The mother and son were very happy together, but Harold winced as if a sore were touched when he spoke of their meeting.

I was anxious that he should hear of nothing to vex him that night, for there was more than enough to annoy him another day, and I talked on eagerly about the arrangements for the wedding. Hippolyta had insisted on making it a mingled archery and hunt-wedding. She was to wear the famous belt. The bridegroom, her brothers, and most of the gentlemen were to be in their pink; we bridesmaids had scarlet ribbons, and the favours had miniature fox brushes fastened with arrows in the centre; even our lockets, with their elaborate cypher of E's, A's, and H's, depended from the head of a fox.

Prometesky looked amazed, as well he might. "Your ladies are changed," he said. "It would formerly scarcely have been thought feminine to show such ardour for the chase."

"Perhaps it is not now," I said.

"Or is it in honour of the lady's name? Hippolyta should have a Midsummer wedding, and 'love the musick of her hounds,'" continued the old gentleman, whom I found to have Shakespeare almost by heart, as one of the chief companions of his solitude.

As soon as Harold heard his boxes arriving, he went to work to disinter the wedding present he had provided—a pretty bracelet of New Zealand green jade set in gold. There was a little parcel for me, too, which he gave me, leading me aside. It was also a locket, and bore a cypher, but how unlike the other! It was a simple A; and within was a lock of silver hair. There was no need to tell me whose it was. "She said she wished she had anything to send you," were Harold's words, "and I cut off this bit of her hair;" and when I wondered over her having taken thought of me, he said, "She blessed you for your kindness to me. If I could only have brought her to you—"

I secured then, as the completion of his gift, one of his thick curls of yellow-brown hair. He showed me the chain he had brought for Dora, and gave me one glance at a clear, pure, crystal cross, from spar found in New Zealand, near the gold-fields. Would he ever be able to give it? I answered the question in his eyes by telling him a certain Etruscan flower-pot had stood in a certain window at Arked House all the winter, and was gone to London now.

Our home breakfast had to be very early, to give time for the drive to Therford, but Harold had been already into Mycening, had exchanged countless hearty greetings, roused up an unfortunate hair-cutter, to trim his locks, bought a hat, and with considerable difficulty found a pair of gloves that he could put on—not kid, but thick riding-gloves; white, at least—and so he hoped that they would pass in the crowd, and Eustace would not feel himself disgraced. He had not put on the red coat, but had tried to make himself look as satisfactory to Eustace as possible in black, and (from a rather comical sense of duty) he made me look him over to see if he were worthy of the occasion. He certainly was in splendid looks, his rich, profuse beard and hair were well arranged, and his fine bronzed face had not lost its grave expression when at rest, but had acquired a certain loftiness of countenance, which gave him more than ever the air, I was going to say, of a demigod; but he had now an expression no heathen Greek could give; it was more like that of the heads by Michael Angelo, where Christian yearning is added to classic might and beauty.

Prometesky preferred staying at home. He seemed suffering and weary, and said that perhaps he should wander about and renew his acquaintance with the country; and so Harold and I set off together on the drive, which, as I well knew, would be the most agreeable part of the day.

Very lovely it was as we passed in the morning freshness of the glowing summer day through lanes wreathed with dog-roses and white with May, looking over grass-fields with silvery ripples in the breeze into woods all golden and olive-green above with young foliage, and pink below with campion flowers, while the moorland beyond was in its glory of gorse near at hand, and purple hills closing the distance. I remember the drive especially, because Harold looked at the wealth of gay colouring so lovingly, comparing it with the frequently parched uniformity of the Bush, regretting somewhat the limited range, but owning there were better things than unbounded liberty.

When we reached Therford he would not go to the house with me, nor seek to see Eustace before the wedding, saying he should wait in the churchyard and join us afterwards. So in I went into the scene of waiting, interspersed with bustle, that always precedes a wedding, and was handed into the bed-room where the bridesmaids were secluded till the bride was ready, all save Pippa and the most favoured cousin, who were arraying her. There were a dozen, and all were Horsmans except Dora and me. The child made one great leap at me, and squeezed me, to such detriment of our flimsy draperies that she was instantly called to order. Her lip pouted, and her brow lowered; but I whispered two words in her ear, and with a glance in her eye, and an intent look on her face, she stood, a being strangely changed from the listless, sullen, defiant creature she had been a minute before.

Therford was one of those old places where the church is as near as possible to the manor house, standing on a little elevation above it, and with a long avenue of Lombardy poplars leading from the south porch, the family entrance, to the front door of the house, so this was that pretty thing, a walking, instead of a carriage, wedding. As one of the procession, I could not see, but the red and white must have made it very pretty, and the Northchester paper was quite poetical in its raptures.

All this was, however, forgotten in the terrible adventure that immediately followed. The general entrance was by the west door, and close to this I perceived Harold following his usual practice of getting into the rear and looking over people's heads. When the service was over, and we waited for the signing of the registers, most of the spectators, and he among them, went out by this western door, and waited in the churchyard to see the procession come out.

Forth it came, headed by the bride and bridegroom, both looking their very handsomest, and we bridesmaids in six couples behind, when, just as we were clear of the porch, and school-children were strewing flowers before the pair, there was a strange shuddering cry, and the great bloodhound, Kirby, with broken chain and foaming jaws—all the dreadful tokens of madness about him—came rushing up the avenue with the speed of the wind, making full for his mistress, the bride. There was not a moment for her to do more than give a sort of shrieking, despairing command, "Down, Kirby!" when, just as the beast was springing on her, his throat was seized by the powerful hands that alone could have grappled with him, and the terrible head, foaming, and making horrid choking growls, was swung round from her, and the dog lifted by the back of the neck in the air, struggling and kicking violently.

Everyone had given back; Hippolyta had thrown herself on Eustace, who drew her back, crowding on us, into the porch; Harold, still holding the dog at arm's length, made his voice heard in steady tones, "Will some one give me my other glove?"

One hand, that which grasped the dog, was gloved, but the free hand was bare, and it was Dora who first understood, saw the glove at his feet, sprang to his side, and held it up to him, while he worked his hand into it, and she pulled it on for him. Then he transferred his grasp from one hand to the other, and in that moment the powerful bloodhound made a desperate struggle, and managed to get one paw on the ground, and writhe itself round so as to fly at his face and make its teeth actually meet in his beard, a great mouthful of which it tore out, and we saw it champing the hairs, as he again swung it up, so that it could only make frantic contortions with its body and legs, while he held it at arm's length with the iron strength of his wrists.

This had taken hardly three seconds, and in that time Jack Horsman and a keeper or two had been able to come up, but no one unarmed could give efficient aid, and Harold said, "I'll take him to the yard."

Mr. Horsman led the way, and as the keepers followed with several of the gentlemen, I was forced to let Harold vanish, carrying at arm's length that immense dog, still making horrible rabid struggles.

I don't clearly remember how we got back to the house. Somebody had fainted, I believe, and there was much confusion; but I know nothing but that there was the report of a pistol, and, almost immediately after, I saw Harold coming up to the hall door with Dora lying back in his arms. Then my eyes and ears grew clear, and I flew forward to ask the dreadful question. "No," he said, "she is only a little upset." Unperceived, that child had followed him down, holding the broken chain in which he might have tripped, and had stood by even while he set the poor beast on his feet, and held it for the merciful death shot. It seemed that her purpose had been to suck the wound if he had been bitten, and when once she heard Mr. Horsman exclaim, "All safe, thank God!" she clung to Harold with an inarticulate gasp, in one of those hysterical agonies by which her womanhood from time to time asserted itself. She could not breathe or speak, and he only begged for a place to lay her down. Old Marianne Horsman, the quiet one of the family, took us to her own den, and, with me, insisted on looking well at Harold's hands and face. What might not that horrid leap have done? But we convinced ourselves that those fangs had only caught his beard, where there was a visible gap, but no sign of a wound; and those riding-gloves had entirely guarded his hands. How blessed the Providence, for ordinarily he never touched gloves, and common white kid ones would have availed little. There was scarce time to speak of it, for the child required all our care, and was only just becoming calmer, as Harold held her, when the bride and bridegroom came in, she, red and eager, he, white and shaken, to summon us to the breakfast. "Don't go!" was her moan, half asleep.

Harold bade me go, and as the bride declared they could not sit down without him, he answered, "Not yet, thank you, I couldn't." And I remembered that his prompt deed of daring had been in defiance of a strong nervous antipathy. There was a spasmodic effort in the smile he attempted, a twitching in the muscles of his throat; he was as pale as his browned cheeks could become, and his hand was still so unsteady that he was forced to resign to me the spoonful of cordial to put into Dora's mouth.

And at that moment Eustace turned and said, "Have you brought the nuggets?"

Without speaking Harold put his hand into his pocket, and laid them in Eustace's hand.

"These? you said they were golden apples; I thought they would be bigger."

"They are wonderful," said Hippolyta; "no one ever had such a wedding-gift."

"Not that—a debt," said Harold, hoarsely; but Pippa Horsman came and summoned them, and I was obliged to follow, answering old Marianne's entreaties to say what would be good for him by begging for strong coffee, which she promised and ordered, but in the skurry of the household, it never came.

The banquet, held in a tent, was meant to be a brilliantly merry one. The cake had a hunt in sugar all round it, and the appropriate motto, "Hip, hip, hurrah!" and people tried to be hilarious; but with that awful shock thrilling on everybody's nerves we only succeeded in being noisy, though, as we were assured, there was no cause for alarm or grief. The dog had been tied up on suspicion, and had bitten nothing but one cat, which it had killed. Yet surely grave thankfulness would have been better for us all, as well as more comfortable than loud witticisms and excited laughter. I looked at the two or three clerical members of the clan and wondered at them.

When the moment for healths came, the bride called to her brother, the head of the house, by his pleasing name of Baby, and sent him to fetch Harold, whom he brought back with him. Dora was sound asleep, they said, and room was made for Harold in the bridal neighbourhood in time to hear the baronet, who had married a Horsman of the last generation, propose the health of the bride with all the conventional phrases, and of the bridegroom, as a gentleman who, from his first arrival, had made it his study to maintain the old character of the family, and to distinguish himself by intelligent care for the welfare of his tenants, &c., &c.

Hippolyta must have longed to make the speech in return. We could see her prompting her husband, and, by means of imitations of Lord Erymanth, he got through pretty well with his gracious acceptance of all the praises.

Baby Jack proposed the health of the bridesmaids, adding, more especially, that of the absent one, as a little heroine; and, after the response, came a ponderous speech by another kinsman, full of compliments to Harold's courage in a fulsome style that made me flush with the vexation it must give him, and the annoyance it would be to reply. I had been watching him. As a pile of lumps of ice fortunately stood near him, he had, at every interval, been transferring one to his glass, filling it up with water, guarding it from the circling decanters, and taking such a draught at every toast that I knew his mouth was parched, and I dreaded that sheer worry would make him utter one of his "young barbarian" bluntnesses; but what he did was to stand up and say simply, "It is very kind of Colonel Horsman to speak in this way of my share in the great mercy and deliverance we have received to-day. It is a matter of the greatest thankfulness. Let me in return thank the friends here assembled for their welcome, and, above all, for their appreciation of my cousin, whose position now fulfils my great wish. Three years ago we were friendless strangers. Now he has made himself one with you, and I thank you heartily for it."

I felt rather than heard Nessy Horsman muttering, "pretty well for the large young man;" and it seemed to occur to no one that friends, position, and all had been gained for Eustace by Harold himself. He was requesting permission to take Dora back with us, and it was granted with some demur, because she must be with Mrs. Randal Horsman on her return to town on the Monday; a day's lessons could not be sacrificed, for she was very backward, and had no application; but Harold undertook that she should meet the lady at the station, and gained his point.

Clan Horsman knew too well what he had done to deny him anything he asked. A man who had not only taken a mad dog by the throat, but had brought home two hundred and twenty pounds worth of gold to lay on the table, deserved something at their hands, though ice was all he actually received; but Eustace, when he came to us while the bride was changing her dress, was in a fretful, fault-finding mood, partly it may be from the desire to assert himself, as usual, above his cousin.

He was dissatisfied with the price paid for Boola-Boola. Someone had told him it would realise four times as much, and when Harold would have explained that this was unreasonable, he was cut short with the declaration that the offer ought not to have been accepted without reference to the other party concerned.

Next he informed Harold, in an off-hand way, that some of the new improvements at Arghouse would not work, and that he had a new agent—a *responsible* agent—who was not to be interfered with.

There was a certain growl in Harold's "very well," but the climax was Eustace's indignation when he heard of Prometesky's arrival. He had worked himself, by way of doing the country squire completely, into a disgust of the old exile, far out-Heroding what he had heard from Lord Erymanth, and that "the old incendiary" should be in his house was a great offence.

"He shall not sleep there another night, neither will I," said Harold, in a calm voice, but with such a gleam in his eyes as I had seen when he fell on Bullock.

It had at least the effect of reducing Eustace to his old habit of subordination, and he fell into an agony of "No, I did not mean that, and—" stammering out something in excuse about not liking the servants and all to think he was harbouring a returned convict.

I had taken care of that. I knew how "that that there Fotsky" was the ogre of the riots, and I had guarded against his identification by speaking of our guest as the foreign gentleman who had come home with Mr. Harold, and causing him to be called Count Stanislas; and, on hearing this, Eustace became so urgent in his entreaties, that Harold, though much hurt, relented so far as to promise at any rate to remain till Monday, so that Dora should not detect the offence.

We saw the happy pair off, among the old shoes, to spend some months abroad, while the old house was revivified for them, and then we had our own drive home, which was chiefly occupied with Dora, who, sitting on Harold's knee, seemed to expect her full rescue from all grievances, and was terribly disappointed to find that he had no power to remove her from her durance in the London school-room, where she was plainly the dunce and the black sheep, a misery to herself and all concerned, hating everyone and disliked by all. To the little maiden of the Bush, only half tamed as yet, the London school-room and walks in the park were penance in themselves, and the company of three steady prim girls, in the idealess state produced by confinement to a school-room, and nothing but childish books, was as distasteful to her as she was shocking to them, and her life was one warfare with them and with their Fraulein. The only person she seemed able to endure was Nessy Horsman, who was allowed to haunt his cousin Randal's house, and who delighted in shocking the decorous monotony of the trio of sisters, finding the vehement little Australian far more entertaining, while, whether he teased or stimulated her, she found him the least uncongenial being she met in Paddington. But what struck me most was the manner in which Harold spoke to her, not merely spoiling her, and giving her her own way, as if he were only a bigger child, but saying "It will all get better, Dora, if you only try to do your best."

"I haven't got any best to do."

"Everybody has."

"But I don't want it to be better. I want to be with you and Lucy."

Then came some reasoning about impossibilities, too low for me to hear in the noise of the wheels, but ending with "It is only another thing to conquer. You can conquer anything if you only try, and pray to God to help you."

"I haven't said my prayers since I went away. They ordered me, and said I was wicked; but you don't, Harold, do you?" she cried triumphantly, little expecting the groan she met in answer, "Yes, indeed I do, Dora. I only wish I had done so sooner."

"I thought it was no use," she said, crying at his tone. "It was so unkind to take me away from Lucy," and whereas she hardly ever shed tears and was now far from restored after the fright, when she once began we could hardly stop her weeping, and were thankful when she was soothed into another sleep, which we durst not peril by a word.

It deepened and lasted so that Harold carried her upstairs still asleep, and laid her on her own little bed. Then he came out with me into my dear old sitting-room, where, without another word, he knelt in the old place and said, "*That* psalm, please Lucy."

"I think we ought to give thanks in church," I said, presently.

"Whatever is right," he said fervently.

"It was the greatest escape you ever had," I said.

"Yes," he said, shuddering; "at least it seemed so. I really thought the dog had bitten me when he flew in my face. It felt just like it, and I was very near giving up. I don't mean letting him go, but not heeding whether he touched me or not. It kept on haunting me till I was alone with Dora, and could examine at the looking-glass."

Of course I was not content till I had likewise again convinced myself by searching into the beard, and then I added, "Ah! this is worse than the lion, though then you were really hurt."

"Yes, but there one knew the worst. Besides," he said, again overcoming a shudder, "I know my feeling about dogs is a weakness owing to my sin. 'Deliver me from the power of the dog,' to me expresses all the power of evil."

Then he sat down and took a pen to write to Mr. Crosse. "Harold Alison wishes to give thanks to Almighty God for a great mercy."

And after that he never alluded to the adventure again. I told the story to Prometesky in his absence, and we never mentioned it more.

Indeed the next thing Harold said, as he addressed his envelope, was, "It is a pity to lose this room."

"There is one that I can fit up like it," I said. "All the things here are mine." And then I was glad to divert his attention by proposing to go and inspect Mount Eaton, as soon as he had had some much-needed food, since Prometesky was out, and we at once plunged into the "flitting" affairs, glad in them to stifle some of the pain that Eustace had given, but on which we neither of us would dwell.

Was Harold changed, or had he only gone on growing in the course he had begun? He was as simple and unconsciously powerful as ever, but there was something there was not before, reminding me of the dawning of Undine's soul.

He was called off in the middle of our consultation as to the house, which was our common property, by a message that Mr. Crabbe would be glad of a few minutes with him.

"Was there any fresh annoyance about the Hydriots?" I asked, when he came back.

"Oh, no! The rascal is come over to my side. What do you think he wanted to say? That he had been to look at my grandfather's will, and he thinks you could drive a coach and horses through it; and he proposes to me to upset it, and come in as heir-at-law! The scoundrel!"

"After all," I said, after a pause, "it would be very good for poor Arghouse if you thought it right."

"*I* should not be very good for Arghouse if I did such a thing as that," returned Harold. "No, poor old Eu, I'm not going to disturb him because he has got out of my hands, and I think she will take care of the people. I daresay I bullied him more than was bearable."

Would Harold have so forgiven even Eustace's ingratitude three years ago?

CHAPTER XIV
SUNSET GOLD AND PURPLE

We had a happy time after that; our Sunday was a very glad and peaceful one, with our thanksgiving in the morning, and Dora's pleasure in the dear old children's service in the afternoon. Poor child, she liked everything that she had only submitted to when she was with us, and Harold took her away on the Monday in a more resigned frame of mind, with a kind of promise that she would be good if the Horsmans would let her.

Then came the removal, and I must say there was some compensation for the pain of leaving my old home in that sense of snugness and liberty in our new plenishing, rather like the playing at doll's houses. We had stable room for Harold's horse and my pony—the kangaroo, alas! had pined and died the winter that Harold was away; the garden was practicable, and the rooms were capable of being made home-like and pleasant.

The Tracys were out of reach for the present. Dermot was gone to Ireland, and Lady Diana and her daughter were making a long round of visits among friends, so that there was nothing for it but waiting, and as it was hopeful waiting, enlivened by Viola's letters to me, Harold endured it very happily, having indeed much to think about.

There was Prometesky's health. It was ascertained that he must undergo an operation, and when we found that all the requisite skill could be had near at hand, I overruled the scruples about alarming or distressing me. I knew that it would be better for him to be watched by George Yolland, and for Harold to be at home, and I had come to love the old man very heartily.

One day of expectation, in which he was the most calm and resolute of us, one anxious day when they sent me to Miss Woolmer, until Harold came, thankful and hopeful to fetch me, a few more of nursing accepted with touching gratitude, and he was soon downstairs again, a hale old man, though nearly seventy, but more than ever bent on his retreat to La Trappe. It distressed us much. He seemed so much to enjoy intelligent talk with Miss Woolmer and the Yollands; he so delighted in books, and took such fresh interest in all, whether mechanical or moral, that was doing at the Hydriots—of which, by-the-by, as first inventor, the company had contrived, at Harold's suggestion, to make him a shareholder to an extent that would cover all his modest needs, I could not think how he would bear the change.

"My dear young lady," he said to me, when I tried to persuade him out of writing the first letter, "you forget how much I have of sin upon me. Can years of negation of faith, or the ruin of four young lives, and I know not of how many more, be repented of at ease in your pleasant town, amid the amiable cares you young people are good enough to lavish on the old man?"

I made some foolish answer about his having meant all for good and noble purposes, but he shook his head.

"Error, my dear madam, error excusable, perhaps, in one whose country has been destroyed. I see, now that I have returned, after years alone with my God, that the work I tried to precipitate was one of patience. The fire from heaven must first illuminate the soul, then the spirit, and then the bonds will be loosed of themselves; otherwise we do but pluck them asunder to set maniacs free to rush into the gulf. And as to my influence on my two pupils, your brothers, I see now that what began in filial rebellion and disobedience could never end well. I bless God that I have been permitted to see, in the next generation, the true hero and reformer I ought to have made of my Ambrose. Ah! Ambrose, Ambrose! noble young spirit, would that any tears and penance of mine would expiate the shipwreck to which I led thee!" and he burst into tears.

He had, of course, seen the Roman Catholic priest several times before encountering the danger of the operation, and was a thoroughly devout penitent, but of his old Liberalism he retained the intense benevolence that made the improvements at the potteries a great delight to him, likewise the historical breadth of understanding that prevented his thinking us all un-Catholic and unsafe.

It was a great blessing that Harold was not held back but rather aided and stimulated by the example of the man to whom he most looked up; but with his characteristic silence, it was long before I found that, having felt, beside his mother's death-bed, how far his spiritual wants had outgrown me, he had carried them to Ben Yolland, though the old morning habit remained unbroken, and he always came to the little room I had made like my old one.

Ben Yolland had become more entirely chaplain to the Hydriots. Those two brothers lived together in a curious way at what we all still called the "Dragon's Head," each with his own sitting-room and one in common, one fitted as a clergyman's study, the other more like a surgery; for though

George had given up his public practice since he had been manager of the works, he still attended all the workpeople and their families, only making them pay for their medicines "when it was good for them."

Thus the care of the soul and bodies of the Hydriots was divided between the two, and they seemed to work in concert, although George showed no symptom of change of opinions, never saying anything openly to discredit his brother's principles, nay, viewing them as wholesome restraints for those who were not too scientific to accept them, and even going to church when he had nothing else to do, but by preference looking up his patients on a Sunday. He viewed everything, from religion to vice, as the outcome of certain states of brain, nerves, and health; and so far from being influenced by the example of Prometesky, regarded him as a proof of his own theory, and talked of the Slavonic temperament returning to its normal forms as the vigour of life departed.

Nevertheless, he did not seem to do harm to the workpeople. Drunkenness was at least somewhat restrained, though far from conquered, and the general spirit of the people was wonderful, compared with those of other factories. Plans were under discussion for a mission chapel, and the people themselves were thoroughly anxious for it.

Lord Erymanth returning, kindly came to call on me in my new house, and as I was out of the drawing-room at the time, he had ten minutes' conversation with the gentleman whom he found reading at the window, and was so much pleased with him that when making the tour of our small domain, he said, "You did not introduce me, Lucy. Is that an Australian acquaintance of Harold Alison's? I did not expect such high cultivation."

"An Australian acquaintance, yes," said I, "and also a Polish count."

"Prometesky!"

"Prometesky," said I, to whom the name had begun to sound historical. "I did not know you did not recognise him."

I was afraid my old friend would be angry with me, but he stood still and said, "I never saw him except at his trial. I can understand now the fascination he was said to have possessed. I could not conscientiously assist your nephew in his recall, but I highly honour the generous perseverance with which he has effected it; and I am happy to acknowledge that the subject is worthy of his enthusiasm. Animosity may be laid aside now, and you may tell Mr. Harold Alison that I heartily congratulate him."

"And he—Count Stanislas we call him—sees now that he was mistaken," I said.

"Does he? That is the best of the higher stamp of men, my dear. They know when they are wrong, and own it. In fact, that's the greatest difference between men. The feeble and self-opinionated never acknowledge an error, but the truly sincere can confess and retrieve their hallucinations and prejudices. Well, I am glad to have seen Prometesky, and to be disabused of some ideas respecting him."

Count Stanislas, on the other hand, received me with, "So that is Erymanth! The tyrant, against whom we raged, proves a charitable, benevolent, prosy old gentleman. How many illusions a few decades dispel, and how much hatred one wastes!"

Lord Erymanth had told me that his sister would soon be at home, and in September I was surprised by a call from Dermot. "Yes, I'm at Arked," he said, "Killy Marey is full of Dublin workmen. My uncle has undertaken to make it habitable for me, like an old brick, and, in the meantime, there's not a room fit to smoke or sleep in, so I'm come home like a dutiful son."

"Then your mother is come?"

"Oh yes; she is come for six weeks, and then she and the St. Glears are to join company and winter at Rome."

"At Rome?"

"Prevention, you see," said Dermot, with a twinkle in his eye, as if he were not very uneasy. "The question is whether it is in time. She will have Piggy's attentions at Christmas. He is to come out for the vacation."

Then he further told me that his mother had brought home with her a Mrs. Sandford with a daughter, heiress to L60,000, and to a newly-bought estate in Surrey, and newly-built house "of the most desirable description," he added, shrugging his shoulders.

"And what sort of a young lady is she?"

"Oh, very desirable, too, I suppose."

"But what is she like?"

"Like? Oh, like other people," and he whistled a little, seeming relieved when "Count Stanislas" came in, and soon after going to hunt up Harry at the Hydriot works.

It made me uncomfortable; it was so evidently another attempt on his mother's part to secure a rich home for him in England, and his tone did not at all reassure me that, with his easy temper, he would not drift into the arrangement without his heart in it. "Why should I be so vexed about it? It might be very good for him," said I to myself.

No, his heart was not in it, for he came back with Harold, and lingered over our fire beyond all reasonable time, talking amusing random stuff, till he had left himself only ten minutes to ride home in to dinner.

The next day Harold and I rode over to Arked together. Dermot was the first person we saw, disporting himself with a pug-dog at the door. "The fates have sped you well," said he, as he helped me down from my pony. "My mother has taken Mrs. Sandford in state to call on Mrs. Vernon, having arranged that Viola and I should conduct the sixty-thousand pounder to admire the tints in the beech woods. The young ladies are putting on their hats. Will it be too far for you, Lucy, to go with us?"

Wherewith he fraternally shouted for "Vi," who appeared all in a rosy glow, and took me upstairs to equip me for walking, extracting from me in the meantime the main features of the story of the bloodhound, and trembling while she gave exulting little nods.

Then she called for Nina (were they so intimate already?) and found that young lady in a point device walking dress, nursing the pug and talking to Dermot, and so we set forth for the beech-woods, very soon breaking our five into three and two. Certainly Lady Diana ought to have viewed Dermot's attentions to the sixty-thousand pounder as exemplary, for he engrossed her and me so entirely with the description of Harold's victory over a buck-jumper at Boola Boola, that it was full a quarter of an hour before she looked round to exclaim, "What is become of Viola?" And then we would not let her wait, and in truth we never came again upon Viola and Harold till we overtook them at the foot of the last hill, and they never could satisfy Miss Sandford where they had been, nor what they had seen, nor how they had missed us; and Dermot invented for the nonce a legend about a fairy in the hill, who made people gyrate round it in utter oblivion of all things; thus successfully diverting the attention of Miss Sandford, who took it all seriously. Yes, she certainly was a stupid girl.

Every moment that lengthened the veritable enchantment of that autumn afternoon was precious beyond what we knew, and we kept Miss Sandford prowling about the garden on all sorts of pretexts, till the poor girl was tired out, as well she might be, for we had kept her on her feet for three hours and a half, and she made her escape at last to join Viola.

I always think of Harold and Viola, as I saw them at that moment, on the top of the western slope of the lawn, so that there was a great ruddy gold sky behind them, against which their silhouettes stood out in a sort of rich dark purple shade.

"Oh, they are looking at such a sunset!" cried Miss Sandford, climbing up the hill.

"Query!" murmured Dermot, for the faces were in profile, not turning towards the sun in the sky, but to the sunbeams in one another's eyes—sunbeams that were still there when we joined them, and, in my recollection, seem to blend with the glorious haze of light that was pouring down in a flood over the purple moorland horizon, and the wood, field, and lake below. I was forced to say something about going home, and Viola took me up to her room, where we had one of those embraces that can never be forgotten. The chief thing that the dear girl said to me was, "Oh, Lucy. How he has suffered! How shall I ever make it up to him?"

Poor dear Viola, little did she think that she was to cause the very sharpest of his sufferings.

Nay, as little did he, when we rode home together with the still brilliant sky before us. I never see a lane ending in golden light, melting into blue, and dark pine trees framing as it were the brightness, with every little branch defined against it, without thinking of that silence of intense, almost awe-struck joy in which Harold went home by my side, only at long intervals uttering some brief phrase, such as "This is blessedness," or "Thank God, who gives women such hearts."

He had told her all, and it had but added a reverent, enthusiastic pity and fervour to that admiring love which had been growing up so long, and to which he had set the spark.

His old friend was admitted to share their joy, and was as happy as we were, perhaps doubly so, since he had beheld with despair Harold's early infatuation and its results, which had made him fear, during those three wretched years, that all the lad's great and noble gifts would be lost in the coarse excesses of his wild life, with barbarous prosperity without, and a miserable, hardening home. That he should have been delivered from it, still capable of refinement, still young and fresh enough for a new beginning, had been a cause of great joy, and now that all should be repaired by a true and worthy love, had seemed beyond hope. We built our castles over the fire that evening, Harold had already marked out with his eye the tract of Neme Heath which he would reclaim; and the little he had already set me on doing among the women and children at the potteries, had filled us with schemes as to what Viola was to carry out.

Some misgivings there were even then. Lady Diana was not to be expected to like Harold's L1,200 a year as well as Piggy's heirship to the Erymanth coronet, or any of the other chances that might befall an attractive girl of twenty.

For coldness and difficulties we were prepared, but not for the unqualified refusal with which she met Harold the next morning, grounding all on the vague term, "circumstances," preventing his even seeing Viola, and cutting short the interview in the manner of a grande dame whose family had received an insult.

Dermot, however, not only raging, but raving, on his side, assured him of the staunchness of his sister, and her resolve to hold by him through everything; and further, in sundry arguments with his mother, got to the bottom of the "circumstances." She had put away from herself the objection to the convict birth and breeding, by being willing to accept Eustace, to whom exactly the same objections applied; and when she called Eustace a man of more education and manners, her son laughed in her face at the comparison of "that idiot" with a man like Harold.

Then came the "past life," a much more tangible objection, but Dermot was ready there, declaring that whatever Harold had done, considering his surroundings, was much less heinous than his own transgressions, after such a bringing up as his, and would his mother say that nobody ought to marry him? Besides, to whom had she given Di? They were not arguments that Lady Diana accepted, but she weakened her own cause by trying to reinforce it with all the Stympson farrago, the exaggeration of which Dermot, after his own meeting with Henry Alison, and with Prometesky to corroborate him, was fully prepared to explode, to the satisfaction even of Lord Eryinanth.

Harold himself was deeply sensible of the stain and burthen of his actual guilt, more so, indeed, than he had ever been before, both from the religious influences to which he had submitted himself, and from the sense of that sweet innocence of his Viola's; but his feeling had come to be that if his Heavenly Father loved and forgave him, so, in a lesser way, Viola forgave him because she loved him. He did not wonder at nor complain of Lady Diana's not thinking him worthy of her good and lovely child. He would be thankful to submit to any probation, five, seven, ten years without any engagement, if he might hope at last. Even Lord Erymanth, when he saw how his darling's soul was set on it, thought that thus much might be granted.

But Lady Diana had still another entrenchment which she had concealed, as it were, to the last, not wishing to shock and pain us all, she said. Though she said she had reason to complain of not having been told from the first that Harold had once been insane, nothing could induce her to sanction her daughter's marriage with a man whose mind had been disordered; nay, who had done mortal injury in his frenzy. It was a monstrous idea!

Dermot's reply to this was, that nobody, then, ought to marry who had had a delirious fever; and he brought Prometesky over to Arked to testify to her how far the attack had been from anything approaching to constitutional insanity. The terrible fall, of which Harold's head still bore the mark, the shock, the burning sun, were a combination of causes that only made it wonderful that he should have recovered the ensuing brain fever, and the blow to his rival had been fatal by the mere accident of his strength. A more ordinary man would have done no serious harm by such a stroke, given when not accountable. Lady Diana answered stiffly that this might be quite true, but that there had been another cause for the temporary derangement which had not been mentioned, and that it was notorious that Mr. Alison, in consequence, had been forced to avoid all liquors, and she appealed to Dermot as to the effects of a very small quantity on his friend's brain.

Poor Dermot! it was bitter enough for him to have that orgie at Foling brought forward against his friend. Nor could any representation appease Lady Diana.

I thought her very cruel and unreasonable then, and I am afraid I believe that if Harold had had ten, or even five thousand a year, these objections would never have been heard of; but after years and experience have cooled my mind, it seems to me that on several grounds she was justified in her reluctance, and that, as Viola was so young, and Harold's repentance had been comparatively recent, she might fairly have insisted on waiting long enough to see whether he were indeed to be depended upon, or if Viola's affection were strong enough to endure such risk as there might be.

For Dermot, resolute to defend his friend, and declaring that his sister's heart should not be broken, was the prime mover in Harold going up to consult the most eminent men of the day on mental disease, Prometesky going with him as having been his only attendant during his illness, to give an account of the symptoms, and Dermot, who so comported himself in his excitement as to seem far more like the lover whose hopes might have depended on the verdict on his doubtful sanity, than did the grave, quiet, self-contained man, who answered all questions so steadily.

The sentence was so far satisfactory that the doctor confirmed Prometesky's original view, that concussion of the brain, aggravated by circumstances, had produced the attack, and that there was no reasonable ground for apprehension of its recurrence, certainly not of its being hereditary. But he evidently did not like the confession of the strange horror of dogs, which Harold thought it right to mention as having been brought on by the circumstances of his accident, and he would not venture to say that any "exciting cause" might not more easily affect the brain than if nothing had ever been amiss. Yet when Dermot tarried, explaining that he was the brother of a young lady deeply concerned, the doctor assured him that whereas no living man could be insured from insanity, he should consider the gentleman he had just seen to be as secure as any one else, since there was no fear of any hereditary taint, and his having so entirely outgrown and cast off all traces of the malady was a sign of his splendid health and vigour of constitution.

But Lady Diana was still not satisfied. She still absolutely refused all consent, and was no more moved at the end of three weeks than before. Dear Harold said he did not wonder, and that if he had seen himself in this true light, he would have loved Viola at a distance without disquieting her peace, but since he had spoken and knew she loved him, he could not but persevere for her sake. We could see he said it with a steady countenance, but a burning heart. Neither he nor I was allowed to see Viola, but there was Dermot as constant reporter, and, to my surprise, Viola was not the submissive daughter I had expected. Lady Diana had never had any real ascendancy over her children's wills or principles. Even Viola's obedience had been that of duty, not of the heart, and she had from the first declared that mamma might forbid her to marry Harold, or to correspond with him, and she should consider herself bound to obey; but that she had given him her promise, and that she could not and would not take it back again. She would wait on for ever, if otherwise it could not be, but he had her troth plight, and she *would* be faithful to it. She would not give up her crystal cross, and she sent Harold her love every day by her brother, often in her mother's very hearing, saying she was too proud of him to be ashamed. She had resolved on her own line of passive obedience, but of never renouncing her engagement, and her brother upheld her in it; while her uncle let himself be coaxed out of his displeasure, and committed himself to that compromise plan of waiting which his sister viewed as fatal, since Viola would only lose all her bloom, and perhaps her health. Nothing, she said, was so much to be deplored for a girl as a long engagement. The accepting a reformed rake had been always against her principles, and she did not need even the dreadful possibility of derangement, or the frightful story of his first marriage, to make her inexorable. Viola, we were told, had made up her mind that it was a case for perseverance, and all this time kept up dauntlessly, not failing in spirits nor activity, but telling her brother she had always known she should have to go through something, but Harold's love was worth it, and she meant to be brave; how should she not be when she knew Harold cared for her; and as to what seemed to be objections in the eyes of others, did they not make her long the more to compensate him?

"She has to make all her love to me, poor little woman, and very pretty love it is," said Dermot.

Whether Harold made as much love in return to their ready medium I cannot tell, for their conferences were almost always out of doors or at the office, and Harold was more reserved than ever. He was not carrying matters with the same high hand as his little love, for, as he always said, he knew he had brought it all on himself.

He never complained of Lady Diana, but rather defended her to her son for not thinking him fit for her daughter, only adhering to his original standpoint, that where there was so much love, surely some hope might be granted, since he would thankfully submit to any probation.

We all expected that this would be the upshot of our suspense, and that patience and constancy would prevail; and by the help of immense walks and rides, and a good deal of interest in some new buildings at the potteries, and schemes for the workmen, Harold kept himself very equable and fairly cheerful, though his eyes were weary and anxious, and when he was sitting still, musing, there was something in his pose which reminded me more than ever of Michel Angelo's figures, above all, the grand one on the Medicean monument. He consorted much more now with Mr. Yolland, the curate, and was making arrangements by which the school chapel might expand into a Mission Church, but still I did not know that he was finding the best aid through this time in the devotions and heart-searchings to which the young clergyman had led him, and which were the real cause of the calm and dignified humility with which he waited.

At last Lady Diana, finding herself powerless with her daughter, sent a letter to Harold, beginning: "I appeal to your generosity." A very cruel letter in some ways it was, representing that he had acquiesced in her judgment, that there were certain unfortunate passages in his past life which made it her painful duty to prevent her child from following the dictates of an inexperienced heart. Then she put it to him whether it were not a most unfortunate position for a young girl to be involved in an engagement which could never be fulfilled, and which was contrary to the commands of her only remaining parent, and she showed how family peace, confidence, and maternal and filial affection must suffer if the daughter should hold fast persistently to the promise by which she held herself bound. In fact, it was an urgent entreaty, for Viola's own sake, that he would release her from her promise. Dermot was shooting at Erymanth, and neither he nor I knew of this letter till Harold had acted. He rode at once to Arked, saw Lady Diana, and declared himself convinced that the engagement, having no chance of sanction, ought to be given up. Rather than keep Viola in the wearing state of resistance and disobedience her mother described, he would resign all hopes of her.

Lady Diana went to her daughter with the tidings, that Mr. Alison saw the hopelessness of his suit, and released her from her promise.

"You have made him do so, mamma," cried Viola. "If he releases me I do not release myself."

Finally, Lady Diana, astonished to find Harold so reasonable and amenable, perceived that the only means of dealing with her daughter was to let them meet again. Of course no one fully knows what passed then. Harold told me, the only time he spoke of it, that "he had just taken out his own heart and crushed it!" but Viola dwelt on each phrase, and, long after, used to go over all with me. He had fully made up his mind that to let Viola hold to her troth would neither be right nor good for her, and he used his power of will and influence to make her resign it. There was no concealment nor denial of their mutual love. It was Viola's comfort to remember that. "But," said Harold, "your mother has only too good reasons for withholding you from me, and there is nothing for it but to submit, and give one another up."

"But we do not leave off loving one another," said poor Viola.

"We cannot do what we cannot."

"And when we are old—"

"That would be a mental reservation," said Harold. "There must be no mutual understanding of coming together again. I promised your mother. Because I am a guilty man, I am not to break up your life."

He made her at last resign her will into his, she only feeling that his judgment could not be other than decisive, and that she could not resist him, even for his own sake. He took her for a moment into his arms, and exchanged one long burning kiss, then, while she was almost faint and quite passive with emotion, he laid her on the sofa, and called her mother. "Lady Diana," he said, "we give up all claim to one another's promise, in obedience to you. Do we not, Viola?"

"Yes," she faintly said.

He gave her brow one more kiss, and was gone.

He took his horse home, and sent in a pencil note to me: "All over; don't wait, for me.—H. A."

I was dreadfully afraid he would go off to Australia, or do something desperate, but Count Stanislas reassured me that this would be unlike Harold's present self, since his strength had come to be used, not in passion, but in patience. We dined as best we could without him, waited all the evening, and sat up till eleven, when we heard him at the door. I went out and took down the chain to let him in. It was a wet misty night, and he was soaked through. I begged him to come in and warm himself, and have something hot, but he shook his head, as if he could not speak, took his candle, and went upstairs.

I made the tea, for which I had kept the kettle boiling all this time, and Prometesky took his great cup in to him, presently returning to say, "He is calm. He has done wisely, he has exhausted himself so that he will sleep. He says he will see me at once to my retreat in Normandy. I think it will be best for him."

Count Stanislas was, in fact, on the eve of departure, and in a couple of days more Harold went away with him, having only broached the matter to me to make me understand that the break had been his, not Viola's; and that I must say no more about it.

Dermot had come over and raged against his mother, and even against Harold, declaring that if the two had "stood out" they would have prevailed, but that he did not wonder Harold was tired of it.

Harold's look made him repent of that bit of passion, but he was contemptuous of the "for her sake," which was all Harold uttered as further defence. "What! tell him it was for her sake when she was creeping about the house like a ghost, looking as if she had just come out of a great illness?"

Dermot meant to escort his mother and sister to Florence, chiefly in order to be a comfort to the latter, but he meant to return to Ireland as soon as they had joined the St. Glears. "Taking you by the way," he said, "before going to my private La Trappe."

Prometesky took leave of me, not quite as if we were never to meet again, for his experimental retreat was to be over at Christmas, and he would then be able to receive letters. He promised me that, if I then wrote to him that, Harold stood in need of him for a time, he would return to us instead of commencing the novitiate which would lead to his becoming dead to the outer world.

Harold was gone only ten days, and came back late on a Friday evening. He tried to tell me about what he had done and seen, but broke off and said, "Well, I am very stupid; I went to all the places they told me to see at Rouen and everywhere else, but I can't recollect anything about them."

So I let him gaze into the fire in peace, and all Saturday he was at the potteries or at the office, very busy about all his plans and also taking in hand the charge for George Yolland, for both brothers were going on Monday to take a fortnight's holiday among their relations. He only came in to dinner, and after it told me very kindly that he must leave me alone again, for he wanted to see Ben Yolland. A good person for him to wish to see, "but was all this restlessness?" thought this foolish Lucy.

When he came in, only just at bed-time, there was something more of rest, and less of weary sadness about his eyes than I had seen since the troubles began, and as we wished one another good night he said, "Lucy, God forgives while He punishes. He is better to us than man. Yolland says I may be with you at church early to-morrow."

Then my cheeks flushed hot with joy, and I said how thankful I was that all this had not distracted his thoughts from the subject. "When I wanted help more than ever?" he said.

So in some ways that was to me at least a gladsome Sunday, though not half so much at the time as it has become in remembrance, and I could not guess how much of conscious peace or joy Harold felt, as, for the first and only time, he and I knelt together on the chancel step.

He said nothing, but he had quite recovered his usual countenance and manner, only looking more kind and majestic than ever, as I, his fond aunt, thought, when we went among the children after the school service, to give them the little dainties they had missed in his absence; and he smiled when they came round him with their odd little bits of chatter.

We sat over the fire in the evening, and talked a little of surface things, but that died away, and after a quarter of an hour or so, he looked up at me and said, "And what next?"

"What are we to do, do you mean?" I said, for I had been thinking how all his schemes of life had given way. We spoke of it together. "Old Eu did not want him," as he said, and though there was much for him to do at the Hydriot works and the Mission Chapel, the Reading Room, the Association for Savings, and all the rest which needed his eye, yet for Viola's peace he thought he ought not to stay, and the same cause hindered the schemes he had once shared with Dermot; he had cut himself loose from Australia, and there seemed nothing before him. "There were the City Missions," he said, wearily, for he did not love the City, and yet he felt more than ever the force of his dying father's commission to carry out his longings for the true good of the people.

I said we could make a London home and see Dora sometimes, trying to make him understand that he might reckon on me as his sister friend, but the answer was, "I don't count on that."

"You don't want to cast me off?"

"No, indeed, but there is another to be thought of."

Then he told me how, over my letters to him in New South Wales, there had come out Dermot's account of the early liking that everyone nipped, till my good-girlish submission wounded and affronted him, and he forgot or disliked me for years; how old feelings had revived, when we came in contact once more; but how he was withheld from their manifestation, by the miserable state of his affairs, as well as by my own coldness and indifference.

I made some sound which made Harold say, "You told me to keep him away."

"I knew I ought," I remember saying faintly.

"Oh—h—!" a prolonged sound, that began a little triumphantly, but ended in a sigh, and then he earnestly said, "You do not think you ought to discourage him now? Your mother did not forbid it for ever."

"Oh no, no; it never came to that."

"And you know what he is now?"

"I know he is changed," was all I could say.

"And you will help him forward a little when he comes back. You and he will be happy."

There might be a great surging wave of joy in my heart, but it would not let me say anything but, "And leave you alone, Harold?"

"I must learn to be alone," he said. "I can stay here this winter, and see to the things in hand, and then I suppose something will turn up."

"As a call?" I said.

"Yes," he answered. "I told God to-day that I had nothing to do but His service, and I suppose He will find it for me."

There was something in the steadfast, yet wistful look of his eyes, that made me take down the legend of St. Christopher and read it aloud. Reading generally sent him into a doze, but even that would be a respite to the heartache he so patiently bore, and I took the chance, but he sat with his chin on his hand and his eyes fixed attentively on mine all the time, then held out his hand for the book, and pondered, as was his thorough way in such matters. At last he said, "Well, I'll wait by the stream. Some day He will send me some one to carry over."

We little thought what stream was very near!

CHAPTER XV
THE FATAL TOKEN

Tuesday morning brought a strange little untidy packet, tied with blue ribbon, understamped, and directed to Harold Alison, Esquire, in the worst form of poor Dora's always bad handwriting. Within was a single knitted muffatee, and a long lock of the stiffly curling yellow hair peculiar to Dora's head. In blotted, sloping roundhand was written:—

> "My Dear Harry,—
>
> "Good-bye, I do fele so very ill, I can't do any more. Don't forget I allwaies was your wiffe.
>
> "I am your affex., D. A."

We looked at each other in wonder and dismay, sure that the child must be very ill, and indignant that we had not been told. Harold talked of going up to town to find out; I was rather for going, or sending, to Therford for tidings, and all the time, alas! alas! he was smoothing and caressing the yellow tress between his fingers, pitying the child and fancying she was being moped to death in the school-room.

We determined on riding to Therford, and Harold had hastened to the office to despatch some business first, when Mr. Horsman himself came in—on his way to the Petty Sessions—to explain matters.

Mrs. Randall Horsman had arrived with her children at Therford the day before, flying from the infection of smallpox, for which the doctor had declared Dora to be sickening. The whole family had been spending the autumn months at the seaside. Nessy Horsman had been with them and had taken Dora about with him much more than had been approved. In one of these expeditions he had taken her into the shop of a village ratcatcher, where, it had since been ascertained, two children were ill of smallpox. She had been ailing ever since the party had returned to London; the doctor had been called in on Monday, and had not only pronounced the dreadful name of the disease, but, seeking in vain for the marks of vaccination on her arms, he greatly apprehended that she would have it in full and unmitigated virulence.

Mrs. Randall Horsman had herself and her children vaccinated without loss of time and fled to the country. Her husband would spend all day in his chambers, and only sleep at home on the ground-floor with every precaution, and Dora had been left in the charge of a young under-house-maid, whose marked face proved her safety, until the doctor could send in a regular nurse. It was this wretched little stupid maid who was ignorant enough to assist the poor child in sending off her unhappy packet, all unknowing of the seeds of destruction it conveyed.

I had had a slight attack of undoubted smallpox when a young child, and I immediately resolved on going to nurse my poor Dora, secure that she would now be left to me, and unable to bear the thought of her being among strangers. I went at once to the office to tell Harry, and Baby Jack walked with me as far as our roads lay together, asking me on the way if it were true that Harold Alison was engaged to Miss Tracy, and on my denial, saying that Mrs. Randall had come down full of the report; that Nessy had heard of it, and, on Sunday afternoon, had teased Dora about it to such a degree that she had leaped up from the sofa and actually boxed his ears, after which she had gone into such a paroxysm of tears and sobs that she had been sent to bed, and in the morning the family mind began to perceive she was really ill. The poor child's passionate jealousy had no doubt prompted her letter, as well as her desire to take leave of the object of her love; and knowing her strange character as I did, I was sure the idea was adding tenfold to the misery of the dreadful illness that was coming on her.

I had to pursue Harold to the potteries, where one of the workmen directed me to him, as he was helping to put in order some machine for hoisting that was out of gear. "Bless you, ma'am," said the man, "he is as strong as any four of we."

When I found him, his consternation was great, and he quite agreed with me that I had better go up that very afternoon and take charge of Dora, since Baby Jack answered for it that Randall Horsman would be most grateful and thankful.

Harold found out the hours for the trains, and did everything to expedite me. He made it certain that poor little Dora had not been vaccinated. When she was born, no doctor lived within sixty miles of Boola Boola, and nobody had ever thought of such a thing.

"And you, Harry?" I asked, with a sudden thrill of alarm.

"Do you expect me to remember?" he asked with a smile.

I begged him to look for the moons upon his arm, and at any rate to undergo the operation again, since, even if it had been done in his infancy, the effect might have worn out, and it was only too probable that in the case of a child born on board a sailing vessel, without a doctor, it had been forgotten. He gave in to my solicitude so far as to say that he would see about it, but reminded me that it was not he who was going into the infection. Yes, I said, but there was that lock of hair and the worsted cuff. Such things did carry contagion, and he ought to burn them at once.

"Poor Dora!" he said, rather indignantly.

Oh that I had seen them burnt! Oh that I had taken him to Dr. Kingston's for vaccination before I went away, instead of contenting myself with the unmeaning, half-incredulous promise to "see about it!" by which, of course, he meant to mention it when George Yolland came home. Yet it might have made no difference, for he had been fondling and smoothing that fatal curl all the time we were talking over the letter.

He came to the station with me, gave me the kindest messages for Dora, arranged for my telegraphing reports of her every day—took care of me as men will do when they seem to think their womankind incapable without them, making all the more of me because I did not venture to take Colman, whom I sent to visit her home. He insisted on Mr. Ben Yolland, who had been detained a day behind his brother, going in a first-class carriage with me. I leant out at the window for the parting kiss, and the last sight I had of my dear Harold, as the train steamed out of the station, was bearing on his shoulder a fat child—a potter's—who had just arrived by the train, and had been screaming to his mother to carry him, regardless of the younger baby and baskets in her arms. It might well make my last sight of him remind me of St. Christopher.

That journey with the curate was comfortable in itself, and a great comfort to me afterwards. We could not but rejoice together over that Sunday, and Ben Yolland showed himself deeply struck with the simplicity and depth that had been revealed to him, the reality of whatever Harold said, and his manner of taking his dire disappointment as the just and natural outcome of his former life. Many men would have been soured and driven back to evil by such a rejection. Harold had made it the occasion of his most difficult victory and sharpest struggle; yet all the time he was unconscious how great a victory it was. And so thorough was the penitence, so great the need of refreshment after the keen struggle for self-mastery, and so needful the pledge of pardon, that though he had never been confirmed, there was no doubt as to making him welcome at once to the Heavenly Feast. Well that it was so!

The "What next" concerned Mr. Yolland as much as it did me. He could not bear to think of relinquishing one who—all unknown to himself—

did more to guide and win the hearts of those Hydriots than teaching or sermons could ever do, and yet no one could advise Harold to remain after this winter. In the reprieve, however, we both rejoiced, and Ben then added, "For my brother's sake, especially."

"Do you think the example tells on him?" I ventured on asking.

"I can hardly say it does," was the answer. "George used to point to Harold Alison as a specimen of a vigorous physical development so perfectly balanced as to be in a manner self-adjusting, without need of what he called imaginative influences. I always thought he was a little staggered that evening that he had to summon you, Miss Alison, to his help; but he had some theory of sentiment to account for it, and managed, as people do, to put it aside. Lately, however, he has been looking on, he says, with curiosity—I believe with something more. You see he reveres Alison for what he is, not for what he knows."

"Of course not; your brother must know far more than Harold."

"But the strength of character and will impresses him. The bending of such a nature to faith, the acceptance of things spiritual, by one *real*, unimaginative and unsophisticated, and, above all, the *self* conquest, just where a great Greek hero would have failed, have certainly told on George, so that I see more hope than I have ever done before."

So careful of me was Mr. Yolland, that he only parted with me at Randall Horsman's door, where I was gladly welcomed by the master of the house, and found my poor little niece a grievous spectacle, and so miserable with the horrible illness, that she only showed her pleasure in my coming by fretting whenever anyone else touched her.

She had it badly in the natural form, but never was in immediate danger, and began in due time to recover. I had ceased my daily telegrams, and had not been alarmed by some days' intermission of Harold's letters, for I knew that Dermot was at Arked alone, and that by this time the Yollands would be returned and my nephew would have less time to spend on me.

One dismal wintry afternoon, however, when I was sitting in the dark, telling Dora stories, a card was brought up to me by the little housemaid. The gentleman begged to see me. "Mr. Tracy" was on the card, and the very sight startled me with the certainty that something was amiss.

I left the girl in charge and hurried down to the room, where Dermot was leaning over the mantel-shelf, with his head against his arms, in a sorrowful attitude, as if he could not bear to turn round and face me, I flew up to him, crying out that I knew he was come to fetch me to Harold; Dora was so much better that I could leave her.

He turned up to me a white haggard face, and eyes with dismay, pity, and grief in them, such as even now it wrings my heart to recall, and hoarsely said in a sunken voice, "No, Lucy, I am not come to fetch you!" and he took my hand and grasped it convulsively.

"But he has caught it?" Dermot bent his head. "I must go to him, even if he bids me not. I know he wants me."

"No!" again said Dermot, as if his tongue refused to move. "Oh, Lucy, Lucy, I cannot tell you!"

And he burst into a flood of tears, shaking, choking, even rending him.

I stood, feeling as if turned to stone, and presently the words came out in a sob, "Oh, Lucy, he is dead!" and, sinking on the nearest seat, his tempest of grief was for the moment more frightful than the tidings, which I could not take in, so impossible did the sudden quenching of that glorious vitality seem. I began in some foolish way to try to console him, as if it were a mere fancy. I brought him a glass of water from the sideboard, and implored him to compose himself, and tell me what made him say such terrible things, but he wrung my hand and leant his head against me, as he groaned, "I tell you, it is true. We buried him this morning. The noblest, dearest friend that ever—"

"And you never told me! You never fetched me; I might have saved him," was my cry; then, "Oh! why did you not?"

Then he told me that there had been no time, and how useless my presence would have been. We sat on the sofa, and he gasped out something of the sad story, though not by any means all that I afterwards learnt from himself and from the Yollands, but enough to make me feel the reality of the terrible loss. And I will tell the whole here.

Left to himself, the dear fellow had no doubt forgotten all about vaccination, or any peril to himself, for he never mentioned it to Dermot, who only thought him anxious about Dora. On the Saturday they were to have had a day's shooting, and then to have dined at Erymanth, but Harold sent over in the morning to say he had a headache and could not come, so Dermot went alone. When the Yollands came home at nine at night a message was given that Mr. Alison would like to see Mr. George as soon as he came in; but as the train had been an hour late, and the message had not been delivered immediately on their coming in, George thought it could not concern that night, so he waited till morning; but he was awaked in the winter twilight by Harold at his door, saying, "Doctor, I'm not quite right. I wish you would come up presently and see after me."

He was gone again, while he was being called to wait; and, dressing as fast as possible, George Yolland went out after him into the dark, cold, frosty, foggy morning, and overtook him, leaning on the gate of a field, shivering, panting, and so dizzy, that it was with difficulty he was helped to the house. He made known that he had felt very unwell all the day before, and had had a miserable night, in which all the warnings about infection had returned on him. The desire to keep clear of all whom he might endanger, as well as a fevered—perhaps already half-delirious—longing for cool air, had sent him forth himself to summon George Yolland. And already strong shivering fits and increased distress showed what fatal mischief that cold walk had done. All he cared now to say was that he trusted to his doctor to keep everybody out of the house; that I was not to be called away from Dora, and that it was all his own fault.

One person could not be kept away, and that was Dermot Tracy. He came over to spend the Sunday with his friend, and finding the door closed, and Richardson giving warning of smallpox, only made him the more eagerly run upstairs. George could by that time ill dispense with a strong man's help, and after vaccinating him, admitted him to the room, where the checking of the eruption had already produced terrible fever and violent raving.

It was a very remarkable delirium, as the three faithful watchers described it. The mind and senses seemed astray, only not the will. It was as if all the vices of his past life came in turn to assail him, and he was writhing and struggling under their attacks, yet not surrendering himself. When—the Sunday duties over—Ben Yolland came in, he found him apparently acting over some of the wild scenes of his early youth, with shreds of the dreadful mirth, and evil words of profane revelry; and yet, as if they struck his ears, he would catch himself up and strike his fist on his mouth, and when Ben entered, he stretched out his arms and said, "Don't let me." Prayer soothed him for a short interval, but just as they hoped that sleep might come, the fierce struggle with oppression brought back the old habits of violent language, and then the distressed endeavour to check himself, and the clutch at the clergyman's aid. Ben Yolland saw, standing in the room, a great rough wooden cross which Harold had made for some decorating plan of mine. He held it over him, put it into his hand, and bade him repeat after him, "Christ has conquered. By Thy Cross and Passion; by Thy precious Death and Burial, good Lord deliver us."

So it went on hour after hour, evening closing into night, the long, long night brightening at last into day, and still the fever raged, and the fits of delirious agony came on, as though every fiend that had ever tempted him were assailing him now. Yet still he had the power to grasp the Cross when it was held to him, and speak the words, "Christ has conquered," and his ears were open to the prayer, "By Thy Cross and Passion, by Thine Agony and Bloody Sweat, good Lord deliver us!"—the prayer that Ben prayed like Moses at Rephidim. Time came and went, the Northchester physician came and said he might be saved, if the eruption could only be brought out, but he feared that it had been thrown inwards, so that nothing would avail; but of all this Harold knew nothing, he was only in that seething brain, whose former injury now added to the danger, living over again all his former life, as those who knew it could trace in the choked and broken words. Yet, as the doctors averred, that the conscience and the will should not be mastered by the delirium was most unusual, and proved the extraordinary force of his character and resolution, even though the conflict was evidently a great addition to his sufferings.

Worst of all was the deadly strife, when with darkness came the old horror of being pursued by hell hounds, driven on by Meg and the rival he had killed—nay, once it was even by his little children. Then he turned even from the Cross in agony. "I cannot! See there! They will not let me!" and he would have thrown himself from his bed, taking the hands that held him for the dogs' fangs. And yet even then a command rather than a prayer from the priest reached his ears. He wrestled, with choking, stifling breath, as though with a weight on his chest, grappling with his hands as if the dog were at his throat; but at last he uttered those words once more, "Christ has conquered;" then with a gasp, as from a freed breast, for his strength was going fast, fell back in a kind of swoon. Yes, he was delivered from the power of the dog, for after that, when he woke, it was in a different mood. He knew Ben, but he thought he had little Ambrose sitting on his pillow; held his arm as if his baby were in it, and talked to them smiling and tenderly, as if glad they had come to him, and he were enjoying their caresses, their brightness, and beauty. Nor did the peace pass away. He was so quiet that all hoped except George Yolland, who knew the mischief had become irreparable; and though he never was actually sensible, the borderland was haunted no more with images of evil or of terror, but with the fair visions fit for "him that overcometh." Once they thought he fancied he was showing his children to Viola or to me. Once, when Dermot's face came before him, he recurred to some of the words used in the struggle about Viola.

"I don't deserve her. Good things are not for me. All will be made pure there."

They thought then that he was himself, and knew he was dying, but the next moment some words, evidently addressed to his child, showed them he was not in our world; and after that all the murmurs were about what had last taken up his mind—the Bread of Heaven, the Fruit of Everlasting Life.

"To him that overcometh will I give to eat of the Fruit of the Tree of Life, which is in the midst of the Paradise of God." That was what Mr. Yolland ventured now to say over him, and it woke the last respondent glance of his eyes. He had tasted of that Feast of Life on the Sunday he was alone, and Ben Yolland would even then have given it to him, but before it could be arranged, he could no longer swallow, and the affection of the brain was fast blocking up the senses, so that blindness and deafness came on, and passed into that insensibility in which the last struggles of life are, as they tell us, rather agonising to the beholder than to the sufferer. It was at sundown at last that the mightiest and gentlest spirit I ever knew was set free.

Those three durst not wait to mourn. Their first duty was to hasten the burial, so as to prevent the spread of contagion, and they went at once their different ways to make the preparations. No form of conventional respect could be used, but it was the three who so deeply loved him who laid him in the rough-made coffin, hastily put together the same evening, with the cross that had served him in his conflict on his breast, and three camellia buds from Viola's tree. Dermot had thought of her and ridden over to fetch them. There had been no disfigurement. If there had been he might have lived, but still it was a comfort to know that the dear face was last seen in more than its own calm majesty, as of one who lay asleep after a mighty conquest. Over the coffin they placed the lion's skin. It had been left in the room during his illness, and must have been condemned, and it made his fit pall when they took it to be buried with him. It was before daybreak that, with good old Richardson's help, they carried him down to a large cart belonging to the potteries, drawn by the two big horses he used to pet, and driven by George Yolland himself. They took him to our own family burial-place in Arghouse churchyard, where the grave had been dug at night. They meant no one to be there, but behold! there was a multitude of heads gathered round, two or three hundred at least, and when the faithful four seemed to need aid in carrying that great weight the few steps from the gate, there was a rush forward, in spite of the peril, and disappointment when no help was accepted.

Ben Yolland read the service over the grave, and therewith there was the low voice of many, many weepers, as they closed it in, and left him there among his forefathers, under his lion's skin; and even at that moment a great, golden, glorious sun broke out above the horizon, and bathed them all over with light, while going forth as a giant to run his course, conquering the night mists.

Then they turned back to the town, and Dermot came by the next train to town to tell me. But of all this I at first gathered but little, for his words were broken and his voice faint and choked, not only with grief, but with utter exhaustion; and I was so slow to realise all, that I hardly knew more than the absolute fact, before a message came hurriedly down that Dora was worse, and I must come instantly. Dermot, who had talked himself into a kind of dull composure, stood up and said he would come again on the morrow, when he was a little rested, for, indeed, he had not lain down since Saturday, and was quite worn out.

I went up, with heart quailing at the thought of letting that passionately loving creature guess what had befallen her, and yet how could I command myself with her? But that perplexity was spared me. The tidings had, through the Horsman family, reached the house, and, in my absence, that same foolish housemaid had actually told Dora of them point-blank. She said nothing, but presently the girl found her with her teeth locked and eyes fixed in what looked like a convulsion, but was in reality such suppressed hysteria as she had had before.

She soon came out of that attack, but was exceedingly ill all that night and the next day, her recovery being altogether thrown back by feverishness and loss of appetite; but, strange child that she was, she never named Harold, nor let me speak of him. I think she instinctively shrank from her own emotion, and had a kind of dread and jealous horror of seeing anyone else grieve for him.

Dermot did not come the next day, but a note was brought me, left, the servant said, by the gentleman in a cab. It told me that he felt so ill that he thought it wisest to go at once to the smallpox hospital, and find out whether it were the disease, or only vaccination and fatigue. It was a brave unselfish resolve, full of the spirit he had imbibed, and it was wise, for the illness was upon him already, the more severe from his exhausted state and the shock he had undergone. Mr. Randall Horsman, who was very kind, managed that I should hear of him, and I knew he was going on fairly well, and not in any special danger.

But oh! that time seems to me the most wretched that ever I passed, up in those great London attic nurseries, where Dora and I were prisoners—all winter fogginess, with the gas from below sending up its light on the ceiling, and Dora never letting me sit still to grieve. She could not bear the association or memory, I believe, and with the imperious power of recovery used to keep me reading Mayne Reid's storybooks to her incessantly, or else playing at backgammon. I hate the sound of dice to this hour, and when I heard that unhappy French criminals, the night before their execution, are apt to send for Fenimore Cooper's novels, it seemed to reveal Dora's state of mind.

After two or three days, George Yolland came up to see me. He had been to see Dermot, and gave me comfort as to his condition and the care taken of him; but the chief cause of the visit was that they wanted my authority for the needful destruction of whatever had been in that room, and could not be passed through fire. Mr. Yolland had brought me my Harold's big, well-worn pocket-book, which he said must undergo the same doom, for though I was contagion proof, yet harm might be laid up for others, and only what was absolutely necessary must be saved.

First of all, indeed, lay in their crumpled paper poor Dora's fatal gifts, treasured, no doubt, as probably her last; and there, in a deep leathern pocket, was another little parcel with Viola's crystal cross, which her mother had made her return. She might have that now, it would bear disinfecting; but the Irish heath-bells that told of autumn days at Killey Marey must go, and that brief note to me that had been treasured up—yes, and the quaint old housewife, with D. L. (his aunt's maiden initials), whence his needles and thread used to come for his mending work. An old, worn pencil-case kept for his mother's sake—for Alice was on the seal—was the only thing I could rescue; but next there came an envelope with "My will" scrawled on it. Mr. Yolland thought I ought to open it, to see who had authority to act, and it proved that we alone had, for he was made executor, with L1,000. A favourite rifle was bequeathed to Eustace, an annuity of L50 to Smith, and all the rest of the property was to be shared between Dora and me. It was in the fewest words, not at all in form, but all right, and fully witnessed. It was in the dear handwriting, and was dated on the sad lonely Saturday when he felt himself sickening. The other things were accounts and all my letters, most of which could follow the fate of all that he had touched in those last days. However, the visit was a comfort to me. George Yolland answered my questions, and told me much more than poor Dermot could do in his stupefaction from grief, fatigue, and illness, even if I then could have understood.

He told me of the grief shown by all Mycening and Arghouse, and of the sobbing and weeping of mothers and children, who went in a broken pilgrimage on Sunday afternoon to the grave at Arghouse, of the throngs at the church and the hush, like a sob held back, when the text was given out: "Thanks be to Him who giveth us the victory through Jesus Christ our Lord."

Yet on the Saturday evening there was something more noted still. The men stood about when they had come up for their wages to the office, where, but a week before, Harold had paid them, with a sore struggle to see and to count aright, as some even then had observed; and at last their spokesman had explained their great desire to do something themselves in memory of "the best friend they ever had," as they truly called him. Some of them had seen memorial-windows, and they wanted Mr. Yolland to take from each a small weekly subscription throughout the winter, to adorn the new chapel with windows. "With the history of Samson a killin' of the lion," called out a gruff voice. It was the voice of the father of the boy whom Harold had rescued on Neme Heath.

"So," said George Yolland, as he told me, "the poor fellows' hearty way was almost more than one could bear, but I knew Alison would have me try to turn it to some sort of good to themselves; so I stood up and said I'd take it on one condition only. They knew very well what vexed Mr. Alison most in themselves, and the example he had set—how he had striven to make them give up making beasts of themselves. Wouldn't they think with me it was insulting him to let a drunkard have a hand in doing a thing to his memory? So I would manage their collection on condition they agreed that whoever took more than his decent pint a day—or whatever else sober men among them chose to fix it at—should have his money returned on the spot. Poor fellows, they cheered and said I was in the right, but whether they will keep to it is another thing."

They did keep to it. All that winter, while the chapel was building, there were only five cases in which the money had to be returned, and two of those took the pledge, pleaded hard, and were restored. Indeed, I believe it was only the habitually sober who ventured on the tolerated pint. Of course there were some who never came into the thing at all, and continued in their usual course; but these were the dregs, sure to be found everywhere, and the main body of the Hydriot potters kept their word so staunchly, that the demon of intoxication among them was slain by those Samson windows, as Harold had never slain it during his life.

Beautiful bright windows they are, glowing with Samson in his typical might, slaying his lion, out of the strong finding sweetness, drinking water after the fight, bearing away the gates, and slaying his foes in his death. But Samson is not there alone. As the more thoughtful remarked, Samson was scarce a worthy likeness for one who had had grace to triumph. No, Samson, whose life always seems like a great type in shattered fragments, must be set in juxtaposition with the great Antitype. His conflict with Satan, His Last Supper, His pointing out the Water of Life, His Death and His victory over death, shine forth, giving their own lesson of Who hath won the victory.

We ventured to add two little windows with St. George and St. Christopher, to show how Christ's soldiers may follow in the conquest, treading down the dragon, and bending to the yoke of the Little Child who leads them out of many waters.

That winter of temperance proved the fulcrum that had been wanting to the lever of improvement. Schools of art, concerts, lectures, choir preparation, recreation, occupation, and interests of all sorts were vigorously devised by the two Yollands; and, moreover, the "New Dragon's Head" and the "Genuine Dragon's Head," with sundry of their congeners, died a natural death by inanition; so that when the winter was over, habits had been formed, and a standard of respectability set up, which has never entirely fallen, and a spirit which has withstood the temptation of strikes. Of course, the world has much to do with the tone of many. What amount of true and real religion there may be, can only be tested by trial, and there are many who do not show any signs of being influenced by anything more than public opinion, some who fall below that; but, as everyone knows, the Hydriot works have come to be not only noted for the beauty and excellence of their execution, and the orderliness, intelligence, and sobriety of their artisans, but for their large congregations, ample offertories, and numerous communicants.

Of course all this would never have kept up but for the Yollands. The Hydriots are wife, children, everything to him who is now called Vicar of St. Christopher's, Mycening. He has refused better preferment, for he has grown noted now, since the work that Harold had begun is still the task he feels his charge.

And whatever is good is led by the manager of the works, whose influence over the workmen's minds has never failed. Even when he talked to me on that day, I thought there was a change in his tone. He had never sneered (at least in my hearing) nor questioned other men's faith, but when he told me of Harold his manner had something of awe, as well as of sorrow and admiration, and I could not but think that a sense had dawned out that the spiritual was a reality, and an absolute power over the material.

The great simple nature that had gradually and truly undergone that influence had been watched and studied by him, and had had its effect. The supernatural had made itself felt, and thenceforth he made it his study, in a quiet, unobtrusive manner, scarcely known even to his brother, but gradually resulting in heart-whole acceptance of faith, and therewith in full devotion of heart and soul.

Did Harold rejoice in that victory, which to him would have been one of the dearest of all?

CHAPTER XVI
CONCLUSION

I must finish my story, though it seems hardly worth telling, since my nephew, my tower of strength and trust, had suddenly sunk away from me in the prime of his manhood.

The light seemed gone out of the whole world, and my heart felt dull and dead, as if I could never heed or care for anything again. Even Dermot's illness did not seem capable of stirring me to active anxiety in this crushed, stupid state, with no one to speak to of what lay heavy on my heart, no one even to write to; for who would venture to read my letters? nay, I had not energy even to write to poor Miss Woolmer. We got into a way of going on day after day with Dora's little meals, the backgammon, and the Mayne Reid, till sometimes it felt as if it had always been thus with us from all time, and always would be; and at others it would seem as if it were a dream, and that if I could but wake, I should be making tea for Harold in our cheerful little drawing-room at Mount Eaton. At last I had almost a morbid dread of breaking up this monotonous life, and having to think what to do or where to go. The Randall Horsmans must long for our departure, and my own house was in a state of purification, and uninhabitable.

The doctor said that Dora must be moved as soon as it could be managed, for in that London attic she could have no impulse towards recovery; and while it still seemed a fearful risk, he sent us off to St. Clement's, a little village on the south coast, where he knew of rooms in a great old manor-house which had sunk to farmer's use, and had a master and mistress proof against infection.

When I brought my tired, worn-out, fretting charge in through the great draughty porch, and was led up the old shallow oak stairs to a big panelled room, clean and scantily furnished, where the rats ran about behind the wainscot, and a rain-laden branch of monthly rose went tap, tap against the window, and a dog howled all night long, I thought we had come to a miserable place at the end of the earth. I thought so still the next morning, when the mist lay in white rolls and curls round the house; and the sea, when we had a peep of it, was as lead-coloured as the sky, while the kind pity of the good wife for Dora's weak limbs and disfigured face irritated me so that I could hardly be civil.

Dora mended from that day, devoted herself to the hideous little lambs that were brought in to be nursed by the fire; ate and drank like a little cormorant, and soon began to rush about after Mr. and Mrs. Long, whether in house or farm-yard, like a thing in its native element, while they were enchanted with her colonial farm experience, and could not make enough of "Little Missy."

I had a respite from Mayne Reid, and could wander as far as I pleased alone on the shingle, or sit and think as I had so often longed to do; but the thoughts only resulted in a sense of dreariness and of almost indifference as to my fate, since the one person in all the world who had needed me was gone, and I had heard nothing whatever of Dermot Tracy. He might be gone out to his mother and sister, or back to Ireland. Our paths would never come together again, for he thought I did not care for him. Nay, was I even sure of his recovery? His constitution had been much tried! He was in a strange place, among mere professional nurses! Who could tell how it had been with him?

Everything went from me that had loved me. Even Dora was to leave me as soon as people ceased to be afraid of her.

Letters had found out the married pair on their return from the cataracts of the Nile. Eustace had immediately been vaccinated fourteen times, but he was shocked and appalled, and the spirit of his letter was—

> O while my brother with me stayed,
> Would I had loved him more,

and I forgave him much.

Hippolyta likewise wrote with feeling, but it rather stung me to be thanked for my care of "her poor little sister," as if Dora were not my child before she was hers. As soon as it was considered safe, Dora was to be returned to Horsman keeping, and as the Randall party declined to receive her again, Philippa would convey her to a school at Baden-Baden.

And Dora declared she was glad! There was none of the angry resistance with which she had left me in the spring; when I had done nothing for her compared with what I had gone through for her now; but I believe I was dull company, and showed myself displeased at her hardness and wild outbreaks of spirits, and that the poor child longed to escape from all that reminded her of the unbearable sorrow at the bottom of her heart. But it was a grievance to a grievance-making temper, such as I feel mine was.

The most wholesome thing I received was a letter from Prometesky, to whom I had written the tidings that Harold would never need his comfort more. The old man was where the personal loss was not felt, and he knew more deeply than anyone the pain which that strong fervent heart suffered in its self-conquests, so that he did not grieve for Harold himself; but he gave me that sympathy of entire appreciation of my loss which is far better than compassion. For himself, he said his last link with the world was gone, he found the peace, and the expression of penitence, his soul required, in the course he was about to embrace, and I might look on this as a voice from the grave. I should never hear of him more, but I should know that, as long as life was left him, it would be spent in prayers for those whose souls he had wrecked in his overboiling youth. He ended with thanks to all of us, who he said had sent him to his retreat with more kindly and charitable recollections than he should otherwise have carried thither. I never did hear of him again; Dermot went to the convent some years later, and tried to ascertain if he lived, but the monks do not know each others' names, and it failed.

The village of St. Clement's, a small fishing-place, was half-a-mile off, through lanes a foot deep in mud, and with a good old sleepy rector of the old school, not remarkable for his performances in Church. I was entering the little shop serving as the post-office, where I went every day in the unreasonable expectation of letters, when I heard a voice that made me start, "Did you say turn to the right?"

And there, among the piles of cheeses, stood a figure I knew full well, though it had grown very thin, and had a very red and mottled face at the top.

We held out our hands to one another in silence, and walked at once out of hearing. Dermot said he was well, and had been as kindly looked after as possible, and now he had been let out as safe company, but his family and friends would hardly believe it, so he had come down to see whether he could share our quarantine.

Happily a few cottages of the better sort had accommodation for lodgers, and one of them—for a consideration—accepted "the gentleman's" bill of health. He walked on by my side, both of us feeling the blessing of having someone to speak to. He, poor fellow, had seen no being who had ever heard of Harold, except George Yolland, who came when he was too ill to talk, and we went on with the conversation that had been broken off weeks before, with such comfort as it could give us in such a loss as ours.

He walked all the way back with me, and I was frightened to see how tired he looked. I took him to Mrs. Long for the refreshment she loved to give, and begged for the pony for him to ride home on, and a boy to fetch it back.

It was wonderful how much more blue there was in the sea the next day, how the evergreens glistened, and how beautiful and picturesque the old house grew; and when I went out in the morning sunshine, for once, inclined to admit some beauty in the staggering black-legged and visaged lambs, and meditating a walk to the village, I saw Dermot coming across the yard, so wearily and breathlessly, that I could only say, "How could you?"

He looked up piteously. "You don't forbid me?" he said.

I almost cried as I told him it was only his fatigue that I objected to; and indeed he was glad enough to take Dora's now vacated place on the great sofa, while we talked of Viola. Writing to her had been, of course, impossible for him, and he had only had two short notes from her, so meaningless that I thought she wrote them fearing to disturb him while he was ill; but he muttered an ominous line from Locksley Hall, vituperated Piggy, and confessed that his ground for doing so was that his mother reported Viola as pleased with foreign life, and happy with her cousins. I said it was his mother's way, and he replied, "Exactly so; and a girl may be worried into anything." A slight dispute on that score cheered him a little, for he showed himself greatly depressed. He was going—as soon as he had gathered a little strength—back to the duties he had promised to fulfil on his own property, but he hated the thought, was down-hearted as to the chances of success, and distrustful of himself among discouragements, and the old associations he had made for himself. "It is a different thing without Alison to look to and keep one up," he said.

"There are higher motives," was my stupid speech.

"It is precious hard on a poor fellow to be left alone with his higher motives, as you call them, before he has well begun to act on his lower."

And then, I don't know how, he began talking drearily, almost as if I was not there, of his having once begun to fancy he could do something creditable enough to make me some day look on him as I used to do in the good old times. My heart gave a great bound, and remembering how Harold said I discouraged him, out came, "How do you know that I don't?"

How he sprang up! And—no, I can't tell what we said, only we found it was no new beginning, only taking up an old, old precious thread—something brought it all out. He had talked it all over with Harold when he came back from Florence, and had taken home a little hope which he said had helped him through the solitary hours of his recovery. So it was Harold who, after all, gave us to one another.

Outspoken Dora informed us, before the day was much older, that the Longs had asked whether that was her brother, or my young man. So we took them into our confidence, and even borrowed "the trap" for one of the roughest and the sweetest drives that ever we had, through those splashing lanes, dropping Dermot at his lodgings to write his letters, while the harvest moon made a path over the sea, no longer leaden, but full of silvery glittering light. There had something come back into the air which made us feel that life was worth living, after all!

Next morning the good people, who were much excited about our affairs, sent the pony for him, and he came in full force with that flattering Irish tongue of his, bent on persuading me that, old lovers as we were, with no more to find out about one another, there was nothing to wait for. 'How could he go back by himself (what a brogue he put on! yet the tears were in his eyes) to his great desolate castle, with not a living man in it at all at all, barring the Banshee and a ghost or two; and as I had nothing to do, and nowhere to go, why not be married then and there without more ado? If I refused, he should think it was all my pride, and that I couldn't take that "ornary object," as he had overheard himself described that day. (As if I did not love him the better for that marred complexion!) His mother? His uncle? They had long ago repented of having come between us ten years ago, and were ready to go down on their knees to any dacent young woman who would take him, let alone a bit of an heiress, who, though not to compete with the sixty-thousand pounder, could provide something better than praties and buttermilk for herself at Killy Marey.'

I could not help thinking dear Harold might have remembered Killy Marey's needs when he gave me that half of his means. And as to going back to Mount Eaton, ghosts of past times would meet me there, whose pain was then too recent to have turned into the treasure these recollections are to me.

There would be just time, Dermot declared, if he put up our banns the very next Sunday, to go through with it before the time Pippa had appointed for receiving Dora, and it would save all the trouble of hunting up a surrogate and startling him with his lovely face.

However, he did startle the poor old parish clergyman effectually by calling on him to publish the banns of marriage between Dermot Edward St. Glear Tracy and Lucy Percy Alison, both residing in this parish. He evidently thought we were in hiding from someone who knew of some just cause or impediment; but whereas we certainly did full justice to our ages twenty-eight and twenty-six, he could only try to examine us individually very politely, but betraying how uncomfortable he was.

It was most amusing to see how his face cleared up when, two days later, he met us on the beach with a dignified old white-haired gentleman, though Dermot declared that the imposing title mentioned on the introduction made him suspect us of having hired a benignant stage father for the occasion.

The dear old uncle Ery had actually come down to chaperone us, and really act as much as possible as a father to me; and as I had likewise sent for Colman and a white silk dress, the St. Clement's minds were free to be pleasantly excited about us. Lord Erymanth had intended to have carried us off to be married from his castle, but we begged off, and when he saw Dermot, he allowed that it was not the time to make a public spectacle of what (Dermot was pleased to say) would have the pleasing pre-eminence of being "the ugliest of weddings," both as to bridegroom and bridesmaid. For he and Dora used to make daily fun of their respective beauties, which were much on a par, since, though she had three weeks' start of him, the complaint having been unmitigated in her, had left much more permanent-looking traces. Those two chose to keep each other up to the most mirthful nonsense-pitch, and yet I am sure none of us felt so light of spirit as we must have appeared, though, perhaps, the being on the edge of such a great shadow made the sunshine seem brighter.

We had considered of beginning with a flying visit to see how poor Viola really was, but the Italian letters prevented this. Lady Diana accepted me cordially and kindly as a daughter, and said all that was proper; but she actually forestalled us by desiring her son not to come out to her, for she thought it much better for Viola not to have painful recollections revived, and Viola herself wrote in a way that disappointed us—loving indeed, but with a strain of something between lightness and bitterness, and absolutely congratulating her brother that there was no one on my side to bring up bygones against him. One half of her letter was a mere guide-book to the Roman antiquities, and was broken off short for some carnival gaiety. Lord Erymanth clearly liked his letters as little as we did. In the abstract, in spite of the first cousinship, I am afraid he would rather have given Viola to Pigou St. Glear than to Harold Alison, but he had thought better of his niece than to think she could forget such a man so soon.

However, the day came. Dora slept with me, and that last night when I came to bed, I found the true self had made a reassertion in one of those frightful fits of dumb hysteria. Half the night Colman and I were attending to her, but still she never opened to me, more than by clinging frantically round my neck in the intervals. She fell asleep at last, and slept till we actually pulled her out of bed to be dressed for the wedding; but we agreed that we could not expose our uncle (who was to escort her to Northchester station) to being left alone with her in one of these attacks, and, as our programme had never been quite fixed, we altered it so far as to pass through Northchester and see her safe into Baby Horsman's hands.

She was altogether herself by day, gave no sign of emotion, and was as merry as possible throughout the journey, calling out to Dermot airily from the platform that she should send him a present of sour krout from Baden. Poor child, it was five years before we saw her again!

We had scarcely had time to settle in at Killy Marey before Lady Diana implored us to meet her in London, without explaining what was the matter. When we came to Lord Erymanth's house, we were met by Viola, very thin, but with a bright red colour on her usually pale cheeks, and a strange gleaming light in her eyes, making them larger than ever; and oh, how she did talk! Chatter, chatter, about all they had seen or done, and all the absurdities of the people they had met; mimicking them and making fun, and all the time her mother became paler and graver, looking as if she had grown ten years older. It went on so all dinner-time. She talked instead of eating, and all the evening those bright eyes of hers seemed to be keeping jealous watch that no one should exchange any words in private.

Nor could we till poor Lady Diana, with a fagged miserable face, came to my room at night, and I called Dermot in. And then she told us how the child had "seemed to bear everything most beautifully," and had never given way. I believe it was from that grain of perversity in Viola's high-spirited nature, as well as the having grown up without confidence towards her mother, which forbade her to mourn visibly among unsympathising watchers; and when her hope was gone led her in her dull despair to do as they pleased, try to distract her thoughts, let herself be hunted hither and thither, and laugh at and play with Pigou St. Glear quite enough to pass for an encouraging flirtation, and to lead all around her to think their engagement immediately coming on. The only thing she refused to do was to go to the Farnese Palace, where was the statue to which there had more than once been comparisons made. At last, one day, when they were going over the Vatican Galleries, everyone was startled by a strange peal of laughter, and before a frieze of the Labours of Hercules stood Pigou, looking pale and frightened, and trying to get Viola away, as she stood pointing to the carrying home of the Erymanthian boar, and laughing in this wild forced way. They got her away at last, but Piggy told his father that he would have no more to do with her, even if their uncle left her half his property, though he never would tell what she had said to him.

Since that time she had gone on in this excited state, apparently scarcely eating or sleeping, talking incessantly, not irrationally, but altogether at random, mockingly and in contradiction to everyone; caring chiefly to do the very thing her mother did not wish, never resting, and apparently with untiring vigour, though her cheeks and hands were burning, and she was wasting away from day to day.

Lady Diana really thought her mind was going, and by this time would have given all she had in the world to have been able to call Harold back to her. Diana Enderby tried reproofs for her flightiness, but only made her worse; with Dermot she would only make ridiculous nonsense, and utter those heartrending laughs; and when I tried to soothe her, and speak low and quietly, she started away from me, showed me her foreign purchases, or sang snatches of comic songs.

Dermot went at last to consult the same doctor to whom, half a year before, he had taken Harold; and it was contrived that he should see and hear her at a dinner-party without her knowledge. He consoled us very much by saying that her mind was not touched, and that it was a fever on the nerves, produced by the never having succumbed to the unhappiness and the shock which, when he heard in what manner she had lost Harold, he considered quite adequate to produce such effects. Indeed, he had been so much struck with Harold himself, that he was quite startled to hear of his death, and seemed to think an excess of grief only his due. He bade us take her to her home, give her no external excitement, and leave her as much as possible to go her own way, and let her feel herself unwatched, and, if we could, find her some new yet calming, engrossing occupation.

We took the advice, and poor Lady Diana besought us to remain with her for the present; nor, indeed, could we have left her. Our chief care was to hinder her oppressing her daughter with her anxiety; for we found that Viola was so jealous of being watched that she would hardly have tolerated us, but that I had real business in packing up my properties at Mount Eaton. For the first week she took up her old occupations in the same violent and fitful way, never sitting long to anything, but rushing out to dash round the garden, and taking long walks in all weathers, rejecting companionship.

From various causes, chiefly Lady Diana's wretchedness and anxiety, Dermot and I had to wait a week before we could have the pony-chaise and go together to Harold's grave. The great, massive, Irish granite cross was not ready then, and there was only the long, very long, green mound, at my mother's feet. There lay two wreaths on it. One was a poor thorn garland—for his own Hydriot children had, we heard, never left it untended all the winter—the other was of a great white-flowered rhododendron that was peculiar to the Arked garden.

Was it disloyal to Harry that we thought more of Viola than we did of him that first time we stood by his grave? It was an immense walk from

Arked to Arghouse Church, over four miles even by the shortest way, which lay through rough cart-tracks which we had avoided in coming, but now felt we had better take.

Nearly half way home, under a great, old pollard ash, we saw a little brown figure. It was Viola, crouched together with her head on her knees, sitting on the bank. She started up and tried to say something petulantly joking about our always dogging her, but she broke down in a flood of tears to which sheer weariness conduced. She was tired out at last, footsore, and hardly able to move a limb, when Dermot almost lifted her into the carriage, the dreadful, hard self-control all over now, when, in those long lanes, with the Maybushes meeting overhead, she leant against me and sobbed with long-pent anguish, while her brother walked at the pony's head.

She had quite broken down now, and her natural self was come back to us. When we came home, I got her up to her own room and Dermot went to his mother. She had a long, quiet sleep, lying on her bed, and when she woke it was growing dark on the May evening. She looked at me a little while without speaking, and her eyes were soft again.

"Lucy," she said, "I think I have been very naughty, but they made me so."

I said, as I kissed her, that I thought "they" had done so.

"*He* would not have let anybody make him so," she said. "I was the bad one. I was almost unfaithful. I told him so to-day."

"Not unfaithful, dearest, only harassed and miserable beyond all bearing."

"Nothing is beyond bearing. I said so to myself over and over again. That was why I would let no one see that I minded."

"You tried to bear it proudly, all by yourself," I said; "that was what made it so dreadful."

"He said it was God's will," said poor Viola, "but I knew it was mamma's. I did what he told me, Lucy; I did not get so wrong as long as he lived, but after that I did not care what became of me, and yet I did love him as much as ever."

She seemed to look on me as his representative, and was now ready to take any persuasion of mine as coming from him. She admitted her mother, was gentle and natural with her, ate and drank at her bidding, and went to bed pale and worn down, but not ill. She never gave in or professed indisposition, but for more than ten days she "went softly," was very tired, and equal to nothing but lying on the sofa and sitting in the garden; and it was in those days that sometimes with her brother, sometimes with me, she went over all that we could tell her, or she tell us, of him who had been so dear to us all. The first time she was alone with Dermot, she kissed every remaining mark she could find in his face, and said she had ached to do it every time she saw him. All those wells of deeper thought that had been so long choked by the stony hardness of a proudly borne sorrow seemed suddenly to open, when she gave herself up to the thought of Harold. She even arrived at sorrow for the way she had treated her mother; when he had given up his own hope rather than make her disobedient. She asked Lady Diana's pardon. She had never done so voluntarily in her whole life. She was met by tears and humility that softened and humiliated her in her sorrow more than aught else. Her precious flower-pot was in her window with its fragrant verbena, and I gave her the crystal cross again, telling her where I had found it, and she held it a moment and said, "Some day it will be buried with me. But I must do something to feel as if I deserved it. You know it comes to me like a token out of the sea of glass like unto crystal, where they stand that overcome! I think I'll only wear it at night when I think I have done something, or conquered a bit of my perverseness with mamma."

A sudden idea came over me. Mr. Benjamin Yolland was in dire want of a lady as reference to a parish woman for his Hydriots. I had begun, but had been called away. Miss Woolmer had tried, but was not well enough, and there was no one else whom he thought capable. I was to stay at Arked for six weeks more; should I put Viola in the way? It would be work for him.

She caught at it. Lady Diana bridled a little as she thought of the two young men who managed the Hydriots, but the doctor's prescription recurred to her mind, and she consented.

Need I tell you how dear Aunt Viola's soul and spirit have gone forth with those Hydriot people, how from going once a week to meet the parish woman at Miss Woolmer's, she soon came to presiding at the mothers' meetings, to knowing everybody, and giving more and more of her time, her thoughts, her very self to them and being loved by them enormously. The spirit, fun, and enterprise that were in her fitted her, as they began to revive, for dealing with the lads, who were sure to be devoted to anything so pretty and refined. When she began, the whisper that she was the love of their hero, gave them a romantic interest, and though with the younger generation this is only a tradition, yet "our lady" has won ground of her own, and is still fair and sweet enough to be looked on by those youths as a sort of flower of the whole world, yet their own peculiar property. For is she not a Hydriot shareholder, and does she not like to know that it was to Harold's revival of those shares that she chiefly owes her present means? Since her mother's death she has lived among them at the house that was old Miss Woolmer's, and is tranquilly happy in finding happiness for other people, and always being ready when any one needs her, as our dear old uncle does very often, though I think her Hydriot boys have the most of her.

Hippolyta made Eustace a good wife, and watched over him well; but there was no preventing his deficiency from increasing; it became acknowledged disease of the brain, and he did not survive his cousin six years. Happily none of his feebleness of intellect seems to have descended to Eustace the third, who is growing up a steady, sensible lad under his mother's management; and perhaps it is not the worse for Arghouse to have become a Horsman dependency.

It was the year before Eustace's death that the conductress of the school at Baden wrote to Mrs. Alison about Dora. The sad state of her brother had prevented her coming home or being visited, and though I exchanged letters with her periodically, we had not sufficient knowledge of one another for any freedom of expression after she had conquered the difficulties of writing.

When she was a little more than sixteen, came a letter to tell that she was wasting away in either atrophy or consumption, and that the doctors said the only hope for her was home and native air. Poor child! what home was there for her, with her sister-in-law absorbed in the care of her brother, whose imbecility was no spectacle for one in a critical state of health and failing spirits? We were at Arked at the time, and offered to go and fetch her (it was Dermot's kind thought), leaving the children to Viola's care.

Poor dear, what a sight she was! Tall in proportion to the giant breed she came of, but thin to the most painful degree, and bending like a fishing-rod, or a plant brought up in the dark, which, by-the-by, she most resembled, with her white face and thin yellow hair. Her complexion had recovered, but her hair never had, nor, as it proved, her health, for she had been more or less ailing ever since she came, and the regimen of the frugal Germans had not supported the fast-growing English girl's frame, any more than the strict and thorough-going round of accurate education had suited the untrained, desultory intellect, unused to method or application. Nor did the company of the good, plodding, sentimental maedchens give any pleasure to the vehement creature, whose playfellow from babyhood had been a man—and such a man! Use did no good, but rather, as the childish activity and power of play and the sense of novelty passed, the growth of the womanly soul made the heart-hunger and solitude worse, and spirit and health came yearly to a lower level.

She was too languid to be more than indifferent when she saw us, and the first sign of warmth that she gave was her kiss, when I went back to visit her after putting her to bed at the hotel. She looked up, put her arms round my neck, and said, "This is like the old days."

We brought her by slow stages to London, where Hippolyta came up to see her for one day, and was terribly shocked. The doctors were not hopeful, but said she might go where she pleased, and do what she liked, and as her one wish was to be with us, my dear husband laughed to scorn the notion that, whatever had been dear to Harold, should not be his sacred charge, and so we took her back.

And there, she did not die. She lay on the sofa day after day, watched the children at play, and listened dreamily to the family affairs, rested and was petted by us both, called it very comfortable, and was patient, but that whole winter seemed to remain where she was, neither better nor worse. With the spring came a visit from George Yolland, a prosperous man, as he well deserved to be, and the foremost layman in all good works in the neighbourhood since dear old Lord Erymanth had been disabled. In the forenoons, when I was teaching the children, and Dermot was busy, he was generally in the drawing-room, talking to Dora, whose blue eyes had a vivid silent intelligence, like no one but Harold's. From the first day he had confirmed my conviction that, at any rate, she was not dying now, and she began to start into strength. She sat up all the evening, she walked round the garden, she drove out, she came down to breakfast. The day after that achievement, she came to me sobbing for joy with something inaudible about "his sake," while George was assuring Dermot that there was only one woman in the world for him!

So, on a bright summer day, we gave her to the friend Harold had gained on the same day as Dermot, and she went to be the happy mistress of Mount Eaton, and reign there, an abrupt woman, not universally liked, but intensely kind and true, and much beloved by all who have cared to penetrate through her shell.

There! my work is done, though I fear it is a weaker likeness of my young Alcides than even the faded photograph by my side, but I could not brook that you, my children, should grow up unknowing of the great character to whom your father and I owe one another, and all besides that is best in our lives. There are things that must surprise you about your dear father. Remember that he insisted on my putting them in, and would not have them softened, because, he said, you ought to have the portrait in full, and that, save at his own expense, you could not know the full gratitude he feels to the man who made a new era in our lives. He says he is not afraid either of the example for you, or that you will respect him less, and I know you will not, for you will only see his truth and generosity.

L. P. T.

All that your mother has written is true—blessings on her!—every word of it, except that she never could, and I hope none of you ever will, understand the depth and blackness of the slough Harold Alison drew me out of, by just being the man he was; nor will she show you—for indeed she is blind to it herself—that it was no other than she, with her quiet, upright sweetness and resolution, that was the making of him and of both of us. Very odd it is that a woman should set it all down in black and white, and never perceive it was all her own doing. But if you see it, young people, what you have to do is to be thankful for the mother you have got and try to be worthy of her, and if the drop of Alison blood in you should make one of you even the tenth part of what Harold was, then you'll be your father's pride, and much more than he deserves.

D. E. ST. G. T.

Thank you, dear brother, for having let me see this, though I know Lucy did not intend it for my eyes, or she would not have been so hard on poor mamma. It shows me how naughty I must have been to let her get such a notion of our relations with one another, but an outsider can never judge of such things. For the rest, dear Lucy has done her best, and in many ways she did know him better than anybody else did, and he looked up to her more than to anyone. But even she cannot reach to the inmost depth of the sweetness out of the strong, nor fully know the wonderful power of tender strength that seemed to wrap one's mind round and bear one on with him, and that has lasted me ever since, and well it may, for he was the very glory of my life.

V. T.

I am glad to have read it, because it explains a great deal that I was too much of a child to understand; but I don't like it. I don't mean for putting in the fatal thing I did in my ignorant folly. I knew that, and she has softened my wilfulness. But there's too much flummery, and he was a hundred times more than all that. I had rather recollect him for myself, than have such a ladylike, drawing-room picture; but Lucy means it well, and it is just as he smoothed and combed himself down for her. Nobody should have done it but George. He would have made a man of him.

D. Y.

As if George could have done it! A lady must always see a man somewhat as a carpet knight, and ill would betide both if it were not so. But, allowing for this, and the want of "more power to her elbow," I am thankful to Mrs. Tracy for this vivid recall of the man to whom I and all here owe an unspeakable debt. For my own part, I can only say that from the day when I marvelled at his fortitude under the terrible pain of the lion's bites, to that when I saw the almost unexampled triumph of his will over the promptings of a disordered brain, he stood before me the grandest specimen of manhood I ever met, ever a victor, and, above all, over himself.

G. Y.